Winterkill

Force of Nature

"An excellent wilderness adventure . . . A violent, bloody, and quite satisfying thriller . . . A rush."
—*The New York Times Book Review*

"Proceeds at warp speed." —*The Denver Post*

Cold Wind

"A nonstop thrill ride not to be missed." —*BookPage*

"Keen insight and dark beauty." —*The Washington Post*

Nowhere to Run

"His best yet!" —Michael Connelly

Below Zero

"Pickett [is] one of the most appealing men in popular fiction." —*Chicago Tribune*

Blood Trail

"[A] riveting thriller." —*The San Diego Union-Tribune*

Free Fire

"[*Free Fire* is] Yellowstone in all its dangerous glory."
—*The Wall Street Journal*

In Plain Sight

"Edge-of-the-chair suspense . . . Heart-stopping action."
—*Library Journal*

Out of Range

"Intelligent [and] compassionate."
—*The New York Times*

Trophy Hunt

"Keep[s] you guessing right to the end—and a little beyond." —*People*

Savage Run

"The suspense tears forward like a brush fire."   —*People*

Open Season

"A muscular first novel . . . Box writes as straight as his characters shoot, and he has a stand-up hero to shoulder his passionate concerns about endangered lives and liberties."   —*The New York Times Book Review*

"Superb . . . Without resorting to simplistic blacks and whites, Box fuses ecological themes, vibrant descriptions of Wyoming's wonders and peculiarities, and fully fleshed characters into a debut of riveting tensions. Meet Joe Pickett: He's going to be a mystery star."
     —*Publishers Weekly* (starred review)

"Box's book has it all—suspenseful plot, magnificent scenery and a flawed male hero who is tough but truly connected to his family. . . . Profoundly memorable."
     —*Boston Herald*

"A high-country *Presumed Innocent* that moves like greased lightning."   —*Kirkus Reviews* (starred review)

"Riveting suspense mingles with flashes of cynical backcountry humor and makes Box an author to watch. I didn't want this book to end."   —Margaret Maron

"A motive for murder that is as unique as any in modern fiction."   —*Los Angeles Times*

Titles by C. J. Box

The Joe Pickett Novels

The Stand-Alone Novels

Short Fiction

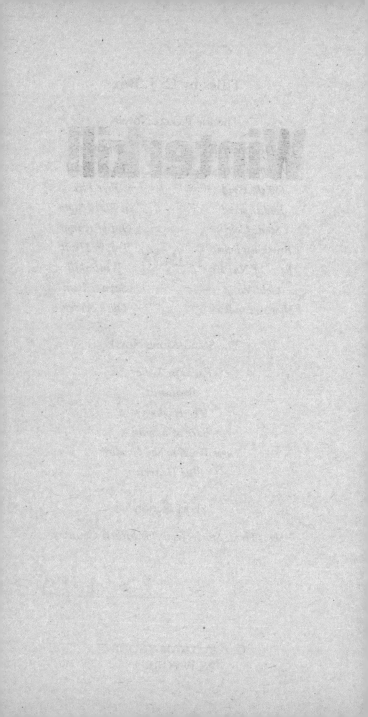

Winterkill

C. J. BOX

G. P. PUTNAM'S SONS
NEW YORK

G. P. PUTNAM'S SONS
Publishers Since 1838
An imprint of Penguin Random House LLC
375 Hudson Street
New York, New York 10014

Copyright © 2003 by C. J. Box
Excerpt from *Trophy Hunt* copyright © 2004 by C. J. Box

First G. P. Putnam's Sons hardcover edition / May 2003
First Berkley Prime Crime mass-market edition / May 2004
First G. P. Putnam's Sons premium edition / July 2016
G. P. Putnam's Sons premium edition ISBN: 9780399575709

Printed in the United States of America
9   10

For Morris and Joanna Meese
and for Laurie, always

PART ONE

Severe Winter Storm Warning

1 *Twelve Sleep County, Wyoming*

A STORM WAS COMING TO THE BIGHORN MOUNTAINS.

It was late December, four days before Christmas, the last week of the elk hunting season. Wyoming game warden Joe Pickett was in his green four-wheel-drive pickup, parked just below the tree line in the southern Wolf range. The terrain he was patrolling was an enormous wooded bowl, and Joe was just below the eastern rim. The sea of dark pines in the bowl was interspersed with ancient clear-cuts and mountain meadows, and set off by knuckle-like granite ridges that defined each small drainage. Beyond the rim to the west was Battle Mountain, separated from the Wolf range by Crazy Woman Creek, which flowed, eventually, into the Twelve Sleep River.

It was two hours away from nightfall, but the sky was leaden, dark, and threatening snow. The temperature had dropped during the afternoon as a bank of clouds moved over the sky and shut out the sun. It was now twenty-nine degrees with a slightly moist, icy breeze. The first severe winter storm warning of the season had been issued for northern Wyoming and southern Montana for that night and the following day, with another big Canadian front forming behind it. Beneath the high ceiling, clouds approached in tight formation, looking heavy and ominous.

Joe felt like a soldier at a remote outpost, listening to the distant rumble and clank of enemy artillery pieces being moved into place before an opening barrage.

For most of the afternoon, he had been watching a herd of twenty elk move cautiously from black timber into a windswept meadow to graze. He had watched the elk, then watched the sky, then turned back to the elk again.

On the seat next to Joe was a sheaf of papers his wife Marybeth had gathered for him that had been brought home from school by his daughters. Now that all three girls were in school—eleven-year-old Sheridan in fifth grade, six-year-old Lucy in kindergarten, and their nine-year-old foster daughter April in third grade—their small state-owned house seemed awash in paper. He smiled as he looked through the stack. Lucy consistently garnered smiley-face stamps from her teacher for her cartoon drawings. April wasn't doing quite so well in rudimentary multiplication—she had trouble with 5's, 8's, and 3's. But the teacher had sent notes home recently praising her improvement.

Sheridan's writing assignment had been to describe what her father did for a living.

MY DAD THE GAME WARDEN
BY SHERIDAN PICKETT
MRS. BARRON'S CLASS, 5TH GRADE.

My Dad is the game warden for all of the mountains as far around as you can see. He works hard during hunting season and gets home late at night and leaves early in the morning. His job is to make sure hunters

are responsible and that they obey the law. It can be a
scary job, but he's good at it. We have lived in Saddlestring for 3 and one-half years, and this is all he has
done. Sometimes, he saves animals from danger. My
mom is home but she works at a stable and at the library . . .

JOE KNEW HE WASN'T ALONE on the mountain. Earlier,
he had seen a late-model bronze-colored GMC pickup
below him in the bowl. Swinging his window-mounted
Redfield spotting scope toward it, he caught a quick look
at the back window of the pickup—driver only, no passenger, gun rack with scoped rifle, Wyoming plates with
the buckaroo on them—and an empty truck bed, indicating that the hunter hadn't yet gotten his elk. He tried
to read the plate number before the truck entered the
trees, but he couldn't. Instead, he jotted down the description of the truck in his console notebook. It was the
only vehicle he had seen all day in the area.

Twenty-five minutes later, the last of the elk sniffed
the wind and moved into the clearing, joining the rest of
the herd. The elk seemed to know about the storm warning, and they wanted to use the last hours of daylight to
load up on food in the grassy meadow before it was covered with snow. Joe thought that if the lone hunter in
the bronze pickup could see the meadow there would be
a wide choice of targets. It would be interesting to see
how the scenario would unfold, if it unfolded at all.
There was just as much chance that the hunter would
simply drive by, deep in the trees, road-hunting like 90
percent of all hunters, and never know that an entire
herd of elk had exposed themselves above him in a clearing. Joe sat in his pickup in silence and waited.

*   *   *

WITH A SHARP CRACK, THEN three more, the calm was shattered. The shots sounded like rocks thrown against sheet metal in rapid succession. From the sound, Joe registered at least three hits, but because it often took more than a single bullet to bring down a big bull elk, he couldn't be sure how many animals had been shot. Maxine, his yellow Labrador, sprang up from where she had been sleeping on the pickup seat as if she'd gotten an electric shock.

Below, the herd had come alive at once and was now running across the meadow. Joe could see that three brown dots remained behind in the tall grass and sagebrush.

One hunter, three elk down. Two more than legal.

Joe felt a rush of anger, and of anxiety. Game violations weren't uncommon during hunting season, and he had ticketed scores of hunters over the years for taking too many animals, not tagging carcasses, having improper licenses, hunting in closed areas, and other infractions. In many cases, the violators turned themselves in because they were honorable men who had lived and hunted in the area for years. Often, he found violations as he did random checks of hunting camps. Sometimes, other hunters reported the crimes. Joe Pickett's district took up more than 1,500 square miles, and in four years, he had almost never actually been present as a violation occurred.

Snatching the radio transmitter from its cradle, Joe called in his position over a roar of static. Distance and terrain prohibited a clear signal. The dispatcher repeated his words back to him, Joe confirmed them, and he described the bronze pickup and advised that he was going to approach it immediately. The answer was a high-pitched howl of static he was unable to squelch. At least, he thought, they knew where he was. That, unfortunately, hadn't always been the case.

"Here we go, Maxine," Joe said tersely. He started the motor, snapped the toggle switch to engage the four-wheel drive, and plunged down the mountain into the dark woods. Despite the freezing air, he opened the windows so he could hear if there were more shots. His breath came in puffs of condensation that whipped out of the window.

Another shot cracked, followed by three more. The hunter had obviously reloaded, because no legal hunting rifle had more than a five-shot capacity. The lead bull elk in the herd tumbled, as did a cow and her calf. Rather than rush into the trees, the rest of the herd inexplicably changed direction just shy of the far wall of trees in a looping liquid turn and raced downhill through the meadow, offering themselves broadside to the shooter.

"Damn it!" Joe hissed. "Why'd they turn?"

Two more shots brought down two more elk.

"This guy is *nuts*!" Joe said to Maxine, betraying the fear he was beginning to feel. A man who could calmly execute six or seven terrified elk might just as easily turn his weapon on a lone game warden. Joe did a quick mental inventory of his own weapons: the .308 carbine was secured under the bench seat, a .270 Winchester rifle was in the gun rack behind his head, his twelve-gauge Remington Wingmaster shotgun was wedged into the coil springs behind his seat . . . none of them easily accessible while he drove. His sidearm was a newly issued .40 Beretta to replace the .357 Magnum that had been destroyed the previous summer in an explosion. He had barely qualified with the Beretta because he was such a poor pistol shot to begin with, and he had little confidence in the piece or his ability to hit anything with it.

Using a ridge line as a road, he found an old set of tire tracks to follow as he descended. Although the forest was criss-crossed with old logging roads, he didn't know of one that could take him directly to where he needed to be. Plus there was the fairly recent problem of the local U.S. Forest Service closing a number of the old roads by digging ditches like tank traps across them or blocking access with locked chains, and Joe wasn't sure which ones were closed. The track was rough, strewn with football-sized boulders, and he held the wheel tightly as the front tires jounced and bucked. A rock he had dislodged clanged from beneath his undercarriage. But even over the whining of his engine he could hear still more shots, closer now. The old road was still open.

THERE WAS AN IMMEDIATE PRESENCE in the timber and a dozen elk—all that was left of the herd—broke through the trees around him. He slammed on his brakes as the animals surged around his truck, Maxine barking at them, Joe getting glimpses of wild white eyes, lolling tongues, thick brown fur. One panicked bull ran so close to the truck that a tine from his heavy spread of antlers struck the pickup's hood with a sharp *ping,* leaving a puckered dent in the hood. A cow elk staggered by on three legs, the right foreleg blown off, the limb bouncing along in the dirt, held only by exposed tendons and a strip of hide.

When they had passed him, Joe accelerated, throwing Maxine back against the seat, and drove through the stand of trees much too quickly. The passenger-side mirror smacked a tree trunk and shattered, bent back against the door.

Then the trees opened and he was on the shooter.

Joe stopped the truck, unsure of how to proceed. The hunter was bent over slightly, his back to Joe, concentrating on something in front of him, as if he hadn't heard Joe's approach, smashed mirror and all. The man wore a heavy canvas coat, a blaze-orange hunting vest, and hiking boots. Spent brass cartridges winked from the grass near his feet, and the air smelled of gunshots.

Out in front of the shooter, elk carcasses littered the slope of the meadow. A calf bawled, his pelvis shattered, as he tried to pull himself erect without the use of his back limbs.

Joe opened his door, slid out of the pickup, and un-snapped his holster. Gripping the Beretta and ready to draw it if the shooter turned around, Joe walked to the back and right of the man, so that if he wheeled with his rifle he'd have to do an awkward full turn to set himself and aim at Joe.

When Joe saw it, he couldn't believe what the shooter was doing. Despite violent trembling, the man was trying to reload his bolt-action rifle with cigarettes instead of cartridges. Dry tobacco and strips of cigarette paper were jammed in the magazine, which didn't stop the man from crushing another cigarette into the chamber. He seemed to be completely unaware that Joe was even there.

Joe drew the Beretta and racked the slide, hoping the sound would register with the hunter.

"Drop the weapon," Joe barked, centering his pistol on the hunter's upper torso. "DROP IT NOW, then turn around slowly,"

Joe hoped that when the hunter turned he wouldn't notice Joe's hands shaking. He gripped the Beretta harder, trying to still it.

Instead of complying, the man attempted to load an-other cigarette into the rifle.

Was he deaf? Joe wondered, or crazy? Or was it all a trick to get Joe to drop his guard? Despite the cold, Joe felt prickling sweat beneath his shirt and jacket. His legs felt unsteady, as if he had been running and had just stopped for breath.

"DROP THE WEAPON AND TURN AROUND!"
Nothing. Shredded tobacco floated to the ground.
The mortally wounded elk calf bleated in the meadow.

Joe pointed the Beretta into the air and fired. The
concussion was surprisingly loud, and for the first time
the hunter seemed to wake up, shaking his head, as if to
clear it after a hard blow. Then he turned.

And Joe looked into the pale, twitching, frightened
face of Lamar Gardiner, the district supervisor for Twelve
Sleep National Forest. A week before, the Gardiners and
the Picketts had sat side by side and watched their daughters perform in the school Christmas play. Lamar Gardiner was considered a dim, affable, weak-kneed
bureaucrat. He wore a wispy, sandy-colored mustache
over thin lips. He had practically no chin, which gave
him the appearance of someone just about to cry. Locals,
behind his back, referred to him as "Elmer Fedd."

"Lamar," Joe yelled, "What in the *hell* are you doing?
There are dead elk all over the place. *Have you lost your
mind?*"

"Oh, my God, Joe . . ." Gardiner whispered, as if
coming out of shock. "I didn't do it."

Joe stared at Lamar Gardiner. Gardiner's eyes were
unfocused, and tiny muscles in his neck twitched. Even
without a breeze, Joe could smell alcohol on his breath.
"What? Are you insane? *Of course* you did it, Lamar," Joe
said, not quite believing the situation he was in. "I heard
the shots. There are spent casings all over the ground.
Your barrel's so hot I can see heat coming off of it."

In what appeared to be a case of dawning realization,
Gardiner looked down at the spent cartridges at his feet,
then up at the dead and dying elk in the meadow. The
connection between the two was being made.

"Oh, my God," Gardiner squeaked. "I can't believe it."

"Now drop the rifle," Joe ordered.

Gardiner dropped his gun as if it had suddenly been electrified, then stepped back away from it. His expression was a mixture of horror and unspeakable sadness.

"Why were you putting cigarettes into your rifle?" Joe asked.

Gardiner shook his head slowly, hot tears welling in his eyes. With a trembling hand, he patted his right shirt pocket. "Bullets," he said. Then he patted his left. "Marlboros. I guess I got them mixed up."

Joe grimaced. Watching Lamar Gardiner fall apart was not something he enjoyed. "I guess you did, Lamar."

"You aren't really going to arrest me, are you, Joe?" Gardiner said. "That would mean my career. Carrie might leave me and take my daughter if that happened."

Joe eased the hammer down on his Beretta and lowered it. Over the years he had certainly cited people he knew, but this was different. Gardiner was a public official, someone who made rules and regulations for the citizens of the valley from behind a big oak desk. He wasn't someone who broke the law, or, to Joe's knowledge, even bent it. Gardiner would lose his job, all right, although Joe didn't know his family situation well enough to predict what Carrie Gardiner would do. Lamar was a career federal bureaucrat, and highly paid compared to most residents of Saddlestring. He probably wasn't many years away from retirement and all of the benefits that went with it.

The bleating of the wounded calf, however, brought Joe back to the scene in the meadow. The calf, its spine broken by a bullet, pawed the ground furiously, trying to stand. His back legs were splayed behind him on the grass like a frog's, and they wouldn't respond. Past him, steam rose from the ballooning, exposed entrails of a cow elk that had been gut-shot.

Joe leveled his gaze at Gardiner's unfocused eyes.

"I'm arresting you for at least a half-dozen counts of wanton destruction, which carries a fine of a thousand dollars per animal as well as possible jail time, Lamar. You may also lose your equipment and all hunting privileges. There may be other charges as well. Given how I usually treat slob hunters like yourself, you're getting off real easy."

Gardiner burst into tears and dropped to his knees with a wail that chilled Joe to his soul.

And just like that, the snow began to fall. The barrage had begun.

WALKING THROUGH THE HEAVY SNOWFALL in the meadow with his .270 rifle and his camera, Joe Pickett killed the calf with a point-blank head shot and moved on to the other wounded animals. Afterward, he photographed all of the carcasses. Lamar Gardiner, who now sat weeping in Joe's pickup, had shot seven elk: two bulls, three cows, and two calves.

Joe had locked Gardiner's rifle in the metal evidence box in the back of his truck, and he'd taken Gardiner's keys. In the bronze pickup were a half-empty bottle of tequila on the front seat and several empty Coors Light beer cans on the floor. The cab reeked of the sweet smell of tequila.

Although he had heard of worse incidents, this was as bad as anything Joe had personally witnessed. Usually when too many game animals were shot, there were several hunters shooting into a herd and none of them counting. Although it was technically illegal for a hunter to down any game other than his or her own, "party" hunting was fairly common. But for one man to open up indiscriminately on an entire herd . . . this was remarkable and disturbing.

The carnage was sickening. The damage a high-powered rifle bullet could do when badly placed was awful.

Equally tragic, in Joe's mind, was the fact that there were too many animals for him to load into his pickup to take back to town. The elk averaged more than 400 pounds, and even with Gardiner's help, they could only load two of the carcasses at most into the back of his vehicle. That meant that most of them would be left for at least one night, and could be scavenged by predators. He hated to see so much meat—more than 2,000 pounds— go to waste when it could be delivered to the halfway house, the county jail for prisoners, or to people on the list of the county's needy families that his wife Marybeth had compiled. Despite the number of dead elk to take care of, the sudden onslaught of the storm meant one thing: *get off the mountain.*

By the time he got back to his pickup and Lamar Gardiner, Joe was seriously out of sorts.

"How bad is it?" Gardiner asked.

Joe glared. Gardiner seemed to be asking about something he wasn't directly involved in.

"Bad," Joe said, swinging into the cab of the pickup. Maxine, who had been with Joe and was near-delirious from sniffing the musky scents of the downed elk, jumped reluctantly into the back of the pickup, her regular seat occupied by Lamar Gardiner.

"Help me field-dress and load two of these elk," Joe said, starting the motor. "That'll take about an hour, if you'll help. Maybe less if you'll just stay the hell out of the way. Then I'm taking you in, Lamar."

Gardiner grunted as if he'd been punched in the stomach, and his head flopped back in despair.

* * *

JOE'S HANDS WERE STAINED RED with elk blood and
gore, and he scrubbed them with handfuls of snow to
clean them. Even with Lamar's help, field-dressing the
elk had taken over an hour. The snow was coming down
even harder now. Joe climbed back in the truck and
drove slowly out of the meadow toward the logging road
Gardiner had used earlier. Joe tried to connect with the
dispatcher on his radio, but again all he got was static.
There was nothing for him to do but try again when he
reached the summit.

Joe was acutely aware of his situation, and of how
unique it was in law enforcement. Unlike the police or
Sheriff's Department, who had squad cars or SUVs with
back doors that wouldn't open from the inside and cage-
wire separating prisoners in the backseat from the driver,
Joe was forced to transport violators in his pickup, sitting
right next to him in the passenger seat. Although Lamar
hadn't threatened Joe in any way, Joe was acutely aware
of his proximity within the cab of the truck.

"I just can't get over what I've done," Gardiner
moaned. "It's like something took over my brain and
turned me into some kind of a maniac. A mindless
killer . . . I've never done anything like that before in my
life!"

Gardiner said he had hunted elk for sixteen years, first
in Montana and then as long as he had been stationed in
Wyoming. He whined that when he saw the herd of elk
in broad daylight, something inside him just snapped.
This was the first year he'd actually got one, and he
guessed he was frustrated.

"Lamar, are you drunk?" Joe asked, trying to sound
understanding. "I saw the bottle and the empty beer
cans in your truck."

Gardiner thought about it before answering. "Maybe
a little," he said. "But I'm sort of over that now. You

know, I see elk all the time when I'm not hunting." It was a familiar complaint. "But when I'm hunting I can't ever seem to find the bastards."

"Until today," Joe said.

Gardiner rubbed his face and shook his head. "Until today," he echoed. "My life is ruined."

Maybe so, Joe thought. Lamar would certainly lose his job with the forest service, and Joe doubted he'd find another in town. If he did, it would most likely offer only a fraction of the salary and benefits that cushioned a longtime federal employee. On top of that, Joe knew Saddlestring's local newspaper and the breakfast coffee gossips would tear Lamar Gardiner apart. Never popular, he'd now be a pariah. Unlike other crimes and criminals, there was no patience—and virtually no compassion— for game violators. The elk herds in the Bighorns were considered a community resource, and their health was a matter of much concern and debate. A large number of local residents endured Twelve Sleep County's low-paying jobs and dead-end prospects primarily for the life-style it offered—which in large part meant the good hunting opportunities. Nothing provoked more vitriol than potential damage to the health and welfare of the big game habitat and population. While it was perfectly permissible—even encouraged—for hunters to harvest an elk each year, the stupid slaughter of seven of them by one man would be an absolute outrage. Especially when the guy at fault was the federal bureaucrat who was in charge of closing roads and denying grazing and logging leases.

Joe couldn't comprehend what could have come over Lamar Gardiner. If that kind of rage lurked under the surface of a milquetoast like Gardiner, the mountains were a more dangerous place than Joe had ever imagined.

*　　*　　*

THE TWO-TRACK ROAD TO THE summit was rugged and steep, and the buffeting waves of snow made it hard to see it clearly. The pickup fishtailed several times on the wet surfaces. *It might be difficult to get back into the bowl even tomorrow if the snow continued like this,* Joe thought.

They were grinding through a thick stand of trees when Joe remembered Maxine in the back with the elk. In his mirror, he could see her hunkered against the cab, snow packed into her coat and ice crystals around her mouth.

"You mind if we stop and let my dog in?" Joe asked, pulling over on a short level stretch that led to another steep climb.

Gardiner made a face as if *this* were the last straw, and sighed theatrically.

"Everything in my life is completely and totally destroyed," he cried. "So I might as well let a stinking wet dog sit on me."

Joe bit his tongue. Looking at Gardiner, with his tear-streaked face, bloodshot eyes, and chinless profile, he couldn't remember anyone quite so pathetic.

When Gardiner turned to open his door to let Maxine in, his knee accidentally hit the button for the glove box and the latch opened, spilling the contents—binoculars, gloves, old spare handcuffs, maps, mail—all over the floor. Maxine chose that moment to bound into the truck, tangling with Gardiner as he bent to pick up the debris.

Gardiner cried out and pushed the dog roughly into the center of the bench seat.

"Calm down," Joe said, as much to Maxine as to Gardiner. Shivering, Maxine was ecstatic to be let in. Her wet-dog smell filled the cab.

"I'm soaked, my God!" Gardiner said, holding his

hands out in front of him, his voice arcing into hysteria: "*Goddamn it, Goddamn YOU!* This is the worst day of my entire life!" His hands swooped like just-released birds and he screeched: "*I'm cracking up!*"

"CALM DOWN," Joe commanded.

The human desperation that filled the cab of the pickup, Joe thought, contrasted bizarrely with the utter and complete silence of the mountains in the midst of a heavy snowfall.

For a moment, Joe felt sorry for Lamar Gardiner. That moment passed when Gardiner leaned across Maxine and snapped one of the handcuffs on Joe's wrist and the other on the steering wheel in a movement as quick as it was unexpected. Then Gardiner threw open the passenger door, leaped out, and was still running with his arms flapping wildly about him when he vanished into the trees.

THE HANDCUFFS HAD BEEN AN old set that required a smaller type of key than the set he now used. Joe tore through the glove box, his floor console, and a half-dozen other places where he might have put the keys, but he couldn't find them. Like every game warden he knew, Joe practically lived in his vehicle, and it was packed with equipment, clothing, tools, documents . . . *stuff.* But not the right key for the old handcuffs.

It took twenty minutes and his Leatherman tool to pry the cap off the steering wheel and loosen the bolts that held it to the shaft. Maxine laid her wet head on his lap while he worked, looking sympathetic. Thick falling snow from the still-open passenger door settled on the edge of the bench seat and the floorboard. A hacksaw would have cut through the wheel, or through the chain of the cuffs and freed him, but he didn't have one.

Seething, Joe strode through the timber in the storm. He carried his shotgun in his left hand while the steering wheel, still attached by the handcuffs, swung from his right.

"Lamar, damn you, you're going to die in this storm if you don't come back!" Joe hollered. The storm and the trees hushed his voice, and it sounded tinny and hollow even to him.

Joe stopped and listened. He thought he had heard the distant rumble of a motor a few minutes before, and possibly a truck door slamming. He guessed that whoever drove the vehicle was doing what he himself should be doing—retreating to a lower elevation. The sound may have come from beyond the stand of trees, but the noises were muffled, and Joe wasn't sure.

Tracking down Lamar Gardiner should go quickly, he thought. He listened for branches snapping, or Gardiner moaning or sobbing. There was no sound but the storm.

He sized up the situation he was in, and cursed to himself. Lamar Gardiner wasn't the only one having a miserable day. Joe's prisoner had escaped, he was out of radio contact, it had already snowed six inches, there was only an hour until dark, and he had a steering wheel chained to his wrist.

He thought bitterly that when he found Gardiner he would have the choice of hauling him back to the truck or shooting him dead with the shotgun. For a moment, he leaned toward the latter.

"Lamar, YOU'RE GOING TO DIE OUT HERE IF YOU DON'T COME BACK!"

Nothing.

Gardiner's tracks weren't hard to follow, although they were filling with snow by the minute. Gardiner had taken a number of turns in the trees and had been stymied several times by deadfall, then changed direction.

He didn't seem to have a destination in mind, other than away from Joe.

The footing was deteriorating. Under the layer of snow were crosshatched branches slick with moisture, and roots snatched at Joe's boots. Gardiner had fallen several times, leaving churned-up snow and earth.

If he's trying to get back to his own vehicle, Joe thought, *he's going the wrong way. And what was the chance that he had a spare set of keys with him, anyway?*

A snow-covered dead branch caught the steering wheel as Joe walked, jerking him to a stop. Again he cursed, and stepped back to pull the wheel free. Standing still, Joe wiped melting snow from his face and shook snow from his jacket and Stetson. He listened again, not believing that Gardiner had suddenly learned how to move stealthily through the woods while Joe crashed and grunted after him.

He looked down and saw how fresh Gardiner's tracks had become. Any minute now, he should be on him.

Joe racked the pump on the shotgun. That noise alone, he hoped, would at least make Gardiner *think.*

The trees became less dense, and Joe followed the track through them. He looked ahead, squinting against the snow. Gardiner's track zigzagged from tree to tree, then stopped at the trunk of a massive spruce. Joe couldn't see any more tracks.

"Okay, Lamar," he shouted. "You can come out now."

There was no movement from behind the tree, and no sound.

"If we're going to get to town before dark, we've got to leave NOW."

Snorting, Joe shouldered the shotgun and looped around the spruce so he could approach from the other side. As he shuffled through the snow, he could see one of Gardiner's shoulders, then a boot, from behind the trunk. Steam wafted from Gardiner's body, no doubt because he had worked up a sweat in the freezing cold.

"Come out NOW!" Joe ordered.

But Lamar Gardiner couldn't, and when Joe walked up to him he saw why.

Joe heard himself gasp, and the shotgun nearly dropped out of his hand.

Gardiner was pinned to the trunk of the tree by two arrows that had gone completely through his chest and into the wood, pinning him upright against the tree. His chin rested on his chest, and Joe could see blood spreading down from his neck. His throat had been cut. The snow around the tree had been tramped by boots.

The front of Gardiner's clothing was a sheet of gore. Blood pooled and steamed near Gardiner's feet, melting the snow in a heart-shaped pattern, the edges taking on the color of a raspberry Sno-Cone. Joe was overwhelmed by the pungent, salty smell of hot blood.

His heart now whumping in his chest, Joe slowly turned to face the direction where the murderer must have been, praying that the killer was not drawing back the bowstring with a bead on *him*.

Joe thought:

. . . His job is to make sure hunters are responsible and that they obey the law. It can be a scary job, but he's good at it. We have lived in Saddlestring for 3 and one-half years, and this is all he has done. Sometimes, he saves animals from danger . . .

2

SHERIDAN PICKETT, ELEVEN YEARS OLD, SLUNG HER backpack over her shoulder and joined the stream of fourth, fifth, and sixth graders out through the double doors of Saddlestring Elementary School into the snow-storm. It was the last day of school before the two-week Christmas break. That, coupled with the storm, seemed to supercharge everyone, including the teachers, who had dealt with the students' growing euphoria by simply showing movies all day and watching the clock until the bell rang for dismissal at three-thirty P.M.

A dozen fifth-grade boys, her classmates, surged through the throng. They hooted and ran, then squatted in the playground to try and gather up the winter's first good snowballs to throw. But the snow was too fluffy for packing, so they kicked it at the other students instead. Sheridan did her best to ignore the boys, and she turned her head away when they kicked snow in her direction. It was snowing *hard,* and there was already several inches of it on the ground. The sky was so close and the snow so heavy that it would be difficult, she thought, to convince a stranger to the area that there really were mountains out there, and that the humped backs of the Bighorn mountain range really did dominate the western horizon. She guessed it was snowing even harder up there.

Free of the crowd, she turned on the sidewalk at the end of a chain-link fence and walked along the side of the redbrick building toward the other wing of the school. It was a part of the school building she knew well. Saddlestring Elementary was shaped like an H, with one wing consisting of kindergarten through third grade and the other fourth through sixth, two classes of each. The offices, gym, and lunchroom separated the two wings. Sheridan had moved into what was known as the "Big Wing" the previous year, and had once again been in the youngest group of the crowd. At the time, she thought fifth graders were especially obnoxious; they formed cliques designed solely, it seemed, to torment the fourth graders. Now she was in fifth grade, but she still thought it was true. Fifth grade, she thought, was just no good. There was no point to fifth grade. It was just *in the middle*.

The sixth graders, to Sheridan, seemed distant and mature, and had already, at least socially, left elementary school behind them. The sixth-grade girls were the tallest students in school, having shot up in height past all but a few of the boys, and some were wearing heavy makeup, and tight clothing to show off their budding breasts. The sixth-grade boys, meanwhile, had morphed into gangly, honking, ridiculous creatures who lived to snap bra straps and considered a fart the single funniest sound they had ever heard. Unfortunately, the fifth-grade boys were beginning to emulate them.

As she had done after school every afternoon since September, Sheridan went to meet her sisters when they emerged from the "Little Wing" and wait with them for the bus to arrive. She was torn when it came to her sisters and this particular duty. On one hand, she resented having to leave her friends and their conversations to make the daily trek to a part of the school building that she should have been free of forever. On the other, she felt protective of April and Lucy and wanted to be there if anyone picked on them. Twice this year she had chased away bullies—once male, once female—who were giving her two younger sisters a hard time. Six-year-old Lucy, especially, was a target because she was so . . . *cute*. In both instances, Sheridan had chased the bullies away by setting her jaw, narrowing her eyes, and speaking calmly and deliberately, so low that she could barely be heard. She told them to "get away from my sisters or *you'll find out what trouble really is.*"

The first time, Sheridan had been mildly surprised that it worked so well. Not that she wasn't prepared to fight, if necessary, but she wasn't sure she was a good fighter. When it worked the second time, she realized that she could project the determination and strength that she often felt inside, and that it unnerved the bullies. It also thrilled Lucy and April.

While she waited for the doors of the Little Wing to open, Sheridan tried to find a direction to stand where the snow wouldn't hit her and melt on her glasses. Because the snowflakes were so large and light and swirly, she had no luck. Sheridan hated her glasses, but especially in the winter. Snow smeared them, and they fogged when she went indoors. She planned to lobby her parents even harder for contact lenses. Her mom had said that once she was in junior high they could discuss it. But the seventh grade seemed like a long time to wait, and her parents seemed overly cautious and more than a little old-fashioned. There were girls in her class who not only had contacts, but had asked for pierced navels for

Christmas, for Pete's sake. Two girls had announced that their goals, upon entering seventh grade, were to get tattoos on their butts!

Sheridan searched the curb for her mother's car or her dad's green pickup, hoping against hope that they would be there to pick her up, but they weren't there. Sometimes, her dad surprised them by appearing in his green Wyoming Fish and Game Department pickup truck. Although it was tight quarters inside with all three girls and Maxine, it was always fun to get a ride home with her dad, who would sometimes turn on his flashing lights or whoop the siren when they cleared Saddlestring and drove up the county road. Generally, he would have to go back to work after unloading them all at home. At least, she thought, her mom would be home from her part-time jobs at the library and the stables when the three girls got off of the bus. Arriving home in this storm, on the last day of school for the calendar year, had a special, magical appeal. She hoped her mom would be baking something.

The street where the bus parked beside Saddlestring Elementary was also marked as a secondary truck route through town. It shot straight through town, merged with Bighorn Road, and, eventually, curled into the mountains. So the heavy rumble of motors and vehicles on the street wasn't, in itself, unusual enough for Sheridan to look up.

But when she did, tilting her head to avoid falling snow, she recognized that this was something strange: a slow but impressive column of rag-tag vehicles.

They passed her one by one. There were battered recreational vehicles, old vans, trucks pulling camping trailers, and school buses that didn't look right because they were full of cardboard boxes. Four-wheel-drives pulled trailers piled high with crates, and the arms and legs of furniture poked out from water-beaded plastic tarps. It was as if a small neighborhood's residents had gathered their possessions before a coming threat and fled. Sheridan thought of the word she had learned in social studies. Yes, the caravan reminded her of *refugees*. But in Wyoming?

The license plates were from all over: Montana, Idaho, New Mexico, Nevada, Colorado, North Dakota, Georgia, Michigan, and more. This in itself was odd, especially in the winter, when most people avoided traveling long distances because of the weather. Many of the drivers seemed rough and woolly; the men had big beards and they were bundled in heavy coats. Some of them looked at her, others looked away. One bearded man rolled down his window while he passed and shouted something about "government schools." He didn't say it in a nice way, and she instinctively stepped back toward the building and the chain-link fence. There were more men than women in the vehicles, and Sheridan saw only a few children, their hands and faces pressed against the windows as they passed. It was then that she noticed Lucy and April. They were standing on each side of her in their coats, hats, and mittens, watching the transient convoy rumble by. Under her coat, Lucy wore a dress and shiny shoes, fashionable as always. She was undeniably cute. April wore more practical corduroy bib overalls, the legs of which poked out from a hand-me-down parka that used to be Sheridan's.

Sheridan noticed the regal, dignified profile of a big man at the wheel of a newer-model Suburban. The man turned his head as he passed, and he smiled. For a moment, their eyes locked. There was something kindly about him, and Sheridan picked him as the leader of the group simply by the way he sat up straight. He had confidence.

"Where's our bus?" Lucy asked.

"Probably behind all of these cars and trucks," Sheridan answered, looking for the end of the procession to see if the familiar yellow bus was there. She couldn't see beyond the end of the block through the snow, and her wet glasses didn't help.

"Who are all these people?" Lucy again.

"I don't know," Sheridan said, reaching back for Lucy's and April's hands. "One of them shouted at me."

"If they yell again, let's go in and tell the principal!" April said with some force, gripping Sheridan's hand in its red cotton glove.

The three girls stood and waited while the parade slowly passed. They all had blonde hair and green eyes. It would take a discerning observer to notice that April didn't share Lucy's and Sheridan's rounded features and big eyes. April's face was angular, and her demeanor stoic and inscrutable.

A battered blue Dodge pickup, the last of the caravan, swerved slightly and slowed as it approached. The back was piled high with bulky shapes covered by a soaked canvas tarp. Behind the pickup, Sheridan could see the red lights of the bus approaching, and Lucy pointed at it and yelled "Yay! Here it comes . . ."

But the Dodge stopped in the street directly in front of the three girls. Sheridan watched as a water-streaked window rolled down. A tiny, pinched-faced woman looked out at them. Her hair was mousy brown and had blond streaks in it, and her eyes were piercing and flinty. A cigarette hung from her lips, and it bobbed as she rolled the window down all the way.

Sheridan stared back, scared, squeezing tighter on her sisters' hands. The woman's look was meaningful, hard, and predatory. It took a moment for Sheridan to realize that the woman was not looking back at her, but lower and to the side. She was staring at April.

The truck started to roll again and the woman swung her head inside and barked something at the driver. Again, the pickup stopped. The school bus was now right behind it, crowding the blue Dodge, the bus driver gesturing at the stopped vehicle in front of him and the faces of children filling the windows to see what the problem was.

The woman continued to look at the three girls. Slowly, she reached up, pulled the cigarette from her mouth, and tapped the ashes into the snow. Her eyes were slits behind the curl of cigarette smoke.

The bus driver hit his horn, and the moment was over. The pickup lurched forward and the window rolled up. The woman had turned her head to yell at the driver. The blue Dodge raced off to join the rest of the caravan, and the big school bus turned into the bus stop.

As the accordion doors wheezed open, Sheridan could hear the raucous voices of children from inside the bus, and feel a blast of warm air.

"That was creepy," Sheridan said, leading Lucy and April toward the door.

"I'm scared," Lucy whined, burrowing her face into Sheridan's coat. "That lady scared me."

April stood still, and Sheridan tugged on her arm, then turned. She found April pale and shaking, her eyes wide. Sheridan pulled harder, and April seemed to awaken and follow.

On the bus, April sat next to Sheridan instead of Lucy, which had never happened before. She stared straight ahead at the back of the seat in front of her. She was still shivering. The bus driver had finally stopped complaining about the "gol-danged gypsy hoboes" who had blocked his route all the way into town.

"Where in the heck is that group headed?" the driver asked no one in particular. "No one in their right mind camps in our mountains in the middle of the gol-danged *winter*."

"Are you cold?" Sheridan asked April. "You're still shaking."

April shook her head no. The bus pulled onto the road. Long windshield wipers, out of sync, painted rainbows across the front windows against the snow.

"Then what is it?" Sheridan asked, putting her arm around her foster sister. April didn't shrug the arm away, which was unusual in itself. Only recently had April started to show, or willingly receive, real affection.

"I think that was my mom," April whispered, looking up at Sheridan. "I mean, the mom who went away."

3

WITH THE STORM MOVING IN, JOE FOUND HIMSELF WITH
no backup, no ability to communicate, and a dead district supervisor of the Twelve Sleep National Forest.
Standing in the timber with Gardiner's body pinned to
the tree and fresh snow quickly covering their tracks back
to his pickup, Joe needed to make some decisions and he
needed to make them now.

He had just returned from the stand of trees where he
assumed the arrows had been fired, assured that the killer
was gone. Enough snow had fallen that the tracks left by
the killer, or killers, were already filling in.

Joe looked skyward into the swirl of falling snow. He
wasn't sure what to do. *Of course* he should leave a crime
scene undisturbed.

Suddenly, Gardiner's body shivered and a fresh hot
gout of blood coursed down his chest between the arrows. Joe leaped back involuntarily, his eyes wide and his
breath shallow. He pulled off a glove and felt Gardiner's
neck for a pulse. Amazingly, there was a tiny flutter beneath the cooling skin. Joe shook his head. He hadn't

even considered, given the wounds, that the man could still be alive.

Joe tried to pull one of the arrows out. He grunted with effort, but it was stuck fast. He tried to break off the back end of the arrow, but the graphite shaft was too strong. Finally, he lifted Gardiner from beneath the arms, Joe's face pressing into Gardiner's bloody parka, and pulled him free, sliding his body up and over the arrows' fletching.

Fueled by adrenaline and desperation, Joe heaved the body over his shoulder, still dragging the steering wheel at the end of the handcuffs. He turned clumsily and started back toward the truck. Snow fell into his eyes as he walked, melting into rivulets that ran down his collar. He realized belatedly that moving Lamar this way might do more damage than good, but he didn't see an alternative.

Despite his own heavy breathing, Joe tried to listen for signs of life from Gardiner. Instead, as Joe staggered through a stand of shadowed saplings, he heard the sound of death. A deep fluttery rattle came from Gardiner's throat, and Joe felt—or thought he felt—a release of tension in the body. Now Joe had no doubt that Lamar Gardiner was dead.

Joe finally reached his truck on the road. A layer of snow had already covered the roof and hood. Leaning Gardiner's body against the front wheel with as much dignity as he could, Joe opened the passenger door. He dragged the body around the open door, then tried to lift it into the passenger seat, but Lamar's long legs had stiffened with cold and death and would not bend. The body maintained the posture it had assumed over Joe's shoulder, with Gardiner's outstretched arms parallel to his legs and his head turned slightly to the side, as if sniffing an armpit.

For a brief, horrifying second, Joe pictured himself as

if from above, struggling to bend or break a body to make it fit into the cab of his truck while the heavy snow swirled around him.

Joe gave up, and dragged Gardiner's body to the back of the truck and unlatched the tailgate. To make room, he hauled one of the still-warm elk carcasses out of the back, and it fell heavily to the ground. Then he lifted Gardiner's body into the back of the truck next to the remaining carcass. Gardiner's eyes were wide open, his mouth pursed.

Joe's muscles quivered and burned with the effort. The steam of his sweat curled up from his collar, head, and cuffs. He closed the tailgate. He covered the body as well as he could with two blankets and a sleeping bag. He searched through the toolbox in the bed of his pickup. Finding a set of bolt cutters he wished he had thought of earlier, he severed the chain between the handcuffs. Then he reattached the steering wheel to the column. Finally, utterly exhausted, he sank back against the driver's seat and started the engine.

By the time he got to the summit, it was dark. He drove down the mountain with the body of Gardiner and the remaining elk carcass in the back of the pickup, stopping several times to scout the road ahead. In the back, blood and ice from both Gardiner's body and the elk had melted and mixed and had filled the channels of the truck bed. The reddish liquid spilled from under the tailgate to spatter the snow each time he stopped.

As he drove, he thought of Mrs. Gardiner—how she might feel if her husband's body had been simply left where it was for the night. The forest was home to coyotes, wolves, ravens, raptors, and other predators who could have found the body and fed on it. *This is best,* he thought, despite the gruesome circumstances of carrying the body out.

*   *   *

THE STORM OBSCURED THE OUTSIDE view as he labored to stay on the road. The swirling snow, lit up in his lights, was mesmerizing. Beyond the illuminated flakes, he could see nothing beyond. With no posts or road markers to guide him, Joe turned off his lights, extinguishing the pinwheel of snowy fireworks, and drove by feel. When he felt the dry crunch of sagebrush under his tires, he would search again for the road, saying a prayer each time his wheels again found the two-track.

Normally, in the distance, he could have seen the lights of Saddlestring in the river valley, looking like sequins flung across black felt. But he could see nothing. He could hear the fluid sloshing against the cab now that he was driving downhill.

The situation he was in was maddening, and frightening. For the first time, he realized that he still wore one blood-soaked glove and that his bare, thawing hand was red with dried gore.

"Damn you, Lamar," he said aloud, "*damn* you." Maxine looked to him with her condolences.

Now that he should be within radio range, Joe reached for the mike and tried to put together the words he would use to report what had happened.

O. R. "BUD" BARNUM, TWELVE Sleep County's longtime sheriff and a man Joe had tangled with before, was livid when Joe brought Lamar's body to the hospital.

As Joe backed into the lighted alcove of the hospital emergency entrance, Barnum stepped out of the well-lit lobby through the double doors and angrily tossed a half-smoked cigarette in the direction of the gutter. Two of his deputies, Mike Reed and Kyle McLanahan, followed Barnum. Joe and McLanahan went back four years, ever since McLanahan had carelessly wounded Joe with a poorly aimed shotgun blast.

"Tell me, Warden Pickett," Barnum drawled, his voice hard, "why is it that every time someone gets murdered in my county, you're right in the middle of it? And how are we supposed to investigate this murder when you've destroyed the crime scene by bringing Lamar down in the back of your truck?"

Barnum had obviously been rehearsing his opening remarks for the benefit of his deputies.

Joe climbed out and glared at Barnum, who was harshly lit by overhead alcove lights that made his aging face and deep-set eyes look even more severe than they really were. Barnum glared back, and Joe saw Barnum's eyes narrow at the sight of Joe's appearance.

"He was alive when I found him," Joe said. "He died as I carried him back to my truck."

Barnum harrumphed, not apologizing, and shined his Maglite flashlight into the back of the truck. "I see a big elk," he said, and then the ring of the beam settled on the snow-covered blanket. Barnum reached in and peeled back the fabric.

"Jesus, somebody butchered him," Barnum said.

Joe nodded. The gaping wound on Lamar's neck looked savage and black in the harsh white light of Barnum's flashlight.

Deputy Reed told Joe that the county coroner was on his way, fighting through the snowdrifts on the road to the hospital.

Joe and the sheriff's team stepped aside as hospital orderlies pulled Gardiner's body from the back of Joe's pickup and strapped him onto a gurney. The four of them followed the gurney into the building, then waited in the admissions area. As the orderlies rolled the body down the hallway, McLanahan said it reminded him of the elk he had brought down from the mountains during hunting season.

"Seven-point royal," McLanahan boasted. "Just shy of the Boone and Crockett record book. We had to quarter him just to get him to fit into the back of the truck."

At this, Barnum turned, smirking, toward Joe. "Well, Warden Pickett," he said, "I'm surprised you didn't gut Lamar before you brought him in."

JOE DROVE TO THE GARDINER house to break the news to Mrs. Carrie Gardiner. He had volunteered for the job, tough as it would be. He was grateful to get away from Barnum and McLanahan. Even in the cold, his cheeks burned. He stung from Barnum's comments, and fought his welling anger at them. As he drove, however, thoughts of what had happened that afternoon, and what he was going to tell Carrie, crowded out Barnum's words. He still couldn't believe Gardiner had used the handcuffs—or that Gardiner had gone on his shooting rampage in the first place. Or that he had been randomly murdered in the middle of a forest during a snowstorm.

As Joe pulled up in front of the Gardiners' house, the realization of what he was about to do hit him, and he sat in the truck for a moment, working up his courage before pushing himself out into the cold and up the front steps of the house. When Lamar Gardiner's daughter opened the door in her nightgown, Joe felt even worse than he had before.

"Is your mom home?" Joe asked, his voice stronger than he expected.

"You're Lucy's daddy, right?" the girl asked. She had sung next to Lucy at the Christmas play. Joe couldn't remember her name. He wished he were anywhere other than where he was at the moment, and felt ashamed of his wish.

Carrie Gardiner emerged from the kitchen wiping her hands in a towel. She was a heavy woman with an attractive, alert face and short dark hair.

"Let Mr. Pickett in and close the door, honey," she said. Joe stepped in and removed his Stetson, which was soaked through and heavy.

The door closed, and both Carrie Gardiner and her daughter waited for him to speak. The fact that he didn't, but simply looked at Mrs. Gardiner, said enough.

Her eyes moistened and flashed.

"Go watch TV, honey," she told her daughter in a voice that would be obeyed.

Joe waited until the girl had left the room and took a deep breath. "There is no way to tell you this other than to tell it straight out," he said. "Your husband Lamar was murdered in the mountains while he was elk hunting. I found his body and brought him down."

Carrie Gardiner looked both stunned and angry, and she almost lost her balance. Joe stepped forward to steady her but she refused his hand. She let out a yelp, and threw the hand towel she was clutching at his boots.

"I'm so sorry," Joe said.

She waved him away, excusing him as the bearer of bad news. Then she turned and walked back into the kitchen.

"Please call me or my wife if there is anything we can do at all," Joe said after her.

She came back into the living room.

"How did he die?"

"Somebody shot two arrows into him." He chose not to mention the cut throat.

"Do you know who did it?" she asked.

"Not yet," Joe admitted.

"Will you find him?"

"I think so. The sheriff is in charge."

"Is that Lamar's blood on you?"

"Yes," Joe said, flushing, suddenly aware that his coat was blackened with blood, and profoundly angry with himself for not realizing it earlier. He should have taken it off in the truck before he knocked on the door. "I'm sorry," he said. "I . . ."

She shook him off, bent and picked up the towel, and touched her face with it.

"I was afraid something like this would happen," she said, and again walked away. She didn't elaborate, and Joe didn't follow up.

Joe let himself out and stood on the porch for a moment. Inside, a wail began and grew louder and louder. It was awful.

AT THE SHERIFF'S OFFICE, BARNUM was already giving assignments for the coming day. Joe stood uncomfortably in the back of the briefing room. He had been asked to give a statement earlier, but had insisted on going to the Gardiner house first, promising to return later. Barnum told his deputies to forget whatever they were doing and to focus entirely on Lamar Gardiner's murder. He explained that he'd already called the state Division of Criminal Investigation, and notified the Forest Service. As soon as they could, he said, they would follow Joe Pickett to the crime scene to retrieve the arrows and any other kind of evidence they could find. Gardiner's staff would be questioned, as would his wife and friends, ". . . if he had any." This brought a muffled guffaw from someone. Gardiner's office would be searched, with the goal of gathering credible evidence of threats or conflicts. The records and sign-in sheets of the public meetings Gardiner had recently held about road closures, lease extensions, and other access issues would be gathered. Barnum wanted the names of everyone in Twelve Sleep Valley who had confronted Gardiner or expressed disagreement over public-policy decisions that had been made by the forest service. Joe had attended the meetings, and he knew that Barnum was likely to end up with a lot more names than he wanted.

"I want this investigation to proceed quickly and I want somebody rotting in my jail by Christmas," Barnum barked. "Pickett, we need your statement."

The deputies in the room, many wearing the sloppy civilian clothes they'd had on when they were abruptly called into the department, turned and looked at Joe, seeing him back there for the first time.

"You're a damn mess," one of them said, and somebody else laughed.

IT WAS TWO-THIRTY IN THE morning before Joe got home, and he drove by his house twice before seeing the yellow smudge of the porch light that looked like an erasure in the storm. The wind had come up, turning a heavy but gentle snowfall into a maelstrom.

After bucking a three-foot snowdrift that blocked the driveway and sent him fishtailing toward the garage, he turned off the motor and woke Maxine. The Labrador bounded beside him through the front lawn, leaping over drifts. Joe didn't have the energy to hop, so he plowed through, feeling snow pack into the cuffs of his Wranglers and into his boot-tops for the second time that day. Snow swirled around the porch light like smoke. Christmas decorations, made by the girls in school, were taped inside the front window, and Joe smiled at the Santa drawing that Sheridan had done the previous year.

Unnoticed by most, Sheridan had added a familiar patch, with a pronghorn antelope profile and the words WYOMING GAME AND FISH DEPARTMENT, to Santa's red coat-sleeve.

The small house had two storeys, with two small bedrooms, a detached garage, and a loafing shed barn in the back. Forty years old, the house had been the home and office of the two previous game wardens and their families. Across Bighorn Road was Wolf Mountain, which dominated the view. In back, beyond rugged sandstone foothills, was the northwest slope of the Bighorn range. He could see none of it in the dark and through the snow.

The people he met in the field were mostly hunters, fishermen, ranchers, poachers, environmentalists, and others Joe lumped into a category he called "outdoorsmen"—but his home was filled with four blonde, green-eyed females. Females who were verbal. Females who were emotional. He often smiled and thought of this place as a "House of Feelings." If the expression of feelings produced a physical by-product, Joe could imagine his house filled with hundreds of gallons of an emotional goo that sometimes spilled out of the windows and doors and seeped from the vents. But his family was everything to him; this place was his refuge, and he wouldn't have had it any other way.

He shut out the storm as he closed the door, and he clumsily peeled off his first layer of clothing in the tiny mudroom. He hung his bloody parka on a peg and unbuttoned his green wool Filson vest. He stamped packed snow out of his trouser legs, then left the Sorel pac boots on a bench to dry. His wet black Stetson went crown-down on an upper shelf.

Sighing, wondering why Marybeth still had her light on, he entered the living room in the dark, banged his shin on the foot of the fold-out couch bed, and fell on top of his sleeping mother-in-law. She woke up thrashing, and Joe scrambled to his feet.

"What are you *doing*, Joe?" she asked, her tone accusatory.

Up the stairs, another light came on. Marybeth had heard the commotion, Joe hoped.

"I didn't want to turn on a light," Joe answered, sheepishly. Not adding: *I forgot Marybeth told me you'd be here.*

When Joe had called home earlier from the sheriff's office, Marybeth had said that her mother, Missy Vankueren, might be staying with them tonight. Apparently, Missy had been flying to Jackson Hole to go skiing with her third husband, a wealthy and politically connected Arizona real estate baron, when the weather diverted the plane to Billings. So Missy had rented a car, driven the two hours to Saddlestring, and arrived just as the storm moved in. Mr. Vankueren was to meet her in a couple of days, after some important meetings in Phoenix. And now Joe Pickett, the man her favorite daughter had chosen despite Marybeth's incredible potential and promise, had just awakened her in a half-dressed state by falling on her bed.

"Hi, Missy," Joe grunted. "Nice to see you." Missy clutched her blankets to her chin and peered over them at him. Without the expertly applied mask of makeup she usually wore, she looked all of her sixty-two years. Joe knew she hated being seen when she wasn't prepped and ready.

Marybeth came down the stairs tying her bathrobe, instantly sized up the situation between her mother and her husband, and forced a smile. Joe wanted to mouth *help me, save me*, but he didn't dare for fear Missy would see. The small front room was filled not only with the length of the couch bed but the seasonal addition of the Christmas tree that stood silent and dark in the corner. Floor space was at a minimum, and Joe had to scuttle sidewise like a crab to cross the room.

"Sorry, Mom," Marybeth said, tucking the disturbed sheet corners back under the mattress. "Joe's had a very bad day."

"And I'm having a bad night," Missy said, averting her gaze from Joe. "I'm supposed to be in our condo in Jackson Hole."

"But instead you're on our crummy couch bed in our lousy living room," Joe finished for her, deadpan as he headed for the stairs. Marybeth shot him a look over her shoulder as she finished re-tucking her mother. He listened as Marybeth calmed Missy, told her that it was still snowing, asked her if she was warm enough, asked her . . . something else, which he didn't pay attention to.

Missy Vankueren was the last person Joe wanted to see in his home right now. The day had been a nightmare. *Now this,* he thought, as he slowly climbed the stairs.

MARYBETH LOOKED TIRED AND WORN out, but she had listened in wide-eyed silence as he told her everything. When he came to how he had found the body, she had pressed her hands to her mouth and winced.

"Are you going to be okay?" she asked in a whisper when he was through talking.

"Yes," Joe said, but really wasn't sure about that.

Marybeth held him and looked him over. "I think you should take a shower, Joe." He nodded dumbly.

In the shower, he wanted to see blood wash down the drain so he could feel clean. But the blood from Lamar Gardiner had been on his coat and clothes, and it had not seeped through to his skin.

*   *   *

JOE DRIED AND SLID INTO bed next to Marybeth. Her bed lamp was still on, and he asked her about it.

"It's been a bad day for the girls and me as well," she said, turning to him. "Jeannie Keeley is back in town."

Joe ran a hand over his face and rubbed his eyes. Now he understood why Marybeth looked so drawn and tired. He had originally thought she had been worried about him, or because of the unexpected visit by her mother. It was those things, he realized, and more.

Marybeth told Joe what the girls had seen after school—the procession of vehicles and particularly the one that stopped. She said April had described the woman who stared as "the mom who went away."

"Joe, why do you think Jeannie Keeley is back?" Marybeth asked.

Joe shook his head, not knowing. He was too tired to think clearly.

Waves of exhaustion washed over him, pounding at him. He moaned at the possibility of further delays, or a fight for April.

The hard fact was that April's situation was precarious. Although she had been with them for four years and was as much a daughter as Sheridan or Lucy, April was not legally theirs.

April's biological mother, Jeannie Keeley, had dropped two things off at the local branch bank when she left town after her husband Ote had been murdered: her house keys and April. Marybeth had heard about it and immediately offered to keep the girl until the issue could be resolved.

Eventually, they had petitioned the court for consent to adopt, and Judge Hardy Pennock had started proceedings to terminate Jeannie Keeley's parental rights.

But then Pennock had been hospitalized with a brain tumor, and the proceedings languished in his absence. Finally, the matter had gone to another court—but the original paperwork had been lost. Another delay had resulted when the new court received a letter from Jeannie Keeley saying she was coming back for her daughter. But that was six months ago now, in the summer, and Jeannie Keeley had never come. A technicality in Wyoming law stated that parental rights couldn't be terminated if there had been contact from the birth parent at least once a year, and the letter qualified, which again delayed the proceedings. Judge Pennock was now back on the bench, but hopelessly backlogged. Joe had tried to expedite the case, with some success, but the rights hearing had not yet been held.

The legal proceedings had been frustrating and endless, but Marybeth and Joe had remained optimistic that a resolution would come.

"As soon as you can, you need to look into this," Marybeth said.

"I will," Joe said.

"That woman scares me, Joe. If she's back, we've got real trouble on our hands."

"That we do," he said, and put his arm around her, pulling her close.

"I've got to lead the sheriff to the crime scene first thing tomorrow," Joe said. "Then I'm sure they'll want to get rid of me, so I should have some time."

"Wherever it stands, when school starts back up, we've got to try and pick up the girls ourselves after school," Marybeth said, her voice rising. "I don't want to take the chance that something will happen to April."

Joe nodded, trying to fight sleep. He knew Marybeth needed him, that she'd been worried about this all afternoon with no one to talk to about it. He wanted to say something that would make her feel better, that would calm her, but his tongue felt thick and heavy and his eyes kept dropping shut. He felt immensely guilty about not being able to emerge from the problems and horrors of the afternoon and night he had just experienced, because he knew that her concerns were real. But he was slipping away, into unconsciousness.

TWO HOURS LATER, JOE AWOKE sweating. He had dreamed that he was back in the timber, suffering under the weight of Lamar Gardiner. The wounded man's coat had been caught in the branch of a tree, and Joe had swung his shoulders to tear it free. A spatter of bright red blood had flecked the snow . . .

He rose quietly and went to the window. An icy breeze flowed under the sill—he would need to pack it with insulation tomorrow, he thought.

It was still dark, still snowing, and the wind was still blowing.

He turned and looked at Marybeth, who had finally fallen asleep under the quilts. Then he tiptoed downstairs and looked in on Sheridan—Maxine was asleep at the foot of her bed—and on Lucy and April, who shared a bunk bed. He could not see their faces, only tangles of blonde hair. After gazing at them for a moment, he returned to his bedroom.

He stared out at the storm, mesmerized. The wind had increased. There was now a bare spot on the front lawn where the brown grass showed through. It was never just the snow in Wyoming that caused problems. It was always the snow plus the wind that sculpted it into something hard, shiny, and impassible. A foot-high stream of blowing snow, like cold smoke, coursed across the ground.

It struck Joe as he stood there, the floor cold beneath his bare feet, that Lamar's murder had an oddly personal feel to it. Saddlestring was not a violent place, and murders were almost unheard of, yet someone had hated Lamar Gardiner so much that he not only shot him with arrows but slashed his throat open, bleeding him like a wounded deer.

Joe wondered if the killer was still out there, caught in the storm. Or if the killer, like himself, had made it off of the mountain. And he wondered if the killer was also standing at a window somewhere, his gut churning, his mind replaying what had happened that day, as the storm pummeled Twelve Sleep Valley.

4

JOE WAS BEING GENTLY SHAKEN AWAKE BY MARYBETH, who held a telephone out to him.

"It's Sheriff Barnum," she said, cupping her hand over the phone. He sat up quickly in bed, rubbed his face hard, and looked around. Marybeth was fully dressed. The curtains were drawn, but on the ceiling and walls were blooms of muted light. The digital clock radio showed that it was 8:20 A.M. *That's impossible,* Joe thought.

His immediate fear was that Barnum had assembled his deputies, the state Division of Criminal Investigation unit, and the county emergency team, and that they were in town—all waiting for him.

Marybeth read the panic in his eyes, and shook her head. "Don't worry," she said, her hand still covering the telephone. It was his cell phone, instead of the handset to the telephone near the bed. "You won't believe the snow outside."

"Why didn't you wake me up earlier?" Joe asked, groggy. "I can't believe I slept this late."

"You needed the rest. And I don't think anybody is going anywhere this morning."

Joe took the phone while he swung out of bed. "Sheriff?"

Barnum's voice was gravelly. "Have you looked outside?"

"I'm doing that now," Joe said, opening the curtains. The blast of pure white light temporarily blinded him. For a moment, he got a sense of vertigo. There was no sky, no grass, no trees or mountains. Only opaque white.

"I can't even see the road," Joe marveled.

"Neither can the snowplow drivers," Barnum grumbled. "We've got thirty-six inches of snow and the wind's supposed to hit fifty miles per hour this afternoon. Everything's closed—the highways, the airport, even our office officially. The phone lines are down again, and half the county doesn't have power. The DCI boys started up here in a state plane and made it as far as Casper before they turned back. The storm was right on their ass, so they had to outrun it and ended up somewhere in Colorado."

Joe squinted. He could make out ghostly shapes of his pickup, and a snow-covered pine in his yard below.

"So what's the plan?" Joe asked.

"Shit, I don't know," Barnum sighed. "I'm trying to get ahold of a Forest Service Sno-Cat to take up there. But I can't reach anybody who can find the keys."

Joe thought briefly about using snowmobiles but it was too far.

"Keep your cell phone on," Barnum barked. "As soon as we can move around here we'll try to assemble and get up there. You'll have to get to town when that happens so you can show us where Gardiner got rubbed out."

"I'll chain up all four tires," Joe said, ignoring the "rubbed out" comment. "I'll be ready when you are."

"You've got power, then?" Barnum asked.

"For now."

"Keep that cell phone charged," Barnum said again. "Who knows when they'll get the lines fixed."

"Sheriff?" Joe asked, before Barnum hung up.

"What?"

"Good thing I brought him down, wouldn't you say?" Joe turned to Marybeth, who had a satisfied look on her face.

Barnum hung up.

"Are you up for making pancakes?" Marybeth asked. "The girls want to know."

Joe looked again out of the window. What little he could see looked like a freeze-frame of a storm at sea, with bucking waves of snow and ground blizzards instead of spray.

"You bet," Joe said, smiling. "I'm not going anywhere for a while."

"The girls will like that."

Then he remembered: "Your mother."

"What about her?"

"Oh," Joe moaned, "nothing."

JOE STOOD AT THE WINDOW after he dressed, blinking at the whiteout, a combination of feeling the frustration and dread churning within him. His thoughts from the night before still haunted him. He fought a wave of nausea as he recalled the brutality of Lamar's murder. The fact that the murderer had sliced Gardiner's throat—and while Gardiner was still alive and pinned to the tree—was particularly hideous. Whoever had done it was unimaginably brutal, and Joe couldn't help but think that there wasn't any randomness about it. He assumed that the killer had known Gardiner, or at least known who and what he represented. The longer it took to begin the investigation, the more time the murderer would have to get rid of evidence, wipe out his tracks, and build his alibi. The crime scene itself was inaccessible, with potential evidence—hair, fibers, blood—being pummeled and scattered by ice and wind.

Joe felt that, unlike hunters, who often policed themselves, whoever had killed Lamar Gardiner was not wracked with guilt. The killer was likely local, possibly someone Joe knew, possibly someone who would not stop with killing Lamar Gardiner if he felt threatened. Someone without a conscience.

And the murderer was out there, shielded by the fury of the storm.

BEFORE BREAKFAST, JOE RETREATED TO his office to type up the report on Lamar's murder for his supervisor, Terry Crump. He wouldn't be able to e-mail it to him until the phones were back up, but he wanted to get the details down while they were still fresh in his mind. As a game warden, one of only fifty-five in the entire state of Wyoming, Joe Pickett had unique duties and obligations. Within his district, he worked virtually alone. His office was in a small anteroom off the living room in his house, and he had no administrative or secretarial staff. Marybeth, and sometimes Sheridan, took messages and served as unpaid assistants. The job of a Wyoming game warden was supposed to consist of one-third public contact, one-third harvest collection, and one-third law enforcement— with no area to exceed 35 percent. Supposedly, the percentages would balance out over the year. The hours ranged from 173 to 259 per month. Joe was paid $32,000 per year in salary by the state of Wyoming and provided with housing and a vehicle. He was supervised, sort of, by District Supervisor Terry Crump, a game warden as well, who was 250 miles away in Cody. Crump's supervision consisted of an occasional telephone call or radio dispatch, usually after Joe had sent in his monthly report via e-mail attachment. Generally, Terry simply wanted to bullshit or trade departmental gossip. He had never called Joe to task, even when Joe's activities had enraged the bureaucrats in Cheyenne, where the headquarters were. Although Joe sometimes worked in tandem with the county sheriff's office or the Saddlestring police department, and even with federal agencies like the U.S. Fish and Wildlife Service, the U.S. Forest Service, the BATF, and the FBI, he was almost always on his own. He liked the autonomy, but there were problems inherent in it that came up when he encountered situations like he had the day before.

Joe was just finishing up his report when he looked up to see Sheridan, April, and Lucy crowding the door. They were still wearing their pajamas and slippers.

"If we don't eat breakfast soon, I think I shall faint," Lucy said dramatically.

BREAKFAST ACTUALLY WENT QUITE WELL, the euphoric mood of his children carrying them all through it. Joe flipped pancakes to them from the stove, and they caught them on their upraised plates while squealing. For Marybeth and Missy Vankueren, Joe delivered pancakes to the table. Missy picked at her breakfast, foregoing both bacon and syrup.

"Do you have any idea how many fat grams there are in these pancakes?" she asked Joe. The three girls looked up, waiting for his answer. He didn't disappoint them.

"Ten thousand apiece?" Joe speculated. Even Marybeth laughed at that. Missy made a dismissive face.

For his girls, a storm that forced all the adults to stay

inside, play with them, and cook for them constantly was the best of all possible worlds. With the mood created by the Christmas decorations and the wrapped packages under the tree—as well as the unexpected visit by their grandmother—there was simply no better time. Sheridan said she loved storms. She declared that the worse the storm, the better she liked it.

As the girls ate, Marybeth did an inventory of her cupboards and the refrigerator, and declared with obvious relief that they had enough food and milk to last for several days without a trip to the grocery store. Joe added that the freezer in the garage was filled with elk and pronghorn antelope steaks, roasts, and burger.

"We can't just eat red meat!" Missy protested.

"Why not?" Joe asked. The three girls laughed.

"He has a captive audience," Marybeth observed to her mother.

"I see that," Missy said, sipping her coffee

ALTHOUGH IT LOOKED IMPOSSIBLE, JOE wanted to see if he could get his pickup running and free of the drifts. Wearing insulated Carhartt coveralls, a knit cap and facemask, and knee-high boots, Joe turned away from the wind and let the snow hammer his back. Despite the heavy clothing, the pure relentless ferocity of the storm chilled him. He'd had to dig into a drift that had formed around his pickup to find the tires before he could even start putting the chains on them. It had taken an hour on his hands and knees to slide the chains over the rear tires and secure them, and the icy steel links had frozen his fingers through his thick gloves. Two tires down, two to go. He kicked through the heavy snow until he found his already covered shovel.

As he dug out the front wheels, he looked up at the

house. Lucy and April were watching him through the window. They were still in their pajamas, and both had candy canes stuck jauntily in their mouths like cigars. They waved, and Joe waved back. They watched him for a while as he put the remaining snow chains on. When he finally stood up and knocked packed snow from his clothes, they were gone.

Joe found himself staring at the window even though they were no longer there, specifically the spot where April had been.

April had appeared after Marybeth had been shot in the stomach, and their own unborn baby lost. There would be no more children. If Jeannie Keeley was in town and wanted April, there would be a battle. Marybeth wouldn't stand idly by. Neither would Joe.

SHAKING HIS THOUGHTS ASIDE, JOE climbed into his pickup and started the engine, slamming the truck forward, then back, letting the chains bite into the drifts. Gradually, he was able to maneuver around so that the truck faced the road. In an emergency, it would be easier to go forward than to try to back out. That was as much as he could do for a while, he thought, until the road was cleared. No one was going anywhere today.

Lumbering through the drifts like a monster, he fought his way back to the house.

Inside, after shedding his outer clothing, he found Marybeth, Missy, and the three girls crammed into the small room that housed the washer and dryer.

"Dad, you've got to see this," Sheridan called out.

They parted to let him look.

The dryer's door was open, and snow filled every inch of it. Apparently, the swirling winds outside had forced snow up through the outside wall vent, packing it inside.

"This is amazing," Marybeth laughed.

Joe smiled—it would be a day of playing board games, baking cookies, and unusual proximity in their small house. As much as he felt he should get back out to the mountain, he simply couldn't. He listened on his radio as one of Barnum's deputies tried to reach the mountain by snowmobile, only to get lost in the blizzard, clip a tree, and turn back. All Joe could do was to stay in contact with dispatch and wait out the storm like everyone else.

He finally resolved to embrace his immobility, and he changed from his uniform to sweat clothes and made chili for everyone for dinner. He cubed elk steaks to brown with diced onions and peppers in his cast-iron pot. As the chili simmered, he added more ingredients and the aroma of tomato sauce, garlic, and meat filled the house. It was a good smell. Cooking also meant he got to stay in the kitchen while Marybeth and Missy visited in the living room, which was fine with all of them.

THAT EVENING, THE GIRLS CLEARED the chili bowls and silverware from the table while Missy tried in vain to call her husband on her cell phone.

"He never leaves it on," she said angrily as she sat down at the table. "He only turns it on when *he* wants to tell somebody something." Her tone was bitter, and Joe exchanged glances with Marybeth. Neither really knew Missy's third husband well, but there had been rumors lately about the possibility of his indictment for land-use fraud. Missy had said little of this, except that the impending "issues" were one of the reasons they'd wanted to get away to their condominium in Jackson Hole in the first place.

"I guess you're stuck with us," Sheridan said as she opened the box of a Monopoly game.

Missy patted her on the head. "I *enjoy* being with you, darling." Sheridan rolled her eyes as soon as Missy looked away.

"Sit with me, Princess," Missy directed Lucy, who gladly did as she was told. Missy liked Lucy's sense of style, and Lucy liked Missy's huge traveling bag of makeup and hairspray.

After a protest from April, Sheridan returned to the table with Pictionary instead of Monopoly. They divided up into teams. Joe was on Missy's team, which meant that he gave himself permission to have another bourbon.

During the game, while the sand ran through the one-minute timer and the designated "artists" drew frantic sketches on pads for their teammates to guess at, Joe found himself paying special attention to April. She was the most determined artist on his team, and she drew very deliberately. When her pictures were complete, she was deliriously happy with herself, and she beamed. Joe had noticed before that April didn't have the lively features and sparkling eyes that Sheridan and Lucy had. Marybeth had said that "the sparkle got beaten out of April early on." He remembered that phrase as he watched her now.

After a round that Joe and Missy won by correctly identifying April's drawing, April whooped and punched the air with pure joy.

"I like it that you're getting more normal," Lucy said to April. "You're not so weird anymore."

"Lucy!" Marybeth said, alarmed.

But April didn't explode and start swinging, or withdraw and freeze her face into a pinched glare, as she had in the past. Instead, she smiled and reached across the table and mussed Lucy's hair. Both girls laughed. Joe thought April seemed flattered. Sheridan beamed with relief, her eyes sliding from her mom to her dad.

During the second game, with Joe about to draw and Sheridan poised to flip the timer over, Joe suddenly looked up. *"Listen,"* he said.

"What?" Missy asked, alarmed.

"Do you hear that?"

"I don't hear anything."

"That's right," Joe said. "The wind stopped."

"Too bad," Sheridan chimed, turning the timer over and setting it down. "This is fun."

"Sherry's right," Lucy smiled, her eyes wide. "Storms are good for our family."

Joe smiled and sipped his bourbon, enjoying the moment despite the ticking of the timer. April tugged on his sleeve, her face was urgent.

"DRAW SOMETHING!" April pleaded. "We're running out of time!"

5

IT WAS TWO DAYS BEFORE THEY COULD GET BACK ONTO the mountain, and they needed three borrowed Sno-Cats to do it. The meeting point was at a clearing outside Winchester where the road ascended into the mountains. There were more people in the assemblage than Joe expected.

After the weather delay, the DCI agents had arrived in their state plane at the Twelve Sleep County Airport with two additional passengers, a U.S. Forest Service official and a female journalist. The Forest Service official had also brought two small dogs with her, a Yorkie on a leash and a cocker spaniel that she clutched to her breast. Joe noticed an attractive, dark-haired woman with the official who seemed to be keeping a close eye on the proceedings. A lone Saddlestring *Roundup* reporter, a twenty-three-year-old blonde wearing a Wyoming Cowboys basketball parka and driving a ten-year-old pickup, approached the gathering carrying a notebook opened to a blank page.

The Forest Service official intercepted the reporter in mid-stride, and an interview was begun. Joe was helping a deputy hook his snowmobile trailer to the back of a Sno-Cat, and he was close enough to overhear their exchange.

"My name is Melinda Strickland," the Forest Service official said. She spelled her name for the benefit of the reporter.

"I'm here on special assignment on behalf of the U.S. Forest Service as the head of a special investigative team that needs to remain classified and off of the record for the time being."

"Why?" the reporter asked vacantly. Joe wondered the same thing. The Forest Service was not a law enforcement agency, although individual rangers had some regulatory responsibility within their jurisdiction, and while Joe assumed it was possible, he had never before heard of a "special investigative team" sent by the agency. He thought it more likely that the agency would ask the FBI to intervene.

"You'll be told in due course, if we confirm some of our suspicions," Strickland said.

The reporter obviously didn't know how to react. The woman sounded so . . . official.

The Yorkie pulled at Melinda Strickland's pant cuff, but was ignored.

"You'll be the first to get the information when we decide to release it, but if you burn me by printing something before that, I'll have your ass," Melinda Strickland said, her eyes narrowing.

This got Joe's attention, and he watched the reporter nod meekly. The brittle edge in Strickland's voice seemed out of place and unnecessarily severe.

What, Joe asked himself, *is she implying, beyond the murder itself? What suspicions is she referring to?*

The Yorkie, frustrated, growled and pulled on Strickland's pant leg, nearly knocking her off balance. She wheeled, and Joe watched with alarmed interest as she drew back a foot, seemingly about to kick the dog hard in the ribs. But something stopped her, and she quickly looked up to see Joe looking at her. To the side, the Yorkie yipped and cowered.

"That dog is going to get seriously hurt if he keeps it up," Melinda Strickland said through gritted teeth. "I picked him up at the shelter to be a companion for Bette, here," nodding at the cocker spaniel she held in her arms. "But it *isn't* working out."

Joe said nothing. Strickland turned from him back to the reporter, whom she dismissed with a few short words. Joe watched Strickland turn and look at the idling Sno-Cats as if nothing had just happened.

Joe was taken aback. She had restrained herself at the last possible moment, but it was obvious to him by the Yorkie's reaction that he'd been kicked before. The incident left Joe feeling unsettled.

The DCI agent-in-charge, Bob Brazille, turned away from another conversation, and walked up to Joe. Brazille had an alcoholic's mottled face and heavy-lidded eyes, and he made the introductions.

"Melinda Strickland, this is Game Warden Joe Pickett and Sheriff Bud Barnum."

With a chilly smile, Melinda Strickland stepped forward and extended a gloved hand from under the belly of the cocker spaniel. Barnum shook it; Joe followed suit, but more warily. He expected her to mention the Yorkie again, but she just smiled as if nothing had happened.

Melinda Strickland had wide hips, medium-length copper-colored hair, a long sharp nose, and dark eyes that made Joe think of a raven's. Wrinkles framed the corners of her mouth like parchment parentheses. She smiled with her mouth only—the eyes remained dark. Her manner of speaking contained lilt and chuckle, as if she were leading up to a punch line that didn't come.

"I understand there are some folks up here who aren't real crazy about the Forest Service, or the U.S. government, you know?" she said, as if sharing common knowledge. "And that Lamar Gardiner wasn't well liked because he strictly interpreted Forest Service policies."

"I doubt that was the reason," Joe answered, puzzled.

"I've been *hammered* by calls from people who want to know what's going on up here," she said, as if Joe had just agreed with her assessment.

"We need to get going," Barnum interjected, and for once Joe was grateful for the sheriff's brusqueness.

IN A RUMBLING, CLANKING, slow-motion procession, the tracked vehicles ascended on the still-unplowed road. Joe Pickett was in the one in front, sitting next to the driver, with two DCI agents wedged into the backseat. Joe's snowmobile and trailer-sled were hitched to the back of the Sno-Cat. Breathing diesel fumes and keeping the windows clear of fogging with a towel, Joe pointed out the turnoff from the highway into the forest, which had been transformed by the heavy snowfall. In the second Sno-Cat were the sheriff, his two deputies, and a photographer from the Saddlestring police department. The third vehicle contained Melinda Strickland, the attractive journalist shadowing her, two more DCI agents, and Melinda Strickland's two dogs.

The sky was sharply blue and the sun's reflection off the cover of snow was blinding. They passed from sun into shadow and into sun again as they approached the Wolf Mountain bowl. Snow ghosts—pines so packed and coated with snow that they looked like frozen spectral beings—stood sentry as the three battered, spewing vehicles passed below.

"So he grabbed your handcuffs and locked you to the

steering wheel, huh?" Bob Brazille asked Joe from the back. Brazille was overdressed in a mammoth down parka, and beads of sweat dotted his forehead.

"Yup," Joe answered over the engine noise. His voice was flat.

"That son-of-a-bitch, huh?" Brazille said.

"Turn here," Joe told the driver.

"The Feds are hot about this, judging by the temperament of that Strickland woman," Brazille continued, shouting over the roar of the engine. "Governor Budd got a call from some Washington mucky-muck. That's probably why Strickland is here. They don't like it when a federal employee gets whacked. The governor showed special interest in you, I was told. How does he know you?"

Joe felt a hot, embarrassed flush spread up his neck. "I arrested him a few years ago for fishing without a license."

Brazille's eyes widened, and he shook his head from side to side. "So you're the one, huh? I heard about that."

Joe nodded and looked away.

After a half-hour of silence, Brazille tapped Joe on his shoulder to get his attention.

"That info-babe with Strickland is a looker, eh?" Joe agreed, although he refused to admit that to Brazille. The journalist with Melinda Strickland was tall and thin and dressed in chic ski-wear: black tights, faux fur-lined boots, and a puffy yellow parka. She had short black hair, green eyes, very white skin, high cheekbones, and bee-stung red lips.

"What did you say her name was?" Joe asked.

"Elle Broxton-Howard," Brazille said, using a mocking British accent. "She's actually American, but she's lived in London for fifteen years or so. Some stuffy Brit magazine has her writing a story on Melinda Strickland."

"What's so significant about Melinda Strickland that they'd do a story on her?" Joe asked.

"I asked Elle Broxton-Howard that," Brazille answered, butchering the accent even worse than before. "She said Melinda Strickland heads up some task force on the increase of violence against federal land managers by local yay-hoos 'out here in the American outback,' as she put it. And Melinda's a woman in a man's world, so yada-yada-yada."

Joe turned to ask Brazille what "increase of violence" he was referring to, but the driver downshifted and the racket within the cab was too loud to continue the conversation.

THE SNO-CAT NOSED OVER the rim, and the wooded bowl was spread out in front of them. The brilliance of the snow hurt Joe's eyes. The snow had changed everything; the melded, muted greens, grays, and blues of the meadows and tree-covered folds of before were now portrayed in stark black and white, as if someone had adjusted the contrast of the picture to its most severe. The day had warmed up and the sunshine was lustrous. Pinpricks of reflected light flashed like sequins from the snow in the flats and meadows.

The next thing Joe observed was that something was wrong in the meadow where the elk had been killed. The area should have been undisturbed, but it was crisscrossed with tracks. Tapping him on the shoulder to get his attention, Joe asked the driver to stop, and swung outside the Sno-Cat. Standing on the running board, he raised his binoculars. Behind him, he heard the other two vehicles approach and stop, their motors idling.

It looked like a circus down there. He could see where

the snow had been dug up and piled in places, and spots where the snow was discolored.

Joe reentered the cab and closed the door. He turned to Brazille. "When you boys are through with me I need to take my snowmobile down there and look around."

"What's the problem?" Brazille said.

"It looks like somebody found those elk," Joe said.

"Who in their right mind would be up here?" Brazille asked. "Who would give a shit about dead elk in these conditions?"

Joe shook his head. He was wondering the same thing. He turned back toward the front. "Me," he said, more to himself than to Brazille.

"If we find whoever it was, we've got to question them about Lamar Gardiner's murder," Brazille said. "Maybe they heard something, or saw something."

Joe nodded.

"Hell," Brazille said, raising his eyebrows, "Maybe they were the ones who did it."

JOE LED ALL OF THEM through the heavy timber toward the tree where he had found Gardiner. The snow was thigh-high, with the consistency of flour. The men grunted and cursed behind him, and Joe felt a thin film of sweat growing between his skin and his first layer of clothing.

"How much farther?" Deputy McLanahan called out, between breaths.

"It's right up ahead," Joe answered, gesturing vaguely. It was hard to get his bearings, and he hoped he wouldn't walk beyond the tree.

"You *carried* Lamar all this way?" Barnum asked, his voice wheezing. "Jesus!"

"The snow wasn't as deep," Joe explained.

"Can we rest for a minute? I need some air," Melinda Strickland said, supporting herself against a tree trunk while she got her breath.

"Plus I've got some important calls to make," she said as she pulled a cell phone from her coat. She looked at the phone. "Shit, I don't have a signal up here."

"Don't you remember me saying that I couldn't get a signal from up here?" Joe asked, annoyed that she hadn't listened during the briefing that morning.

"Let's take a break before proceeding," she said, as if Joe hadn't spoken.

"You'd think she was leading the investigation," Barnum grumbled, although not loudly enough for Strickland to hear him. But the reporter, Elle Broxton-Howard, caught his remark and shot him a withering look.

"I don't think you're being fair to her," Broxton-Howard sniffed. "She is an amazing woman."

"Right," Barnum coughed, rolling his eyes toward Joe.

"When a man takes charge like that, he's a leader," Broxton-Howard said. "When a woman does it she's a nasty bitch."

Joe waded away from them in the fresh snow. He felt a sharp tug in his stomach. *First, an elk slaughter. Then a murder. Then a storm. Now this Melinda Strickland. What in* hell *is her official involvement?*

HE FOUND THE TREE, SPOTTING it by the glint on the twin shafts of the arrows. He had been concerned that the killer might have returned and dug them out of the soft wood with a knife blade. Finding the arrows brought a sense of relief.

Joe stopped and pointed. "I found him right there."

The party stopped and caught their breath. Billows of steam rose from them and dissipated above. The morning was eerily quiet, almost a vacuum. The storm had stilled the birds and the squirrels, who usually signaled the presence of strangers. The only natural sound was the occasional hushed *whump* of heavy snow falling from tree branches. One of the DCI men slid his day-pack from his shoulders and let it drop at his feet before unzipping it to dig out his evidence kit.

Joe stepped aside while the sheriff's officer and DCI men approached the tree.

"These arrows are Bonebuster-brand broadheads," one of the DCI agents said, leaning close to the thick, camouflage-colored shafts, but not touching them. "They have chisel-point tips that'll cut right through the spine of a big animal. These arrows are vicious bastards, and judging by how far they're sunk into the tree, whoever shot them had a compound bow with a hell of a pull on it. It's going to be tough to get these suckers out."

Joe shot a glance toward Strickland, who had had been quiet up until then. She stood in the trail, again cradling her cocker spaniel, cooing into the dog's ear. The Yorkie had been left to follow her, and did so by leaping through the deep snow in clumsy arcs. Strickland had not offered any advice, or suggested any procedure, since they had found the crime scene. Joe wondered if she really knew anything about conducting an investigation.

As if reading Joe's mind, Melinda Strickland spoke. "Elle needs to take some digital pictures of it," Strickland said, nodded to her. "We can use them in our investigation," she said.

"I can?" Elle Broxton-Howard asked, honored.

The local photographer had attached a filter to his lens to cut down the glare, and his camera made a distinctive sipping sound as he shot. Elle Broxton-Howard was obviously new to both her camera and this kind of photography, and she mimicked his actions with her digital camera. Getting the hint, the photographer offered to assist her. When she bent over to retrieve a dropped lens cap, McLanahan and Brazille eyed her form-fitting tights and exchanged boyish grins.

"I don't know what in the hell we can possibly find up here besides these arrows," Barnum complained. "This is a whole different world than it was three days ago."

Brazille shrugged, and agreed. Then he ordered one of his team to fire up the chain saw they had brought. Brazille's idea was to cover the arrows with a bag and cut down the tree, which was about a foot thick. They would then cut the trunk again, above the arrows, and transport the section back to town, where it would be shipped to the crime lab in Cheyenne. This way, he said, they wouldn't damage the arrows or smudge prints by trying to remove them from the wood.

"McLanahan, go through the trees over there to the other road and look for tracks or yellow snow," Barnum barked at his deputy. "If you find anything, take a picture of it and then bag it."

McLanahan made a face. "You want me to bag yellow snow?"

"It can be tested for DNA," one of the DCI agents said.

"Shit," McLanahan snorted.

"That, too," Barnum said flatly, which brought a laugh from Brazille. McLanahan scowled.

As one of the agents primed the chain saw, Joe turned.

"Do you need me for anything else?" he asked Brazille and Barnum. "If not, I need to check out that meadow."

Brazille waved Joe away. Barnum just glared at Joe, clearly still annoyed that Joe was there at all, butting in on his investigation.

Joe said nothing, accepting the fact that Barnum had a problem with him. The feeling was mutual.

But if Joe had been given the choice to decide who would head up the investigation—Sheriff Barnum or Melinda Strickland—well, he was glad he didn't have to choose.

The chain saw coughed and then started, the high whine of it invasive and loud, cutting a swath through the silence of the morning.

JOE SLOWLY CRUISED through the meadow on his snow-mobile, half-standing with a knee on the seat, studying the tracks and re-creating what had happened. There had been at least three snow machines in the meadow, he judged. Two of them were similar, with fifteen-inch tracks and patterns. The third track was slightly wider, with a harder bite, and the machine that made it had been towing some sort of sleigh with runners. The visitors had been there the evening before, since a few fingers of fresh white snow had blown into the tracks during the night.

Whoever had been there had ignored Gardiner's pickup, which was encased in snow near the tree line. Two deputies were in the process of digging their way to it so they could photograph the inside of the cab.

The piles of snow he had seen from above were where the elk had been found and butchered. The visitors had found all of them.

The discoloration in the snow was from flecks of blood, hair, and tissue. The hindquarters and tenderloin strips had been removed from the elk and, Joe assumed, loaded onto the sleigh. He noted scald marks in the snow, and tissue blowback from where the cutting had been done. They'd used chain saws. Although Joe was grateful that the meat hadn't gone to waste, the circumstances of its harvesting were bizarre. It wasn't likely that three snowmobilers had been out for recreation the night before, as the storm finally let up. Their tracks showed that they had entered the meadow from the west, from the Battle Mountain area, and had left the way they'd come. They had driven directly to the meadow, then scouted it in wide circles until they began to find the lumps of the carcasses. He could see that their tracks dug deeper on the way out than when they entered, no doubt due to the thousand pounds of meat they had hauled.

More than a thousand pounds of meat, Joe thought, and whistled. Who had the manpower, the equipment, and the acumen to butcher five elk during a mountain blizzard? How had the visitors known the elk were there? And, obviously, was there a connection between the snowmobiles in the meadow and the murder of Lamar Gardiner?

Joe used his hand-held radio to contact Barnum and Brazille.

"They took *five* elk somewhere on snowmobiles?" Barnum asked. He heard Brazille ask Barnum for the radio.

"Can you see any tracks heading up this direction?" Brazille asked.

"Nope," Joe said.

"Then it's unlikely these meat-lovers knew about Gardiner being up here, or I think they would have checked on him," Brazille concluded.

"That's possible," Joe said. "But they could have done that earlier. It's been two days. There's been a lot of new snow since Gardiner was killed, so it's impossible to see if they were up here before last night."

"Hold on just a second," Brazille asked, and clicked off.

A few minutes later, Brazille came back on and asked for Joe.

"McLanahan found some yellow snow near the other

road," Brazille reported. "He bagged it. So we've got a little something to go on."

The thought of McLanahan grumbling and digging through the powder made Joe smile to himself.

"I think I'll find out where these tracks end up," Joe said. "They go west toward Battle Mountain."

He heard Brazille consulting with Barnum for a moment, then Brazille came back on.

"Don't confront anyone if you find them," Brazille said. "And keep your radio on at all times."

"Will do," Joe said.

"Sheriff Barnum asked me to tell you not to do anything that will piss him off."

"I don't think I can do that," Joe said.

Joe and Barnum had never been close, but their working relationship had been strained further since the previous summer. Joe had suspected Barnum of complicity and corruption in regard to the events that took place at Savage Run. But there was no proof, and the sheriff had fessed up to nothing. There was now an underlying hostility between them, and Joe knew that someday it would break out into something ugly.

BEFORE RESTARTING HIS MACHINE, Joe photographed the tracks, the remnants of the carcasses, and the blowback and jotted his observations in his spiral notebook. He patted his coat to make sure he had everything he might need: binoculars, handcuffs, pepper spray, batteries for the radio, his .40 Beretta.

Then he fired the motor, goosed it, and sat back as he entered the timber, staying in the tracks of the visitors.

*   *   *

OVER THE TOP OF THE west rim, six miles into the forest, the tracks stopped at a forest service road. Joe was out of the wind now, on the south side of the mountain, and the snow was not as deep. The vehicle that had pulled the snowmobile trailer up the mountain was long gone, but Joe could see footprints in the road where someone had loaded the machines, and where the truck had turned around. He took more photographs.

The reception was scratchy, but he was able to reach Brazille on his radio and tell him what he had found.

"Never mind that," Brazille answered. "We just got a report that a rancher saw a vehicle coming down the mountain that night about the same time as you did. The rancher says he identified the vehicle and the driver and that he's some bad-ass local yahoo who lives alone out in the sticks. So we've got to get back down in the valley and regroup. And get this," Brazille continued. "He's a bow hunter."

Then Joe heard Strickland's voice from somewhere near Brazille: "Let's get that bastard."

WHEN JOE RETURNED, the team was trudging back to the Sno-Cats carrying the section of tree with the arrows in it. Joe shuttled back and forth between them and the vehicles, giving rides on the back of his snowmobile. The Sno-Cats roared back to life and started clanking down the mountain, but then Joe saw the lead machine stop abruptly. The driver crawled out, and was peering under his vehicle. Joe got out of the cab and walked over to him. They were joined by Melinda Strickland.

"Aw, I'm so goddamned sorry about this," the driver said, clearly upset. "I saw that little dog dart right under my track and felt the bump before I could do anything about it."

Joe squatted, trying to see any sign of the dog under the heavy metal track. He could see a tuft of hair on the snow, and the still paw of the Yorkie sticking out from beneath the metal cleat.

He braced himself for the explosion. It didn't come.

"The only place that dog could run was in the packed down snow from the Sno-Cats. It's too deep everywhere else," the driver said. Joe noticed that his eyes were moist and he looked like he was about to be ill.

More of the team had gotten out and were standing around the lead Sno-Cat, looking down at what remained of the dead Yorkie.

"How did the dog get out of the Sno-Cat?" Joe asked.

"I didn't let it in," Strickland said.

Joe felt a chill. It had nothing to do with the cold.

"Ma'am, I'm so . . . ," the driver started, but Strickland dismissed him with a wave of her hand. Joe watched her walk clumsily back through the snow toward her vehicle. If she was upset, he couldn't tell.

As she opened the door to climb back in her vehicle, she glared at the men still standing in the snow.

"We need to stop wasting time here," she snapped. "Lamar Gardiner's killer isn't going to wait for *us*."

Everyone stood there for a moment, then silently shuffled back to their Sno-Cats. The first machine lurched forward and resumed its pace. From the second, Joe saw a flat, tan, pie-shaped object in the road. He winced as he rolled over it, but there was no bump.

THE SUSPECT'S NAME WAS Nate Romanowski, and he lived on a small tract of land south of Saddlestring near the river. Joe had heard the name before, somewhere, but he couldn't place it. The procession of vehicles made their way along a county road toward Romanowski's cabin.

Sheriff Barnum had called ahead and ordered a county snowplow driver to start clearing the road toward the river. By the time the sheriff's department, the DCI team, and Joe Pickett had taken the Sno-Cats back down the mountain to the highway and gotten back into their trucks, the snowplow driver had reported that 75 percent of the road had been cleared. The snowplow operator was attacking the last 25 percent when the parade of four-wheel drive vehicles caught up with him and settled in behind.

While the plow roared ahead of them, tossing wind-hardened plates of snow to the shoulder like winter flagstones, Joe thought that he must be taking part in the slowest-moving raid in law enforcement history.

He had listened to the conversations on the radio while they drove. A local rancher, Bud Longbrake, had told the dispatcher that he'd been checking on his cattle in his winter pasture at the confluence of Bitter Creek and Crazy Woman Creek when the storm hit. He had gotten disoriented in the heavy snowfall, taken a wrong turn, was briefly lost, then found out where he was when he hit the road that led down from Wolf Mountain. As he turned onto the road in the blizzard, he was almost broadsided by an older-model Jeep that was screaming down the two-track. As the Jeep passed him, Longbrake said, he could see the driver clearly in his headlights. He recognized the profile, as well as the long blond ponytail. It was Nate Romanowski, all right. And Longbrake said Romanowski was a strange son-of-a-bitch—a recluse who hunted for all of his food with a bow and arrow and who raised birds of prey to hunt with as well.

Now Joe remembered where he had heard the name before. Romanowski had sent in an application for a falconry permit. It was the only falconry-hunting application he had ever encountered on the job.

6

NATE ROMANOWSKI LIVED IN A STONE HOUSE ON THE banks of the north fork of the Twelve Sleep River. Across the river, a steep red bluff rose sixty feet into the air, topped by a crew-cut juniper brush that this morning supported sixteen inches of frosting-like snow. The sun lit up the red face of the bluff. The deep river was slowed by its cargo of slush.

Inside the stone house, Romanowski threw off his quilts after a midday nap. The inside walls of the house were cold, and the only light was a quarter-inch shaft from the edge of the shuttered window. He opened the shutters and squinted at the snow. After lighting a wood fire in his stove, he pulled on a pair of insulated coveralls and a tall pair of black rubber Wellington boots. He tied his blond hair into a ponytail with a leather thong, clamped on his cowboy hat, and started to cook a late lunch of pronghorn antelope steak, eggs, and toast.

After he'd eaten, he stepped outside into the deep snow. The sun had begun to soften it, and it crunched slightly as he high-stepped through it. Rocky Mountain winters were nothing like most people perceived, he thought. In the foothills and flats, the snow didn't stay on the ground all winter like it did in the Northeast or Midwest. It snowed, blew around, then melted, then snowed again. The mountains were a different situation.

He thought he heard the sound of a motor in the distance. He stopped and cocked his head. He was too far from the highway to hear traffic, so the sound of a motor usually meant someone was either lost, stuck, or coming to see him. The rushing sound of the river was loud this morning, and he didn't hear the sound again.

IN THE SHACK, OR "MEWS," where the birds were, strips of light caught swirling dust mixed with crystals of ice. The peregrine falcon and the red-tailed hawk perched on opposite corners of the mews on dowel rods. They were motionless. A slash of sunlight striped their breasts.

Romanowski pulled on a welder's glove and extended his right arm. In a leather hawking bag slung from his belt, two pigeons struggled. The hawk stepped from the dowel rod and gripped the weathered leather of the glove. Romanowski raised his arm and studied the bird, turning it slowly to see the tail feathers. They were still broken off evenly, but were regrowing. In two months, the hawk would once again be in the air. It was a much-changed bird from the one he had found crumpled on the side of the highway, stunned and still from bouncing off of the windshield of a cattle truck. The hawk had eaten well and filled out, and its eyes had regained their cold black sharpness, but it wasn't out of danger yet. For the first six weeks, while it recovered, Romanowski had kept the leather hood over its eyes to keep the bird calm. Dark meant calmness. Only recently had he begun to re- move the hood for short stretches of time. At first, the hawk had reacted poorly, screeching hysterically. But now the bird was getting used to the light, and the outside stimuli.

He dug for a pigeon with his free hand and brought it up flapping. Nate trapped the pigeons in barns and on top of old stores in downtown Saddlestring. He stuffed the head of the pigeon between his gloved fingers while the hawk watched, very intent. When the pigeon was secured, the hawk bent down and took the pigeon's head off.

The hawk ate the entire pigeon—feathers, bone, and feet—his gullet swelling to the size of a small fist. When the pigeon was gone and the hawk's beak and head were matted with bloody down, Romanowski put the bird on a perch outside the mews. The peregrine now stepped up to his fist.

Romanowski took the falcon out into the dry cold. Jesses—long leather straps attached to the bird's legs— were wrapped in Romanowski's gloves. The other pigeon lay motionless in the hawking bag.

The peregrine had not yet focused attention on the sack; it had locked its eyes on something beyond the stone house and through the triad of formidable cottonwoods, out toward the sagebrush plains. *Perhaps,* Romanowski thought, *the peregrine heard a motor too.*

Romanowski released the peregrine, who flapped loudly upward until it caught a thermal current near the river. The bird circled and rose, soaring up in a tight spiral. He watched the falcon until it merged with the sun.

He reached down into his bag and pulled out the pigeon. He tossed it into the air, and the bird flapped furiously downriver for the cover of the trees.

Romanowski's eyes moved from the falcon to the pigeon and back.

At the altitude of a thousand feet, the peregrine

tucked its wings, contracted its talons, rolled onto its back, and dropped head-first like a bullet. It cut through the air in a wide, daredevil arc, slicing across the fabric of the light-blue Wyoming sky. Sensing this, the pigeon increased its speed, darting from bank to bank, close to the surface of the water.

The peregrine, feet tight like fists, connected from above with a sound like a fastball hitting a catcher's mitt. The pigeon exploded in blood and feathers. The peregrine caught air a few inches above the river, pitched up, and dived again quickly to snatch the largest chunk of the pigeon before it hit the water. Then the peregrine settled gracefully on a narrow sand spit and devoured the dead bird.

Pigeon feathers floated down softly all over the water and swirled downriver on the way, eventually, to the town of Saddlestring.

Romanowski whistled in awe, and rubbed his forearm until the goose bumps flattened.

ROMANOWSKI HEARD THE SOUND AGAIN, and this time he saw what was making it. He cupped his hands around his eyes to shade them against the glare of the snow, and saw the top of a snowplow on the flat, and a procession of other vehicles behind it. The fleet shimmered in the distance.

"Here we go," he said aloud.

7

UPON ORDERS FROM THE SHERIFF, THE SNOWPLOW stopped short of the final sagebrush crest that rose between the road and the river. Joe saw the snowplow veer to the left, off of the road, and the brake lights of the sheriff's Bronco light up. Then, doors were flying open and heavily armed men were pouring out of the vehicles into the deep snow. Barnum walked back from his Bronco and stopped at the rental DCI Yukon to gather everyone around him.

Joe Pickett dug for his shotgun behind the seat. It was a new model, slicker and lighter than the old Wingmaster he'd bird-hunted with until recently. That shotgun, like his sidearm and pickup, had been replaced after they were destroyed a year ago during his flight through Savage Run. He and Marybeth were still scouting for a new horse to replace Lizzie.

As he quietly closed his pickup door, Joe felt oddly removed from the rest of the unit. He was a game warden, after all, not an assault-team member. He was used to working alone. But the sheriff had jurisdiction now, and Joe was in a mandated support role.

Joe looked around him at the DCI agents and the deputies from the Sheriff's Department. Although he assumed they had all received some kind of training, this situation was well beyond what he or any of them was used to. The police-blotter column that ran every week in the Saddlestring *Roundup* consisted of small-time domestic disputes, dogs without tags chasing sheep, and moving violations. This was no SWAT team. The men were doing their best, though, Joe thought, to look and act as if they were big-city cops on another routine raid. Given the pent-up aggression they no doubt had and their general lack of experience, Joe hoped the situation would stay under control. He had seen Deputy McLanahan empty his shotgun at tents and pull the trigger to hit Stewie Woods in a cow pasture. How much restraint would he use when confronted with a brutal murderer?

Once again, he thought of how he had found Lamar Gardiner—sitting among the elk carcasses and stuffing cigarettes into his rifle. No one could have anticipated Gardiner's state of mind, or his subsequent actions. If Joe had had a secure location in his vehicle, or if he'd had backup, this could all possibly have been avoided. But Joe hadn't had either of those things. He was expected to bring lawbreakers to jail, but wasn't exactly equipped for it if they were hostile or resisted arrest. Nonetheless, what had happened in the mountains had triggered this chain of events. He felt guilty, and responsible. And he wanted, and needed, to see this thing through, even though this was the last place he wanted to be. Only when he was convinced that Nate Romanowski had killed Lamar Gardiner, and that Romanowski was in custody, would Joe's conscience let him rest.

It was the day before Christmas, after all, and the

place he should be was home. Instead, he loaded six double-ought buckshot shells into his shotgun, racked the slide, and approached the group of officers who were clustered around Barnum.

"SPREAD OUT NOT MORE THAN twenty feet from each other and form a skirmish line as we approach," Barnum said. "I want Agent Brazille on the left end and I'll be on the right. I want this Romanowski perp to think a thousand men are advancing on him. As we approach the cabin, Brazille and I will close on it and flank it from both sides in a pincer movement. I want everyone in the line to move from cover to cover, but keep moving forward. Imagine you're kick-returners in football. No lateral movements. Keep advancing up the middle toward that cabin."

Barnum sounds impressive in these kinds of situations, Joe thought. This was Joe's first raid of this kind, however, so he couldn't compare Barnum's orders or plan to anything he had experienced before. Watching the DCI agents, Saddlestring police officers, and sheriff's deputies loading and checking weapons, he was reminded of Barnum's theory of addressing every situation with overwhelming firepower, which they certainly had.

"I'll take the point, if you want," Deputy McLanahan offered, slamming the clip into a scoped M-16 semiautomatic rifle. As if for maximum effect, McLanahan worked the bolt as well, sliding a cartridge into the breech.

"No way, McLanahan," Barnum said, sounding tired. "We don't need cowboys."

Joe watched McLanahan carefully, noting the sting as McLanahan's eyes narrowed in embarrassment and anger.

"No firing unless it's in self-defense," Brazille interjected, eyeing McLahanan as well as his own men.

"I've heard he has some kind of big fucking hand-gun," McLanahan said. "If he goes for it—the party's over."

Barnum and Brazille exchanged worried glances. "If he goes for his big gun," Barnum said, "we turn him into red mist."

Joe grimaced. "Red mist" was a term prairie-dog hunters used when they hit the indigenous rodents with high-powered rifle bullets and the impact reduced the animals, literally, into puffs of spray.

"I've got some questions for him when you've got him in custody," Melinda Strickland said, speaking for the first time since they had arrived.

Again, Joe wryly noted that although Strickland seemed to want to be in charge of something, she had no apparent experience with tactics or strategy. And she seemed more than willing to stay out of danger.

"That's fine," Barnum agreed. "But please stay back here since you're not armed."

"That won't be a problem," Strickland chortled.

ODDLY, JOE PICKETT THOUGHT OF his children as he approached the stone house in the skirmish line. He thought of his girls getting ready for the Christmas Eve church service; trying on dresses and tights, asking Marybeth what she thought of their outfits, furtively checking out the brightly wrapped presents under the tree. It was a Pickett family tradition that, after a supper of clam chowder and a trip to church, the children could choose one present to unwrap. Except for Lucy, the girl with style, it was a catastrophe if the present they chose turned out to be clothing. Sheridan, especially, wanted games or books to tide her over until Christmas morning. April claimed she wanted a toaster oven. (She wasn't getting one.) She had explained that she used to warm up her own meals when she was with her mother and father, and would like to be able to do that again. Marybeth had assured her that there would be plenty to eat, but April didn't seem to completely understand.

Joe shook his head to clear it knowing he needed to focus on the situation at hand. He snapped his shotgun's safety off, and tried to keep the recommended distance between himself and two DCI agents as they neared the crest. A stand of cottonwoods crowned by snow provided the only "cover" he could see.

He approached the crest as he would if he were hunting or patrolling—inch by inch. He saw the snow-covered roof of the stone house, then the ragtop of the Jeep. Above them was the bloodred rim of the wall on the other side of the river.

Then he rose far enough to see a surprising, and jarring, sight: Nate Romanowski stood in plain view near a clapboard shed. The suspect stood tall and ready, with both hands empty and away from his body. He was facing the skirmish line, as if waiting for them to come.

Joe stared at Romanowski, and was impressed—and intimidated—by his size and his calm. Romanowski stood stock-still, but Joe could see the man's eyes move from deputy to deputy at they approached. Joe didn't see alarm or threat in Romanowski's demeanor, just that steely calm.

In his peripheral vision, Joe saw both Barnum and Brazille appear from the sides with their weapons drawn. Romanowski saw them too, and leisurely raised his hands.

Then the skirmish line broke and they were on him, a half-dozen high-powered weapons trained on the breast pocket of Romanowski's coveralls. Brazille held his pistol to the suspect's temple with one hand and ran his other hand over Romanowski's person, checking for weapons. When he got to the empty hip sack, he jerked it away to the ground. Barnum barked an order, and the suspect put his hands behind his head and laced his fingers together.

The skirmish line stood erect and began to crowd Romanowski. Joe lowered his shotgun and followed. Two of the DCI agents peeled off and walked toward the stone house.

"You want to confess now or wait until you get into my nice warm jail?" Barnum asked, his voiced raspy.

Romanowski sighed deeply, and looked straight at the sheriff.

"I'm just surprised that they sent the local yokels," Romanowski said. "Do you think there are enough of you?"

Sheriff Barnum didn't know what to make of Romanowski's comment. Neither did Joe. They looked toward Brazille, who shrugged.

Joe tried to read Nate Romanowski. The man certainly didn't display any fear, which seemed unnatural—and suspicious—in itself. Joe realized with a chill that he had no trouble picturing Romanowski drawing a bow and firing two arrows into an unarmed Lamar Gardiner, then walking up and drawing a knife across his throat while his victim watched him, wild-eyed.

"I understand you're a bow hunter," Barnum asked.

Suddenly, from inside the mews, there was a rustling noise and a screech. Deputy McLanahan turned on his boot heels and, his M-16 on full auto, blasted a solid stream of fire at the structure, which heaved and collapsed in on itself in a cloud of dust and feathers. The smell of gunfire was sharp in the air and the thundering echoes of the shots washed back from the bluffs. The snow was scattered with steaming brass shell casings.

"Nice job," Romanowski hissed through clenched teeth. "You just killed my red-tailed hawk."

Miraculously, the hawk was unharmed. Squawking with an annoyed *reep-reep-reep* chorus, the bird extricated itself from under fallen boards and hopped to the top of the new pile. With several heavy flaps of its wings, it clumsily caught air and began to rise.

McClanahan started to raise his weapon and Joe reached out and caught the barrel.

"What are you doing, McLanahan?" Joe asked, annoyed.

"Leave it be," Barnum said to his deputy who, with a scowl at Joe, relaxed and swung his rifle back to Romanowski.

A DCI agent tumbled from the stone house, clearly alarmed by the gunfire. He righted himself, and looked to Brazille. "We've got a compound bow and a quiver of arrows in there. And this . . ." He held up a leather shoulder holster filled with a massive, long-barreled stainless-steel revolver. This, Joe guessed, was the "big fucking handgun" that McLanahan had mentioned earlier.

This guy is no complete innocent, Joe thought. He had never seen a handgun as large.

Melinda Strickland, who had been far behind in the raid, now strode into the gathering.

"Do you hate the government, Nate?" Melinda Strickland suddenly asked Romanowski. Elle Broxton-Howard was at Strickland's shoulder, scribbling notes on a pad.

Romanowski seemed to think about it for a minute. Then he turned toward her slightly—not quick enough to elicit a reaction from the trigger-happy team—and said, "All of a sudden I don't have any idea what we're talking about."

Joe studied Romanowski. What he saw, for the first time, was confusion.

"What I do know is that you people came onto my property with firearms and tried to kill my recovering falcon," Romanowski said, his calmness eerie and out of place. "Who is the Barney Fife in charge of this outfit?"

As a response, McLanahan stepped forward and slammed Romanowski in the mouth with the butt of his rifle. Romanowski's head snapped back, and he stumbled. But he didn't lower his hands. Despite the slash of burbling crimson and bits of broken teeth on his lips, Romanowski sneered at McLanahan.

Joe had taken a step toward McLanahan again, but Barnum had flung his arm out to stop him. Joe couldn't believe what the deputy had just done.

"You people have no idea what you've just gotten yourselves into," Romanowski warned, his voice barely perceptible.

"Neither do you," Melinda Strickland said, her face hard.

"Hit the son-of-a-bitch again," she ordered. And despite Joe's shout to stop it, McLanahan did.

8

JOE WAS PLEASED TO SEE THAT THE PLOW HAD COME down Bighorn Road that day as he drove home. It had cut a single lane through the drifts, and massive flag-stone-sized plates of wind-hardened snow had been flung onto both sides of the cut, making the edges look jagged and incomplete. He smiled slightly to himself, thinking how disappointed the girls would be that they would have to go to church after all.

But, he thought, *I need to go to church, even if they don't.* He needed to leave the blood, gore, and violence of the last few days behind him. The Christmas Eve service wouldn't wash him clean, but it might, at the very least, change the subject to something better and more hopeful. The apprehending of Nate Romanowski left a sour taste in his mouth. Although from the outside, it might look like a highly successful investigation and arrest—hell, they identified the killer and captured him all in the same day, and in miserable conditions—to Joe things seemed tainted. His mind melded the death of Melinda Strickland's little dog with the rifle-butt beating of Nate Romanowski. He couldn't get the image of Romanowski's face pulled tight with confusion out of his mind. Given the eyewitness testimony and the discovery of what appeared to be the murder weapon, there was no reason to think that Romanowski wasn't the killer— except that something in Romanowski's face bothered Joe. It was as if the man had expected to be arrested, but for something else. Or, Joe thought, as if Romanowski thought he had a perfect alibi but no one was biting. *Something* . . .

Joe wanted a sense of massive relief that this was over, that the murder investigation was complete, that the thing he had started had finally ended. But he didn't feel that way.

Maybe I'm asking for too much, he thought. Maybe these things just weren't as neat and clean as he hoped they would be. His experience pointed in that direction, after all. Maybe this was a hangover of success, and tomorrow he would see it all in a different light.

He needed to put it out of his mind, at least for a while. And he needed to go to church.

WHILE THEY DRESSED, JOE TOLD Marybeth about what had happened during the day. She listened intently.

Moments before, Marybeth had entered the living room where the girls were playing, clapped her hands sharply and announced, "Ladies, we are going to church."

Sheridan was silent, but glared at her mother. April had moaned. Lucy had begun to chatter about what she would wear.

"So we might have wrapped this thing up," he said now. "Like a Christmas present to Saddlestring."

Marybeth paused a beat. "Why don't you sound convinced?"

He saw his own bitter smile in the mirror.

"I'm not sure," he said. "I need to sort it out in my mind, I guess."

She nodded, but kept her eyes on him. He had tried to sound upbeat, but she always read him correctly. He could see her reflection watching his.

"That poor little dog," she said, shaking her head.

"Yup."

"Do you think it was deliberate?" she asked.

"That's my suspicion. Either she wanted to punish the dog by making it run behind the Sno-Cats, or to leave it up there, or to set the stage for what happened. I just don't know."

"She might have let that dog in the Sno-Cat if you or someone had said something," Marybeth said. "Maybe out of shame, if nothing else."

Joe whistled. "I don't know, darling. I don't think anyone knew the dog was out. And she doesn't seem the type who feels shame."

Marybeth shook her head. "At least now she'll go back to wherever she came from."

"Let's hope," Joe said, admiring his wife in her dress. "You look like ten million bucks, you know."

IN A TIE AND HIS unfashionable topcoat, Joe Pickett herded his children into the aged minivan after the Christmas Eve church service. Missy, dressed to the nines in black formal wear and pearls she had packed for Jackson Hole cocktail parties, joined her grandchildren in the backseat with a sigh. Marybeth slid into the passenger seat.

The service had been good, Joe thought. Surrounded by his family while the songs and message washed over him, he felt partially cleansed of the scene of unnecessary

savagery he had witnessed earlier in the afternoon. Lamar
Gardiner or no Lamar Gardiner, there had been no reason
for McLanahan and Barnum to beat Nate Romanowski.
He said a prayer for Mrs. Gardiner, and a little prayer for
the dead dog, but he felt self-conscious doing it.

Sheridan was seated directly behind Joe in the van.

"How about two presents, just in case the first one is
clothes?" she asked.

"Sheridan has a point," April said from the back.

Joe grunted as he started the motor. The influx of
bodies into the car steamed all of the windows. The
night was clear so far, although snow had once again
been predicted, and the moon was framed by a secondary halo.

If it came to a philosophical debate, he knew he would
lose on passion points. He was inclined to let them open
everything. Just as he was inclined to back Marybeth.

"It's tradition. One present on Christmas Eve," Marybeth interjected, turning in her seat. "And besides, you
need clothes."

"But I don't *want* clothes," Sheridan whined.

"Me neither," April added sourly.

"I do," Lucy squealed, cutely. Missy laughed.

"We *know*!" Sheridan shouted. "And maybe you expect some pearls like Aunt Missy's."

Joe said nothing. His mother-in-law liked to pretend
she was not a grandmother, but an aunt. She suggested
that the girls call her "Aunt Missy" in mixed company.
Joe thought it was ridiculous. This was a sore point.
Sheridan had obviously picked up on it.

"Let's all be kind to each other," Marybeth said, in
her most calming tone. *"It's Christmas Eve."*

It worked. Joe felt Sheridan give up her debating
points and settle into her seat. Marybeth was amazing,
Joe thought.

They drove through Saddlestring with the heater on high and the defroster at full strength. The girls pointed out the good decorations and dissed the poor ones.

After they had cleared the town limits, Joe sped up. They passed the feed store, the Saddlestring Burg-O-Pardner (the lighted outdoor sign beckoned: ROCKY MOUNTAIN OYSTERFEST FREE WITH PURCHASE OF SAME), and the Mini-Mart. But it was the unusual number of parked cars at the First Alpine Church of Saddlestring that made Joe slow down and look.

"I've never seen so many cars at *that* church since we moved here," Marybeth said.

Neither had Joe, and he often passed the church on his way home from work. The number of parked vehicles—more than thirty—was unusual in itself, but it was the license plates that caught his attention. There were campers, vans, battered four-wheel-drives, and SUVs from Montana, Idaho, New Mexico, Nevada, Colorado, North Dakota, Georgia, Michigan, and Wyoming. The small parking lot was filled with them, and late arrivals had lined up bumper to bumper along the entrance road.

"I'm pulling over," Joe announced. He wanted to check this out, even if it wasn't his business. As expected, his children responded with a collective moan.

Marybeth gave him a look. "Joe, you can take the night off."

"Wait," Sheridan suddenly said from the backseat. "It's all of those cars we saw in front of the school."

Joe shot a glance in the rearview mirror at April, to gauge her reaction. Her eyes had suddenly grown very large. But she said nothing.

"It'll just be a minute," he said.

Marybeth started to say something—Joe knew it was going to be a "be careful" admonition—but caught herself for the sake of the children and her mother.

"Don't be long," she said instead, turning to comfort the children, and especially April.

Joe left the van's engine running and the heater on, and walked down the middle of the road that led to the church. It had started to snow, and the moon was now blocked by swift-moving storm clouds.

The First Alpine Church of Saddlestring was a small structure made of logs with an adjoining double-wide trailer that served as living quarters for the "unconventional" Reverend B. J. Cobb and his wife, Eunice. The Reverend Cobb normally served a small congregation of Twelve Sleep County's survivalists and the dispossessed. These were the people who had chosen Saddlestring because it was the end of the road—people who built bunkers, stockpiled weapons and food, and reported sightings of black helicopters to the Sheriff's Department. Normally, even on Christmas or Easter, there were not more than a half-dozen cars at the church. The tiny congregation provided so little income that the Reverend Cobb supported himself and his wife by working full-time as a certified welder. Eunice was the Welcome Wagon lady, who met with new residents and gave them coupons to local retail stores.

The footing was icy. Large flakes wafted through the air and settled into vague cotton-ball shapes on the ice. The three steps to the front door were slick, and Joe steadied himself on the handrail as he climbed them. The church was heated inside by a stove; the sweet smell of woodsmoke hung in the air.

He stopped at the door, his fingers around the elk-antler handle. He could hear the Reverend Cobb finish a passage with a flourish. When Eunice began to play the electric piano—the church was too small and poor for an organ—he opened the door and stepped inside. A harsh mixture of woodstove heat, candlewax, and body odor assaulted him. Eunice was playing *Silent Night*. Most of the congregation sang in English, but a few were singing the words in poor German.

> *Stille Nacht! Heil'ge Nacht!*
> *Alles schläft, einsam wacht . . .*

The rough-hewn pews were packed with visitors wearing big, weathered coats. Their backs were to him. He recognized no one except for the Cobbs, and two locals, Spud Cargill and Rope Latham, who co-owned a company called Bighorn Roofing. He had recognized their identical white Ford pickups outside—the ones with the company logo of winged roofing shingles on the doors. Joe suspected them of poaching, but had never caught them in the act.

As the congregation began the second verse, Reverend Cobb noticed Joe standing in the back. Still singing, the minister skirted the row of pews and greeted Joe with a handshake.

> *Schlafe in himmlischer Ruh'*
> *Schlafe in himmlischer Ruh'*

Reverend B. J. Cobb was a blocky ex-Marine who had served in Vietnam. He had short-cropped silver hair and a big jaw. His wife, Eunice, was just as short and just as blocky, with a mat of iron-gray curls on the top of her head. She had also been a Marine.

"Can the Lord, or this humble servant help you, Mr. Pickett?"

Joe surveyed the wall of turned backs and heavy coats.

"Maybe both of you can," Joe said. "Who are all these people?"

The Reverend Cobb smiled, and shrugged happily.

"They're here to worship and celebrate Christmas. Who am I to question that?"

Joe looked sharply at Cobb.

"I don't know them all yet," Cobb confessed. "I was happily surprised when they showed up for services."

Joe felt a pair of eyes on him and looked over Cobb's shoulder. A big, bearlike man had turned slightly in the back row. The man had a massive head with deep, soft eyes and fleshy lips. His expression was alert, but somehow calming. The man looked Joe over carefully, and Joe looked back. *He must be the one Sheridan described as their leader,* Joe thought. The man turned back to his hymnal.

"They've established a camp in the forest on Battle Mountain," Cobb said. "They all drove down tonight."

"You're kidding," Joe said, alarmed. "In the national forest?"

"That's what they told me. I haven't visited it yet."

"That sounds like trouble in the making," Joe mumbled.

Cobb smiled sweetly. Despite Cobb's unique take on things, Joe liked the man.

"I might give you a call in a few days," Joe said, thanking Cobb and shaking his hand good-bye. "Merry Christmas."

"And a merry Christmas to you, Joe Pickett," the reverend said.

Joe turned toward the door but paused before he opened it, feeling eyes on him again. He wondered if the big man had once again turned, to make sure Joe was leaving.

Slowly, Joe looked over his shoulder. The big man still had his back turned, and was singing. Then Joe saw her.

Because she was small, she couldn't see him over the congregation, so she had to lean out into the aisle. Her face was thin and pinched, her eyes so hard and cold that Joe shuddered.

The first time he had met Jeannie Keeley was at her husband Ote's funeral. She had walked up to Joe, pulling April behind her like a rag doll, and said: "Aren't you the motherfucking *prick* who wanted to take my Otie's outfitting license away?"

And now she was back.

AFTER MAKING THREE PILES OF Santa's gifts for discovery in the morning, and after eating the cookie and drinking the milk left for Santa by Lucy (with plenty of telltale crumbs), Joe and Marybeth said good night to Missy. She acknowledged them by raising her pinkie finger above the rim of her just-filled wineglass. That annoyed Joe, who was still on edge from seeing Jeannie Keeley.

Later, Joe joined Marybeth at the sink in their bathroom.

"So it was her for sure?" Marybeth asked, while removing her makeup in the bathroom mirror.

"Yup."

"How awful, Joe."

"I know."

"That poor little girl. I feel like she's a target, and she doesn't even know it."

When Marybeth had finished washing her face, she removed her clothes and slid her nightgown over her head. She walked to the bedroom, threw back the covers, and slid into bed.

Joe climbed into bed, exhausted. He could hear Christmas music playing from the radio downstairs. He arose and firmly shut the door, something they had done ever since Missy had arrived. Usually, the door was open in case any of the girls needed anything. As he walked back, Marybeth spoke.

"Joe, I know my mother gets to you, but you're getting worse at disguising your feelings. You make this . . . face . . . like the one you just made a few minutes ago. I know she notices it."

"I make a face?"

She nodded, and tried to imitate it.

"I look that bad?"

"Yes."

"I'll work on it," he said. "Marybeth, I seem to be annoying you quite a bit lately."

"I'm sorry, Joe. I don't mean to needle you. It's this thing with Jeannie Keeley. I have a very bad feeling about it. I'm on edge."

"I understand."

"Merry Christmas," she said. "And come to bed. Now."

Joe recognized her tone and was genuinely surprised. "What about that thing you have about not enjoying sex if your mother is under the same roof?"

"I need to get over that," Marybeth said, raising her eyebrows. "She might be here awhile."

"Aw . . ."

"Joe, get in this bed."

He did.

PART TWO

Snow Blind

9

CHRISTMAS WAS PLEASANTLY CLAUSTROPHOBIC, AND
Joe and Marybeth realized that with their growing children—and the addition of just a single extra person—
how small their home had become.

Joe roasted wild pheasant and grouse, while Marybeth and her mother made wild-rice casserole, mashed
potatoes, fresh bread, vegetables, and pecan pie. The
girls had been up early, of course, and their gifts were
opened, played with, tried on, and strewn about the living room. Because of their limited finances, Marybeth
budgeted throughout the year to provide a substantial
Christmas for the children, and she and Joe economized
on their own gift-giving. Marybeth gave Joe a new fly-
fishing vest, and Joe reciprocated with two pairs of Canadian-made Watson riding gloves. Marybeth loved the
gloves, which were suede, and lined with a thin layer of
fleece. She said they were supple enough for reining her
horses while riding, but tough enough to withstand stall-
mucking and other stablework.

Missy spent most of the afternoon on the telephone

in Joe's office with the door closed, talking with her husband, and came out wiping away tears. She might be staying awhile, she announced. Mr. Vankueren was being indicted, his assets had been frozen, and she was *quite angry* with him. Marybeth offered support, and the couch bed. Joe greeted the news with the false courage he hoped he would display one day when the doctor told him he had one month to live.

ON CHRISTMAS EVENING, AFTER THE melancholy period when the girls became quiet because the day was nearly over, Joe sat with Marybeth on the couch with his arm around her. They sipped red wine in the glow of the Christmas tree lights, enjoying a rare moment of quiet. The girls were down the hall getting ready for bed and Missy was napping.

"Joe, are you still fretting about Lamar Gardiner and Nate Romanowski?" Marybeth asked.

He started to protest, but realized she was right. "I guess," he said. "It's a hard one to just put away."

She nodded, and burrowed closer to him.

"And to make things even more complicated," Joe said, "we've got Jeannie Keeley back in town. And . . ."

He stopped himself.

"What?" she asked, then frowned. "Oh—my mother."

"Not that she's as bad as . . ."

"Hush, Joe."

He took a drink of wine, and wished he hadn't started down that road. Luckily, she seemed willing to let it go.

"I wish we could just stay snowed in," Marybeth whispered. "With our family all together under our roof. Where no one, and nothing, can get us." Her voice trailed off.

They sat without speaking, surrounded by the soft

sounds of Missy's breathing and the internal popping of the woodstove. Joe drank the last of his wine as he thought about what Marybeth had said.

"We can't control what's happening," he said softly. "All we can do is stay focused and be prepared. That means first things first: We need to find out what Jeannie Keeley's intentions are."

Marybeth looked up. "How?"

"I'll ask her," Joe said. "It may be that we're worried over nothing."

"God, I hope that's the case. Did you see how happy April was today? She had a glow I've never seen before."

Joe nodded. "I'll just flat-out ask her," he said, almost to himself. Which meant he needed to approach the rag-tag group of men and women who had been at the First Alpine Church of Saddlestring on Christmas Eve.

"Are you guys okay?" It was Sheridan, standing in the doorway in her new flannel pajamas. Joe and Sheridan shared a special look. She had been through a lot, and seemed specially tuned to gauging the moods and concerns of her parents. *She's getting older, more mature,* Joe thought. She was becoming formidable, like her mother.

"We're fine," Joe answered. "Go to bed, honey."

"Merry Christmas," she said, padding over to them for a hug and kiss.

"Merry Christmas, darling."

THE NEXT DAY, JOE PULLED on his wool vest and parka over his red uniform shirt and drove toward the mountains. He intended to see if he could find out if Jeannie Keeley was at the camp on Battle Mountain.

Snow had been cut sharply on each side of the road, and he had the feeling of driving through a tunnel. The top reflectors of delineator posts nosed out just above the surface of the snow at the level of his pickup windows. Another storm like the last would bury the tops of the posts for the rest of the winter, and the snowplow driver would be without landmarks in finding the road to plow, and would give up on it until spring.

While his tire chains bit into the snowpacked road, and the sun beamed off of the icy glazed surface, he thought about the stories he had read in the *Roundup* over breakfast. It was the first day that the newspaper had been delivered since the storm of a week ago. The arrest of Nate Romanowski commanded the front page. A photo of Romanowski in handcuffs, his eyes fixed boldly and contemptuously on the photographer, appeared under a headline that stated LOCAL MAN ARRESTED IN USFS SUPERVISOR MURDER. An old photo of Lamar Gardiner, looking particularly chinless, was inserted within the text. There was also a photo of Melinda Strickland, and she was quoted extensively throughout the article. Joe learned new information that Barnum had not passed along to him.

In addition to the compound bow found at Romanowski's home near the river, the DCI investigators had found two Bonebuster-brand broadhead arrows in a quiver, as well as a credit-card receipt for the purchase of four. Also found in the stone house were copies of letters Romanowski had sent to Lamar Gardiner protesting the closure of specific Forest Service roads that Romanowski claimed he used for accessing falcon traps and for hunting. With the account by the rancher placing Romanowski near the scene, the apparent murder weapon, the specific arrows, and the letters providing a motive, Melinda Strickland had "strongly speculated" that justice had been served.

The additional evidence was incriminating, Joe thought, and furthered the case against Romanowski. In a way, it surprised him. The doubts that he'd had when he saw Romanowski up close still nagged at him. But Joe had thought more about it over the past few days, and a few explanations had arisen. One, Joe recognized a tendency in himself to assume morality and rationality in others because he aspired to those qualities himself. Joe knew that if he was guilty of a murder, he certainly wouldn't be able to hide it. Hell, he'd confess to Marybeth so fast he'd leave skid marks. So Joe assumed others, even bad guys, would possess at least some of the same rationality and guilt, and that the guilt would be obvious in some way. But a person capable of the kind of cruelty that surrounded Lamar Gardiner's murder might not be rational at all, or even feel guilt in a conventional sense. Murderers and molesters of children were beyond Joe's comprehension, for example. And to assume that morality or guilt played a role in the mind of a molester was simply naïve. Maybe he was just as naïve about Nate Romanowski.

Two, Joe had followed his instincts before on occasions when it was later discovered that there was more to a crime than the obvious. This couldn't be the case every time, he conceded. Years ago, Barnum had told Joe that sometimes things are exactly what they seem. In the case in question then, Barnum had turned out to be wrong. But there was truth in that statement and Joe knew he needed to recognize it.

Nate Romanowski was not an average citizen, after all. He was a loner with a mysterious past and present. He lived alone, trained hawks, and carried a huge pistol. He was feared and talked about, but no one could really say why, except for his manner. He was just someone who seemed suspect from the start.

"This is only the beginning," Melinda Strickland was quoted near the end of the article. "The antigovernment movement that resulted in Lamar Gardiner's tragic murder still exists. Mr. Romanowski was merely a soldier. Our investigation, and my task force, will continue."

Joe had been troubled by that, just as he had been troubled when she first brought up the prospect to him. Unless he had been stubbornly oblivious—a possibility, he conceded—he could not see the "antigovernment" threat she seemed so sure of. Certainly, there were hunters, loggers, cattlemen, and now, apparently, *outlaw falconers,* who objected to some forest-service policies. But the opposition wasn't violent, or even organized, as far as Joe Pickett could tell. He wondered if Melinda Strickland headed up a federal task force in search of a task. And he wondered how long she would remain in Twelve Sleep County.

10

THE FIRST THING JOE SAW AS HE APPROACHED THE BATtle Mountain campground were the strands of barbed wire strung through the timber and stapled into the trunks of trees. There were several signs, two of them nailed over the top of the ubiquitous dark-brown Forest Service signs identifying the campground. Hand-painted in crude block letters. They read:

THE NATION OF
THE ROCKY MOUNTAIN SOVEREIGN CITIZENS.
ALL TRESPASSERS WILL BE VIOLATED.

The Sovereign Citizens, or "Sovereigns" as they called themselves, had literally taken over the old Forest Service campground. Their trailers, RVs, and pop-up campers occupied all of the camping spaces. Trails tramped down in the snow wound from unit to unit and clothing and equipment hung from ropes strung between trees. Crossbeams had been roped up to hang garbage, and possibly wild game, Joe surmised. In the center of the compound, tipi poles had been lashed together, but no canvas or hide had been attached yet. To Joe, the Sovereign Citizen compound looked like a twenty-first-century version of a Plains Indian winter camp. The road into the compound was blocked by a barbed-wire gate with orange ribbons tied to it for visibility.

Joe stopped in front of the gate, and stayed in his pickup while it idled. He decided not to enter unless invited in.

Two men wearing insulated coveralls who had been working on the tipi poles stopped what they were doing and stared at Joe. One of them raised a single-bladed axe and let it rest on his shoulder. The other walked to the nearest and biggest travel trailer and loudly knocked on the side of it with his knuckles.

There were only two Sovereigns visible, but Joe had no doubt that there were others watching him. Although the camp was cleared except for a few large trees, the forest walls on both sides were thick and dark, with trails from the compound leading into it.

Joe considered backing up and driving away, now that he had seen the camp. Judging by the lack of tire tracks in the snow, he was their first visitor since the plow had come through. His heart whumped in his chest. As usual, he had no backup, and Marybeth was the only person who knew where he was. But with the two men still staring, and his goal incomplete, he took a deep breath, steeled himself, and slowly opened his door. His boots squeaked as they hit the snowpacked road. Although the compound seemed deserted, Joe noted the hiss of propane tanks feeding the trailers and curls of steam and smoke rising from chimney pipes. And there was a cooking smell—of meat, but—something sweeter than roasting beef or chicken. Wild game was being prepared—pronghorn antelope, or elk.

Joe was about to ask the two men where the leader of the camp was, but the distinctive metal-on-metal sound of a slide being racked on a shotgun stopped him.

"You need some help, mister?"

Joe turned toward the sound and the voice. Someone stood behind a bulwark of downed green timber and piled snow. He saw the dull glint of metal between two evergreen branches, and guessed he was looking into the opening of a barrel. He could not see the man who spoke.

"Game Warden Joe Pickett," he said. "Please put the weapon away." His voice sounded steadier than he thought it would.

The barrel withdrew from the timber, but the man behind it said nothing.

Joe turned back toward the compound and watched as a door opened on the trailer the tipi worker had knocked on. The large man who emerged was the same one Joe had seen in the church—the man Sheridan had guessed was the leader.

Slowly, the man walked down the slope toward the gate, his outline bearlike, with wide, slumped shoulders, a massive head, and a fleshy mouth framed by pouchy jowls. Joe guessed his height at six-foot-five, his weight at least 290. Joe noted in his peripheral vision that a few curtains had been inched back and blinds raised in some of the campers. He tried not to think about how many weapons might be pointed at him. He knew that if the situation suddenly deteriorated and he was forced to fumble through his coat for his handgun—the shotgunner in the trees, and perhaps dozens of others, would have the time to fire.

Clamping on a floppy brown felt hat, the man approached the barbed-wire gate. He didn't open it, or invite Joe in, but extended a gloved hand through the strands.

"Wade Brockius," the man said. Brockius read Joe's name badge. "How can I be of service, Mr. Pickett?" Joe shook Brockius's hand, and tried to mask his own trepidation, although he guessed that he failed at that.

Wade Brockius had a profoundly deep gravel voice with a hint of a Southern accent, and soft, soulful eyes.

"I was hoping you could answer a couple of questions," Joe said. He could hear the *tick-tick-tick* of the radiator cooling from the grille of his pickup directly behind him.

Brockius smiled slightly. "Is it about the elk we found in the field?"

"That's one of the questions."

"We harvested them," Brockius declared. "They provided enough food for our entire group for months to come. I don't think we broke any laws doing it."

"No, you didn't." Joe shook his head. "Actually, I'm glad the meat didn't go to waste out in the meadow."

Brockius nodded, studying Joe and waiting for what would come next.

"How did you know about them?" Joe asked, watching Brockius carefully.

"Our advance team heard the shots," Brockius answered easily, without hesitation. "Five of our party were up here holding the campground until we got there. They heard a bunch of shooting way up there on the mountain and after the rest of us had arrived, they took some snowmobiles out to see what had happened. That's when they found the dead elk."

Joe nodded. He saw no holes in that.

"Did your people see or hear anyone else up there in that meadow?"

Brockius shook his head. "It was the next morning when they went up there," he said. "There's no way they could have gone up that night in that storm."

That was the first day I was snowed in, Joe thought. The time line made sense. He changed the subject.

"You know, of course, that you're in a national forest."

"Yes, we're aware of that."

"So you know there's a limit to the number of nights you can camp?"

Brockius's eyes narrowed, and the softness Joe had noted earlier hardened. "Are you an agent of the Forest Service as well?"

"Nope," Joe said quickly. "Not at all."

"Good," Brockius responded. "Because I really don't want to have an argument about this with you. As far as we can tell, this is a *public* campground in a *national* forest. By definition, that means that the forest is owned by the citizens of the United States. We own this, as do all American citizens. So I'm pleased to hear that you're not asking us to leave our forest."

Joe tensed. "There are others . . . Forest Service officials . . . who may want to make an issue of it, though. Stringing that barbed wire is an invitation for trouble."

Wade Brockius started to speak, then sighed deeply.

"The Forest Service are servants of the people, are they not?" Brockius didn't so much ask as state it. "They work for us. They are our employees, I believe. *I* didn't elect them, did you? So who are they to tell me where I can set up a camp in a place owned and operated by the people?"

"I'm not going to argue with you," Joe said. In fact, he wasn't sure he could make an argument with much effectiveness. "I just wanted to pass that along."

"Noted," Brockius said, his features softening once again.

"Do you know anything about the murder of Lamar Gardiner, the Forest Service supervisor here?" Joe asked suddenly, hoping to startle Brockius into revealing something.

"No, I do not," Brockius answered with gravity. "I heard about it on Christmas Eve. It's unfortunate. And I assume he was the man who shot all the elk in the meadow."

"Yes he was. Do you know a man named Nate Romanowski?"

"Never heard of him," Brockius said.

There was a beat of silence, and Joe heard the shot-gunner shift his position behind the timber.

"Do you plan to stay here long?"

Brockius looked heavenward, then his deep eyes settled on Joe. "I honestly don't know. We might, we might not. In many ways, this seems like a good place to settle in for a while. It feels like the end of the road, the end of our journey. You see, we've been traveling, and I'm very, very tired."

Joe's face obviously betrayed his confusion.

"There are about thirty of us," Brockius said. "From all over the country. We've found each other, and are bound together through mutual tragedies and experiences. Nearly all of us are the last of our kind, the survivors of places and situations that are just incredibly sad."

Brockius turned and pointed to a pop-up camper at the south of the compound. Joe noted the Idaho FAMOUS POTATOES license plate. "Ruby Ridge," Brockius said. "They were there when the FBI snipers shot the dog, the boy, and the woman as she stood at her door holding her baby. If you'll recall, no one on the federal side was ever prosecuted for that. Only the survivors." He pointed toward a camper on a pickup with Montana plates. "Jordan," he said. "The last of the Montana Free-men, only recently released from prison. They lost their liberty, their land, their prospects, everything. No one on the federal side was prosecuted for that, either."

Joe felt an icy shiver crawl up his spine as Brockius spoke. *How can this be happening, right here, right now?* he thought. Brockius could be putting him on. Joe hoped like hell he was.

"Waco," Brockius intoned, motioning toward a fifth-wheel trailer with a Texas plate parked next to his. "They lost their two young sons in the fire. No arrests were made of the officers or politicians who were there."

Brockius turned to Joe. His voice was still soft, but it suggested steel wrapped in velvet: "We see this place as our refuge, at least for a while. We pose no threat to anyone. We're beaten down and unbelievably tired. We've been wronged, but we just want to be left alone, and we intend to leave others alone. We need this place to rest."

Joe found himself staring back at Brockius. Oddly, he believed the man.

"It was nice meeting you, Mr. Pickett." Brockius thrust his hand through the fence again. "I think I've talked too much. It's a bad habit of mine."

Joe reached out, but felt weak.

"One more question."

Brockius sighed again. His expression was pained.

"Is a woman named Jeannie Keeley with you? And is she intending to contact the little girl she left in Saddlestring?"

"I understand it's her daughter," Brockius said.

"And mine," Joe said, his voice hard and low. "My wife and I are her foster parents. Jeannie Keeley abandoned April when Jeannie cleared out of Saddlestring five years ago. My wife and I are attempting to adopt her."

"Oh," Brockius said. "This is personal, then. And complicated."

"Not really."

"Yes, it is." Brockius looked apologetic. "I hope you understand that I have no control over the Sovereigns. They're here on their own free will, and can come and go as they please. They have their own business and personal interests. And if one of them is involved in legal action for custody of her daughter, that is no concern of mine or any of the others."

"Custody?" Joe repeated. His heart sank.

"She's not in camp right now," Brockius said, shaking his woolly head. "I'm not sure when she'll be back. But I'll tell her you were here."

Joe thanked Wade Brockius and watched as the big man trudged back toward his trailer.

Joe heard his own heartbeat in his ears. He had been hit with two hard blows within a few minutes. The explanation of who these people were. And the news that Jeannie had come back for April.

HEADING BACK DOWN BIGHORN ROAD, Joe was grateful for the walls of snow on either side of the road, because without them he'd be likely to drive right off it.

Was it really possible that the survivors, criminals, accessories, sympathizers, and victims of several of America's worst events had grouped together and decided to set up a compound in *his* mountains? Or that one of them, Jeannie Keeley, was there to take April back?

It was too much, too fast. Then his cell phone rang.

"This is Nate Romanowski," the voice said. Romanowski spoke with a kind of drawled sarcastic lilt. "I've got one phone call and I'm calling you, buddy. Can you meet with me?"

"Why aren't you calling a lawyer?" Joe asked, stunned.

"Because I'm calling you," Romanowski said, sounding annoyed. "Because I thought about it for two days and *I'm calling you*, mister."

"This is ridiculous."

"It sure is," Romanowski agreed. Joe assumed Romanowski was referring to the case against him. "I'll be waiting for you. I'll clear my schedule."

"Clear your . . ."

But Romanowski had hung up.

A FEW MINUTES LATER, HIS phone rang again.

Joe snatched it up.

"Please hold for Melinda Strickland," an unfamiliar female voice commanded.

"How did you get my number?" Joe asked. He knew he'd never given it to Strickland.

"Please hold for Melinda Strickland."

Joe held, anger welling up inside of him. He heard a click as the call was put through.

"Uh, Joe, why is Nate Romanowski calling you?" Strickland's voice was strained, as if barely under control.

"I'm not exactly sure," Joe answered. "But how did you know that, and how did you get my cell phone number?"

"I don't like being kept in the dark about things like this," she said icily, ignoring his questions.

Joe was confused.

"He *just* called. Just minutes ago. And why should I report that to you, anyway?"

"Because, Joe Pickett, I am in charge of this investigation. A man was murdered, you know." Her voice was dripping with sarcasm. "I *need* to be kept in the loop. I *can't have* this kind of thing happening behind my back."

"I don't know what you're talking about," Joe said, raising his voice. He felt his scalp twitch. "And there's nothing going on behind your back."

"He called *you*!" she shouted. "The man who murdered a federal employee on federal land called *you*, of all people!"

Joe stared at his cell phone as if it were a hyena. Then he raised it to his ear. She was still shouting.

"I'm losing my signal," he lied, then turned the phone off and tossed it angrily aside onto his truck seat.

11

BUCKING A ROOSTER TAIL OF PLOWED SNOW IN THE county building's lot, Joe parked in the designated visitors section and got out. Three floors of institutional blond brick housed the sheriff's office, the jail, the attorney, the court, the assessor, the treasurer, and other county administration offices. The sandstone inscription over the front doors read:

TWELVE SLEEP COUNTY—
WHERE THE PAVEMENT ENDS
AND THE WEST BEGINS

The slogan was an endless source of amusement, especially among a group of retired men who drank coffee every morning at the Burg-O-Pardner. They'd petitioned the Saddlestring *Roundup* for years with slogans that they preferred:

TWELVE SLEEP COUNTY—
TRAILHEAD FOR THE INFORMATION COWPATH

TWELVE SLEEP COUNTY—
MILLENNIUM? WHAT MILLENNIUM?

TWELVE SLEEP COUNTY—
TEN YEARS BEHIND WYOMING,
WHICH IS TEN YEARS BEHIND EVERYWHERE ELSE

Joe was still shaken from the events of the morning. The word "custody" hung in the air and wouldn't go away. Joe hoped like hell that Brockius was wrong. And where was Jeannie Keeley, if she wasn't in the camp?

Melinda Strickland's rantings had angered and confused him further. She had sounded unhinged, hysterical. When would she go away?

And now this. Nate Romanowski.

After hanging up on Strickland, Joe had decided to visit Nate at the county jail. He was curious as to why the man had called him. He hoped as well that talking to Nate would dispel the lingering doubts he had about his guilt. And Joe also hoped it would really piss off Melinda Strickland. A newly installed metal detector and security desk were manned by a semi-retired deputy wearing a name tag that identified him as "Stovepipe." He'd received the nickname years before in an elk camp when he fell over a woodstove in a tent and brought the chimney down all over himself. Joe had met Stovepipe during the previous summer when Joe had driven up on him to check out his fishing license. Stovepipe had fallen asleep on the bank of the river, where he had been bait fishing, and was angered to discover when he awoke that a trout had not only taken his bait, but had dragged his rod into the river.

This time, Stovepipe was awake, although barely.

"You ever find your fishing rod?" Joe asked, while he unbuckled his gunbelt and slid it across the counter.

Stovepipe shook his head sadly. "That was a hundred-dollar Ugly Stik with a Mitchell 300 reel. I bet you that fish must have been seven pounds."

"Maybe," Joe said, patting his pockets for metal items.

"Don't worry about it," Stovepipe said conspiratorially, leaning forward over the counter to see if anyone else was around. "The machine's broke anyway. It hasn't worked since July."

THE SHERIFF'S OFFICE AND COUNTY jail were on the second floor. Joe mounted the steps and pushed through frosted glass doors. Barnum's door was shut and his office was dark, but Deputies Reed and McLanahan sat at desks, staring into computer monitors.

"Which one of you told Melinda Strickland that Nate Romanowski called me?" Joe asked.

Reed was obviously puzzled by the question. That left Deputy McLanahan. When McLanahan looked up, Joe noticed two things. The first was a barely disguised hatred—a snake-eyed, thin-lipped countenance similar to a horse about to bite. The second thing he noticed were the stitches that appeared to fasten McLanahan's nose to his face.

"What can I help you with, Mr. Pickett?" McLanahan asked, the question posed as a bored statement.

"What happened to you?" Joe asked, taking his coat off and hanging it on a hook. He kept his cowboy hat on.

"Nate Romanowski happened to him," Reed volunteered from across the room. McLanahan glared at Reed.

"When did he do that?"

"Two days ago," Reed answered again, ignoring McLanahan.

"What are you, my goddamned mouthpiece?" McLanahan asked, rising from his desk. He turned to Joe.

"I looked in Romanowski's cell and he was on his bed trying to choke himself. He had his hand in his mouth, and I told him to knock it off," McLanahan explained, his voice nasal due to his injury. "He wouldn't quit, so I went in there to make him stop."

"And Romanowski decked him," Reed said, pointing toward McLanahan. "Romanowski cleaned McLanahan's clock, then kicked him outside his cell, and shut his own door. He doesn't like Deputy McLanahan very much."

"SHUT UP!" McLanahan seethed. Reed looked away, obviously hiding a smile.

Joe looked from Reed to McLanahan. McLanahan's face was red, and his anger had caused tiny beads of bright red blood to leak through his stitches.

"He didn't try to escape?" Joe asked. "Seeing that you were on the floor and he could have stepped over you and walked away?"

McLanahan shook his head. "Maybe he knows what I would have done to him if he'd tried."

"I'm sure that's it," Joe said, deadpan. Reed continued to look away, but Joe could tell he was smiling by the way Reed's cheeks bulged out in profile.

McLanahan tried to gauge Joe's comment. He looked ready to fight—and if not Joe, then Reed. Anybody. *But, Joe thought, McLanahan is at his best in a fight when he's surrounded by armed agents and his opponent is defenseless. Like Nate Romanowski was.*

"Has he admitted to the murder?" Joe asked.

"He denies everything," McLanahan said. "He hasn't even requested a lawyer. Instead, he called you."

"Maybe you should have hit him again with your rifle butt," Joe said.

Reed turned back, expectant. McLanahan tried to grimace, but it clearly hurt his face to do so.

"Why exactly did he call *you*?" McLanahan asked.

"I don't know."

"Why the game warden and not a lawyer?" Reed wondered.

Joe shrugged.

"You going to meet with him?" McLanahan asked, looking at Joe with a suspicious eye.

"That's why I'm here."

McLanahan and Reed exchanged a glance, each waiting for the other to make a decision of some kind.

"It's his funeral," Reed said dismissively, "If Romanowski wants to talk to the game warden, he has every right to do so."

McLanahan crossed his arms over his chest. "Something about this doesn't sound right to me."

"Me either," Joe said truthfully. "I don't know the man."

"You're sure?"

Joe rolled his eyes. "Of *course* I'm sure."

Reed stood up, jangled his ring of cell keys, and threw Joe a "follow me" nod.

"You left your gun and everything with Stovepipe, right?"

"Yup."

"Watch that son-of-a-bitch," McLanahan called after them. "If he jumps you, I may not hear it."

As they entered the hallway, Reed looked over his shoulder at Joe. "I'll hear it," he said.

NATE ROMANOWSKI LOLLED ON HIS COT with his hand in his mouth, just as McLanahan had described. His other arm was flung over his eyes. One of his feet was on the concrete floor of the cell and the other hung over the foot of the bed. He wore a sky-blue one-piece county

jumpsuit and standard-issue slip-on boat shoes—no belt
or shoelaces that he could harm himself with.

The cell was ten feet by ten feet square, with a cot, an
open toilet, a desk and chair bolted to the wall and floor,
and a stainless-steel sink with a faucet that leaked a thin
stream of water into the basin. The single window was
thick opaque glass reinforced with wire.

Joe Pickett had never been in the county jail itself. He
had been in the anteroom, where, on two occasions, he
had brought in game violators because they were either
drunk or drugged and he didn't want to run the risk of
leaving them out in the field. Unlike Lamar Gardiner,
they had sat quietly in Joe's pickup while being transported to town.

Although it was uncomfortably warm, the bare walls
and metal furnishings made the cell seem cold. Not for
the first time that day, Joe asked himself what he was
doing here, and questioned whether he should have
come. He wondered if he was thinking clearly enough
after his encounter with Wade Brockius and the Sovereigns. Maybe, he thought, he should have run this by
Terry Crump, his supervisor.

But the door closed behind him, and Nate Romanowski was sitting up, both his feet on the floor now,
fixing sharp, cold, lime-green eyes on Joe. Romanowski's
head was bowed forward slightly, and he was looking out
at Joe from under a thick shelf of brow bone that made
him seem even more menacing. Romanowski was lanky
and all angles, his sharp elbows and long arms jutting out
from broad shoulders, his nose beaklike above a V-
shaped jaw. His blond hair was thinning on top.

"Thanks for coming," he said. His hand remained in
his mouth slurring his voice.

"I'm not sure why I'm here," Joe said honestly.

Romanowski smiled with his eyes, then ever so slowly

withdrew his fingers from his mouth. Joe noticed that Romanowski was working his mouth gently with his tongue, probing his teeth. Then he realized what Romanowski had been doing: holding the teeth that had been knocked free by the rifle butt in the sockets they had come from, so they would reattach.

"Think that's going to work?" Joe asked, impressed.

"It seems to." Romanowski shrugged. "They're loose—but my two front teeth are back in. They should stay there and firm up as long as I don't use 'em."

"You mean, like eating?"

Romanowski nodded. "Soup's okay. Broth is better."

"There *are* dentists in Saddlestring," Joe offered. "One could be sent up here."

Romanowski shrugged again. "It gives me something to do. Besides, I don't know if Barnum would be that helpful."

Romanowski's voice was low and soft. The cadence of his speaking rhythm was sarcastic, making him sound a little like Jack Nicholson. Joe strained to hear him.

Romanowski seemed oddly comfortable with his surroundings. He was the kind of man, Joe thought, who was probably comfortable in his own skin wherever he was. He was cool, confident—and intriguing. *And charged with murder,* Joe reminded himself.

"Why'd you clean Deputy McLanahan's clock?" Joe asked.

Romanowski snorted and pulled down the collar of his jail overalls. Joe could see two small burn marks, like snakebites, on Romanowski's neck. Joe recognized the marks as the aftereffects of the Taser stun-gun that McLanahan carried on his belt. McLanahan, Joe guessed, hadn't been checking up on Romanowski as he'd claimed. He had been harassing him, probably trying to elicit a confession.

"I'll get right to it," Romanowski said. "I want to ask you two favors. If you can do either one of them I'll be in your debt. If you can do 'em both, I'll owe you a life. Mine, I mean."

Joe shook his head. What was *this*?

"First, you should try to get me out of here."

"Why would I do that?"

"Because," Romanowski said, displaying either a smirk or a smile—Joe was unsure which—"I didn't kill Lamar Gardiner. Not that I might not have if I was given the chance and considering the circumstances. I heard about those dead elk. Any asshole that shoots seven elk deserves a couple of arrows in his heart. But I'm innocent on this one."

"Why aren't you telling your lawyer this?"

Romanowski fixed his gaze on Joe. "My public defender is a twenty-six-year-old named Jason. He still has notes from college classes in the same legal pad he brought with him to see me. I'm his second client ever. When he was making conversation, he asked me if I listened to hip-hop."

Joe listened blankly.

"My lawyer is a twenty-six-year-old named Jason," Romanowski repeated, his voice rising for the first time.

It was if Romanowski had said all he was going to say about this subject, and Joe should readily agree. But Joe didn't.

"Maybe you ought to be calling a real private-practice criminal lawyer instead of me."

Romanowski shifted slightly, and closed one eye as if to see Joe Pickett from a different angle.

"But I didn't. I called you."

Joe shifted in his chair, uncomfortable.

"How can I prove you didn't murder Lamar Gardiner?" Joe asked. "They've got your bow and the arrows, you were seen coming down from the mountain that afternoon, and you've got a motive. You've got to give me something to go on."

Romanowski snorted. "I *was* coming down that road. I was coming from the Longbrake ranch, where I had returned a certain item of clothing to Mrs. Longbrake."

"A certain item of clothing?" Joe asked.

"Her black thong underwear. I found it under a juniper bush at my house. I guess it had been there since the summer." Romanowski paused. "Mary Longbrake and I had a certain thing together. She would come out to my place when Bud was out of town. I'd wait for her naked in my tree. When she got out of her truck, I'd come down and get her. We would do it outside. Sometimes on my picnic table, sometimes on the bank of the river, sometimes *in* the river. She was a lonely woman, and I helped. Hell, I made her *whoop!*"

Joe didn't know whether to laugh or call for Reed to let him out.

"So did you tell the sheriff?"

"I did," Romanowski sneered. "He said he called Mary and she swore she's never heard of me. When she talked to Barnum she was packing for an around-the-world cruise and planned to be gone for a few months. She's lying about me, I understand that. Not about the cruise, though. Besides, Bud would pound her into jelly if she came clean."

"Okay," Joe said. "What about the bow and the Bonebuster arrows?"

Romanowski nodded. "I've hunted with a bow, and I own that brand of arrows. But it's not my weapon of choice. Even for a lowlife like Gardiner, I would use my weapon of choice."

"Which is?"

"My .454 Casull," Romanowski said, smiling. "A five-shot revolver made by Freedom Arms in Freedom, Wyoming. It's the most powerful handgun in the world. It's four times more powerful than a .44 Magnum."

Joe remembered hearing about it, and seeing the butt of the revolver in a holster at Romanowski's home.

"And the motive?" Joe asked, as if playing the game through.

"I already told you, I would have likely popped Gardiner given the circumstances, but I wasn't there. He was a bureaucratic little turd, floating in a bowl. He shut off the roads to where I trap falcons, and imposed policies and restrictions on the citizens of this county that were heavy-handed and dictatorial. I sincerely disliked the son-of-a-bitch, but somebody got to him first. And good for them."

Joe thought: *That ought to convince a jury.* The cadence of Nate's words was odd as well—a series of short, edgy pulses. Joe couldn't decide if he was credible or not.

"When we came to your place," Joe said, "You seemed to be expecting us."

Romanowski nodded.

"But when Barnum and Melinda Strickland started accusing you of Lamar Gardiner's murder, you looked confused. Did I read that right?"

"Absolutely," Romanowski said, nodding. "Absolutely."

"So explain."

Romanowski sighed, and looked away. "Let's just say I got into a little trouble a year and a half ago in Montana. I know there's a warrant, but I wasn't sure when they'd find me. So when the vehicles pulled up out there, I figured my time had come to go back to the Treasure State."

"What did you do up there?" Joe asked.

Romanowski winced. "I don't know how it can help me to tell you."

"You're probably right about that," Joe said. "But you're asking me to trust you. How can I trust you if you won't tell me the truth?"

A slow smile tugged at Romanowski's mouth. Joe waited.

Romanowski turned back. "I was in the Special Forces in a unit that doesn't officially even exist. If you try to check up on me, you won't find anything about it. I was involved in some things in other countries. Some of the countries are friendly, but most of them aren't. It was covert, and it was nasty.

"But I had a conflict with a supervisor," Romanowski said, weighing and measuring each word in an attempt, Joe thought, to tell his story without getting too specific. "I guess I don't deal with authority all that well, especially when there's a philosophical difference with regard to policy. Like when I get sent out to do things to people simply to further the career of a supervisor, and not to serve my country. In my opinion, at least."

Joe nodded for him to go on.

"So I quit, which isn't an easy thing to do in the first place. But I sent some letters about my supervisor before I left, and I named names and literally told them where some bodies were buried. That didn't make me very popular with my superiors, and they tracked me down. I knew they would, eventually."

Romanowski gazed at the ceiling, pausing. Then he lowered his sharp eyes until they locked with Joe's.

"The people they sent after me met with some trouble in Montana. Up by Great Falls. A car crash or something. Somebody told the local authorities that I might have been involved, might have seen something. But they couldn't find me, because I had left the state."

Joe sat silently as Romanowski finished, trying to judge what he had just heard. Romanowski was a convincing speaker, although his admission that he "didn't deal with authority all that well" didn't help his case. Lamar Gardiner had certainly been "an authority."

Romanowski seemed to be reading his thoughts, because he lowered his voice, leaned forward so that Joe was less than two feet from him, and said: "Forget Lamar Gardiner. He was an insect, and not worth swatting. Melinda Strickland is who you need to watch out for."

Joe was genuinely surprised at this, and he cocked his head.

"Why?"

"She's a psycho. She's real trouble."

"Do you know her?" Joe asked.

Nate shook his head. "I could feel it when she approached. It *emanated* from her. She reminded me a lot of my former supervisor, in fact."

Joe sighed. For a moment there, he'd been taken in.

Romanowski held up his hand. "No, I don't mean she is my former supervisor. She just reminds me of her. You just have to look into her eyes to realize she's trouble.

"I know these things," Romanowski said, looking hard at Joe. There was no hint of a smirk now. "That's why I ended up here in Wyoming. As far away from government bullshit as I thought I could get. How was I to know I'd find another one like her?"

"What are you talking about?" Joe asked, leaning back away from Romanowski.

Romanowski's eyes got hard. "Make no mistake, Joe—Melinda Strickland is a cruel woman, who doesn't give a shit about anyone but herself. I knew I was in the presence of someone evil. Even though that idiot deputy knocked my teeth in, I recognized him for the dumb, redneck cracker he is. There's a hint of evil with that sheriff, but nothing like what I felt from Melinda Strickland. It's like my gut seized up when she looked at me."

"Do you know who killed Lamar Gardiner?" Joe asked abruptly, breaking into Romanowski's monologue. Joe suddenly realized that he had crossed over; that he believed Nate Romanowski was telling the truth. He wasn't sure he really wanted to believe that, but he did.

"I don't have a clue. But from the details I've heard, I think it was a local thing, maybe a business or a family thing, even," Romanowski said.

Joe tried not to react: to say that Romanowski had just echoed his own thoughts from before.

"The bastard who did it is still out there," Romanowski said. "You might even know him."

Joe felt his own stomach knot. This was exactly what he had been thinking.

"Can Melinda Strickland really be as bad as you say?" Joe asked.

Nate held Joe's gaze for a long count. "Maybe worse. She'll climb over the dead body of her mother to get what she wants. "

Joe sat and thought in silence, staring at Nate Romanowski, not sure what to think of this dangerous, fascinating man.

"I believe in right and wrong, and I believe in justice," Romanowski said. "I believe in my country. It's the bureaucrats, the lawyers, and the legal process I have a problem with."

"Okay, then," Joe said, slapping his knees and standing up. "I think we're through here." He admitted to himself that he was thoroughly conflicted, and confused. He had not entered this cell expecting to be convinced of Romanowski's innocence.

Joe stood, looking at Romanowski as he would a suspect, trying to assume that the man was guilty. He looked for a facial tic, for the averted eyes, bitten lip, or furtive glance of a liar. But Romanowski exuded calm, even a hint of righteousness. Or arrogance. Or self-delusion.

"So what was the other favor?" Joe asked.

"My birds," Romanowski said. "I've got a peregrine falcon and a red-tailed hawk out at my place. I left them pretty abruptly, as you know. They're probably circling, hanging around. I fed them just before I left, and there are wild rabbits and ducks around the river, but I'm worried about them. I was hoping you could go out there and feed them."

"I think I could do that," Joe said. "But understand that I'm doing it because I don't want the birds to starve, not because I believe you."

"The peregrine is a suspicious little bitch," Romanowski said. "But she was coming around. She just doesn't know who to trust."

"Sounds familiar," Joe said, thinking of his own predicament.

Romanowski smiled in an understanding, slightly defeated way.

"Do you know a man named Wade Brockius? Or the people who call themselves the Rocky Mountain Sovereign Citizens?" Joe asked, watching Romanowski carefully.

"I've heard of them," he said, his tone conversational. "I don't know any of them, but I overheard the deputies out there talking about some camp in the mountains."

Joe nodded and turned to call for Reed, then remembered that one question was still unanswered. "Why did you call *me*?" he asked.

Romanowski nodded. "I know about you. I've been watching you for some time. I followed the situation with the Millers' weasels, and what happened at Savage Run."

Joe said nothing. It unnerved him to know that someone had been observing him.

"You like to fly under the radar," Romanowski said, locking eyes again with Joe. "When you see something that's wrong, you don't give up. You value being underestimated. In fact, you encourage it. Then, if you have to, you turn fucking cowboy and surprise everyone."

"REED!" Joe yelled, turning, ready to get out.

"I trust *you* to do the right thing," Romanowski said evenly to Joe's back.

Joe looked over his shoulder. "Don't put that on me."

"Sorry," Romanowski said, smiling as if he had just touched Joe Pickett during a game of Ultimate Tag. "You're the only guy between me and a needle."

THAT NIGHT, JOE WORKED IN his garage. Under a bare hanging lightbulb, he replaced the spark plugs and belt from his state-issued snow machine so it would be ready when he needed it again. The clear, sunny day had birthed a crisp and bitterly cold night. When he'd last checked, it was fifteen below zero outside and even with the propane heater hissing in the corner of the garage, he could see his breath. The thick gloves he wore made it tougher to unscrew the plugs with his ratchet, but when he took them off, the steel tool burned his skin with cold.

Earlier, after dinner, while he and Marybeth had done the dishes, Joe poured out everything from the day: seeing the Sovereigns, hearing of Jeannie Keeley's intentions, the call from Melinda Strickland, the meeting with Romanowski, and the possibility that the real murderer was still out there. Marybeth listened in silence, her expression becoming more tense and alarmed as he talked. He noticed that she was washing the same plate twice.

"I don't know what to think, Marybeth," he confessed. "And I'm not sure I know what to *do* about any of it either."

"I wish Jeannie Keeley would have been up there, so you could see how serious she really was." Marybeth was focusing on the part most important to her. Earlier in the evening she had told Joe she'd spoken with a lawyer and that the lawyer hadn't been very optimistic about their chances if Jeannie Keeley sincerely wanted April back.

"Why is she back now? It's been five years, Joe—why the hell is she back now?"

Joe looked at his wife, her face pale with anger and fear and wished he had an answer for her.

THE SIDE DOOR OPENED AND Marybeth stepped in wearing her parka. Her arms were crossed, her hands clamped under her armpits.

"It's not much warmer in here than outside," she said, closing the door and huddling back against it. "Are you coming in soon?"

"Is everyone in bed?"

"You mean my mother?" Marybeth sighed. "Yes."

"I'll be in in a minute," Joe said, ratcheting a plug in. It had been a year since he'd replaced the spark plugs.

"I've thought about what you told me tonight. Brockius, Romanowski, Strickland, all of it. I wish I had been with you."

Joe looked up. "Me, too. Maybe you'd have a better read on these people than I do."

"Do you put any stock into what Nate Romanowski said about Strickland?" Marybeth asked. "Could she really be that bad? Or does she just remind him of somebody he hated?"

Joe's socket wrench slipped on a spark plug and he struck his knuckles hard against the engine block and cursed. He looked up. "I don't know, Marybeth. But

that woman gives me the willies. There's something . . .
off . . . about her."

"Then you believe him? Do you think he's innocent,
like he claims?"

Joe pulled the wrench out of the engine, slipped off
his glove, and examined his skinned knuckles. His bare
fingers immediately stiffened in the cold.

"He's either innocent, or he's an excellent liar," Joe
said.

"I do know one thing he might not be lying about,"
Marybeth said, arching her eyebrows. "Mary Longbrake
was seeing a much younger man. It could have been
Nate."

"How in the . . ." Joe caught himself, and rephrased,
"How could you possibly know *that*?"

"From the library," Marybeth said, smiling. "A couple
of the women who work there used to play bridge with
Mary every week. I guess they talk about all sorts of things
in that club. Apparently, Mary made it very clear that her
life had changed for the better since she had met this
man."

12

THE CLOSED-CASKET FUNERAL FOR LAMAR GARDINER was held on the morning of New Year's Eve, while another dark winter storm front was forming and boiling in the northwest. The wind was icy and withering. The service took place at Kenneth Siman's Memorial Chapel on Main Street in Saddlestring and was attended by about fifty mourners, most of whom were family, employees of the Forest Service office, or local law enforcement.

Joe sat with Marybeth in the next-to-last row of chairs. He wore a jacket and tie, and had left his hat on the coatrack. Carrie Gardiner, wearing black, sat in the front row with her two children. Behind them was Melinda Strickland, surrounded by Forest Service employees. Strickland's hair, Joe noted, was a different color than when he had last seen her. Now it was tawny, almost blonde. She wore her Forest Service uniform. Sheriff Barnum and his two deputies occupied a single row of chairs, but they all kept empty chairs between them. Elle Broxton-Howard, with her notebook in her lap, sat alone behind them all.

The ferocity of the wind outside made something flap and bang on the roof while the pastor spoke. Kenneth Siman, the earnestly sober funeral director and county coroner, appeared from a door near the front of the room, looked up to check that nothing within the building had been damaged, and silently disappeared.

When the pastor was done, Melinda Strickland approached the dais and withdrew a folded piece of yellow paper from her uniform pocket. Her demeanor was oddly melodramatic, and she consciously tried to meet the eyes of all of the mourners before she spoke.

"You've heard from Pastor Robbins about the life of Lamar, and I'm here to let you know that he didn't die in vain. No Sirree Bob."

No Sirree Bob? Joe felt Marybeth squirm next to him. And he felt it again when Melinda Strickland paused and forced a blazing, inappropriate smile.

Joe felt a cold shiver run through him. Was it just Strickland, he wondered, or was it Romanowski's manipulation?

"Cassie," Strickland said to Carrie Gardiner, getting her name wrong, "your dutiful husband was the casualty of a war that we must, and will, stop. When citizens turn against their federal government it will not stand, ya know?"

Joe tried to attribute Melinda Strickland's words, gestures, and behavior to nervousness. She was certainly making Joe nervous. And Marybeth seemed to be trying to shrink into her chair.

"Ya know, this little war some citizens have with federal employees has gone too far, don't you think?" She seemed to be looking straight at Joe, and she nodded conspiratorially.

"Ya know, a group of extremists have set up a compound on federal land. That's kind of 'in your face,' don't you think?"

Melinda Strickland went on for another five minutes. Her thoughts seemed random and disconnected, sound bites in search of a paragraph. Joe barely heard her, but he did hear Marybeth groan.

When she was through, Strickland approached Carrie Gardiner and her children, and grasped both of Carrie's hands in hers.

"I'm sorry for your loss, Cassie," Strickland said.

Joe noticed that Elle Broxton-Howard was scribbling furiously in her notepad. As Strickland rejoined her employees, she turned and handed her speech to Broxton-Howard, who accepted it with a grateful smile.

THE RECEPTION/WAKE WAS HELD AT the Forest Service building. Joe noted right away that the Gardiners hadn't come. He felt sorry for Carrie, and especially for her children. The other mourners stood in the reception area, drinking punch in paper cups and eating cookies from plates on the office desks. USFS employees stood uncomfortably behind the desks, urging mourners to have another cookie with a lack of enthusiasm that led Joe to believe that they had been instructed to be good hosts by their immediate supervisor, Melinda Strickland.

Elle Broxton-Howard approached Joe and Marybeth and introduced herself. She wore a high-collared Bavarian wool jacket over black stretch pants. She handed Joe a card.

"*Rumour* magazine," Joe read aloud. He gave her his card, and she slid it absently into a pocket without looking at it.

"It's very popular in the U.K.," Broxton-Howard explained. "It's kind of a cross between your *Maxim* and *People*, with a little of *The New Yorker* thrown in for highbrow literary content. I also freelance."

"I think my mother reads it," Marybeth said, making conversation.

Broxton-Howard nodded at Marybeth, but turned again to Joe. Joe knew how well this would go over with his wife.

"I'm doing a long-form story on the battle between the rural militia types and the U.S. government," Broxton-Howard said, "And I plan to feature Melinda Strickland as my protagonist. I see her as a strong-willed, independent woman in a man's world. A Barbara Stanwyck of our time."

She was interrupted, however, as Melinda Strickland joined them wearing her wide, inappropriate grin. Her cocker spaniel trailed behind her.

"I'm Marybeth Pickett, Joe's wife," Marybeth said, extending her hand, and smiling with a hint of malice, Joe thought.

"Joe's been working very closely with our effort, and we appreciate that immensely," Strickland said, looking at him. "He's been such a help."

"I didn't get that impression when you called me on my cell phone," Joe said.

Strickland reacted as if Joe had slapped her. "I'm sure I don't know what you're referring to," she said. Then her expression softened once again into her hostess face.

Wow, Joe thought.

"So tell me, Joe," Strickland asked, "have the extremist tendencies in this area affected the job you're trying to do?"

Joe thought for a moment. "To be honest, I'm not quite sure what you mean by 'extremist tendencies.' There are a few bad apples, but the community is generally supportive."

Strickland cocked her head skeptically at Joe. *"Really?"* she said, in a way that indicated that she didn't believe him, but didn't want to cause a scene.

Joe shrugged. "Some folks might get a little eccentric and hardheaded when it comes to land policies and rules and regulations. But I've found you can deal with them, if you're reasonable and fair across the board."

" 'Eccentric' is an odd term for the murder of a Forest Service supervisor, I would think," Strickland said, looking to Marybeth and Broxton-Howard for confirmation.

Joe waded in, taking advantage of the moment, wanting to make a point while Melinda Strickland was in front of him.

"I want to let you know," Joe interjected, "that I met a man named Wade Brockius a couple of days ago. He's the spokesman of sorts for the—" But before Joe could get any further, Melinda Strickland suddenly noticed that the cookies were gone from the nearest desk and excused herself to admonish the employee. Broxton-Howard faded into the crowd.

Joe and Marybeth looked at each other.

"Well, *she's* interesting," Marybeth added. "In a bad kind of way."

"Remember what Nate Romanowski said," Joe added.

"You're quoting a murder suspect, Joe," Marybeth smiled.

"I'll stop doing that," Joe said sourly.

"But did you notice how Melinda was acting with you?"

Joe shook his head.

"She wasn't talking with you or even listening to you. She was *assessing* you," Marybeth said.

"Why?"

"To see if you'll be any value to her personally; if you'll buy into her agenda, her career path, or hurt it. Remember when you told me she almost turned back on the mountain? It sounds to me like when it got tough physically, she looked up and saw that probably nobody in that party really mattered to what was important to her. She saw a bunch of local yokels and the state DCI. A bunch of losers. The only person in that group who mattered was the journalist, and she was already in her camp. The rest of you meant nothing. She's a user, and she's dangerous."

"You got all that from a two-minute exchange?"

"Yes."

Marybeth nodded toward Broxton-Howard, who now commanded the attention of McLanahan and Reed.

"She's nice-looking," Marybeth said in a flat tone. "It takes hours to make your hair look that casually wind-tousled."

Joe wisely said nothing.

WHILE MARYBETH SEARCHED FOR THE bathroom, Joe sought out County Attorney Robey Hersig.

"What are your plans tonight, Joe?"

Joe rolled his eyes. Their New Year's Eve plans were the same as they had been since Sheridan was born eleven years ago: They would go to bed early. Missy had asked about parties and celebrations in town, and hinted that she might want to go. Joe had offered her the use of their minivan, and she had wrinkled her nose, but accepted.

"Got a minute?" Joe asked. Hersig nodded and motioned Joe into an office behind them. He entered and sat on a desk and loosened his tie. Joe eased the door closed behind them. The office had been Lamar Gardiner's, but was now, obviously, occupied by Melinda Strickland. A framed photo of her cocker spaniel stood on the desk. Joe hadn't realized that she'd already moved in.

Hersig was from one of Twelve Sleep County's oldest ranching families, and after a bout of college rodeo he had gone into law at the University of Wyoming. His first term as county attorney would end in the coming year, and there was speculation as to whether he would run again. Although almost brutally cautious when it came to prosecuting a case, Hersig had an impressive track record of convictions. The summer before, Hersig and Joe had discovered that they were both fly fishermen, and had floated the Twelve Sleep river together in Hersig's flat-bottomed McKenzie boat. They got along, and made plans to do it again. To both, fishing together successfully created a special bond.

Joe had called Hersig earlier in the week to talk about April, but their conversation had been brief; Hersig's phone was full of static, thanks to damage from the storm.

"We're not sure what we can do about Jeannie Keeley," Joe said. "Can we ask for a restraining order or something?"

Hersig shook his head. "Joe, she has to do something first. Just her presence isn't enough. And legally, since April hasn't been adopted, Jeannie has a damned good chance of getting her back."

Joe winced. "How could a judge possibly give her back to that woman after what she did?"

"Judges do things like that, Joe. Birth mothers carry a lot of clout, even when it's clear that you and Marybeth care for April. In Wyoming, if the mother's maintained contact in some way—even with the judge—the child isn't considered abandoned."

"We love her," Joe said firmly. "She's one of ours."

"Too bad the adoption got delayed so long," Hersig commiserated. "That's where the problem lies."

Joe cursed, and looked away for a moment.

"I wish this punch had a kick," Hersig said idly, looking into his cup as if willing a shot of bourbon into it. "It's New Year's Eve, after all."

"How's the case against Nate Romanowski?" Joe

asked. "You know, he called me the other day—I met with him and he told me he was innocent."

"I heard about that," Hersig said, shaking his head. "Imagine a man in jail claiming *that*." Hersig threw down the last of the punch.

"I wish our case against him was stronger," Hersig confided. "It's compelling, but largely circumstantial. I'd be nervous taking it to a jury without more direct evidence. Did he tell you anything of interest?"

Joe relayed the story about Mrs. Longbrake and what Marybeth had told him about the women at the library, but nothing about what Romanowski had said about Melinda Strickland, or the supposed incident in Montana. Joe wondered why he felt guarded about what Romanowski had said. Joe's allegiance, after all, was supposed to be to Hersig and the law.

"I've got to admit that I found myself questioning his guilt," Joe said.

Hersig turned his head to look at Joe.

"Questioning his guilt, or being taken in?" Hersig asked.

Joe shrugged and admitted, "I'm not sure."

"Mrs. Longbrake is out of the country," Hersig said. "The sheriff checked. So we can't confirm that part of his story yet although now maybe we'll interview the women she played bridge with."

Joe nodded. "What do you know about Nate Romanowski? What's his background?"

"It's pretty mysterious." Hersig raised his eyebrows. "He's a Montana boy, from Bozeman originally. He was appointed to the Air Force Academy and played football for them. Middle linebacker for the Falcons . . ."

"Falcons?" Joe repeated, thinking about Romanowski's birds. He hadn't fed them yet; there had been no time. He *had* to get out there soon.

"Then he vanished off the face of the earth from 1984

through 1998. Nobody can vanish like that unless they've got special help from the Feds."

"Special Forces?" Joe asked. "He said something about that when I saw him at the jail." *Two of Romanowski's claims—about Mrs. Longbrake's dalliances and his Special Forces background—were now much more likely true than false,* Joe thought.

"Really? That's interesting," Hersig said. "I didn't know that. And Romanowski's not cooperating. Even with his P. D."

"I know. He says he's depending on me to help him out," Joe said sourly.

Hersig frowned. "Romanowski's only arrest was in 1999—he was held in Idaho for allegedly beating a rancher. He claimed the guy shot his falcon out of the sky. Spent ninety days in the Blaine County Jail for that."

"Do you see a connection between Romanowski, the Sovereigns, and Lamar Gardiner?" Joe asked. "They all sort of happened at once."

Hersig peered at the ceiling for several beats. "It almost seems like there's got to be one, doesn't it?"

"Maybe so," Joe said.

The door opened and one of the Forest Service employees looked in. "Oops, sorry," he said.

Hersig waved to indicate it was okay. "Leave the door open. We're through, aren't we?"

"Yup."

Hersig heaved himself off of the desk, and they stood in the doorway looking out. Elle Broxton-Howard stood in the middle of a gaggle of midlevel Forest Service managers as well as Reed and McLanahan. Hersig tilted his chin toward her.

"She likes 'em rugged and real, or so she says," Hersig confided to Joe. "Ranchers, cowboys, loggers. Real manly men."

Joe stared at Hersig. "How do you know that?"

Hersig smiled, but his face was flushed. "She told me that. And believe me, she's got a few notches on her lipstick case in this county already."

As if she'd heard Hersig, or read Joe's thoughts, Broxton-Howard suddenly turned, extricated herself from the knot of admirers, and walked boldly up to Joe Pickett.

"You were there when Mr. Gardiner was killed," she stated flatly. Joe was surprised she hadn't known that already.

"Yes."

"You've met with Wade Brockius and the Sovereigns as well."

"Sort of." Joe felt his neck getting warm.

"Then we *must* have an interview," she said, her eyes boring into his, her jaw set with sincerity. Without breaking her gaze, she fished Joe's card out of her pocket and raised it until it came into her view.

"Joe Pickett. Game warden," she said, in a breathy British accent. Then she turned on her heel and walked back to her admirers.

Marybeth entered the room from a dark hallway, looking for Joe. Joe felt both guilty and slightly exhilarated. As Marybeth made her way over, Hersig leaned toward Joe and mocked, "We *must* have an interview!"

"WHAT DID ROBEY SAY ABOUT April?" Marybeth asked, as they drove out of Saddlestring on Bighorn Road. The storm clouds had blocked out the moon and stars, and the wind was relentless. Tiny flakes of snow, like sparks, flashed past the headlights.

"He wasn't encouraging," Joe said. "But he didn't indicate that Jeannie's tried to get April back, either."

"That was a very strange experience back there," Marybeth said, sighing. "The funeral was disturbing, and the reception was even worse. The person I feel for the most is Carrie Gardiner. Or Cassie, as Melinda Strickland calls her. I almost look forward to seeing my mother."

Joe laughed. "Me, too," he said. But he was thinking of Melinda Strickland. And Nate Romanowski. And Elle Broxton-Howard.

"What did she say to you?" Marybeth asked abruptly.

"Who?" Joe asked. He sounded guilty, even to himself.

"You know who," Marybeth snapped. "The chick you and Robey were melting in front of when I came from the bathroom. Ms. Broxton-Howard."

Again, Joe felt his neck get hot.

"She wants to interview me," Joe said.

"I'll *bet* that's what she wants," Marybeth snorted.

Joe didn't say a word. He had learned that, in these kinds of situations, the less he said, the better.

He felt Marybeth looking at him and he turned to her.

"Honey, I . . ."

"JOE!" Marybeth shouted. And Joe looked, saw the ragged form of a man bathed in the white of his headlights, his wide-eyed face black with streaming blood, outstretched frozen hands up as if to shield himself; then he heard the sickening thump despite his violent effort to wrench the car away into the ditch, saw what looked like a scarecrow turned bright red by the taillights bounce and crumple on the glass-slick surface of the snow-packed highway in his rearview mirror, heard Marybeth scream.

13

HIS NAME WAS BIRCH WARDELL, HE WAS AN EMPLOYEE of the U.S. Bureau of Land Management, and Joe hadn't killed him after all. The collision did break Wardell's pelvis, however, which was just one of many injuries he sustained that day after wrecking his truck in a sharp ravine in the breaklands that led up to the foothills of the Bighorn Mountains.

The emergency-room doctor had recognized Joe from when he'd brought Lamar Gardiner's frozen body in.

"I'm seeing more of you than I want to," the doctor said. "And every time you show up, you bring trouble."

Joe agreed with him. *But at least this time,* he thought, *the man's alive.*

JOE SAT IN THE HALLWAY on a molded plastic chair, still in his jacket and tie, outside Wardell's room at the clinic. It was well into New Year's Day. He had called Marybeth to tell her that Wardell was alive and expected to recover. Marybeth thanked God.

"I can't believe that poor man was walking down the middle of the road," she said. "On a night like this."

"I'll try to find out why," Joe said. "Now go to bed and get some sleep."

"How are you going to get home?" she asked.

Joe hadn't thought of that yet. Marybeth had taken the car home after they had brought Wardell to the hospital.

"I'll figure it out," he said.

THE HOSPITAL WAS SILENT and subdued, the lights dimmed for the night. Mrs. Wardell had been in to see her husband after he came out of surgery, and she thanked Joe for bringing him into town.

"But I was the one who hit him," Joe said.

She patted Joe's arm. "I know," she said. Her eyes were puffy and rimmed with red. "But if you hadn't found him, the doctor said there was no doubt he would have died of exposure out there. It's eighteen below."

"I wish I could have missed him, though."

"It's okay, Mr. Pickett," she said soothingly. "He's alive, and conscious. The doctor says he'll be okay."

"You think it would be okay if I talked with him?"

Mrs. Wardell looked over Joe's shoulder for a doctor or nurse but the hall was empty.

"They gave him medication to help him sleep," she said. "I'm not sure he'll make much sense."

BIRCH WARDELL LAY IN HIS hospital bed with his eyes at half-mast. A thin tube of fluorescent light extending from the headboard lit up half his face and threw peaked shadows across his blankets. In addition to his broken pelvis, Wardell also had a broken collarbone and nose.

Stitches climbed from his neck into his scalp like railroad tracks. Joe had overheard the nurses say that the tips of three of his fingers and four of his toes were severely frostbitten.

The man in the bed was stout and in his mid-forties, with a thick mustache and brown eyes. Joe had seen him before while patrolling.

Wardell's eyes found Joe in the doorway, and he raised his good hand slightly in greeting.

"You doing okay?" Joe asked softly.

Wardell seemed to be trying to find his voice. "Much better since they filled me full of drugs. In fact, I'm kind of . . . happy."

Joe approached Wardell. The room smelled of bandages and antiseptic.

"Happy New Year," Joe said, smiling.

Wardell grunted, and then winced because the grunt clearly hurt his ribs.

"Thanks for saving my life. The doctor said I couldn't have stayed out there much longer."

"I'm just sorry I hit you," Joe said. "So what happened? You walked all the way out of the breaklands after you wrecked your truck?"

"I was on my way back to town," he said. "Must have been about four-thirty or so. I had about another half hour, forty-five minutes of light yet. I wanted to get home because Mrs. Wardell and me had tickets for the steak and shrimp feed at the Elks Lodge for New Year's."

Joe nodded, urging him on.

"I seen a white pickup truck on BLM land up on a ridge, past the signs that say the damn road is closed in the winter. You know, in that cooperative Forest Service/ BLM unit?"

Joe had patrolled the area. It was a rough, treeless expanse of sharp zigzag-cut draws and sagebrush that stretched from the highway to the wooded foothills of the Bighorns. The "unit" had been recently designated a research area, jointly managed by the two federal agencies to study the spread of native buffalo grass in the absence of cattle or sheep. The designation had raised the ire of several local ranchers who had grazed their stock in the breaklands for years, and of some local hunters and fishermen who used the roads to get to spring creeks in the foothills. Wardell was the project manager.

"Well, this white truck was in the process of pulling my 'Road Closed' signs out of the ground with a chain. When I seen that, I thought: *'What the hell?'*" Wardell pronounced it "hay-uhl."

"I heard something about signs being vandalized," Joe said.

Wardell nodded his head slightly. It took him a moment to start up again—the sedatives were working. Joe hoped Wardell could finish the story before he went to sleep. "It's been going on for a few months now. Sometimes the signs are gone, and other times they're just run over.

"So I says to myself, *'What the hell?'*" Wardell said again. "And I turned up that closed road and give chase."

"Got it. Can you identify the vehicle?"

"White. Or maybe tan. Light-colored, for sure. Not brand-new. The damn sunlight was starting to go bad on me about then."

"Ford? GMC? Chevy?" Joe asked.

Wardell thought. "Maybe a Ford. The truck was pretty dirty, I noticed that. There was mud or smudges on the doors, I think."

Joe smiled grimly. Finding a Ford pickup in Wyoming was about as hard as finding a Hispanic male in Houston.

"Anyway . . ." Wardell swallowed, and his eyes fluttered. He was tiring. Joe felt a little bit guilty pushing him so hard. Joe looked at his watch: 3:30 A.M.

"Anyway, that truck saw me coming and the driver took off over the hill, still on the closed road. You know how it is out there with all them draws and hills. It's damn easy to get lost or turned around. But whatever . . . I took off after him up that hill anyway."

"Did you try to call anyone?"

"Damn right I tried. But the BLM office closed early, on account it's New Year's Eve. Our dispatcher left early."

"Go on."

"I got to the top of that hill and the whole unit was out there to be seen. The road turned to the left and I started to go that way but then I seen that white Ford halfway down the hill. He had gone off-road and was barreling down the hill toward the bottom. I said '*What the hell?*' and followed him. All I wanted to do by then was get a license plate."

"I think this patient needs some rest," a night shift nurse said tersely from the doorway.

Joe turned. "We're about done."

"You better be," the nurse said.

"Sassy little number," Wardell commented, watching her walk away, her big hips making the hem of her skirt jump.

Joe turned back. "So, you saw the truck at the bottom of the draw. Doesn't it start to get brushy down there?" Joe was becoming convinced that he knew the specific road and hill Wardell was describing.

Wardell nodded, then winced. "Yeah, it gets all tangly down there. And it was getting pretty dark, but I could see those taillights go right into the bush and disappear. Hell, I had no idea there was a way to get across that draw down there in a vehicle."

Joe stroked his jaw. He didn't know of any way to cross there either.

"Then I saw the truck come out of the brush on the

other side and start climbing the hill straight across from me. I said . . ."

"*'What the hell?'*" Joe joined in with Wardell.

"I tried to get a read on the plate through the binoculars, but I couldn't get an angle on it. So I thought, shit, if he could cross down there, *I* can cross down there."

"What about the snow?" Joe asked suddenly. "Wasn't it deep?"

Wardell shook his head. "That hill is on a southern exposure. The wind and sun cleared it down to the grass. The big drifts are all toward the foothills."

"Okay."

"So I followed the tracks straight down that mountain, stayed right in 'em. Right into the big bushes . . . and then WHAM! I was suddenly ass over teakettle, and in the air. I literally was airborne for a second until I hit the bottom of the draw. I hit harder than hell. Good thing I was wearin' my seat belt."

Joe agreed. "You didn't see how the truck crossed down there?"

Wardell said no, he didn't see how anyone could have done it. It was steep on the sides, and there was a frozen little stream on the bottom.

"So how did he get across?" Joe asked.

"I have no earthly idea," Wardell said, his eyes widening with amazement. "No clue at all. But when I was hanging there, suspended by the seat belt with blood pouring out of my head, I could hear laughing."

"Laughing?"

"That son-of-a-bitch in the truck was laughing out loud. I heard his truck start up again, and he just laughed his stupid head off. He must have been sitting up there on that hill watching me. I'm sure he thought he left me there to die."

Joe stood up straight and crossed his arms. The scenario just didn't sound quite right.

"I finally got out of the cab of the truck and started walking. To be real honest, there must have been an angel with me, because I wasn't even sure I was going the right direction toward town."

You weren't, Joe thought. Luckily, though, he had stumbled into Bighorn Road—and then Joe had hit him with his car.

Joe stared at the ceiling tiles, trying to figure it all out.

"I think it was those goddamned Sovereigns," Wardell mumbled.

"What makes you say that?" Joe asked, but although Wardell's eyelids flickered he didn't respond. Wardell was asleep.

The nurse was back at the door. "Good night, Mr. Pickett. Drive safely. It's cold and icy out there."

Joe let himself be ushered out.

In the lobby, the emergency-room doctor was pulling his coat on to leave after his shift.

"Quiet night, except for you," the doctor said, winking, and offered Joe a ride home. Joe accepted gratefully.

Outside, it was still dark and the wind was bitter, and it sliced right through his clothing. The doctor drove a Jeep Cherokee, a vehicle prized locally because of how fast the heater started working.

Joe sank back in the leather seat, realizing how exhausted he was. He liked the doctor because the man felt no compulsion to start up a conversation.

Joe thought about what Wardell had said. He thought about how cruel it was of the driver of the light-colored truck to leave Wardell behind like that. Surely the driver would have seen or heard Wardell crash, and realize that if Wardell wasn't killed on impact, he would likely freeze to death out there. Either way, it was a bad way to die. It had suddenly occurred to Joe when he was talking to Wardell that the viciousness was similar to how Lamar Gardiner had been treated.

If the same person who was responsible for Gardiner's murder was involved in leaving Birch Wardell to freeze to death, then the killer was not Nate Romanowski. The likelihood that the perpetrator was a Sovereign, as Wardell had suggested, didn't make sense to Joe, since Birch had seen the truck well before the Sovereigns had set up camp. It was unlikely, Joe knew, that any of the Sovereigns—including Jeannie Keeley—had the kind of intimate familiarity with the BLM land and the complicated terrain within it to know the secret route that Wardell said the light-colored pickup had taken. Joe shuddered. The more he thought about it, the more convinced he became that neither the Sovereigns nor Nate Romanowski were to blame. And that the real killer was still out there.

THEY DROVE SLOWLY DOWN Main Street while the defroster cleared ever-larger sweating holes in the ice on the windshield. Saddlestring was still. Streetlights illuminated the clouds of heat and steam that escaped from the vents of dark buildings, giving the illusion that they were silently breathing. Joe noticed a few more cars than normal still parked downtown, and guessed they belonged to revelers who would come and get them in the morning.

The only place with lights and cars out front was the Elks Club. As they passed, Joe rolled his head over on the headrest. A couple stood in profile in the front door, backlit by a bare porch light, their outlines in silhouette. The woman wrapped her arms around the man, and his cowboy hat tipped back as he lowered his head to kiss her.

Joe moaned, and turned to stare straight out the front window.

"Are you alright?" the doctor asked.

"Yup," Joe answered. "I just thought I saw my mother-in-law back there."

JOE THANKED THE DOCTOR AND gingerly approached his front door, careful of the ice on the walk. Inside, he confirmed that the couch bed had not been slept in.

Dragging himself upstairs, he wondered how long it would take for word to get out that another federal employee in Twelve Sleep County had been assaulted.

The news would no doubt supercharge Melinda Strickland's crusade.

14

ON SUNDAY, NEW YEAR'S DAY, JOE MIXED PANCAKE BATTER in a bowl with a whisk and watched the snow fall outside the kitchen window. It was a light snow, powdery as flour, and it skittered along over the top of the week-old glaze, settling into cracks and crevices. In the living room, the girls watched the Rose Bowl parade—a sun-drenched pageant of flowers, floats, and Pasadena Parade Committee members in matching blazers—while wrapped in robes and blankets on the floor. Marybeth had made room for them by folding up the couch bed when Missy had finally awakened. Missy was now upstairs preparing herself for the day. Joe had learned that this took about two hours and ten minutes.

Joe let his mind wander as he prepared the batter, unwrapped the bacon, and put the "special" bottle of real maple syrup in a pan to warm. He was tired, and already forecasting an afternoon nap. The night at the hospital, and several sleepless hours afterward thinking about Birch Wardell, Nate Romanowski, the Sovereigns, Lamar Gardiner, Missy Vankueren, and Melinda Strickland had wiped him out. He woke up feeling worried and unfocused. Joe was thankful he had the day off, and the fresh snow was not unwelcome.

He had heard that the Inuit people had scores of words to describe snow, and that had always impressed him until he thought of how many *he* knew. Most described the condition of snow. There was powder, packed powder, slush, wind-groomed, wind-loaded, fluff, glazed, crud, rain crust, cold smoke, and corduroy. Also carvy, sugary, tracked out, white smoke, dust on crust, ice cube, gropple, granular, and wind butter. He knew lots of snow words.

Marybeth came into the kitchen and nodded her approval at the breakfast he was preparing. Then she checked over her shoulder to make sure no one was listening.

"Mom came in at *five-thirty* this morning." Her eyes were disbelieving. "I can't imagine ever coming home that late when I was growing up."

"I told you I saw her last night," Joe said. "She sure doesn't waste any time."

"Joe!" Marybeth scolded, but didn't really argue. "Don't let the girls hear you."

"I won't."

Marybeth leaned forward conspiratorially. "Could you tell who she was kissing?"

"I wasn't sure at the time," he said, pouring palm-sized rounds of batter onto the griddle. "But it might have been Bud Longbrake."

Marybeth moaned. She knew that Longbrake's wife—Nate Romanowski's supposed alibi—was out of the country.

"It fits the profile," Joe said. "One, he's a state senator. Two," Joe held up his hand and raised a finger as he made each point, "He's wealthy. Three, he's sort of single at the moment. Four, she's sort of single at the moment. Five, she apparently needs a man in the on-deck circle in case the one at bat strikes out." He grinned ruefully. "Like if he goes to federal prison or something."

Marybeth shook her head at him, mildly disapproving. "What's gotten into you?" she asked.

"I've got a question for you," Joe said. "How in the *hell* did you ever turn out to be so wonderful?"

She smiled at him. Then, apparently jarred by the earlier mention of Mrs. Longbrake, she told Joe to follow her into his office.

"WHILE I WAS WAITING UP for you last night, I did an Internet search," Marybeth said over her shoulder while she settled into Joe's office chair. "I wanted to see if I could find anything on a car crash in Montana a year and a half ago."

Joe arched his eyebrows and waited for more. She handed him several sheaves of paper that she had hidden under a stack of files.

Joe took them and read. They were stories from the Great Falls *Tribune* from three consecutive days in June eighteen months ago. The first was headlined TWO DEAD IN U.S. 87 ROLLOVER. The story said that a damaged vehicle with out-of-state plates had been called in to the Montana highway patrol twenty-one miles north of town near Fort Benton. The identities of the occupants were unknown at the time, but authorities were investigating.

On the next page, a smaller story identified the victims of a multiple-rollover accident as two men, aged 32 and 37, from Arlington, Virginia and Washington, D.C., respectively. Both were killed on impact. The highway patrol suggested that, judging by the skid marks, it was possible that the engine of the late-model SUV had died on a sharp grade with several turns, and that the driver, unable to negotiate the sharpest of the turns, had blown through a guardrail. The SUV had rolled at least seven times before it reached the bottom of the canyon. The passenger was thrown from the vehicle, and the driver was crushed behind the wheel.

"The engine lost power. No power steering, no power brakes. Yikes," Joe said absently, and read on.

WITNESS SOUGHT IN ROLLOVER INVESTIGATION, the third and smallest headline read. In the story, the highway patrol reported that they were seeking a potential witness to the rollover on U.S. 87 that had killed two men from out of state. Specifically, they were looking for the driver of an older-model Jeep with Montana plates that was seen passing a speed checkpoint near Great Falls. The authorities estimated that the Jeep may have been in the vicinity of the rollover and that the driver could have seen the accident happen.

Joe looked up at Marybeth and put down the papers.

"Doesn't Nate Romanowski drive a Jeep?" Marybeth asked.

Joe nodded. "Yes, he does."

"Interesting, huh?"

"Two guys sent from our nation's capital sent to clear up an internal problem crash on a desolate road in Montana," Joe said. "So what did he do, force the SUV off the road?"

"If the motor of the SUV wasn't working, he wouldn't have to, would he?" Marybeth asked. She had obviously been thinking about this.

"So how could he make a motor die in another car?" Joe asked, but halfway through his question, he guessed the answer.

*   *   *

THEY LISTENED TO THE SHOWER run upstairs while they ate breakfast. The girls ate pancake after pancake, soaking up every drop of the syrup. Because real maple syrup was expensive, it was saved for holidays and special occasions.

"Grandmother Missy takes long showers," Lucy observed.

"She uses up all our hot water," Sheridan grumbled.

"I like the sweet taste of the syrup and the salty taste of the bacon," Sheridan said, savoring it.

"I just like the syrup," Lucy declared. "I wish I could suck that syrup up through a straw." Lucy smiled, pantomiming exactly how she would do it.

"Remember when Mom caught you licking your plate clean of all of the leftover syrup like a dog?" Sheridan asked Lucy, baiting her. Lucy made a face, and Sheridan laughed. "Like Maxine, licking out her dog-food bowl!"

"Stop it!" Lucy howled.

Marybeth shut things down with a look of disapproval.

"What do you like, April?" she asked.

April had been silent through the Rose Bowl parade and breakfast. Joe looked at her from his place at the stove. Sometimes, April withdrew from the rest of them, seeming almost to shrink out of view even though she was in the middle of things—the invisible girl. Other times, like now, she looked lonely and haunted. Joe sometimes thought of her as a living, sweet ghost.

April mumbled something, and stared into her lap.

"What was that, honey?" Marybeth asked.

April looked up. Her face was hard, and pinched. "I said I had a dream my other mom was looking at me last night."

April's words froze everyone at the table.

Marybeth leaned closer to April. Sheridan and Lucy looked from their mother, to April, and back.

"Are you doing okay now?" Marybeth asked softly.

"She was outside my window, looking in at me through the curtains," April said, her eyes still downcast. "She sort of rubbed the window with her hand and smeared the glass. She kept saying 'I love you, April, I miss you, April.'"

April said it in a Southern accent that sounded just like Jeannie Keeley, and it disturbed Joe because he had never heard April talk like that before.

For the first time that morning, Joe was focused. The dull red ball of anxiety, dormant in the pit of his stomach for a few hours, awoke.

Then he realized that Marybeth was trying to catch his eye. When he looked back, Marybeth was using her chin to point toward the back door without April realizing what she was doing. Joe got it: She wanted him to go outside and check the yard. Marybeth obviously believed April, or at least wanted to dispel any lingering possibilities.

AS MARYBETH CLEARED THE DISHES away—leaving a clean one for Missy when she made her morning entrance—and the girls returned to their parade, Joe pulled on his insulated coveralls in the mudroom. As he laced his boots, he looked up. Sheridan was the only one who looked back. She had caught the exchange between Marybeth and Joe, and knew where he was headed. Her eyes slid off of him and back to the television. She was complicit in the plan.

He went out the front door, shoving it hard to break through a small drift that had piled against it. It was bitterly cold outside, with enough of a wind to bite into his exposed skin. Pinpricks of snow stung his eyes. Pulling a stocking cap over his ears, he trudged around the house and into the backyard. His boots broke through the crust of snow, making it hard to walk without moving like Frankenstein's monster.

The girls' room was at ground level. April's and Lucy's bunk bed was near the wall and window, and Sheridan's single bed was near the door. The snow in the yard looked undisturbed except for a recent set of dog tracks and a yellow stain left by Maxine. He approached the back porch and squinted into the wind at the snow beneath the window.

The world was white-on-white—white ground, white sky, snow in his eyes—making it hard to see.

But they were there—two slight indentations beneath the window. They were only a little larger than a child's boot-prints. At least he *thought* he could see something. With the fresh snow filling them and the wind topping them off with powder it was hard to know for sure. Ground blizzards, like water flowing over a dam, rolled over the fence and snaked across the yard, obscuring the depressions under the window.

Joe stopped and closed his eyes. He hoped when he opened them he could see more clearly.

When he opened his eyes they were still there. Kind of. For Jeannie Keeley to have stood beneath April's window, she would have had to park on the road the night before, open the front gate, and walk around the dark house to the back. It had been extremely cold, as he knew. And if she had done it, it had to have been after Marybeth had arrived home from the funeral and Missy had taken the van back into town, or before she returned home that morning. Joe wondered when April thought she'd seen her mother, but knew it was unlikely that she'd noticed the time. He didn't want to upset April more by asking her.

His camera was in his evidence kit in his pickup, and

he retraced his steps to the front to dig it out. If he had hard evidence of his daughter being stalked, it could be used in a custody hearing. Returning, he wondered if the camera's shutter release would be too cold to work properly. Photographing in snow was always difficult.

But it didn't matter. By the time he returned, the boot tracks under the window—if they had ever really been there at all—were gone beneath the shifting rivulets of windborne snow.

AS HE STAMPED THE SNOW off his boots, Marybeth came into the mudroom.

"Well?" she asked.

Joe sniffed and shrugged. "Maybe. It was too hard to tell."

Marybeth shivered, but Joe doubted it was from the cold.

THAT AFTERNOON, JOE SMASHED HIS pickup through snowdrifts on the dirt road to Nate Romanowski's house by the river. In the bed of the pickup were flattened, road-killed jackrabbits that Joe had collected on the highway, and two pheasants from his freezer. Blowing snow flowed like floodwater over the brush, obscuring Romanowski's house and the mews.

On the bank of the river, Joe stopped and opened his door, which snapped away from his grasp as the wind took it and threw it wide open. He leaned against the wind and snow, clamping his hat on his head, and carried the burlap sack of rabbits and pheasants to the river's edge. He tucked the carcasses between large round river stones so they wouldn't blow away. While he did this, he searched vainly in the howling sky for a glimpse of Nate

Romanowski's hawks. If they were there, or watching him from the gorge, he couldn't see them.

As he drove home, his fingers thawing, he hoped the birds were still around and would find the food he had left them.

He was fulfilling one of Romanowski's requests. It was time to get working on the other one, he thought, now that he knew more. Now that he knew that Nate Romanowski had been telling the truth.

15

THE NEXT MORNING, JOE GOT A CALL FROM A LOCAL rancher who complained that elk had knocked down his fence and were in the process of eating the hay he had stacked to feed his cattle during the winter. When Joe arrived at the ranch, the elk had eaten so much hay out of the rancher's haystack that it leaned precariously to one side, ready to topple. The small herd of elk, lazy and satiated, had moved from the stack to the protection of a dark windbreak of trees. Because the animals of Wyoming were the responsibility of the state, ranchers called game wardens when elk, moose, deer, or antelope ate their hay or damaged their property. The warden's job was to chase the animals away and assess the harm done. If the damage was significant, the rancher was due compensation, and Joe would have to submit the paperwork.

Using a .22 pistol loaded with cracker shells, Joe drove toward the sleeping elk while firing out the window. The cracker shells arced over the animals and popped in the air. It worked: The herd rumbled out of the meadow and back toward the mountains, through the place in the barbed-wire fence that they had flattened to get in. *It's going to be a busy winter of chasing elk out of haystacks,* Joe thought. The heavy snow in the mountains would drive them down for feed, and the worst snows of the year, usually in March and April, were still to come.

At least elk are usually pretty easy to clean up after, Joe thought. Moose were far worse. Moose were known to walk through a multi-strand barbed-wire fence as if it were dental floss and drag the fence along with them, popping the strands free from the staples in the posts like buttons from a ripped shirt.

After chasing the elk away, Joe stopped by the rancher's small white house. The rancher, named Herman Klein, was a third-generation landowner who Joe knew to be a good man. Klein had told Joe before, after a similar incident, that he wouldn't mind feeding the elk if the damned things didn't get so *greedy.*

As Joe pulled into the ranch yard, Klein walked out of the barn, where he had been working on his tractor. He wiped grease from his hands on his Carhartt coveralls and invited Joe in for coffee. After they had performed the winter ranch ritual of leaving their boots and heavy coats in the mudroom before walking in stocking feet to the kitchen table, Klein poured Joe a cup of thick black coffee. While Mrs. Klein arranged sugar cookies on a plate, Joe filled out a report to submit to the Game and Fish Commission confirming the loss of hay and the damage to the fence. Joe didn't mind doing this at all. He considered Herman Klein a good steward of the land, a thoughtful manager who improved the range and riparian areas on both his private and leased land.

"Joe, can I ask you a question?"

"Shoot," Joe said, as he finished up the damage claim. Klein tapped the morning Saddlestring *Roundup* on the table. "What in the hell is going on in Saddlestring these days?"

The headline read SECOND FEDERAL EMPLOYEE AS-SAULTED. There was a photo of Melinda Strickland holding a press conference on the steps of the Forest Service office the day before, deploring the "outrageous attack" on Birch Wardell of the BLM by "local thugs."

"Is there really a movement afoot to go after the Forest Service and the BLM?"

Joe looked up. "That's what she seems to think, Herman." The press conference itself was a unique event in Twelve Sleep County.

"Is she serious?"

"I think she is."

"That's complete bullshit," Klein snorted, shaking his head.

"Herman!" Mrs. Klein scolded, placing the cookies on the table. "Watch your language."

"I've heard much worse," Joe smiled.

"Not from Herman, you haven't."

HIS CELL PHONE WAS BURRING in his pickup when Joe climbed in. He plucked it from its holder on the dashboard.

"Game Warden Joe Pickett."

"Joe Pickett?" asked a female voice he didn't recognize.

"That's what I said."

"Please hold for Melinda Strickland."

Joe moaned inwardly. Strickland was the last person he wanted to talk to. He was placed on hold. Background music played. He identified the song as "Last Train to Clarksville" by the Monkees. *Only the U.S. Forest Service would have a waiting tape that old,* he thought.

He held. Maxine watched him hold, and minutes

passed. He assumed that when the President of the United States wanted to talk with the President of Russia, this was how it worked.

"Joe?" It was Melinda Strickland. She sounded chirpy.

"Yes."

"Joe, my friend, how are things going? Are you hanging in there?"

Her tone was that of a lifelong chum who was concerned with his health and welfare, which puzzled him.

"I'm fine," he said haltingly. "Why do you ask?"

"I'm getting hammered by the press asking questions about how you found Birch Wardell out on that road. They want to know how he got hit by your car, and all of that, you know?"

Joe took the phone away from his ear and stared at it. *Hammered by the press?*

"I hit Birch Wardell with my car because he was standing in the middle of the road," Joe said flatly. "It was an accident. Then I took him to the hospital and stayed with him until I was sure he was okay."

"Joe, you don't need to use that tone," she said soothingly. "I'm on your side here, you know? They just keep asking me about you being there when Lamar Gardiner was killed, then you being there again when Birch Wardell was hurt."

Joe felt a flush of anger. "Are you suggesting I had something to do with those incidents?"

"Oh, God no," she said. "I'm on your side."

"What other side is there?" Joe asked. "And who exactly is 'hammering' you with questions?" In Saddlestring, there was the *Roundup,* an FM radio station, and one local AM station that played preprogrammed music, stock reports, and CNN radio newsbreaks.

There was a long pause, and then she filled the silence with a rush of words. "That's not why I called, Joe. Lamar Gardiner scheduled a public meeting for Friday night on the USFS strategic plan for this district . . . you know, the road closures. He announced the meeting quite a few weeks ago and I'm going to go ahead and chair it. I was hoping you would come and offer support. I know Lamar's policies were controversial, and I could use your help on this."

The quick change of direction caught Joe by surprise.

"I can be there," Joe said, although he immediately wished he hadn't.

"Great, great. Thank you, Joe." Her chirpiness resumed. "You be careful out there, my friend. Things may be a little dicey until we get all this stuff figured out with the Sovereigns—and who knows if they'll go after state government representatives as well as federal land managers."

"Are the Sovereigns being targeted for Birch Wardell's ambush?" Joe asked. He had heard nothing of this.

"I'm not at liberty to say,"

Then she wished him a good day and hung up. Joe listened to the silence on the phone for a moment, still not sure what had just transpired.

The conversation left him flummoxed. He wished he had recorded it so he could replay it later, and try to make sense of it. Melinda Strickland seemed to be implying things—that Joe was the subject of controversy and suspicion, that forces were out to get her, that maybe Joe was aligned with those forces—while at the same time assuring him that everything was fine and that she and Joe were working well together. Her backtracking, when he asked her for specifics, he thought wryly, left a smell of burning rubber as she floored it into reverse.

He turned off his cell phone so she couldn't call again.

* * *

INSTEAD OF RETURNING HOME AND to his office, Joe turned toward the BLM joint range-management study area. He wanted a clearer picture of the crash site and the terrain that Birch Wardell described. It took nearly an hour and a half on drifted-in gravel roads to get to the place where Wardell had seen the light-colored pickup that had fled from him and led to the accident.

Joe stopped in the road and looked up the gently rising hill where Wardell said he had first seen the other vehicle. Gunmetal-gray sagebrush dotted the hillside, each bush supporting a shark-fin wedge of drifted snow. The rest of the ground was blown clean of snow, revealing gray dirt and yellow grass. It was the first grass he had seen for a couple of weeks.

From where he sat in the idling truck, Joe could make out tire tracks in the crushed grass that led from the road he was now on to the top of the hill. The tracks, he assumed, were Wardell's. On the top of the hill, against the sky, he could see a broken signpost. It was all just as Wardell had described it.

Joe reached down and shoved the pickup into four-wheel drive, and ascended the hill, staying in Wardell's tracks. At the top, near the broken signpost, he stopped. Beyond him, the breaklands stretched for miles until they melted into the foothills of the Bighorn Mountains. The terrain was deceptive. At first glance, it looked flat and barren, like gentle corduroy folds. But the folds obscured rugged draws and arroyos, and small sharp canyons. Pockets of thick, tall Rocky Mountain juniper punctuated the expanse.

With his binoculars, Joe swept the bottom of the hill, where Wardell said he'd wrecked his pickup. Sure enough, through the thick brush, Joe saw the back bumper of a BLM pickup pointing toward the clouds. The truck had crashed headfirst into a steep draw. It had been there for two days, and the BLM had not yet sent a tow truck to pull it out. For once, Joe was pleased with bureaucratic inertia.

Joe found another set of tracks on the opposite hill that led up and over the top. Those tracks no doubt belonged to the vehicle Birch Wardell had been chasing. Slowly, Joe studied the bottom of the hill and the sharp draw that stretched out from both sides of the wrecked truck like a stiletto slash. He could see no obvious place to cross. There *was* no place to cross. But, damn it, that other driver had done it somehow.

Joe sighed and lowered his glasses. How in the hell did he do it? He thought about the possibility of a ramp or bridge that the vandal had carried with him. Maybe he carried it in the back of his truck, and laid it across the draw. But that was too far-fetched, Joe decided. The distance across the arroyo was too great, and the logistics of carrying, deploying, and retrieving a ramp while being pursued were impractical.

He sat back and thought about it. Maxine crawled across the seat and put her large, warm head in his lap. He studied the opposite hill, the dual sets of tracks up from the bottom of the draw, and the bumper of the wrecked truck, sticking up obscenely from the heavy brush.

While he thought, a pronghorn antelope doe and her yearling twins crossed in front of him. Their coloring was perfect camouflage for this terrain—finely drawn patches of dark tan, white, and black that blended in with the grassy, windswept slopes with their dark brush and dirty snowdrifts. At a distance, they fused so well with the landscape that entire herds were virtually invisible.

Joe smacked the steering wheel with the heel of his hand. "Damn, Maxine," he said aloud, *"I just figured it out."*

Now it would be a matter of finding the light pickup, and letting himself be drawn in.

16

THAT AFTERNOON, MARYBETH WENT TO WORK AT HER part-time job at the stables. Her mother, who had not left the house since her New Year's Eve sojourn, stayed at home with Lucy and April, and Sheridan was at basketball tryouts at school. Joe had left early that morning to respond to Herman Klein's call.

All eight of the horses had stalls in the barn and twenty-four-foot fenced runs outside. They were in the runs when she drove up. She loved being around the horses, who had nickered a greeting when she arrived. There were four sorrels, three paints, and a buckskin. All belonged to boarders who paid monthly for shelter, hay, stall-mucking, and in some cases, grooming and exercise. All of the horses had grown hairy for the winter, and she liked the look of them: frosted muzzles billowing clouds of condensation, and thick, shaggy coats.

She wore her thick canvas barn coat, Watson gloves, and a fleece headband over her ears and under her blonde hair.

The owner of the stables, Marsha Dibble, had left her

an envelope pinned to the bulletin board inside the barn. In it was her paycheck for the hours worked in December, a "Happy New Year" card, and a Post-it note reminding Marybeth to add a nutritional supplement to the grain of one of the older mares. Because Marybeth's arrival meant they would soon get their evening feed, all of the horses had come into their barn stalls to watch her. Using a long hay-hook, she tugged two sixty-pound bales of grass hay from the stack and cut the binding wires. She divided the hay into "flakes"—about one-fifth of a bale per horse—while the horses showed their impatience by stomping their hooves and switching their tails.

It was while Marybeth mixed the granular supplement in a bucket with the grain that she noticed that several of the horses had turned their heads to look at something outside. Their ears were pricked up and alert. Then she heard the low rumble of a motor and the crunching of tires on snow. The engine was killed, and a moment later, a car door slammed shut.

Assuming it was Marsha, Marybeth slid back the barn door to say hello. Her greeting caught in her throat.

Jeannie Keeley stood ten feet away, looking hard at Marybeth through a rising halo of cigarette smoke and condensed breath. Behind Keeley was an old blue Dodge pickup. A man sat behind the wheel, looking straight ahead through the windshield toward the mountains.

"Do you know who I am?" Jeannie Keeley asked. Her Mississippi accent was grating and hard. *Dew you know who Ah yam?*

Keeley wore an oversized green quilted coat. Her small hands were thrust into her front jean pockets. She looked smaller and more frail than Marybeth remembered her from their brief introduction four years before at the obstetrician's office. At that time, both were pregnant. Keeley had six-year-old April with her in the office at the time.

"I know who you are," Marybeth said, trying to keep her voice from catching in her throat. Behind her in the stalls, one of the buckskins kicked at the front of her stall to get her attention. Marybeth ignored the horse, her attention on the small woman in front of her.

"I know who you are, too," Keeley said. Her cigarette tip danced up and down as she spoke. "I want my April back."

The words struck Marybeth like a blow. Until this moment she hadn't realized just how much she had hoped Jeannie Keeley's arrival back in town was benign, that perhaps she was just passing through and making some noise.

"We consider April our daughter now, Jeannie. We love her like our own." Marybeth swallowed. "Joe and I are in the process of adopting her."

Keeley snorted and rolled her eyes.

"That process don't mean shit 'til it's done. And it ain't done if the biological mother don't consent."

"She's happy now," Marybeth said, trying to talk to Jeannie mother-to-mother. "If you could see her . . ." Then she remembered the tracks in the snow and flushed with anger. "Or maybe you did see her. Jeannie, were you outside our house two nights ago? Were you looking into our windows?"

A hint of a smile tugged at Keeley's mouth, and she tipped her head back slightly.

"Your house? That musta' been somebody else." *Ay-else.*

Marybeth tried to keep her voice calm and measured, while what she wanted to do was scream and yell at Jeannie at the top of her lungs. In the back of her mind, Marybeth had been preparing for this fight ever since she heard that Jeannie Keeley was back. But she fought the urge to attack, choosing instead, and with difficulty, to try to appeal to Jeannie's emotions.

"Jeannie, you dropped April off at the bank with your house keys when you left town. I understand how painful losing your husband and your home must have been. But you made the choice to abandon your daughter. We didn't take her from you."

Keeley eyed Marybeth with naked contempt. "You don't understand nothin' at all. I fuckin' *hate* people who say they understand things about me they don't." Her eyes narrowed into slits. "There's nothing for you to understand, Miss Marybeth Pickett, except that I want my baby back. She needs to be with her real mama, the one who changed her diapers. She was a hard birth, lady. She got me to bleedin'. I like to bled to death to bring her into this world." Keeley's voice lowered: "I want my daughter . . . back . . . *now*."

Marybeth glared back. She felt her rage, and her frustration, building. This woman hated her. This stupid, trashy woman hated *her*.

"We love April," Marybeth said evenly. The words just hung there.

"That's mighty white of you," Keeley smirked. *Tha's mah-ty waht uv you.* "But it don't matter. She's not your child. She's my child." *Chile.*

Marybeth realized that Jeannie was trying to bait her, trying to get her to lose her cool and say or do something that would look bad if they ever ended up in court. Jeannie had even brought a witness with her.

Again, Marybeth forced back her rage, and spoke softly.

"Jeannie, I do understand what it's like to lose someone. I lost my baby four years ago. Did you know that? Remember when we met at the doctor's office when we were both pregnant? I lost that baby when a man shot me. He was the same man who killed your husband." Marybeth's eyes probed for a sense of connection or compassion, but neither was forthcoming. "After I got out of the hospital, we found out about April. We took her in as our own. She's part of our family now. She's got wonderful sisters who care for her. Joe and I care for her. Can't you see that . . ."

Marybeth needed to be careful here, and she tried to be. "Can't you see that April is happy, and has adjusted? That the greatest gift a mother can give is to make sure her child is loved and cared for?"

Jeannie Keeley took her eyes off Marybeth, and seemed to be searching the snow for something. Absently, she dug in her coat pocket for another cigarette and placed it in her mouth, unlit.

Marybeth noticed that the man driving the pickup had finally turned his head to look at her. He was severe-looking, older than Jeannie, with an unkempt growth of beard. He wore a dirty John Deere cap. His eyes were sunken and dark, his pupils hard dots.

A match flared, and Marybeth looked back to Keeley as she lit her cigarette. Was it possible she was reconsidering, that Marybeth had touched her?

Keeley let two streams of smoke curl out of her nose. "Fuck you, princess," she hissed. "I want my April back."

Marybeth clenched her teeth, and her eyes fluttered. She thought that in four steps she could be on this horrible woman, pummeling her head with the hay hook that hung within easy reach on an upside-down horseshoe inside the door.

It was as if the man behind the wheel could read her mind, and he quickly opened his door and walked around the front of the truck. He stopped and casually pulled open his coat so that Marybeth could see the faux-pearl grip of a heavy stainless-steel pistol stuck into his greasy jeans.

"We best go, honey," the man said to Jeannie Keeley.

Keeley snorted, her eyes locked in hatred on Mary-beth. The man reached up and put his hand on Keeley's shoulder but she shook it off.

"We best go."

"Look at that bitch," Keeley said, her voice barely a whisper. "Look at her standin' there like some kind of goddamned princess. She loses her baby so she thinks she can just steal mine to make up for it."

That tore at Marybeth, but she stood still and firm. Four steps, she thought.

The man moved behind Keeley, and put his arms around her, squeezing her into him, his head close to her ear, "I said let's go. We'll get April back. The judge said we would."

Jeannie started to resist, but was obviously overpow-ered. She relaxed, and he released his grip. She never broke off her glare at Marybeth.

"What was that about a judge?" Marybeth asked, not able to stop a tremble in her voice.

Keeley smiled, shaking her head instead of speaking. "Never mind that," she said, and backed up past the man, never taking her eyes off of Marybeth until she bumped up against the door of the truck. "You just bet-ter be packing her stuff up so's she'll be ready when we come get her and take her home."

Jeannie Keeley turned and opened the door, climbed in, and slammed the door with a bang.

The man looked vacantly at Marybeth, his face reveal-ing nothing. Then he patted the butt of the pistol with-out looking at it, turned on his heel, and climbed back behind the wheel. Neither looked over at her as they drove away.

*   *   *

MARYBETH STUMBLED INTO THE BARN and slid the door closed. Her legs were so weak that she collapsed on a bale of hay and sat there, staring at the door handle, replaying the scene in her mind, disbelieving what had just happened.

A judge, she said. Joe's experience with Judge Pennock had shown how nonsensical the courts could be in these cases, especially when it came to decisions involving a biological mother.

She could call the sheriff and report the incident, but she knew it would be her word against theirs, and it would go nowhere. Marybeth had not actually been threatened in any way she could prove. *Maybe Joe will have an idea,* she thought, and she tried to call him on his cell phone. She cursed out loud when he didn't pick up. He must have turned it off for some reason. He was due to pick up Sheridan at practice within the hour, and Marybeth would keep trying.

The mare nickered aggressively and she looked up at her.

"You'll get fed," Marybeth said aloud, her voice weak. "Just give me a minute to think and settle down."

AFTER FEEDING THE HORSES, SHE slid open the barn door again. She looked at the tracks that the pickup had made, saw the cigarette butt and spent matches that Jeannie Keeley had dropped in the snow. It was almost as if she could see Keeley standing there again, squinting against the smoke, putrid with hate, spewing filthy words. The dirty man stood next to her, his handgun stuck in his pants.

These two reprobates, these *scum,* wanted her April

with them. The injustice of it filled her with violent passion. Children were not pets, not furniture, not *items* put on earth to bring pleasure to people who owned them, she raged to herself.

She clenched her hands into fists and shook them. She threw the now-empty bucket across the barn, where it clattered loudly against the wall and sent the horses scattering back to the outside runs. Her eyes welled hotly with tears that soon ran down her freezing cheeks.

17

SHERIDAN PICKETT STOOD IN THE BRICK ALCOVE OF THE school and waited for her dad. Her hair was still damp, so she pulled her hood over her head. The basketball try-outs had been held the day before school resumed, and tomorrow she and the other hopefuls would be greeted with a posted list revealing who had made the team.

It was always strange being at the school when it wasn't in session, she thought. The sounds they made in the gym echoed louder, and the hallways seemed twice as wide when empty. She had peeked into her locked class-room to see that her teacher had replaced all of the Christmas decorations with self-esteem motivational posters.

Most of the girls had walked home from school, but that wasn't an option for Sheridan. So she waited, hoping her hair wouldn't freeze.

Sheridan shook her head when she thought about how the tryouts had gone. She doubted that she'd made the team. Although she had hustled—her dad had told her that even if she couldn't shoot, every team needed players who hustled and played defense—the fact remained that she *was* a lousy shooter. In the scrimmage, she had gone 0-for-3, and one of her errant shots had bounced straight up off the top of the backboard. Worse, in one scramble after a loose ball, her glasses had been knocked off and gone skittering across the floor. The coach had whistled a time-out to protect them. The time-out called attention to her, and a couple of the girls giggled when Sheridan obviously had trouble locating her glasses, and the coach, because of her poor vision. When play resumed, and she had her glasses back on, she was called for two fouls in a row. She had hacked one of the girls who had giggled before when the girl went up for a layup, and she'd set a moving pick on another.

The doors wheezed open behind her and the coach, Mr. Tynsdale, who also taught art, came out of the building and locked it up behind him.

"Do you have a ride?" he asked. She tried to judge from the way he looked at her if he was asking out of sympathy or if he wanted to provide transportation to one of his new players. She couldn't tell.

"My dad is supposed to pick me up."

Mr. Tynsdale nodded. "He's the game warden, right?"

"Yes."

"Okay, then." Mr. Tynsdale smiled and walked toward the teacher's parking lot.

"Thanks for offering!" Sheridan called after him, wishing she would have thanked him earlier.

Mr. Tynsdale waved it off. As he started to climb into his car, he gestured toward the main road as if to say, "I think your ride is here."

Sheridan started toward the street, then saw that the big late-model SUV that had pulled to the curb was not her dad's. She stopped as the passenger window descended.

"Do you know where the Forest Service office is?" a man asked. He was thin, almost skeletal, with a close-cropped pad of curly gray hair. He had a long thin nose and wore silver-framed glasses. His eyes were blue and rheumy.

The driver was dark, but didn't look as old as the man who had asked the question. The driver had close-set eyes and a scar that hitched up his upper lip so that it looked like he was snarling.

"You scared her, Dick," she heard the driver tell the passenger, not intending for her to hear.

A slight smile pulled at Dick's thin lips, but he didn't acknowledge his partner's comment.

"Is this a school for the deaf?" Dick asked.

The driver chuckled at the other man's remark. Dick, Sheridan noted, didn't mind trying to intimidate young girls. Sheridan wasn't to be intimidated.

"No, it isn't," she answered a bit testily. "This is Sad-dlestring Elementary. The U.S. Forest Service office is three blocks down and a block to the right." She pointed down Main Street.

"You stand there much longer you're gonna catch a flu," Dick said dryly. The driver laughed.

"And if you keep talking to me, I'm going to call the police," Sheridan snapped, a little surprised that she'd said it.

"Woo-hoo!" the driver laughed.

Dick turned to him, then back to Sheridan. The power window began to whir closed.

"Thanks for your help, you little—" The window sealed tight, and the insult wasn't heard. But through the glass, Sheridan saw the man say the word "bitch."

The vehicle eased away from the curb and continued down the street. Sheridan watched it go. She noticed that the license plates weren't local. They read: U.S. GOVERNMENT.

Sheridan stood there for a moment, still shocked that an adult would call her that. It made her feel numb inside.

Before she could retreat to the alcove, her dad's green pickup appeared. She was relieved and grateful that he was there, and she ran out to greet him.

"Who was that?" her dad asked, nodding toward the SUV that was now two blocks away.

"A couple of men wanted to know where the Forest Service office was," she said, settling in and pulling the seat belt across her. Maxine's tail thumped the back of the seat in greeting. "They were jerks."

She sat in silence as they drove through town. Both Sheridan and her dad glanced down the street where the Forest Service building was and saw the two men getting out of their SUV. Her dad slowed his truck to a crawl as they drove by. The men wore heavy, high-tech winter clothing that looked brand-new. The man named Dick had a large black duffel bag. The driver was sliding a long metal case out of the hatchback of the SUV.

"That's a gun case," her dad said.

She looked over to see if he was concerned or not, but couldn't read his expression.

"Why are we going this way?" she asked, since their home was in the opposite direction.

"I wanted to see these guys," her dad responded. "And I was wondering if you would want to help me check on some birds at a place out by the river."

"Some birds?"

"Falcons," her dad said. "I'm doing a guy a favor."

Sheridan had never seen a hawk up close, and she'd always wanted to.

"You bet, Dad," she said.

Sheridan noticed, however, that her dad wasn't looking at her. His eyes were fixed on his rearview mirror, watching the two men enter the Forest Service office.

"Oh," her dad said, as they cleared Saddlestring on the highway. "I'm sorry. How did tryouts go?"

"Bad, I think," she said.

"Did you hustle?"

She smiled. "That's the one thing I did right."

He winked at her. "That's the most important thing, Sheridan. Even if you're just hustling inside, and anybody who looks at you just sees calm. Always be aware of what's going on around you."

THE WIND PICKED UP AS they drove west. The fresh snow from the day before mixed with the gritty snow from the first storm and whorled in kaleidoscopic ground blizzards. *Snow in Wyoming never stays in one place,* Sheridan thought. *It just keeps moving and rearranging itself, as if it's constantly looking for a better place to live.* They turned off of the highway and drove several miles down a snow-packed gravel road. Drifts were high and sharp on both sides of the pickup.

"There it is," her dad said, pointing through the windshield.

"Is this the house of the man who's in jail?" Sheridan asked.

"Yes, it is. He's a falconer, and he asked me if I would feed his birds."

"Is he a bad man?"

"He's accused of murder."

Sheridan screwed up her face. "Then why are we helping him?"

"We're not," Joe said. "We're keeping the birds alive. There's no reason they should be punished. At least, I hope we're helping them. I didn't see them the last time I was out here to feed them."

There was a broken-down fence, and beyond that a small stone house and a little building of some kind that had collapsed. It wasn't much, she thought, although the steep red bluff on the other side of the river was beautiful and vibrant in the last half-hour of sunshine. Her dad drove into the ranch yard close to the house and turned off the truck. Before getting out, he pulled on a pair of leather gloves.

"It's cold but it's not too bad," he said, opening his door and jumping out. "Nate Romanowski picked a good place here. It's the only spot in the valley where the wind isn't blowing."

Sheridan patted Maxine and closed the door on her. Sheridan didn't need to be told that Maxine should stay in the cab of the truck if they were going to try to feed the birds.

Her dad stood near the front of the truck, looking at the stone house and shaking his head. The house's front door was flung open, and clothes and furniture had been tossed out. Books lay open and facedown in the snow, their pages swelled with moisture so that they were twice their normal size.

"It's been ransacked," her dad said. "They tore the place apart to find evidence."

Sheridan nodded. She thought that maybe her dad was a little ashamed that law enforcement had done this. After all, he was law enforcement, too.

He picked up a few of the books out of the snow. "*The Art of War, Mutiny on the Bounty, Wealth of Nations, Huckleberry Finn,*" he said, looking at the spines. Sheridan picked up two from the ground and followed him toward the cabin. Both of the books she had were about falconry.

Inside, they stacked the books on a counter before

looking around. It was a mess. Cupboard doors hung open, drawers sagged. Their contents littered the floor. The mattress in the bedroom had been sliced open, its innards of cotton and spring exposed. Even sections of the interior walls had been smashed open.

Sheridan watched as her dad went back outside and brought the furniture back in. Most of the pieces— clearly not all that great to begin with—were damaged. "The least we can do is get this stuff out of the weather," he said. It took her dad eight trips to get everything back inside. She helped as much as she could. One thing she could not stop staring at was a framed photo with cracked glass. The photo was faded, but it was of four men standing shoulder to shoulder in the desert. The men wore white robes, and behind them was a camel. Three of the men looked like Arabs, with dark features and beards. The fourth man was fair, with piercing eyes and a slight smile.

Her dad saw her looking at the picture and picked it up.

"That's Nate Romanowski, by God," he said, pointing at the fourth man. Her dad sounded surprised. He nodded at the picture, and pursed his lips as if reaffirming something.

"What is it?" She asked.

"Nothing," her dad answered, but in a way that she knew meant he didn't want to talk about it.

They went outside, and her dad closed the door behind them. Then he scanned the sky.

"There's one of them," he said, pointing toward the river. She followed his sight line, and there it was, all right.

"That's a red-tailed hawk," he said. "He's immature, not older than a year. You can tell because he's still got a brown tail and a speckled dirty breast."

She looked to her dad, and he smiled. "Go ahead and

walk up to him, but give him plenty of space. He needs sort of a cushion between you and him, or he'll get nervous. I'll go get some of their food and be with you in a minute."

The hawk stood on a piece of driftwood near the river. He stood so still that she thought it would be possible to miss him if they hadn't been looking for him. His eyes were on her as she approached.

Her first impression of the bird was that it was smaller than she would have guessed it would be. Still and compact, not revealing his wingspan, the hawk looked to be about the size of a large raven. But unlike a raven, the hawk had a sense of majesty about it, she thought. The bird's head was cocked back slightly, as if looking down on her. Its coloring was finely textured, a beige breast and mottled, bay-colored wings. His large, wrinkled talons gripped the driftwood, and she could see shiny black and curled nails.

From behind, she heard her dad approach. The hawk was now watching him instead of her. She found out why when he approached the bird and lowered a dead sage grouse on the ground in front of it.

The hawk looked at the grouse, looked at Sheridan, looked at her dad. Its movements were precise, almost mechanical.

Then, with a slight shuffle of his wings, he hopped down from the driftwood to the grouse and began to eat.

"This is kind of . . . gross, honey," her dad cautioned.

But she was fascinated. She watched the hawk methodically take apart and consume the entire sage grouse. As he ate, a lump above his breast got bigger and bigger.

"That's called his crop," her dad explained. "It fills as he eats. The food is stored there for later. That's one of the reasons these birds can go so long between meals."

She noticed now that blood flecked the hawk's sharp

beak, and that bits of down from the grouse floated through the evening air. She watched the hawk carefully. Although its eyes were hard and impassive, she sensed a kind of comfort in him now. He was full, and relaxed.

"This bird is somebody's *pet*?" she asked.

"It's not like that," her dad said. "Good falconers don't break the birds, or domesticate them. They work with them, like partners. The birds can fly away any time they choose to leave."

All that was left of the sage grouse was a pair of clawed feet. Sheridan watched as the hawk dipped down and took one of the feet in his mouth and started eating it. The crunching sound reminded her of when she opened peanuts to eat them.

"Here comes the peregrine," her dad whispered.

She looked up and saw it, an airborne "V" cruising upriver like a missile, a few feet from the surface of the water and ice. She could hear it cutting through the air with a hiss as it went by.

"Stay still," her dad said, putting his hand on her shoulder. "I think he'll come back."

"Do you have another sage grouse?" she asked, concerned.

"Yup."

It took a few moments before the peregrine reappeared. This time, it was flying downriver, and a little closer to the bank.

"What a beautiful bird," Sheridan said.

"Peregrines are the ultimate hunters," her dad said. "They're not the biggest falcons, but they're the fastest and the most versatile. They used to be endangered, but now there are lots of them."

She was entranced.

And when the peregrine came back, flared, and lit with a graceful settling of his wings just a few feet away from them, she felt as if something wild, and magical, had happened.

Her dad lowered the other grouse to the ground in front of the peregrine. The little bird, darker and somehow more cocky and warlike than the red-tailed hawk, gracefully tore into it.

"I think I'd rather learn about these falcons than play basketball," she heard herself say.

IN THE PICKUP, AS THEY drove from Nate Romanowski's place in the pre-dark of winter, Sheridan realized just how cold she was. Her teeth chattered as she waited for the heater to warm up. Seeing the falcons had made her forget about the cold, forget about how late it was getting.

She noticed that her dad's cell phone, clipped to the dashboard, was turned off, and she mentioned it.

"I forgot about that, damn it," he said, turning it on. Her dad rarely cursed.

Almost immediately, it rang and he grabbed it quickly. She watched him. His expression seemed to sag, then harden, as he listened.

"I can't believe she said that."

"Is it Mom?" Sheridan asked. But she knew it was.

"I'll be home in half an hour, darling. I'm so sorry this happened. And I'm sorry you couldn't reach me."

Sheridan was concerned. His voice was low, and calm, and very serious. But she knew that inside, he was hustling.

18

THE NEXT MORNING DAWNED GRAY AND COLD, AND there was a bulletin on the radio that said a stockman's advisory had been issued for Northern Wyoming. For their first day back to school, the girls were dressed in clothes they had received for Christmas. Because the girls had become used to sleeping later in the morning over the break, Joe and Marybeth had trouble moving them along so they would be finished with breakfast and ready to go when the bus arrived.

"Christmas is over, ladies," Joe told them. "Back to work we go."

Marybeth was quiet, her eyes tired. She had spent most of the previous night awake and crying about her encounter with Jeannie Keeley. Joe had held her, and shared her rage and frustration. Both Joe and Marybeth were painfully aware of the fact that this might be the last "normal" breakfast with the three girls for a while. And both were determined to see it go smoothly. Neither Marybeth nor Joe had said anything to April, or Sheridan and Lucy about Marybeth's encounter with Jeannie

Keeley the afternoon before. But April seemed prophetic, and was acutely alert. Throughout breakfast, her eyes darted furtively from Marybeth to Joe, as if trying to pick up a signal or read a glance. Just as Maxine always seemed to know when Joe was going to go out of town, April seemed to sense instinctively that something was afoot. Sheridan and Lucy, rubbing sleep from their eyes, were oblivious to the morning drama.

After they'd gathered their coats and backpacks, Joe ushered all three girls outside to meet the bus. As the bus doors opened, April turned and threw her arms around Joe's neck and kissed him goodbye. Joe couldn't remember such an open display of affection from April before. When he returned to the house, it was obvious that Marybeth had seen them from the front window, and she was wiping away tears again.

Before they could talk about it, the telephone rang. Marybeth picked the receiver up, and as she listened, Joe watched her face turn into an ivory mask.

"Who is it?" Joe mouthed.

"Robey Hersig," Marybeth answered in a sharp voice. Joe could not hear the county attorney speaking, but he could tell what Hersig was saying by Marybeth's reaction.

"Robey, I appreciate you letting us know," Marybeth said, and hung up the phone. She looked up at Joe and her eyes were flat and distant. "Robey said that Jeannie Keeley got a judge down in Kemmerer to issue an order for April's return. The judge issued the order last week, and Robey just got a copy of it. He's going to fax it to us."

Kemmerer was a small town in southwestern Wyoming. Joe was puzzled. Why Kemmerer?

"Robey says the judge is a loose cannon, some kind of a nut," Marybeth continued, still eerily matter-of-fact.

"He said the order could probably be overturned in court, but until that happens we're obligated to hand over April if Jeannie wants her."

Joe stood still, his eyes locked with Marybeth's.

"Joe, Robey says that if Jeannie comes for her and we don't turn her over, that *we* could be charged."

Joe shook his head, as if trying to shake away the news.

Her mask cracked and she broke down, and he welcomed her into his arms. "Joe," she asked him, "What are we going to do?"

AFTER MARYBETH REGAINED CONTROL AND seemed to hammer her emotions into the armor of icy resolve, she left for work at the library. Joe, frustrated, spent the day in the field. There was plenty to keep him busy, as always, and he threw himself into it in a barely controlled frenzy. Better to work himself hard physically, he thought, than to sit and contemplate what was happening at home.

He loaded his snow machine and mounting ramps in the back of his pickup, drove up the Crazy Woman drainage as far as the road was plowed, then chained up and continued until he reached a trailhead. He backed the snowmobile down the ramps with a roar, then raced across untracked snow up and over the mountain. In the drainage below was a designated winter elk refuge, and he cruised down through it. Because of the deep snow, most of the elk that normally would have been there had moved to lower ground, even though a contractor had dropped hay for them. Instead of using the refuge, though, the elk were eating Herman Klein's lowland hay, as well as the hay of other ranchers in the valley. Joe didn't particularly blame the elk, but wished they would have stayed around. The few elk that were present on the range were emaciated. He could tell they weren't likely to last through the winter. The storms and the coyotes would get them. They stood dark and mangy, looking pathetic, he thought.

He fought a totally uncharacteristic urge to challenge them with his snowmobile, to charge at them and watch them run. Instead, he turned back and raced up the mountain he had come down, flying though the trees with a recklessness that both frightened and exhilarated him.

He stopped short of his pickup and tried to collect his thoughts. He noted the elk population of the winter range—seventeen sick and starving animals—in his notebook. He would check the other ranges throughout the week, and compile a report for Terry Crump. Joe expected to find the same depressing results in the other refuges as well. A lot of elk were going to die this winter, he concluded. He couldn't protect them. Too damned many would die of winterkill.

ONE THING HAD CRYSTALLIZED IN Joe's mind during his breakneck rush up the mountain: He needed to talk with Jeannie Keeley. He drove toward Battle Mountain and the Sovereign Citizen compound but was stopped by a sheriff's-department truck that was blocking the road. The Blazer was sidewise on the plowed one-track, its front and back bumpers almost touching the walls of snow.

Joe slowed to a stop as Deputy McLanahan emerged from the Blazer and walked toward his truck. McLanahan raised a hood over his head as he approached. A short-barreled shotgun was clamped under his arm.

Joe rolled his window down.

McLanahan's damaged nose was a grotesque blue-black color and there were half-moons of dark green under his eyes. He looked worse than Joe remembered.

"Where are you heading, game warden?"

The way McLanahan said it, "game warden" sounded to Joe like "son-of-a-bitch."

"Patrolling," Joe said, which was not quite accurate. He had intended to go to the compound to see if Jeannie Keeley had returned. And to advise Wade Brockius that April should not be the pawn in the bitter game Jeannie was playing.

"I thought the hunting seasons were over," McLanahan stated. Joe could tell the deputy was in his hard-ass mode, and he guessed that being assigned to roadblock duty by the sheriff might have precipitated it.

"They are," Joe agreed. "But I've got winter range all over these mountains to check. What's going on here, anyway?"

McLanahan's face looked raccoon-like inside the hood.

"Roadblock. I'm supposed to check anyone coming in or going out."

"Because of the Sovereigns?"

"Yep. They've overstayed their welcome as of today. The eight-day camping limit has done run out."

Joe didn't understand. "What?"

"Folks can camp for eight days in this national forest campground. That's it. Then they have to move on. These yay-hoo extremists have not only overstayed their welcome, they've tapped into the electricity and the phone lines up there. I'm freezing my ass off down on this road and those assholes are up there surfing the Internet and using county power to heat their RVs." McLanahan spat, but the cold spittle didn't clear his lips. "Sheriff Barnum and Melinda Strickland want them to get the fuck out of our county. So they posted eviction posters up there last night, and I'm here to see if they leave."

So Barnum and Strickland are working together. How odd, Joe thought.

"And if they don't leave?" Joe asked.

A grim smile broke across McLanahan's face. "If they don't leave there's a plan in place to take care of business. We won't stand for any more incidents like what happened with Lamar or that BLM guy."

Joe rubbed his eyes. He knew it was a nervous habit, something he had the strong desire to do as stress built up inside him. "What's the connection between the Sovereigns and those two?" Joe asked. "Do they really think they're connected in some way?"

McLanahan's eyes were flat pools of bad pond water. "The day the Sovereigns showed up was the day Lamar got killed," he said, deadpan. "The BLM guy was a week later. Both are Feds. These Sovereign nutcases hate the government. We've got one of 'em in jail, but the rest are up in that camp. Is it really that hard to figure out, game warden?"

McLanahan said "game warden" in that way again. Joe controlled his anger, and asked calmly, "What are they going to do?"

"You mean, what are *we* going to do," McLanahan said, the grin still stretched tight. "Melinda Strickland called in a couple of experts in the field. They're in charge of the situation, and they're a couple of bad-ass cowboys."

Joe thought of the two men who had questioned Sheridan, then driven to the Forest Service building. But he said nothing.

"So what are you going to do if they don't leave?" Joe asked again.

McLanahan's bruised and mottled face contorted

even further into a kind of leer. Joe realized that McLanahan didn't have a clue what Barnum, Strickland, and the two "bad-ass cowboys" were planning. But he didn't want Joe to know that.

"Let's just say that we're not going to stand around and scratch our nuts like they did in Montana with those Freemen," McLanahan finally said.

"What's that mean?"

"That's privileged information," McLanahan blustered. He stepped away. "I'm freezing to death standing out here," he said. "I'm going to get in my truck and fire up the heater. You want to go up there you're going to have to clear it with Barnum first."

"Have you seen an older-model blue Dodge pickup come up this road?" Joe asked. "With a man and a woman in it? Tennessee plates?"

"Nope."

Joe watched McLanahan walk away. Joe's mind was swirling with new implications. He rubbed his eyes.

IN THE AFTERNOON, JOE PATROLLED the breaklands. He drove the BLM roads boldly, and took the ones that would crest hills or traverse sagebrush clearings, choosing to fully expose himself. He was looking for the light-colored Ford. He hoped the driver of the Ford, the man (or men) who had lured Birch Wardell into the canyon, would try to do the same to him. He needed some kind of action that would make him feel he was doing something, and occupy his mind to delay the inevitable.

The inevitable would be later in the evening, when he and Marybeth sat down with April to tell her that her mother wanted her back.

19

JEANNIE KEELEY SAT IN THE DIRTY PICKUP WEARING HER best green dress and smoking a cigarette. The defroster didn't work worth a damn, and every few minutes she leaned forward and wiped a clean oval on the foggy windshield. When it was clear, she could see the redbrick façade of Saddlestring Elementary. It was Wednesday morning, the second day the children were back at school.

A bell rang, and despite the cold, children filed out of a set of double doors on the side of the building and across a playground that was mottled with snow and frozen brown gravel. Jeannie noted that there was a playground supervisor—a teacher, she supposed—walking stiffly on the perimeter of the children.

Her eyes squinted and fixed on a blonde girl wearing a red down coat with a hood rimmed with fake white fur. The girl was in the middle of a group of three other girls huddling near the building. The girls, presumably classmates, were talking and gesturing with animation.

"There she is," Jeannie whispered, pressing her finger against the glass. "There's my April."

Clem, her man, cleaned a little oval for himself.

"Which one?"

"By the building. In that red coat."

Clem hesitated. He obviously couldn't pick her out. "Red coat?" he asked. "There's about twenty red coats."

Jeannie waved him off impatiently. "I goddamned know which one is my daughter, Clem."

"Didn't say you didn't," he answered, clearly looking to avoid a confrontation. She knew he would choose to do that. Usually, she wished he wouldn't talk at all. Rarely did he say anything worthwhile. She wished he would just shut up and drive.

JEANNIE HAD MET CLEM IN eastern Tennessee at a Cracker Barrel restaurant. She had been waitressing, just about to quit and move on, and he was seated in her section. He was alone. He had driven her crazy with the length and precision of his order—how, *exactly*, he wanted his eggs cooked (just shy of over-easy with a dollop of butter on the yolk), his gravy ladled (on the side, in a soup bowl and not a cup, with plenty of pieces of pork sausage in it), his fried apples prepared (a double order with extra cinnamon) and his toast toasted (hard on one side, soft on the other). She had stared at the man with his prison pallor and thin dark hair when he'd asked her politely to repeat his order back to him. She did, and then asked him where in the hell he was from that he could order a breakfast like that and expect to get it. Eastern Montana, he said. Jordan. And it wasn't that he could get a breakfast exactly like that in Jordan. It was that he had been dreaming of this particular breakfast for three years in Deer Lodge, Montana, at the penitentiary. He told her his name was Clem. She told him her name was Suzy. She always lied about her name; it was habit.

He ate his breakfast and read a newspaper, and didn't move until lunch, when she came to take his order again.

"How come your name tag says 'Jeannie' if your name is Suzy?" he had asked her.

"If you want lunch, you'll shut your goddamned pie-hole," she answered, and was overheard by the manager, an overeager junior achievement type who didn't even have the guts to fire her in person but sent the accountant to do it.

Jeannie had gathered her few belongings in a bundle and left the Cracker Barrel. Along with her possessions, she took some silverware and a few frozen steaks from the walk-in to her car. But the battery was dead, or something, and the car wouldn't start. She was furious at this turn of events, but Clem had been waiting for her in the parking lot and he had offered her a ride.

That was nine months ago now. Neither one of them had a place to stay, a place to go, or family to move in with. When Clem heard that a man named Wade Brockius planned to provide some refuge for people like him, he told Jeannie about it and they bought a twenty-year-old travel trailer with what little money they had and drove northwest. She had no idea at the time that she would end up in a place she knew, a place she hated, where her husband had been murdered and her daughter lost to her.

"You look purty in that dress," Clem said. She shot a look at him.

Here was a man, she thought, a Montana Freeman, who had held out in a dirty farmhouse outside Jordan, Montana, for months in defiance of local, state, and federal law enforcement. A man who had patrolled the flat scrub earth of eastern Montana wearing a ski mask and carrying a Ruger Mini-14 with a banana clip. (His image had been broadcast around the world during the siege.) A man who had spent three years at the state penitentiary in Deer Lodge rather than tell the authorities what he knew about the Freeman leadership. But a man who was so damned scared of *her* that he flinched when she turned on him and started crying like a eunuch when she threatened to leave him. Clem the Freeman, she thought. *Clem the Freeman*.

The bell rang again. Recess was over. Jeannie watched April and the other girls go back inside the building.

"That woman, Marybeth Pickett, thinks she's a better mother to April than I am," Jeannie said bitterly.

Clem grunted in disapproval of Marybeth.

"She took advantage of me, and my April," Jeannie spat. "She took that child when I was at my worst, when I couldn't care for her. Now that woman wants to keep her because she lost one of her own."

Clem grunted again.

"People been taking things from me all of my damned life. Just because I'm smaller, or had less school than them, they figure they can just *take* what they want from me." Her eyes narrowed to slits, and she lit another cigarette. "My first husband, Ote, took my childhood and my future from me when he moved me out to this damned place so he could be a mountain man. Then that judge in Mississippi took my boy away after that. That damned judge said I abandoned my boy, which was a damned lie. Everybody has a right to go on a vacation, and that's all I done. How could I be blamed for the fact that my baby-sitter, that little bitch, went on vacation, too? But that judge took my boy away anyway."

Jeannie's youngest, her three-year-old daughter, was with Ote's parents in Jackson, Mississippi. They claimed they were going to keep her, but Jeannie had other plans.

She looked at Clem, her eyes blazing. He was shaking his head slowly.

"It's a crying shame," Clem said.

"You goddamned right it is," she said, turning back to the windshield, which was fogging again. "Once we get April, we'll go back for my baby."

Jeannie pulled two envelopes from her purse. One was old and brown, and the other was crisp and white. She shook out a thin sheaf of photos from the brown envelope. Clem watched as she shuffled through the snapshots.

"I'm gonna show these to April to remind her where she comes from," Jeannie said. "This one's her and her brother when they was babies. April used to suck her two fingers all the time, instead of her thumb. Ote said that was unnatural."

She went through all of the pictures again, smiling at some, riffling past others. Then she dropped them back into the brown envelope.

The white envelope contained a court order assigning immediate custody of April to Jeannie. The order was signed by Judge Potter Oliver of Kemmerer, Wyoming.

CLEM HAD BEEN THE ONE who knew of Judge Oliver, and they had driven across the state to meet the judge, after hours waiting in his office. Clem had told her Judge Oliver was "eccentric," but had his heart in the right place. What he meant, she found out, was that Judge Oliver was sympathetic to the Freemen and had okayed several of their most outrageous financial schemes to fund their militia group. Despite petitions and threatened judicial and legislative action to have him removed from the court, Oliver had somehow stayed on. He was now being forced to retire within the year, he told them. Because of his age.

Judge Oliver was massively fat, with a wispy beard and heavy-lidded eyes. A single green-shaded banker's lamp threw garish shadows across the judge and across the room. When he met with them, Oliver wore an ancient three-piece suit that was shiny from wear and stained with grease spots. Because of an attack of gout, Oliver explained, he was forced to wear slippers on his feet instead of shoes. She saw the slippers under his desk. They were big, like elephant slippers.

Jeannie had pleaded her case for April while Clem sat next to her, holding her hand. Judge Oliver listened impassively, his fingers intertwined across his stomach.

When she was through, the judge asked Jeannie to leave the room while he talked with Clem.

She had waited outside the door for less than ten minutes when Clem came outside to retrieve her. He nodded and told her things were going to be okay.

"I have remanded custody of your daughter to you upon your request," Judge Oliver told Jeannie in a wheezy voice. "My clerk is preparing the order as we speak, and we will fax it to Twelve Sleep County."

Jeannie actually cried with joy, and reached across the desk to shake his huge, crablike hand. She was so happy, and so grateful, thanks to Judge Oliver.

Oliver smiled back, but his eyes were on Clem.

Clem ushered Jeannie to the back of the room while the judge sat at his desk. She could tell when she looked at him that Clem had done something awful.

"The judge asked about compensation," Clem had whispered nervously. "I told him we couldn't pay him very much."

"Clem, you asshole," Jeannie had whispered back, furious. "We can't pay him *anything*!"

Clem had hesitated, then gulped, then pulled at his collar.

"What, damn you?" she asked. Her whisper was loud enough, she thought, to be heard by the judge.

Clem continued to look at his own boots. Then she understood. *The judge wanted compensation.*

She turned toward Judge Oliver and smiled sweetly.

"I'll wait for you out in the truck," Clem mumbled, still looking down.

"You bet your bony ass you will," Jeannie said over her shoulder, through smiling teeth.

"I GUESS I DON'T GET it why you want to go into that school and get her," Clem said. "With that order and all, you could march right up to their house and take her."

Jeannie sighed and rolled her eyes. "Clem, sometimes you're even stupider than usual."

He looked away, stung.

"It's been three long years," she said. "Do you want to drag a crying, screaming kid out of somebody's house?"

Clem frowned. "But you're her mother. She'll want to go with you."

She glared at him. "Who knows what kind of crap and filth about me they've put into her head? Who knows what they'll tell her tonight, now that they know we've got this here order?"

Clem shook his head, confused. But it was obvious he didn't want to argue.

"What this order means," Jeannie said, "is that they can't get her *back*."

Clem dropped his eyes to the floorboards of the truck. "I'm just sorry what you had to do to get it."

Jeannie snorted. "I've done worse."

FOR ONCE, JEANNIE KEELEY WAS lucky. She remembered the layout of the school well enough to walk straight to the office without asking anyone where it was.

Her heels clicked on the tile floor and her green dress swished with purpose as she walked down the hallway.

Most of the classroom doors were open, and the sounds of children and teachers came and went like radio stations set on "scan" as she walked.

The school office was empty except for a secretary who sat at a computer behind the front counter. Jeannie had been thinking about this for a long time. This was a small town. Everybody knew damned near everybody else. She had not been inside the school for four years, since April was in kindergarten. She doubted she had made enough of an impression to be remembered. When she finally decided how to play it, it was simple. She operated on one premise: *What would Marybeth Pickett do?* When the secretary looked up, Jeannie smiled at her.

"Hi again. I'm April Keeley's mother," Jeannie said with such familiarity and assurance that the secretary should be ashamed for not recognizing her. "Third grade. I'm here to take her to the dentist."

The secretary looked befuddled, and plunged into a spiral notebook on her desk. "I'm filling in today for the secretary because she came back from Christmas vacation with the flu," the woman explained. "I'm trying to figure out how this works."

Jeannie tried not to whoop with jubilation. She hoped she hadn't looked too elated.

What would Marybeth Pickett do?

"No hurry at all," Jeannie said. "I sent the note with April this morning, so it could be that it didn't even get to you. I don't mean to cause any problems."

The secretary flipped page after page in the notebook, then looked up. Her face was red with embarrassment. "There's nothing here, but that doesn't mean she didn't bring in the note."

Jeannie made a "What can you do?" gesture.

20

SHERIDAN AND LUCY STOOD WAITING AT THE CURB
when their father pulled up to the school to pick them
up. Sheridan held Lucy's hand. It was darker than it had
been all day, and mist tendrils reached down from the sky
like cold fingers. It wasn't really snowing, but ice crystals
hung suspended in the air.

"Where's April?" her dad asked, as Lucy climbed over
the bench seat to the narrow crew-cab backseat and
Sheridan jumped up beside him.

"Mom came and got her this afternoon," Sheridan
said, pulling the seatbelt across her.

Her dad nodded, and began to pull away from the
curb. Then something seemed to hit him and he slammed
on the brakes. Lucy yelled *"Dad!"* to admonish him, but
Sheridan turned in her seat to face her father.

"Sheridan," he said slowly, enunciating clearly, each
word dropping like a stone. *"How do you know your
mother came and got her?"*

"I heard the announcement from the other room,"

she said. "The secretary came on and asked for April to report to the principal's office. That's what they do."

Lucy came to her older sister's defense. "They made an announcement like that for me when Mom came and got me to take me to the dentist. Whenever they do that it means your mom or dad is waiting in the office for you."

"Did you see her?" her dad asked. *"Did you see your mom?"*

Both girls shook their heads. Sheridan had seen a woman in a green dress pass by her classroom door. But it wasn't her mother. She had no idea why their father seemed so upset. Then she realized what must have happened—Jeannie Keeley must have come for April and taken her away. Sheridan clapped her hand to her mouth. She had been afraid something like this would happen. Her parents had never spelled out what was happening with April, but Sheridan knew whatever it was, it wasn't good.

"Your mom was at work all day at the library and the stables," he said.

And their sister April was gone.

Sheridan began to sob, and Lucy joined her. Sheridan felt awful. April was her responsibility because she was the oldest. Her dad closed his eyes tightly, then opened them and drove. He did not say *It's okay, it's not your fault.*

"I need to call your mother," her dad said, his voice resigned.

JOE LAY AWAKE IN BED and waited for Marybeth to join him. It was late, and he was exhausted. He watched Marybeth brush her teeth and clean her face in the vanity mirror. He could hear the murmur of late-night television from downstairs, a nightly habit of Missy Vankueren's.

Marybeth had amazed him once again that night. By

the time Joe got home, Marybeth had again channeled her rage and frustration into usefulness. Her ability to push her emotion aside and develop a strategy was stunning, Joe thought.

She had calmed Sheridan and Lucy as well as she could, and made dinner for them all. While she cooked, she methodically called both the principal and the sheriff to notify them of what had happened. She left after-hours messages with the county attorney and three local attorneys, asking them to call her in the morning.

While the girls bathed and watched television with Missy, Marybeth filled a suitcase and several boxes with April's clothing and toys. At the first opportunity, she announced to Joe, they must make sure Jeannie received April's belongings. She said it with a kind of chilly determination that had unnerved him.

"Jeannie got April before we could prepare our little girl, or kiss her goodbye," Marybeth said. "I will never forgive her for that."

Missy always thought—and often said—that Marybeth would have made an excellent corporate lawyer if she hadn't married Joe Pickett and started having children. Now Joe could see what an efficient and cold-blooded lawyer she could have become.

Marybeth turned the vanity light off and came to bed. Joe held her.

"We're going to get April back," Marybeth said through gritted teeth. "We're going to get her back, Joe."

Three times during the night, Marybeth left the bedroom. Joe slept so fitfully that he woke up and noted her comings and goings each time. He knew what she was doing. She was checking to make sure that her other two girls were still there.

21

ON FRIDAY NIGHT, THE PUBLIC MEETING ON ROAD CLO-
sures in the national forests was held in the cafeteria of
Saddlestring High School, home of the Wranglers. Joe
Pickett arrived late. He parked in the last row of cars in
the lot and shuffled through vehicles toward the building. It was bitterly cold, with a clear sky. The stars looked
blue-white and hard, and he could hear the rattling hum
of an overworked power transformer mounted on a light
pole. A set of fluorescent pole lamps cast chilling pools of
light on the snow and ice in the gravel lot. The storm
predicted by the National Weather Service had skirted
the Bighorns and slammed full-force into the Tetons, the
Absarokas and the Wind River mountains to the west.
Twelve Sleep Valley had received only a skiff of light
snow and single-degree temperatures.

Before he had left his home office, Joe had sent a report to his supervisor outlining the doubts he had about
Nate Romanowski's guilt, and saying that he thought
there was a connection between Lamar Gardiner's murder and Birch Wardell's crash in the foothills. Joe wrote

that he didn't have enough information to take his suspicions to the sheriff or Melinda Strickland, but that he hoped to draw out the driver of the light-colored vehicle. He ended his report to Terry Crump by saying that due to personal circumstances relating to his foster daughter, he might need to request time off in the near future. Then he had sent the e-mail, gathered his parka, walked out through the cold to his pickup, and left to attend the meeting.

JUDGING BY THE NUMBER OF vehicles in the parking lot, Joe expected a full house inside for the meeting. A blast of warm air greeted him as he opened the cafeteria door, and he could see that the room was filled with locals sitting in metal folding chairs. This was definitely an outdoor crowd—hunters, fishermen, outfitters, ranchers. Most of the men wore heavy coats, boots, and facial hair. Melinda Strickland was speaking from behind a podium. Maps were taped to the wall behind her. Joe worked his way toward the back of the room. A few men Joe knew in the audience nodded greetings to him.

Behind him, Melinda Strickland paused in her briefing about the meeting's protocol.

"Glad you could make it, Joe!" Melinda Strickland said with surprising enthusiasm.

Joe waved and felt his face flush as nearly a hundred men turned in his direction before they settled back around toward the podium. For a moment, Joe wondered why she had greeted him so warmly and publicly. When a number of the faces lingered on him with narrowed eyes, he realized why. It was Melinda Strickland's way of announcing to the crowd that he was on *her* side. The realization left him cold.

Several men were already standing behind the crowd,

their backs to the wall, surveying the participants. Two of them, one with curly gray hair and another with hawkish eyes, stood with their arms folded, barely contained smirks on their faces. Joe recognized them as the men who had asked Sheridan for directions. Elle Broxton-Howard, looking smashing in a black outfit with a fleece vest, was there as well. She scribbled earnestly in her pad. Robey Hersig, the county attorney, still wore his jacket and tie from the office and stood off to the side of the crowd, against the wall. He slid over to make room for Joe.

"Any progress with April?" Hersig asked in a whisper out of the side of his mouth.

Joe shook his head. "Nope."

"It's a matter of time," Hersig said. "That's what I told Marybeth. If we can charge Jeannie with abuse or neglect, we can move in and get April back."

Joe turned his head and stared at Hersig. His neck was hot. "That's great, Robey. Let's hope April gets abused or neglected. We'll pray that happens."

"Joe, you know what I meant."

Joe didn't respond.

"Come on, Joe." Hersig leaned over and gently prodded Joe in the ribs. "You know what I meant."

Joe nodded, but didn't look over. Joe knew he was being unfair to Hersig but he didn't care. He was haunted from lack of sleep and frustration.

Hersig was an officer of the court, and Joe's opinion of the legal process right now was poor and getting worse. He was ashamed of the whole system, and angry with the people who made it up. Joe knew Robey wanted to be helpful, but there was little he could do. The situation with April seemed practically hopeless. Judge Potter Oliver's order was valid, if outrageous. An attorney Marybeth had hired (and who they didn't know how they would afford) was filing paperwork to contest the order.

If they were successful in a preliminary hearing, a full hearing would be scheduled. But even without inevitable postponements or delays, the hearing wouldn't likely be for weeks or possibly months. The slow grind of the legal system was diabolical in circumstances like this, Joe had concluded. Who even knew if Jeannie Keeley would be around by the time a hearing was scheduled? And what would happen to April in the meanwhile? Marybeth had called the school to see if April was there, but Jeannie had kept her out of school and out of sight both Thursday and Friday, telling the school that April was sick with some kind of virus.

With each day, April seemed farther away. The emptiness in their house seemed to shout at them. But the shouting would eventually fade. The most frightening thing of all, Joe thought, would be the day when he *didn't* wake up thinking of April—because too much time had passed. The thought depressed him and he shook his head in an attempt to dispel it. He tried to focus on the public meeting at hand.

Melinda Strickland was still talking, holding forth on the policy of road closures. Her voice seemed distant, disconnected, and singsong. Her hair color had been changed again, and was now off-orange.

"What's she saying?" Joe asked.

Hersig quietly scoffed. "What we are witnessing is an amazing display of the most sanctimonious, dysfunctional, cover-your-ass, bureaucratic horseshit I have ever heard. And if you quote me on that I'll deny it."

Taken aback, Joe turned to listen to Melinda Strickland. A retired electrical contractor had been called on, and he asked why a certain road in the Bighorns had been closed to vehicle traffic. He said that he had used the road all his life when he hunted, and that his father had used the road for fifty years before that.

"I wish I had a choice in the matter," Strickland was explaining to the crowd, "But it's not as simple as that. I understand what you're saying, but the policy is in place and there is very little we can do to change it at this juncture. We don't have the manpower or resources to re-evaluate grazing leases or timber allotments in this fiscal year . . ."

Hersig was right, Joe concluded. Strickland was talking in circuitous paths leading nowhere, with confusing little asides thrown in to divert attention from her meaning just as it threatened to become clear. Joe knew that, like Lamar Gardiner, Melinda Strickland had much more discretion in decision-making than she let on. And like Lamar Gardiner, Strickland blamed all of her own unpopular decisions on unnamed, faceless higher-ups, nebulous policy documents, or public meetings that had never been public and that might never have actually occurred.

". . . strike a balance between resource management, recreation, the health and welfare of the ecosystem itself . . ."

As she droned on, several hands were raised in the audience. She looked over the tops of the hands as she spoke, as if she couldn't see them. Joe could sense the rising tension in the room. Men fidgeted and cleared their throats. Many sat back with their arms crossed, staring at the ceiling.

". . . a thorough, top-to-bottom assessment needs to be completed in order to determine the biodiversity needs of the resource in regard to input from a wide range of scientific and recreator-derived opinions . . ."

Finally, one of the men who had raised his hand stood up. As he did so, his flimsy folding chair fell over backward. The sound caught Strickland's attention, and her face betrayed a flash of terror.

It was Herman Klein, the rancher Joe had shared coffee with the previous week. He introduced himself to Strickland and the room.

"Public comments need to be submitted in advance so we can address them, and I don't believe your name is on the list," she said to Klein. "Additional comments can be registered after the presentation. So please, sir, take your seat." Two Forest Service employees who flanked Strickland at the podium stood up to reinforce her statement. But they did so reluctantly, Joe noticed.

Klein put his hands in the front of his jeans in an awshucks manner, but he didn't sit down. "Ms. Strickland, I've been to enough of these things to know that by the time the 'public comment' period rolls around we'll be either out of time or your decision will have already been made."

His words sent a ripple of laughter through the room. Joe watched Melinda Strickland carefully. Her face betrayed fear and contempt. She *hated* this. She *hated* the fact that someone would interrupt her.

"Please excuse me for my stupidity," Klein continued, "but I want to make sure I understand what you're saying up there. Those of us not used to speaking in government rhetoric have a hard time following you." More laughter rumbled through the room.

Joe looked around quickly. All of the faces were turned to Herman Klein. Joe recognized more of the attendees than he had thought he would. Several of Klein's fellow ranchers were scattered throughout. Outfitters who used the forest for hunting and packing trips were there in full force. Local hunters made up the rest of the crowd. In a hunting community like Saddlestring, that meant doctors, lawyers, retailers, and teachers. Spud Cargill and Rope Latham, the roofers, wore their company jackets with the logo of a winged T-Lock shingle on the

backs. Joe remembered them from the First Alpine
Church. But as far as he could tell, there were no Sovereigns in the room. He had wondered if any of them
would attend.

Melinda Strickland was falling into a trap that was being baited by Herman Klein. It was the "I'm just a poor
dumb country boy" ruse that locals loved to spring on
outsiders and especially government officials. Joe recognized the trap from experience.

"My understanding is that just about half of all the
land in the state of Wyoming is owned and managed by
the federal government," Klein said, "Whether it's the
Forest Service, or the BLM, or the Park Service, or whatever. In any case, half of our state is run by federal bureaucrats. Not that I have anything against federal
bureaucrats, of course."

The crowd tittered and even Joe smiled. Melinda
Strickland stood with her hands on her hips and her eyes
cold. One of her employees started to sit down beside
her and she shot him a withering look. He stood back
up.

"The problem I got with this," Klein continued, "is
that there is no accountability. If all this land was run by
the state, or even local politicians, we could vote them
out if we wanted to. If it was run by a corporation we
could buy stock and go to board meetings and raise hell.
But because it's run by bureaucrats who nobody
elected—all we can do is come to meetings like this to
hear what you're going to do to our forests and our
countryside." There were murmurs of assent.

"Excuse me," Melinda Strickland interrupted. "Excuse me. Our agency manages the resources on behalf of
the public. We're not dictators here, ya know." She
looked to the back of the room for approval. The two
men standing next to Robey Hersig nodded to her.

"That may be," Herman Klein agreed, smiling. "But by saying you're managing things on behalf of the public you're basically saying that those of us here in this room who live here *aren't* the public, because you sure as hell never asked us anything."

"That's the purpose of this meeting!" Melinda Strickland countered, exasperated.

"If that's the case," Klein asked, "why did you try to shut me up just a minute ago when I stood up?"

"Because there needs to be order," Strickland said, her face flushed. "We can't do things based on mob rule."

Herman Klein feigned surprise. He slowly looked around the room. "This doesn't look like a mob to me," he said. "This looks like a group of concerned local citizens who came out on a cold-ass night to participate in a public meeting."

"Nailed her," Hersig whispered. "He nailed her."

Joe nodded.

"This," Melinda Strickland said, her voice rising and her finger pointed at Herman Klein, "This is an example of the problem. I've had a district supervisor murdered and a hardworking BLM employee assaulted because of this kind of hateful attitude."

"Me?" Klein asked, genuinely hurt. "What in the hell did I do?"

"You didn't do anything, as far as I know," she said. "But this kind of antigovernment attitude allows things like that to happen! It practically guarantees that things like that will happen!"

Hersig turned his head and he and Joe exchanged glances. The air had been sucked out of the room. Melinda Strickland had, within a minute, successfully shamed the crowd.

"What are you going to do about those Sovereigns?" someone asked.

Melinda Strickland jumped at the chance to change the subject, and compound her momentum.

"A plan is in place to evict the violators," she said. "I'm not at liberty to explain the steps that are being taken, other than to say that a well-thought-out, strategic plan is in place that will end in the desired results."

Several people in the crowd clapped with approval. While they did, Herman Klein quietly sat back down.

"Amazing," Hersig whistled, as he gathered his coat to leave.

AS THE CROWD FILED OUT, Melinda Strickland strode toward Joe in the back of the room. She approached him as if she couldn't wait to shake his hand. The two men in the back joined them. She introduced them to Joe as Dick Munker and Tony Portenson of the FBI.

"This is Joe Pickett," she said to the two men. "He's the game warden I was telling you about."

The gray-haired, skeletal man with the deep voice was Dick Munker. Munker offered Joe a business card.

"Manager, Federal Bureau of Investigation Interagency Special Assignment Unit," Joe read. "What does that mean?"

"We defuse volatile situations." Munker smiled with his mouth, his eyes fixed on Joe. "We're here by special request."

"You two insulted my daughter, I believe," Joe said. "She was the one who gave you directions to the Forest Service office."

Munker looked quickly away, but Portenson stared back at Joe with what looked like anxiety. He seemed to Joe to be wishing that there was not a confrontation with Munker.

Melinda Strickland acted as if the exchange had not

occurred. "They're very familiar with quite a few of the Sovereigns," she said. "That's why I wanted them here. We want to prevent another Ruby Ridge, or Waco."

Joe nodded.

"In Idaho they called it 'Weaver Fever,'" Munker added, taking Strickland's cue, his voice dropping an octave so he couldn't possibly be overheard by the departing crowd. "It's when the community and the press get whipped up into a fury by a standoff situation and things get ugly. We're here to make sure that doesn't happen."

"I thought it was the FBI who got ugly at Ruby Ridge." Joe said.

Munker set his jaw and his eyes bored holes into Joe. "You thought wrong," he said. He shot a look at Melinda Strickland. "Which side is he on, anyway?"

"Geez, I wished I could get away with wearing a hat like that," Tony Portenson interjected, clearly attempting to change the direction of the conversation. He nodded toward Joe's well-worn Stetson. "But I'm from Jersey, and everybody would know I was faking it."

"I know who you are," Munker said, stifling a smile. Portenson's joke hadn't diverted him. "You're the one who had Lamar Gardiner in custody when he escaped. The game warden, right?"

Joe felt a pang of anger and embarrassment.

"Joe," Strickland said, placing her hand on Joe's shoulder, "Mr. Munker and Mr. Portenson are experts in the kind of situation we have here in Twelve Sleep County. They're in demand all over the west. They're here to advise us on how we should proceed with the Sovereigns. They'll be working here, but also in Idaho and Nevada."

"Other hotbeds of insurrection," Munker added. "Where federal officials have been hurt or threatened."

Strickland opened her purse so Joe would look inside.

"They advised me to get *this* to protect myself." He could see the checkered grip of a stainless-steel nine-millimeter Ruger semiautomatic pistol. "I still can't believe I'm actually carrying a gun around with me." Her half-giggling voice belied her words of concern, though, Joe thought.

Joe took his hat off and rubbed his eyes. *Melinda Strickland with a gun.*

He couldn't believe what he was hearing.

"I think saying this is a *hotbed of insurrection* is pretty strong," Joe cautioned. "I live here and I just don't see it. I'm not saying there aren't some real independent characters around, or some hotheads. But I just don't see that it could be organized like you seem to be suggesting."

Tony Portenson and Dick Munker exchanged glances.

"How familiar are you with the extremists up there in that compound?" Munker asked. "Do you know what kind of people they are? What they believe? We know them, and their type. Some of those individuals have been involved in some of the worst situations that have taken place in this country in the past dozen years. You've got ex-cons, and conspirators, and scumbags who just haven't been caught at anything yet. These scumbags have gotten this far because they've been tolerated and coddled. They need to know that not everybody will take their crap."

Joe stared at Munker in disbelief. He felt another hard twist in his stomach as he listened.

"Ms. Strickland has given us carte blanche to deal with the situation," Portenson said, grinning. "For once, we can deal with these assholes the right way."

Melinda Strickland returned his grin. She clearly liked being admired by colleagues. It made Joe slightly sick. "Sheriff Barnum is completely on board with this," she told Joe. "He's volunteered his complete cooperation."

"I met Wade Brockius," Joe confessed. "He told me they just want to be left alone. That they mean no harm."

"And you believed him?" Munker asked, cocking his eyebrow.

"I don't have any reason not to," Joe said.

"How about a dead Forest Service supervisor? How about a BLM employee left for dead?"

Joe felt a slow rise of anger. "Unless there's something you boys can tell me, I can't see the connection between those crimes and the Sovereigns. Nate Romanowski is already in jail for the Gardiner murder. Are you saying Romanowski is connected to the Sovereigns?"

"Maybe Romanowski scouted the mountains for them," Portenson said, raising an eyebrow. "Maybe Romanowski found that campground for them and called his buddies to come join him here in Lost Bumfuck, Wyoming."

Joe turned on Portenson with a withering stare. "Do you have a single shred of proof that what you say is valid?" Joe asked. "You sound like you're making this up as you go along."

"What about your little girl?" Munker asked. "Didn't one of them take her?"

Joe didn't reply. He couldn't believe April had been brought up. The wound was still too fresh.

"Maybe if you help us out, it will help you get her back sooner."

"How?"

Munker started to speak, then caught himself. A wry smile formed. "At least then we'll know whose side you're on."

Joe fought the urge to smash Munker's face with his fist. Instead, Joe fitted his hat back on and walked away.

*   *   *

JOE WAS SITTING IN HIS truck waiting for it to warm up
when Elle Broxton-Howard appeared in his headlights
and approached the passenger-side window. She knocked
on the glass, and Joe gestured for her to come in. She
climbed into the truck and shut the door.

"The heater isn't hot yet," he apologized. "It'll take a
minute to get going."

"It's so cold here," she said, shivering. She was huddled in her dark wool coat. "I don't know how you people can stand it out here."

"Sometimes I wonder that myself," Joe said, making
conversation.

"Melinda was magnificent in there, wasn't she?" Broxton-Howard said, sounding awestruck.

Joe grunted—not a yes, not a no. He was still seething from his encounter with Munker.

As the cab warmed, Joe could smell her scent. The
far-off light from the fluorescent pole lamp profiled her
against the window. She was lovely.

Suddenly, Elle leaned across the seat toward him.
"I'm starting to think you're the key to my story."

"What?" Joe asked, confused. "I thought you were
writing about Melinda Strickland."

"Well . . . it's *about* her. But you seem to be a pivotal
character in all of this." She stared deeply into his eyes as
she spoke. Her eyes glistened. Her lips were parted ever-
so-slightly. Her scent seemed even stronger now, somehow. It both troubled and excited him.

"I heard that you've shot three men? That you
wounded two men three years ago and that you killed a
man last year at a canyon called Savage Run?"

Joe broke off their gaze and stared out the windshield.

"Who told you that?"

"Oh . . . people around town."

He felt his throat constrict, and tried to recover.

"We need to talk . . . soon," she said. "How about dinner?"

She smiled. Her teeth were white and perfect.

"Sure," Joe said, pausing. "At my house. With my wife Marybeth and the kids."

The light went out of her eyes, and although the smile remained it decreased in wattage. She assessed him coolly.

"I guess that would work," she said, businesslike. "Although I was kind of thinking of something more . . ." The sentence trailed off into nowhere. He didn't prompt her to continue.

"I'll give you a call," she said, withdrawing and opening her door. "Your number's in the wonderful little half-inch-thick Saddlestring telephone book, I presume?"

"Yup."

"Do you have a fax machine?" she asked suddenly, half-in and half-out.

He told her the number.

"I'll fax over the list of things I can't eat," she said, and was gone.

DRIVING HOME, HE TRIED TO put the evening into some kind of perspective. He failed. All he could foresee, as he thought about it, was inevitable tragedy. Dick Munker troubled him. The man exuded a smug, chip-on-the-shoulder fanaticism, and he had Melinda Strickland's ear. Munker didn't seem like the kind of person who could *defuse* a situation, as he claimed, but the kind who would ignite one. The kind of guy who would spray a campfire with gasoline. Munker, and Portenson, seemed disdainful of the Sovereigns, the community, and Joe himself. They seemed to revel in being insiders with guns, specialists finally given a green light to do what they saw fit.

Munker, Joe thought, was the kind of guy who would kill somebody and later claim it was for the victim's own good.

He opened his window and let a knife-edge of icy air cut into his face. Maybe, he hoped, it would sweep the scent of Elle Broxton-Howard's perfume from the cab of the pickup.

Joe felt like his head was caught in a vise. And every day, someone applied another half-turn.

MISSY WAS AWAKE IN THE dark, watching television on the couch when Joe got home. As his eyes adjusted to the gloom, he saw things more clearly. There was an empty wine bottle on its side near the foot of the couch, and a half-full bottle gripped in her other hand. Her face was shiny with tears.

"Are you okay?" Joe asked tentatively.

She raised her head, and her unfocused eyes settled somewhere to the left of his nose. She was very drunk.

"Okay?" she asked. "I'm just fucking wonderful."

He regretted that he had asked.

"It's my BIRTHday," she slurred. "I'm sixty-three. Sixty-three goddamned years old without a house, without a husband, without even a boyfriend for the first time in my life."

Yes, you're old, Joe thought, *old enough not to act like this.* He began to mount the stairs.

"It's been a long night," he said, hoping she would stop.

"Stuck here in the middle of nowhere-land, getting older by the minute, and missing my granddaughter April." She sipped from her glass and a bead of red wine ran down her chin. "Even though she's not *really* my granddaughter."

Joe stopped and turned. "That's right," he snapped. "Even though she's not 'really' your granddaughter. How generous of you. I can tell you're pretty busted up about it. You're so upset, you even opened a bottle of wine."

Missy's face fell. "I can't believe you said that to me," she said, tears glistening in her eyes.

"Sorry," Joe said, his voice unsympathetic. "Happy birthday." He turned and resumed climbing the stairs.

"Ah, you don't really care," Missy said behind him. "You know, Joe Pickett, if you weren't my son-in-law, I'd say you were a very self-absorbed man."

Joe hesitated again on the stairs, thought better of it, and proceeded. He heard the clink of the wineglass against her perfect, six-thousand-dollar teeth.

ALTHOUGH THE BEDROOM WAS DARK, Marybeth was awake.

"Joe, were you arguing with my mother?"

Joe stood still, trying to tamp down his anger from a moment before. Instead, something he had been bottling up gushed out.

"Is she going to *live* with us?" he asked. "Is she going to *stay* here?"

Marybeth turned on her bedside lamp. "Joe, she's going through a tough time. I can't believe you're acting this way."

Joe couldn't quit. "*She's* going through a tough time? Look at us, Marybeth. All she has to do is snag another husband and she's home free. We've got the situation with April, and lunatics are running everything . . . I've got a guy who somehow expects me to save his life, and I'm pretty sure there's a murderer out there running loose . . ."

"Joe, lower your voice," Marybeth said sternly.

". . . and I've got a mother-in-law downstairs feeling sorry for herself."

"JOE."

He stopped and caught himself.

"I don't need you to remind me what's going on." Marybeth's eyes flashed. "What do you want me to do, throw her out into the snow? All day long I've been trying to blot out this . . . *'situation'* . . . with April and do something constructive. And you lose your temper and bring it all back."

Joe looked at her, noticed the tears forming in her eyes. But he was still too angry to apologize.

In a silence that was deafening, Joe got ready for bed and climbed in. She switched off the lamp, turned her back to him and he thought she was pretending to sleep. He touched her shoulder but she didn't respond.

You're right, he wanted to tell her now, *I'm sorry.*

Joe rolled back over and stared at the ceiling and listened to the icy wind outside rattle the window.

JOE WOKE A FEW HOURS later, the remnants of another nightmare skittering in his head. He quietly slid out of bed and went to the window. He pressed his forehead against the cold glass and wondered how everything had gotten so bad so quickly.

Things are building up, Joe thought. His family was coming unhinged, and he was not blameless. *Somehow,* he thought, *I need to do more. To try and fix things. Take some kind of action before everything explodes.*

22

THE NEXT MORNING, JOE WAS EATING BREAKFAST EARLY and alone when Marybeth came down the stairs. He could tell by the way she walked that she was still angry with him, and he watched as she went silently into his office, and came out with something in her hand and a glare in her eyes.

"You got a fax." Her voice was not kind. "I heard it come in late last night."

Joe winced, and reached for the single sheet.

"It's from Elle Broxton-Howard," Joe said, reading it.

"I know."

"She wants to interview me. I invited her to dinner with us."

"I figured that out."

"This is a list of things she can't eat. I guess she has a stack of these all made up and ready to send to people when she gets a dinner invitation."

"Apparently."

"Says here she doesn't eat beef, poultry, pork, olive or

canola oil, sugar, processed foods of any kind, or geneti-
cally enhanced products."

"Mm-hmm."

"She has a suggested menu here. Baked trout, steamed
broccoli, and brown rice. Hell, we don't have any of that
stuff," Joe said.

"No, we don't—although I'd be happy to get it for
you and your *friend* for your little dinner."

"That's not necessary, Marybeth."

Marybeth turned on her heel and went up the stairs
to get dressed.

Joe cursed, and crumpled the paper into a ball and
flipped it toward the garbage can in the kitchen.

IN A FOUL MOOD, JOE left the house and drove into the
mountains on the Bighorn Road toward Battle Mountain and the Sovereign Citizen compound. Again, McLanahan's Blazer blocked his path. Joe eased up to it and
stopped, while the sheriff's deputy slowly climbed out
into the cold to greet him.

"Still on roadblock duty, huh?" Joe asked, opening
his window.

"Yes, goddammit," McLanahan said, his teeth chattering. Twin plumes of condensation blew from his nostrils.

"Is there any traffic up here?" Joe asked. "Do the Sovereigns come and go much?"

McLanahan shook his head. "Every once in a while
there's a truck or two. But they also use Timberline Road
on the other side of the mountain, so I don't see 'em all."

"Any activity this morning?"

"Just you," McLanahan said. "Things pick up at
night. Those two FBI guys have been through here a lot.

They had quite a bit of sound equipment with them, and I guess tonight they're planning a new phase."

"A new phase?"

McLanahan shrugged. "Don't ask me. They don't tell me anything, and I'm not here at night. All I know is that that Munker guy is a real prick."

Joe cocked his thumb toward the back of his truck. "I've got some clothes and toys to deliver to the compound for our daughter April."

Marybeth had packed the boxes early that morning, before it was light out. It must have been very hard on her, but she didn't say anything about it. Marybeth was not talking with him, and neither was Missy, which Joe counted as a blessing.

McLanahan shrugged. "I'm supposed to inspect all deliveries."

"Feel free," Joe volunteered.

McLanahan developed a pained look, and Joe could see him weighing the time it would take to search through the boxes in the bitter cold versus climbing back into his warm Blazer. He stepped aside and waved Joe through.

AT THE GATE TO THE compound, Joe stopped as he had before, and got out. A bearded man in a heavy army-surplus parka emerged from the nearest trailer and approached on the other side of the fence. He didn't carry a rifle, but Joe guessed that he was armed. Joe stacked the boxes and suitcase near the barbed wire.

"What you got there?" the man asked.

Joe explained that it was for April Keeley. "Is she here?" Joe asked. "Is Wade Brockius around?"

"I don't give out that kind of information," the man

mumbled. "Is it important?" He reached through the strands and opened the top of the highest box to confirm that it was clothing.

"It's important."

The man lifted the top box over the barbed wire and carried it back to the large trailer that Brockius had come out of the last time Joe was there. "We've gotta go through all this stuff," the man said over his shoulder. "Then I'll be back for the rest. I'll ask about Wade and Jeannie."

"I'll wait."

Joe turned to get back in his pickup, his eyes sweeping through the timber around him. Something seemed out of place, and he tried to figure out what it was.

When he saw it, he was surprised he hadn't noticed it earlier. Four silver speakers poked into the sky above the tops of the trees. Their fluted metal openings were aimed at the Sovereign Citizen compound. The speakers were mounted on poles that were apparently secured to tree trunks within the forest. The speakers were silent, for now.

Munker and Portenson had been busy.

WADE BROCKIUS EMERGED FROM THE trailer and walked slowly down to the fence. His gait suggested arthritis, or a leg injury. Joe went out to meet him.

"This cold weather stiffens me up," Brockius mumbled. "The clothes are thoughtful. Thank you."

"There's two more boxes," Joe said. "Some of April's toys, too."

Brockius nodded, and Joe thought he looked uncomfortable. "Thoughtful," he said again.

Joe looked into the compound at the trailers and RVs. He hoped to catch a glimpse of April, or even Jeannie Keeley, through a window.

"Can I see her to make sure she's okay?"

"She's with her mother right now, Mr. Pickett."

"Does she know I'm here?"

Brockius sized up Joe from beneath his heavy brow. "No, she doesn't."

"Can you tell her?"

Brockius shook his massive head. "I'm sorry. I really don't want to interfere."

Joe swallowed. "I want to let April know that we miss her, and that we love her very much."

Brockius appeared to think it over. Then he shook his head again. "No, I don't think it would be a good idea," he said with finality.

"Just tell me she's here and that she's okay," Joe asked. "It would mean a lot to my wife to know that."

"She's here," Brockius said, in a tone so low that Joe could barely make it out. Then Joe realized that Brockius didn't want to be overheard by anyone in the RVs or hidden away in the brush. "And she seems fine."

"Thank you," Joe said.

"You best move on now, Mr. Pickett." Brockius's voice was raised back to normal now. "We'll make sure the clothes and toys go to good use."

Obviously, the conversation was over as far as Wade Brockius was concerned. He handed the remaining boxes to Brockius, who took them. He and Brockius exchanged a long, silent look. Brockius appeared troubled by the situation with April. *This is not the kind of thing,* he seemed to be communicating, *that I want to be involved in.*

"What comes out of those speakers back there?" Joe asked, as he prepared to leave.

Brockius paused and looked up and over Joe's pickup at the speakers.

"I don't know yet," he said in a bass rumble. "But I suspect we'll be finding out soon."

"Did your people have anything to do with that dirty trick down on the BLM land?" Joe asked, out of the blue.

Joe wanted to see Brockius's reaction to the question.

Brockius's face hardened, as it had before. He was not puzzled by the question, which to Joe meant that the Sovereigns were in communication with someone on the outside—or that they were involved with the ambush. Brockius turned to walk back to his trailer.

"I'd suggest you look a little closer to home, Mr. Pickett," Brockius said over his shoulder.

THE OPPORTUNITY TO LOOK CLOSER to home came almost immediately, as Joe descended from the snowy mountains. He was still in deep snow, with twenty miles of rugged BLM breaklands laid out in a vista below him. The town of Saddlestring, beyond the breaklands, glittered in the morning sun.

His radio crackled to life.

"I think I've got a situation out here." The signal was strong, and the voice belonged to a woman. "This is Jamie Runyan calling BLM headquarters. Does anybody read me?"

Joe heard a rush of static and assumed it was somebody trying to reply to Jamie Runyan from town.

"I didn't get that at all," she said. "Try again."

There was another squawk.

"Damn it," she said. "I don't know whether anyone there can hear me or not, but I'm out in the joint management unit and I see a light-colored pickup up on top of a hill. I think it might be the vehicle Birch Wardell described. I don't know whether to pursue it or not."

Contact, Joe thought. He reached for the microphone, and waited for Jamie Runyan to repeat her message to the dispatcher once again.

"This is game warden Joe Pickett," he said when she was through. "I read you loud and clear. Please stay put. I'm about fifteen minutes away from you."

He increased his speed, and roared down the mountain as fast as he could without sliding off the road.

JAMIE RUNYAN'S TAN PICKUP WITH the BLM logo was pulled to the side of the gravel road with its exhaust burbling. Joe stopped behind her and swung outside. While driving down the mountain, he had unfastened his Remington Wingmaster shotgun from his saddle scabbard behind his seat, and he carried it to her vehicle.

She was thick-bodied and plain, with a wide, simple face. She rolled her window down as he approached.

"Where did you see the truck?" Joe asked, scanning the horizon. Because she had parked in a depression, her truck would be hard to see from a distance.

She gestured up the road, over the hill. "I was going up that hill when I saw it. It was a light-colored, older-model pickup on the top of the next ridge. It looked to me like the guy was pulling our fence down with a chain."

"Did he see you?"

She shook her head. "I'm not sure. I backed down the road out of sight when I saw him."

"Has anyone from your office replied to you?"

She shook her head. "I think I'm out of range in these damn hills. The only person I heard was you."

Joe nodded. "Do you mind if I borrow your truck? You can stay here in my truck and keep warm."

She searched his face while she decided. "What are you going to do?" she asked.

"I've got a theory about what happened," he said. "If you let me borrow your truck I'll look like I'm BLM and I can test it out."

She hesitated. "I don't know. Only authorized government personnel are allowed to drive these vehicles."

"I'm authorized," Joe lied. "The Game and Fish has an inter-agency agreement with the BLM." He thought he sounded convincing, and it worked.

She got out of the cab, remembering to take her sack lunch.

Joe racked a shell into the chamber of his shotgun, then flipped the safety on and slid it muzzle-down onto the floorboards. He narrowed his eyes and gunned the truck up the gravel road.

As he cleared the hill he could see the light pickup Runyan had described. And she was right—it was in the process of pulling a post-and-wire fence down with a chain attached to its bumper. The fence had been erected by the BLM and Forest Service to keep the public off of the management study area.

The truck was about a half-mile from Joe. On his present course, he would soon be on the road beneath it. In his mind, he replayed the scenario Wardell had described to him that night in the hospital: how the truck took off out of sight over a hill while Wardell pursued. Joe wasn't sure of the terrain over the hill, but he assumed it would be similar.

Despite the cold, Joe rolled down his window so he could hear the other vehicle better as he drove. As his BLM truck bucked and pitched on the frozen gravel road, the light-colored truck dropped in and out of view. Soon, Joe could hear the motor of the light-colored truck grinding in the still morning air. In a minute, Joe would be close enough to look up and see the driver, he thought, or perhaps a license plate.

But the next time the truck came into view, it was speeding away. Joe saw its outline against the deep blue sky as it crested the hill and went over it.

Following Wardell's script, Joe jerked the wheel and left the gravel road, pointing the squat nose of his BLM truck up the hill where he had last seen the other truck. He crashed through two crusty drifts, and nearly lost traction as he approached the top of the hill. His back wheels threw plumes of frozen gray dirt as the pickup fishtailed on dirt and ice, but then they caught solid rock and propelled him up and over the top.

Joe's heart pounded in his chest as he crested the ridge and plunged over it. The tire tracks from the other truck went down the hill and vanished into a wide, tall swath of evergreen brush at the bottom.

Joe reached for the shotgun, which had slid toward the passenger door during the rough ride up the hill, and pulled it close to him as he descended.

On cue, a light-colored truck emerged from the brush below and started climbing the opposite slope, directly across from him. The truck labored up the hill as well, sliding a little in loose shale and kicking out puffs of dislodged rock. At the rate Joe was flying down the hill and the other pickup was laboring up the opposite slope, he would be on it in seconds.

Joe tapped the brakes to slow his reckless plunge and gripped the wheel tighter. The tracks he drove in would soon be swallowed in the tangle of ancient juniper.

Suddenly, the brush closed over the top of his BLM truck and branches scratched the sides of his doors like fingernails on a chalkboard. A sap-heavy bough slapped the windshield, leaving needles and gray-blue berries smashed against the glass. He caught a flash of an opening through the branches ahead

But then Joe did something Birch Wardell hadn't done. He slammed on his brakes. Then, throwing the pickup into reverse, he floored the accelerator at the same time that he cranked the steering wheel to the right. The engine whined and the tires bit, and the vehicle flew back and to the side through the brush in a cacophony of snapping branches.

BOOM!

Joe hit something metal and solid so hard that his head jerked back and bounced off the rear-window glass. He slumped forward over the wheel as bright orange spangles washed across his eyes. Then smoke, or steam, enveloped the cab of the truck in darkness. Trying to shake his head clear, he looked up and smelled the steam. It was bitter and smelled like radiator fluid.

The spangles had shrunk to the size of shooting sparks when he fell out of the door of the pickup and landed on his hands and knees in the dirt and snow. His hat was smashed down hard on his head, and he pushed it up so he could see.

The twisted grille of the light-colored pickup furiously spewed green steam. A pool of radiator fluid smoked on the ground, and was beginning to cut its way through the snow toward him. Standing, Joe retrieved his shotgun from the seat. He walked around the back of the BLM pickup toward the vehicle he had smashed into.

The windshield of the light-colored truck was marred by a single spidery star where a man's head would have hit it. Joe skirted the steam and looked into the cab to see a man slumped over the steering wheel, a cap askew over his face and dark rivulets of blood coursing down from under the cap into the collar of his coat. Joe recognized the coat, and the logo that was painted on the truck's door even though a thick smear of mud had been applied to obscure it.

It was a flying T-Lock shingle with wings.

Joe opened the door, and Rope Latham, the roofer, moaned and rolled his head toward him.

"How bad are you hurt, Rope?" Joe asked.

"Bad, I think," Rope said. "I think I'm blind."

Joe reached into the cab and lifted the baseball cap that had fallen over Rope's eyes. A three-inch cut ran along Latham's eyebrows. The cut looked like it would require stitches, Joe thought, but it didn't look much worse than that.

"I can see!" Rope cried.

"Climb on out of there," Joe ordered, prodding Rope Latham in the ribs with his shotgun. "Turn around and put your hands on the truck and kick your feet out."

Moaning, Latham obeyed.

Joe pulled each of Latham's arms back in turn and snapped handcuffs on his wrists. Then he turned Latham and pushed him back into the truck. Joe saw a Motorola Talkabout hand-held radio on the seat that Rope had obviously used to communicate with the other truck.

"Two trucks," Joe said. "Two identical Bighorn Roofing trucks. One goes down the hill and pulls over at the last second into the brush. Another truck that looks just the same starts up the other side of the hill where it's been parked out of sight. Looks like one truck that crosses the draw and goes on up the other side. Makes the poor BLM guy think he can cross the draw just like that other truck just did. Pretty good trick, even though he didn't die out here like you two intended."

Latham grimaced. Blood was pooling in his eyes as it ran down his face.

"There's a six-foot drop down there once you clear the brush, isn't there?" Joe asked.

"Spud thought of it," Latham said. "But we waited a couple days for that BLM guy to bite. It worked pretty good before."

Joe didn't say that seeing twin antelope fawns had led him to think of how they'd pulled it off.

Keeping Rope Latham in his peripheral vision, Joe

stepped back and looked up the opposite slope. Spud Cargill, the other half of Bighorn Roofing, had stopped at the top of the hill and was looking back with binoculars. Joe grabbed the hand-held radio from Spud's pickup and held it up to his mouth.

"We've got you now, you son-of-a-bitch," he said, then tossed the radio back inside. Joe raised his arm and pointed his index finger at Cargill, who was still looking back through binoculars, and pretended to shoot him.

Spud's truck started to move again, and vanished over the top of the hill.

WHILE JOE WAITED FOR JAMIE Runyan to arrive in his pickup, Rope Latham began to tremble. He hoped Latham's injuries weren't worse than they appeared.

Joe read Rope his Miranda rights, then turned on the micro-recorder that he hid in his shirt pocket.

"Why were you targeting the BLM boys?" Joe asked. He leaned against a tree with his shotgun pointed vaguely at Rope Latham. The back of his own head had started to throb from the collision.

"They owed us money," Latham said dejectedly. "So did the goddamned Forest Service."

"They owed you money?" Joe was confused. "What?"

"Those bastards owed us from last summer. Twelve thousand dollars' worth of work we did for them on their buildings. We replaced all the roofs, and paid for the material in advance. But it's been six months and we still haven't been paid." Latham spat bloody saliva into the brush. "Some goddamned problem with the check request the BLM sent to Cheyenne has held it all up, and me and Spud want our money. When it comes to paying their bills, our government is just fucked. 'Maybe next month,' they tell us. Shit, how would those BLM shitheads feel if their paychecks were even a week late, much less six months?"

Joe pushed himself off the tree. The back of his neck was tingling, and it wasn't from hitting the window.

"These people throw money around like it isn't even real, you know? Just look at this stupid 'joint management' area that cost three million dollars between them just to string some fence and put up some signs."

"What did you say before about the Forest Service?"

Latham's voice suddenly caught in his throat. "Nothing."

"No, you said the Forest Service owed you money as well."

"Fuckers." Latham coughed. "They're the worst of all. They owe us fifteen thousand from work we did *last* summer!"

"This would be Lamar Gardiner," Joe said flatly.

"It *was* Lamar Gardiner," Latham said, smiling wickedly. His teeth were pink from a cut in his mouth. "He wouldn't even return our calls about it, and he told Spud that if he didn't stop harassing him, we'd be off the government bid list for good and he'd press charges!"

"Move aside," Joe ordered, and Latham slid along the truck away from the cab.

Reaching inside, Joe pulled the bench seat forward. A well-used compound bow was wedged between the seat and the cab wall. A narrow quiver of arrows lay next to it.

Joe slid one of the arrows out and held it up.

"Bonebuster," Joe said.

Latham's eyes bulged, and his face drained of color. At the same time, the cut on his forehead started to gush again.

Joe was stunned. "This was about some *unpaid bills*? You killed a man and tried to kill another because their agencies owed you money?"

Latham nodded, fear in his face because of Joe's tone.

"I ought to shoot you right here and leave you for the coyotes," Joe said icily. "Do you realize what you two idiots almost set in motion?"

SHERIFF O. R. "BUD" BARNUM sat shell-shocked as Joe Pickett dropped the bow and arrows with a clatter on his desk after he had turned Rope Latham over to Deputy Reed.

"I got one of 'em," Joe said. "Spud Cargill is the other one and he got away. Rope shot the arrows and Spud cut Lamar's throat."

Barnum glared.

"Rope confessed everything on the way into town," Joe said. "I've got it on tape."

"Did you read him his rights?"

"That's on the tape."

"So where's Spud?"

"I don't know," Joe said. "Why don't you find him? You're the sheriff."

Barnum stared at Joe, his eyes darkening.

"I know you're busy with the Sovereigns and Melinda Strickland and *'Phase One'* and all, but Spud's driving a tan pickup with a Bighorn Roofing logo on the door and Wyoming plates. It shouldn't be all that hard to find," Joe said. He put his hands on Barnum's desk and leaned toward him.

"This had nothing to do with any antigovernment movement in the county. It had to do with roofers who didn't get paid when they should have been paid." Joe glared at Barnum. "And it had a lot to do with sloppy police work by the Sheriff's Department."

Veins in Barnum's temples began to throb. But he said nothing.

"When you release Nate Romanowski, please tell him I'm looking forward to talking with him," Joe said. "That is, if your deputy is through hitting him with a hot shot."

Joe turned and walked out.

THAT NIGHT, IN BED, MARYBETH shook Joe awake. When he opened his eyes, he found her staring at him.

"I'm sorry about last night and this morning," she said. "You didn't deserve it."

"Yes, I did. You were right," he said, his mood suddenly lifting. "It's okay. The tension level was pretty high around here."

She smiled, but stayed silent.

"What?" he asked, finally.

"Joe, sometimes you amaze me. Two antelope fawns?"

He laughed.

23

IN THE MORNING, JOE CONFIRMED ROPE LATHAM'S story with Carrie Gardiner. He found her standing in front of her house in a heavy coat, hugging herself with both arms. A big moving truck had backed up to her front door across the yard, and a crew was carrying furniture and boxes up a ramp from her house into the back of the trailer.

"I heard," Joe said, tipping the brim of his hat toward the moving truck. "Where are you going?"

"My parents live in Nebraska." She sighed. "Still on the farm. They've got room for all of us."

"I'm sorry to see you leave."

Her eyes flared briefly. "I'm not," she said.

"You heard about Rope?"

"Yes. The sheriff called this morning. Thank you for arresting him."

"Yup."

"Please tell me what happened," Carrie said.

She listened, staring at her winter boots, while Joe told her everything Rope had said.

When he was done, she nodded.

"I believe it," she said.

"You do?"

She nodded sadly. "I wish it didn't make sense, but it does. The roofers even called our house a couple of times to complain. I spoke with Spud Cargill once, and he told me about it, so I asked Lamar about it when he got home that night.

"Lamar was going through a real tough time last summer. I guess he realized he wasn't going any further in the Forest Service and it was really bothering him. He'd been applying for other districts for the past three years, and jobs at regional headquarters, but he wasn't getting any encouragement. I think he realized that he would always be a midlevel manager, and he didn't take it well at times. It was hard on me, and on the kids."

Joe listened, shifting his gaze occasionally to watch the team of movers emerge from the house with something and disappear into the back of the truck.

"I'm not excusing what Lamar did up there in the mountains," she said. "Shooting all those elk makes me sick to my stomach. But I know that his frustration level was really high. For the first time since we'd been married, he was snapping at me and the kids. He was drinking too much. I was thinking about leaving him just before, well, you know . . ."

"Carrie, what about the roofers?"

"Oh, yes." She flushed. "From what Lamar told me, he did a standard request for bids in the spring to get all the buildings shingled. Bighorn Roofing—Spud and Rope—had the best bid. Lamar said he gave them a verbal okay to start working, then submitted the paperwork to the regional office in Denver. He said that in the past, submitting the paperwork was just a formality.

"But this time, after a couple of months, the regional

office sent him everything back and said he hadn't filled out a couple of the forms properly. Lamar was really angry when they did that, so he resubmitted everything and didn't tell the roofers about it."

"When was this?" Joe asked.

"I think it was about August," she said. "The work was just about done already, and the roofers were getting mad about having to front the Forest Service all of the materials and labor without getting paid. Then the regional office denied the request altogether, because they said Lamar had entered into a contract without their approval."

Joe shook his head.

"Lamar was fit to be tied over that one."

"I can believe that he would be," Joe said.

"They hung him out to dry," she said. "They didn't give one bit of consideration to what it would be like for him out here in the field. They didn't really care that he had to look people in the eye and tell them they wouldn't get paid for the work they did."

It was so . . . *believable,* Joe thought. And so frustrating. It didn't have to happen this way.

He thanked her and told her once again that he was sorry she was leaving.

As he approached his pickup, she called after him.

"Oh, Mr. Pickett—I didn't tell you who at regional headquarters kept sending back Lamar's request."

Joe turned.

"It was Melinda Strickland," she said bitterly. "The woman who thinks my name is Cassie."

THE COMBINED LAW-ENFORCEMENT AGENCIES IN and around Twelve Sleep County scrambled to find Spud Cargill, who was still at large. From the radio in his small office, Joe monitored their progress while writing an overdue report to his supervisor. A rookie deputy sheriff reported that Spud Cargill's empty pickup had been found near the Saddlestring landfill with the driver's-side door open and tracks in the snow indicating that Spud had run toward the two-lane highway. "The suspect's tracks end at the pavement," the deputy said. "He either had another car to climb into, or he stole one, or somebody picked him up on the highway. I don't know where in the hell he is." A citizen in town reported seeing someone who looked like Spud running across the Saddlestring High School football field, and the police were sent to check it out. It turned out to be the boys' basketball team running outdoor windsprints for punishment. An all-points bulletin was issued by Sheriff Barnum, and the Wyoming highway patrol set up roadblocks on all four highways out of Saddlestring to check drivers, passengers, and anything that looked suspicious. Barnum dispatched his deputies to Bighorn Roofing, Spud's residence (where he lived alone except for a caged badger in the garage), and the Stockman's Bar, where Spud liked to drink beer after work.

Spud Cargill could not be found.

IT HAD TURNED OUT TO be a nice day for a manhunt, Joe observed through his window. After he had come home from seeing Carrie Gardiner, the wind had stopped, the sky had cleared, and the sun swelled bright and warm in the western sky. Water from the melting snow dropped like strings of glass beads from the eaves of the house and melted holes in the snow on the ground. The sound of running water through the outside drainpipes sounded like music to Joe. He loved water like a true Westerner. There was never enough of it. It pained him when the

wind kicked up and blew the snow away. It seemed unfair.

He finished the report and e-mailed it to Terry
Crump. He ended it by writing that since Rope Latham
was in jail and Spud Cargill would no doubt soon be
caught, the pressure that had been building in Twelve
Sleep County should ease up.

At least he hoped so. For the first time in days, he
didn't have a dull pain in his stomach.

He wished he could have been there when Melinda
Strickland, Dick Munker, and Tony Portenson heard
that the likely motive for the killing of Lamar Gardiner
and the ambush of Birch Wardell was not crazed, organized, antigovernment hate, but anger at unpaid bills
from federal agencies. Joe couldn't help but shake his
head at that. He wondered if Munker and Portenson
would simply sneak out of town now, and if Melinda
Strickland would follow.

Then he could concentrate on something that mattered: April.

"JOE, THERE'S SOMEONE OUT FRONT," Missy said from
his office doorway. There was concern in her voice.

Joe had dozed off in his chair with his feet on his desk
and his hat pulled down over his eyes. The week had
worn him out.

He stood up and rubbed his face awake with his hands
and looked at his mother-in-law through his fingers. Her
face and hair were . . . perfect, the result of at least two
hours under construction, he guessed. She wore an oversized camel-colored cashmere sweater, pearls, shiny black
tight pants, and shoes with straps and stiletto heels. She
was obviously not dressed for dinner at their house.

Then he remembered why he was suddenly awake.

She stepped aside for him and he parted the curtains in the living room.

"Who is that man?" she asked. "He didn't knock on the door or anything. He's just sitting out there."

A battered and ancient snub-nosed Willys Jeep was outside, its grille and mesh-covered headlights leering over the top of the picket fence like a voyeur. Canvas from the shredded top hung in shreds inside the vehicle from a bent-up frame. Sitting on the hood of the Jeep, with his heavy boots resting on the front bumper, was Nate Romanowski. The setting sun, now dropping into a notch between two mountain peaks, backlit the visitor in a warm and otherworldly glow. The red-tailed hawk sat hooded on Romanowski's shoulder, making him look like a pirate with a parrot. The peregrine gripped Romanowski's fist, flaring his wings for balance.

"I don't know how long he's been out there," Missy said, fretting. "Marybeth and Sheridan will have to pass right by him to get to the house."

That's right, Joe remembered. *Marybeth's picking Sheridan up from basketball practice.*

"His name is Nate Romanowski," Joe said.

Missy gasped and raised her hand to her mouth. "He's the one who . . ."

"He didn't do it," Joe said bluntly.

Joe let go of the curtain and went to find his coat. Although the sun had warmed up the afternoon nicely, it would be much different when the sun dropped behind the mountains.

As he pulled his coat on, he noticed that Lucy had emerged from her bedroom and was standing next to Missy. It was a jarring sight, and he realized he'd done a double-take. Lucy was a miniature version of Missy Vankueren. The sweater, pants, pearls, and shoes she wore were identical to her grandmother's, except that the sweater was cotton and the pearls were fake. Even her swept-up hairstyle was the same.

Joe looked up for an explanation, and found Missy beaming.

"Isn't she adorable?" Missy gushed. "The outfit is a late Christmas present from me. We're going out to dinner tonight, my little granddaughter and me."

"Going out? Like that?" Joe asked, incredulous.

"Show him," Missy commanded.

Lucy swung her little hips and did a slow turn with her arms raised above her head. She looked and moved so much like Missy that Joe cringed.

"What did you do that for?" he asked, refraining from saying *what in the hell* because of Lucy.

Missy looked back, hurt.

"Come on, honey," she said, turning on her heel. "Your daddy doesn't appreciate style." Lucy turned as well, following Missy stride for stride toward the bathroom. Unlike Missy, though, Lucy looked over her shoulder as she entered the bathroom and winked at Joe. Lucy knew it was a joke, even if Missy didn't.

Joe didn't know whether to laugh or run from the house.

"I OWE YOU," NATE SAID, as Joe approached.

"No, you don't."

Nate fixed his sharp eyes on Joe. "I asked you for two things and you did both of them. I knew I could trust you."

Joe stuffed his hands in his pockets and kicked uncomfortably at the snow. "Forget it. I'm just real glad we found the guys."

"Is Spud Cargill still out there?" Nate asked.

"As far as I know."

Nate nodded and seemed to be thinking about that.

"Why? Do you know something?" Joe asked.

There was a hint of a smile. "I know just enough to be dangerous. I overheard a lot of things in that jail—snippets between Barnum and his deputies and between Melinda Strickland and Barnum. And I could tell what they were thinking by what they questioned me about. Things are in motion to get those Sovereigns out of here. The sheriff and Strickland were convinced I was one of them, you know. Dick Munker even tried to get me to admit I was a soldier for the militia types. That whole sick crowd is real disappointed to find out that all the Sovereigns are guilty of at this point is hating the federal government—which isn't a crime—and staying too many nights in a campground. They're trying like hell to pin something on those people up there."

"Maybe now things will ease off," Joe said, hopeful.

"Don't count on it."

"No," Joe said sternly. "It *needs* to happen."

A set of headlights appeared on Bighorn Road from the direction of town. Absently, Joe watched the car approach and the headlights pool wider on the freezing road. It was Marybeth, and Sheridan.

"My wife's home," Joe said. "Would you like to come in? It's getting cold out here."

Instead of answering, Nate studied Joe, his eyes narrowing.

"What?" he asked, annoyed.

"You really are a good guy, aren't you?"

Joe's shoulders slumped. "Knock it off."

"I'm not kidding around," Nate said softly. "I've spent most of my life around hypocrites and assholes. McLanahan and Barnum types. Most of them haven't had a thimbleful of character. So it's just kind of heart-warming to see that there are still some good guys left."

Joe was grateful for the darkness because he knew his face was flushing.

"Are you drunk, Nate?"

Nate laughed. "I had a few. After I saw what they did to my cabin."

"They trashed it, all right. Sheridan and I put a bunch of your stuff back in your house." The minute Joe said it he cringed, because he knew what was coming.

"See!" Nate exclaimed, raising his arm and turning it as if showing Joe off to his peregrine. "See what I mean? You *are* a good man. With a good wife and good children!"

After what seemed like forever to Joe, Marybeth pulled off the road and parked her car next to the Jeep. She got out with an armful of groceries. Sheridan walked around the car, her eyes fixed on Romanowski and the hawks. Joe could tell she was entranced.

Joe introduced Marybeth and Sheridan to Nate Romanowski.

"I was just telling your husband what a nice family you have," Nate said. "I'm happy to find people like you."

Marybeth and Joe exchanged glances.

"It's nice to meet you, Mr. Romanowski . . ."

"Call me Nate," he interrupted.

". . . Nate," Marybeth amended, "But I've got to get these things in and get dinner started."

Nate shook his head ruefully. "And get dinner started," he repeated. "That's lovely."

"Would you like to join us?" Marybeth asked.

"Please?" Sheridan pleaded. "I'd like to ask you some questions about falcons and falconry."

Everyone looked to Joe.

"I already invited him in," Joe grumbled.

*　　*　　*

WHILE MARYBETH PREPARED DINNER IN the kitchen, Joe listened as Nate Romanowski discussed his birds with Sheridan in the living room. Nate spread newspaper on the floor and borrowed two chairs from the table for the birds to perch on. He lowered the birds to the tops of the chairs, where they perched facing backward with their tail feathers down the chairbacks. Missy had taken Lucy to town in the van for dinner. If Nate thought the sight of two identically dressed females with a fifty-something age difference was odd, he didn't say anything.

Nate and the falcons seemed to fill the living room, Joe thought. Although the birds were no more than twelve inches tall on the chairbacks, they projected a much larger aura. Like Nate himself, they seemed to be creatures of a different, wilder, and more violent world.

While Sheridan sat enraptured, Nate explained the accessories on the birds themselves, from the tooled leather hoods that covered their eyes but not their hooked beaks, to the long, thin leather jesses that hung from their ankles. The jesses, Nate said, were how the falconer kept a bird secured on his hand. Gently, he lifted the peregrine on his gloved fist and showed Sheridan how he twined the jesses through his fingers. The grip of the jess in his hand, he said, provided balance and stability for the bird and also prevented it from taking flight or walking up his arm. At the end of the jess was a swivel and a leash.

"What if it tries to fly?" Sheridan asked.

"Then the bird just kind of flops around like a chicken," Nate answered. "You'd be surprised how much lift they've got and how much power. A scared falcon flapping his wings can almost pull you off your feet."

He held the peregrine close to Sheridan, letting her examine it.

"I feel sorry for it, having to wear that hood," Sheridan said, gently stroking the bird's breast with the backs of her fingers.

"Then let's get rid of it," Nate said, pulling two small strings and slipping the hood off.

The falcon cocked its head toward Sheridan, studying her with rapid, almost mechanical snaps of its head. The bird's eyes were preternaturally alert and piercing. Nate told Sheridan how those eyes worked, how they had more cell surface area inside than human eyes so they could see in the dark and catch movement, like a mouse, from more than a mile away.

"I've heard it said that if you look into a falcon's eyes you can see forever," Nate said softly, in his strange blunt cadence. "I've also heard it's bad luck, because looking into a falcon's eyes is like looking into your own black, murderous heart."

Sheridan's own eyes widened at that, and she looked to Joe.

Joe shrugged. "I've never heard either one of those."

Nate smiled mysteriously.

"One thing I do know is that you can tell the difference between a falcon that's wild and a falcon that's broken by the look in their eyes. I've seen it at aviaries and zoos. The falcons there look at you, but something is missing behind the stare."

After a moment, Sheridan said, "Why don't we put his hood back on?" And Nate did.

"How do you get these birds?" she asked.

"Some I trap them when they're young," he said, describing how he mountaineered on cliffs to find the aeries, or nests, to set the mesh webs. He would stay at the site, ready to pounce if a bird hit the trap. "Others I've rescued when they've been hit by a car, or shocked by high wires."

"Falconry is considered the sport of kings in some Middle Eastern countries," Joe added, nodding.

"How long can you keep them?" she asked.

"It's not how long you keep *them*. It's how long they decide to stay with *you*. They can fly away any time they want and never come back. So every time they come back, it's a precious gift."

"What do they hunt?"

Nate explained that while all falcons are hawks, not all hawks are falcons. He said that each bird had its particular specialty, and that falconers often chose the birds based on that. Red-tailed hawks, like the one on the chair, were best on rabbits and squirrels. Falcons were best on sage grouse, ducks, and pheasants—upland game birds. The mere silhouette of a falcon in the sky, he said, would make ducks on the water freeze or seek cover, because a duck in flight would be instantly intercepted and destroyed. Ducks knew the imprint of a falcon from birth, and knew to fear it.

"The peregrine, though, is unique: It will hunt just about anything. That's why peregrines are so prized, and why they were protected for so many years when it looked like they were going extinct. For a peregrine, its specialty is prey in general, and they can hunt ground game, upland game birds, or waterfowl.

"You can't just keep a raptor like a pet and be a true falconer," Nate said. "Falconry requires hours of patience, training, and communicating with your bird. The birds must be exercised daily and kept in top condition— to hunt well, and in case they leave. You have to think like a falcon, like a predator, but at the same time you can't dominate the bird. If you do that, you break it. If it's broken, it's ruined forever. It'll fly off for sure, and its defenses will never again be as sharp. You're imposing a death sentence on a falcon if you break it. So if you respect the bird, you'll work to keep that wild, sharp edge the bird naturally has."

Then he nodded toward a thick glove in his falconry bag.

"You want me to put that on?" Sheridan asked.

"Don't you want to hold the bird?"

"Dad, is it okay?"

Joe wasn't sure what to say. Sheridan's eyes were glowing, and Romanowski continued to smile inscrutably.

"Sure," Joe finally said.

Nate took off the hood and leveled his fist near Sheridan's gloved hand, and slightly swiveled his wrist, urging the falcon to step forward. It did, gracefully, and Sheridan's arm dipped a little from the weight of the falcon on her fist. Nate helped her wrap the jesses through her fingers and pulled them tight near the heel of her hand. It was an oddly intimate moment that made Joe squirm a little. Nate was a big man, with a soothing veneer that was somehow calming as well as magnetic. Sheridan was only eleven years old. As Joe studied the falconer, he sensed the same kind of natural, violent wildness under the surface that Nate described in his birds. *Nate is a raptor,* Joe thought. *He's a hunter and a killer, and he lives closer to the earth than anyone I've ever known.* In a way, Nate was terrifying. He could also be, Joe thought, a hell of an ally.

TO JOE'S CHAGRIN, MARYBETH SERVED meat loaf. It wasn't her fault that she had played to type this way and further entertained Nate's ideal fantasy of the Picketts— happily married, picket fence, loving family, Labrador, and now *meat loaf* for dinner—but that's how it looked.

Nate smiled happily and took a double portion. He moaned almost obscenely as he ate it, which caused Joe and Marybeth to stifle smiles of their own. No one had ever loved Marybeth's meat loaf quite so much, or so obviously. Sheridan picked at her food, spending most of her time either watching Nate or looking over her shoulder at the two birds on chairs in the living room.

The telephone rang and Marybeth left the table to answer it. After a beat, she handed it to Joe.

"Please hold for Melinda Strickland," Marybeth said, mocking what the secretary had told her.

Joe winced, and excused himself. He felt Nate's eyes on his back as he took the telephone into the living room.

After a moment, Strickland came on. "Joe!" She cried, "You got one of the bastards! Good work, Joe!"

"Thank you," he mumbled. He knew that both Marybeth and Nate were quietly listening at the table.

"Too bad he didn't have an accident on the way into town, though."

"Excuse me?"

"You know, too bad the guy didn't try to escape or something."

He knew what she meant, but he wanted her to actually say it. But she was too good a bureaucrat to admit anything outright.

"Is there any news on Spud Cargill?" he asked.

What she told him froze him to his spot. He found himself still standing, still holding the telephone to his ear, long after she had said goodbye and hung up. The dull pain in his stomach that had been with him for days reappeared, and once again he felt the tightening jaws of the vise.

"WHAT'S WRONG?" MARYBETH ASKED AS he sat back down at the table.

"Joe?"

He looked up. "They still haven't found Spud. Melinda Strickland said that someone thinks they saw him in a stolen truck on the way to Battle Mountain, and McLanahan said that a truck fitting that description ran his roadblock just a couple of hours ago."

"Didn't someone also say they saw him on the football field?" Marybeth asked skeptically.

"Yes."

"So why are you acting this way?"

Joe noted that Sheridan was watching him carefully.

Nate leaned back in his chair and he spoke in almost a whisper. "What this means is that Strickland and her FBI hit team can now go after the Sovereign compound. She can say that they're harboring a fugitive suspected of murdering a federal employee."

"I was thinking this thing was going to calm down," Joe said. "But Melinda Strickland is determined to prove there's a war on. And now she's got a much better reason to start it."

Marybeth instantly understood. "She wouldn't do that, would she?" Her eyes flashed. "April . . ."

JOE WALKED NATE ROMANOWSKI TO his Jeep in the dark. The sky was clear and gauzy with stars. The melting snow had frozen into a slick cold skin on the sidewalk and road.

Nate perched his falcons on the top of the backseat and secured the jesses to metal swivels he had installed on the framework for the purpose. Joe watched, his breath condensing into snaky wisps, his mind twenty miles away in the deep snow of Battle Mountain.

When he had secured the birds, Nate reached under his Jeep seat and pulled out a bundle that turned out to be a shoulder holster and his massive revolver. He looped a strap over his head and buckled it below his sternum. Another strap fit around his midsection. The curved black grip of the stainless-steel .454 Casull now offered itself to Joe.

"Why do you carry a gun like that?" Joe asked.

Nate smiled slightly. "Because I know how to use it and it's all I need. It gives me the mobility of a handgun but with more firepower and velocity. It's a Freedom Arms Model 83 with a seven-and-a-half-inch barrel. A hand cannon. I did my research and went to the factory in Freedom, Wyoming and paid twenty-five hundred for it. It shoots a 300-grain bullet and it can literally shoot through a car."

Joe whistled.

"Or I could fire into the trunk and hit the driver. If three bad guys were lined up, I could put a single slug through all of them. And I could do it from three hundred yards away."

Joe had been waiting for this moment. "I suppose you could even knock out the engine of an SUV driving down U.S. Highway 87 near Great Falls, Montana."

Nate turned and leaned against his Jeep, folding his arms across his chest. His uncommonly sharp eyes bored into Joe.

"Theoretically, yes," Nate said evenly. "That could happen. Now I really owe you."

"No, you don't, I told you that."

"Do you want me to get your little girl back?"

Joe paused, and thought. He was torn. The question wasn't unanticipated. Nate was well aware of the empty chair at the table, as they all were.

"We've got a lawyer working on it," Joe said. "That's our only recourse right now."

Nate didn't scoff, but his silence said enough.

"I worry about her, Nate. She's been abandoned once already, then taken away from her school. If you go in and grab her, she might be even more messed up. We love her too much to put her through that right now. Plus the fact that we would be facing kidnapping charges. The law isn't on our side in this."

Nate nodded. "You've thought about it."

"For days."

"Something bad is going to happen up there in that compound. I think we both know that."

Joe rubbed his eyes and sighed, and said nothing.

"Maybe something could happen to Melinda Strickland," Nate said.

Joe looked up, shocked. Nate was deadly serious. He had also crossed a line by threatening Strickland in front of Joe, who had a duty and obligation to take some kind of action. Nate knew all of this.

"Don't ever say anything like that to me again, Nate," Joe said, his voice low and hard.

Nate didn't react.

"Joe, thank you for dinner and the very nice evening. Your wife and daughter are wonderful. Sheridan is something special. I think she would make a good falconer."

Joe nodded, half-hearing Nate. His head was swimming with situations and consequences.

"I'll be available if you need me," Nate said. "Do you hear me, Joe?"

It seemed to have gotten much colder in the past two minutes, Joe thought.

"Joe?"

"I hear you."

24

AT THE SAME TIME ON BATTLE MOUNTAIN, A CONVOY OF vehicles had driven up the road outside the Sovereign compound. As they approached the fence, their engines rumbling, Jeannie, Clem, and April had pulled back the curtain and watched through the trailer window. Clem doused all the lights so they could see out but not be seen.

There were either six or seven vehicles out there. As they came up the road, they turned toward the fence as if they were going to drive through it. But then four of the trucks stopped abreast of each other, their headlights flooding the snow between the road and the compound. The trailing vehicles parked behind the first row. Framed by the rising, glowing clouds of exhaust, the front row of trucks looked like they had risen from a cauldron. Their drivers were silhouetted: Jeannie could see Sheriff Barnum behind the wheel of his Blazer. A woman sat next to him holding a little dog in her arms. A bullhorn squawked, and someone asked for Wade Brockius.

Brockius had been outside his trailer, and he ambled toward the headlights.

"Stop where you are."

Spotlights from two of the vehicles came to life and bathed him in light.

Brockius stopped.

"This is Dick Munker of the Federal Bureau of Investigation. We have reason to believe that you're harboring a dangerous fugitive by the name of Spud Cargill, who is a murder suspect in an ongoing investigation. We would like your permission to conduct a thorough search of the premises."

Brockius raised his arm to block the spotlights from his eyes. His deep voice rumbled through the icy night. He didn't need a bullhorn.

"Permission denied. I don't know what you're talking about."

"We can show up with a court order tomorrow."

"That won't do you any good, Mr. Munker. There's nothing to be found. Mr. Cargill is not here. There are people here who would consider your forced intrusion to be an armed attack."

Wade Brockius paused, and lowered his arm, attempting to see the man with the bullhorn. "We know what happened at Waco, Mr. Munker. I know you were there. I remember your name. You were one of the snipers, as I recall. You were also on Ruby Ridge. You should be in federal prison, Mr. Munker."

Jeannie tried to look into the darkness around her, but her eyes were scalded by the headlights and spotlights. She knew there were armed Sovereigns behind trailers, in the brush, and in the trees. There were probably a half-dozen sets of crosshairs focused on the man with the bullhorn, and open sights trained on Sheriff Barnum.

Munker spoke through the bullhorn, although it wasn't really necessary. "All of the entrances and exits to this compound have been sealed off by deputies of the Twelve Sleep County sheriff's office and the FBI. You're trapped here, and Cargill has nowhere to run. We had planned to keep the power and telephone lines available as long as you were communicating and cooperating with us. But that doesn't appear to be what's happening."

Although Munker lowered his bullhorn to speak to someone else, his muffled voice could be heard saying "Turn off their lights, boys."

At that moment, the electricity was cut to the compound. Lights blinked out. Heaters whirred to a stop. Refrigerators ticked to silence. Almost immediately, the cold began to seep into the trailers.

Jeannie knew that all of the trailers and campers had full propane tanks in addition to a large community tank in the middle of the compound. There were gas powered generators as well as wireless telephones and transmitters hidden under tarps in the woods. So the power outage was simply symbolic, a way of showing who held the cards.

"We've got some musical entertainment lined up for you later, Mr. Brockius. I made it myself and it's one-of-a-kind. It's also on a continuous loop."

They had all seen the speakers above the trees, Jeannie knew, and they had expected something like this to happen eventually. Wade had prepared them.

"We have children here," Brockius said.

"Then you might want to reconsider your position," Munker had said. The contempt in his voice was palpable. "If you do reconsider, call me personally. That's why we kept your telephone line up. Just dial nine-one-one and the dispatcher will track me down day or night. Otherwise, I'll be back in the morning with the court order for Spud Cargill."

"I told you he's not here."

One by one, the vehicles backed up from the line and began to leave. The last remaining car was a dark SUV containing Dick Munker and a driver.

Jeannie knew what was happening. The good people of Saddlestring, along with the Feds, were trying to kick them out. Just like they had kicked her out before. To do so, they were going to make things as miserable as possible.

Her mouth curled into a snarl. *Fuck them*, she hissed.

AFTER MUNKER AND THE TRUCKS left, it took hours for April to calm down. She asked why they hadn't given the men in the trucks what they wanted.

Clem told April to shut up, and Jeannie backhanded him across the mouth. Clem glared at Jeannie, then went outside for a while. When he came back, he was half-drunk and docile, and April was finally sleeping.

LATE THAT NIGHT, FROM INSIDE a heavy black box under the base of a tree near Battle Mountain, there was a dull click. The click was so faint that it could not have been heard beyond a few feet away. Through the snow, two amber lights now glowed, and a digital tape began to spin. Heavy, double-insulated electrical wires crawled up from the box through the snow and were stapled fast on the trunk of the tree. A hundred feet away and twenty-four feet in the air, the two speakers crackled to life. The mountain silence yielded to a swinging back beat, tinny horns, and a young Wayne Newton singing:

> *Danke schoen, darling,*
> *Danke schoen,*
> *Thank you for walks down Lovers' Lane . . .*

*　　*　　*

INSIDE ONE OF THE ICE-ENCRUSTED trailers within the compound, Jeannie Keeley sat bolt upright in her bed. She listened, and realized that the song was not part of her dream. She looked through the gloom toward the rear of the trailer where April slept. April's bed was of a thin fold-down design made of plywood veneer. When the girl tossed or turned, the bed creaked. It was creaking now.

The song finally ended. Within a few seconds, it started up again. The same song, "Danke Schoen," by Wayne Newton. This time the song was slightly louder than before. Clem, sleeping next to Jeannie on the double bed that they built each night by fitting the tabletop between the trailer's two bench seats, had not stirred. As the music increased in volume, April began to cry.

Jeannie was enraged. This was the first night that April had gone to sleep without crying. Since April had been back with her, Jeannie thought, there were lots of signs that she'd turned back into a baby. She had obviously been coddled. The girl cried about everything. April seemed to think that life was supposed to be easy, not tough. Jeannie knew better. April would learn. She would toughen up. She would have to, or else.

Jeannie had just about had it with the girl. There'd been times in the last few days when she wanted to drive April back to the Picketts' house and toss her out the door. It annoyed Jeannie to no end that April referred to the Pickett girls, Sheridan and Lucy, as her "sisters." Jeannie had even rehearsed a "Here, you can have her back" speech in her mind.

But when April slept, she was lovely. When April slept, Jeannie felt some of her motherly feelings come back. When April slept, the girl's face relaxed and gentled and looked like a photo Jeannie had seen of herself when *she* was nine. Which reminded Jeannie that April was *hers*. Now, though, there was this horrible music, music that was almost pleasant at first but that now was otherworldly, awful, and gruesomely out of place.

"Why do they keep playing that song over and over again?" April asked from her bed. Her voice was tiny and rough from crying.

"'Cause they're trying to get rid of us, honey," Jeannie answered.

> *Danke schoen, auf wiedersehen,*
> *Danke schoen . . .*

THE SONG STARTED UP AGAIN, as soon as it was over. Jeannie had heard it six times now. Again, it was louder. The bass beat reverberated through the metal frame of the trailer, sounding to Jeannie like the devil's own heartbeat.

"Why do they keep playing it again and again? Can you make them stop?" April said.

Another sound emerged, layered beneath the snappy tune of "Danke Schoen." The first hints of it were distant: A knife being honed on a sharpening steel. There was a slight pop and the sound of tearing, like fabric being ripped, accompanied by a high-pitched, otherworldly squeal that set Jeannie's teeth on edge. April cried harder, her body shaking. The squealing was now ear-piercing. It began to overwhelm the Wayne Newton song.

"You know what that is?" Clem said, now awake. "That's a rabbit being skinned alive."

Jeannie didn't ask him how he knew that.

Finally, it stopped. The rabbit panted shallowly, then died with a death rattle.

April was now shaking, her hands covering her ears, her eyes closed tight.

Then the brassy music started up again, louder. Then the background sound of the knife being sharpened.

> *Danke schoen, darling*
> *Danke schoen,*
> *Thank you for walks down Lovers' Lane . . .*

PART THREE

Whiteout

25

THE TELEPHONE NEXT TO THE BED BURRED AT 5:05 A.M. and Joe picked it up on the first ring. It was County Attorney Robey Hersig.

"Did I wake you up?"

"It's okay," Joe said. "I've been awake most of the night." Marybeth had slept poorly again, tossing and turning and pining for April. Joe had tried to calm her, with partial success. After she went back to sleep, he replayed in his head the conversation he'd had with Nate Romanowski, playing "What if?" What if, he wondered, he told Romanowski he needed his help? What if he turned Romanowski loose?

"Joe, did anybody notify you about a meeting this morning at the Forest Service office?"

"Nope."

"I didn't think so. Anyway, Melinda Strickland and Sheriff Barnum have called a meeting for seven-thirty. All county law-enforcement personnel have been ordered to be there. They've requested that all state personnel be there as well, so I assume that means the state troopers and you."

Joe closed his eyes and breathed deeply. "What's going on?"

"Hell has broken loose."

THE COFFEE IN HIS ROAD cup tasted bitter and metallic as he drove toward Saddlestring. It was unusually dark out for seven, and it took him a moment to see that the cloud cover was so dense and far-reaching that it blocked out the rising sun. It was as if a sooty lid had been placed over the valley. The only gap in the lid was a razor-thin band of orange that paralleled the eastern sagebrush plains. That band was the only hard evidence that it was daylight.

Joe knew that a big storm was coming.

He remembered the feeling he'd had in the wooded bowl before hearing Lamar Gardiner's gunshots. It was the feeling of artillery being moved into place prior to a barrage. He felt it again—only this time, it was worse.

JOE WAS SHOCKED AT THE number of law-enforcement vehicles parked around the Forest Service office off Main Street. He parked half a block away and approached the building on a buckling concrete sidewalk. The air was still but seemed supercharged with rising humidity and low pressure. It was still unusually dark out, and Joe recalled the otherworldly half-light created by a solar eclipse the previous summer. He looked at his watch and saw that he was right on time for the meeting.

The reception and conference area had been completely transformed since his visit on New Year's Eve. The standard-issue government desks had been turned and shoved against the walls to create more space. Deputies, town police officers, and state troopers milled in the open area drinking coffee. Joe had never seen so many big guts straining against uniform shirt fabric in one place at one time. Although there was little talking this early in the morning, he heard the clump of heavy boots and the creak of leather from holsters and Sam Browne belts. Deputies McLanahan and Reed were missing from the room, and Joe guessed they were still on roadblock duty. He scanned the room for Robey Hersig and found him near the back to the side of the coffee urn.

"Thanks for calling," Joe said to Hersig. "I think."

Hersig looked anxious. "Joe, did you get a fax this morning?"

Joe said that the last fax he'd received from anybody was a list of food items that Elle Broxton-Howard didn't want to eat.

"You're one of the few, then." Hersig reached inside his blazer and handed Joe a folded sheaf of documents. The cover page of the fax was addressed to Robey, and the letterhead showed that it was from the Sovereign Citizens of the Rocky Mountains. After the cover was page after page of dense legalese. Statutes were cited throughout, including the Uniform Commercial Code. Joe was puzzled, and glanced up to Hersig.

"What is this?"

Hersig smiled sourly. "Two things, actually. The first is a subpoena to appear before their court to defend against the charge of impersonating a public official. The second is a lien against the county courthouse, the sheriff's office, and my home for $27.3 million dollars."

"*What?*"

Hersig nodded, and swallowed dryly. "Subpoenas and liens were faxed all over the place during the middle of last night." He held his hand out—Joe noticed it was shaking slightly—and started counting off with his fingers. "The mayor, the town council, the county commis-

sioners, the chief of police, the BLM director, Melinda
Strickland, the governor of Wyoming . . ."

"Governor Budd got one?"

Hersig nodded and continued. "The Interior Secretary of the United States, the national Forest Service director, the director of the FBI, and I don't know who all
else got them nationally. Those are just the phone calls
we've received this morning. That's just the East Coast,
which is two hours ahead of us. We don't know how
many people in the West will call."

"What prompted this?" Joe had never seen Hersig so
shaky.

Hersig's eyes narrowed. Joe thought Hersig was
about to spit a name out when the likely bearer of the
name walked into the room.

Melinda Strickland wore her Forest Service uniform,
and her cocker spaniel trailed behind her on a leash. She
strode purposefully to the front of the room and stationed herself behind a podium. Sheriff Barnum flanked
her on one side, Dick Munker on the other. Munker
sucked on a cigarette with the same intensity as an
asthma victim using an inhaler.

"Thank you all so much for coming," Melinda Strickland said, her manner incongruously pleasant. Joe noted
that her hair was a mousy brown color once again. "As
you know, a situation developed yesterday that com-
pounded during the night. I see Game Warden Joe Pickett in the back there—he somehow learned about this
meeting—and we all have our friend Joe to thank for
bringing at least one of the murderers to justice!"

Joe wished he could worm himself through the back
wall, as officers, deputies, and troopers all turned and
looked at him. His fellow state employees—the
troopers—clapped sharply, but they were the only ones.
Joe knew that the others, especially the deputies, proba-

bly felt they'd been shown up. His intuition was confirmed when he noticed how Barnum was glowering at him from the front of the room. *Someday,* Joe thought, *he and I will need to have it out. There are scores to settle.*

"The important thing . . ." Strickland shouted over nonexistent applause, as if trying to bring the silent room to heel, "The important thing is that we've been anticipating this situation for quite some time and we have everything completely and totally and *awesomely* under control. So now I'd like to turn the briefing over to Dick Munker of the FBI, who is heading up the operation on my behalf."

Munker extinguished his cigarette and turned to the podium, but Strickland thought of something and remained. She raised a thick stack of papers in the air and waved them. Joe recognized them as similar to what Hersig had showed him.

"I don't know how many of you got these during the night, but now you know the kind of twisted people we are dealing with here, ya know!"

Munker lit another cigarette and gave her a moment to leave the podium. When she did, he surveyed the room with amusement in his eyes before stepping forward. He wore a gray sweater over a black turtleneck, and a shoulder holster. A two-way radio was hanging in a case on his belt.

Munker began by nodding toward Joe. "A federal official is murdered while in his custody. The reason he gets murdered is because he manages to escape under the nose of our game warden here. Then our game warden, with a steering wheel handcuffed to his wrist, chases the escapee through the snow only to find him pinned to a tree by arrows." His tone was accusatory, his eyes cold and mocking. "This is the man who is now our little hero. Well done, Game Warden."

Joe felt as if he'd been slapped. Even the deputies who had withheld applause seemed surprised by Munker's nastiness, and they didn't turn around to further embarrass Joe. Only Barnum stared and smirked.

After a long, leisurely drag that allowed his comments to hang in the air even longer, Munker cocked his head to change the subject. "Gentlemen, we are at war, and this is now a war room." Portenson wheeled a large chalkboard into the room. On it was a large-scale diagram of the Sovereign Citizen compound in relation to the two roads that approached it.

"We've had entrance and exit roads blocked," Munker said, pointing at red X's on the map. "The only way out, or in, is via those roads or over the snow to nowhere. As soon as this meeting is over, the roadblocks will be manned again. The compound is currently quiet after a full night of audio PsyOps—psychological operations. We're waiting on a warrant being signed by the judge, and when we have it we can apply even more pressure. Unfortunately, the judge received one of those documents Ms. Strickland showed you earlier and he's a little shaken right now."

Munker smirked, and inhaled.

"These liens and subpoenas are old fucking news, gentlemen. The Montana Freemen invented the trick back in 1995. Those losers found out they could paralyze the local community and all of the goddamned 'officials' in the State of Montana by sending those things out. Nothing makes a politician crap his shorts faster than a threat of legal action. As some of you know, there are some dregs of the Freemen up there in that compound now, so they know how the scheme works."

Joe barely heard what Munker was saying. He was still stinging from the unprovoked attack that started the meeting. It seemed to have come from nowhere. Joe knew that it was calculated. Calculated to do exactly what, he wasn't sure. But it hurt.

When he glanced up, he realized that Elle Broxton-Howard was standing next to him. She looked at him with a mixture of false affection and pity. He hated that.

". . . Sheriff, what can you tell us about Spud Cargill?" Munker asked, turning his head toward Barnum.

"Spud Cargill was thought to have been seen yesterday afternoon in a stolen vehicle driving like a bat out of hell up Battle Mountain Road," Barnum said, passing out copies of Cargill's photograph. Joe took one as the stack went by. It was a Saddlestring *Roundup* photo from two years ago, when Cargill caught a five-and-a-half-pound rainbow trout to win an ice-fishing tournament in Saratoga, Wyoming. "He was seen going up, and blew right through the roadblock, but he wasn't seen coming down. It's possible he came down between the shift change, but we have no information on that. There's too many old Forest Service roads up there to keep watch on all of them, but we've tightened up the security on the main roads as of today. Our assumption is that he is in the Sovereign compound, and the Sovereigns are harboring him. Last night, as many of you know, they refused to turn him over or even let us look for him. This leads us to believe that Cargill may have been in cahoots with them since the beginning."

"There's a leap of logic," Joe whispered to Hersig. Hersig pretended he hadn't heard.

"Cargill's partner, Rope Latham, is currently in custody. He's confessed to assisting Cargill with the murder as well as setting up the BLM employee."

"Has he confessed to being in cahoots with the Sovereigns?" Joe whispered, again for Hersig's benefit.

Hersig shot him an angry look that surprised Joe. Apparently, Hersig was more troubled by the lien and subpoena than Joe had realized. Hersig was dead serious this morning.

"What about the press?" Munker asked rhetorically, nodding toward Melinda Strickland.

She stepped forward as Barnum had. "We've been getting hammered with calls since last night, just hammered."

Joe stifled a smile.

"The Casper and Cheyenne newspapers, radio stations from all over the state, and network affiliates from Billings and Denver have been calling," she said, with a hint of pride. "CNN and Fox have contacted us as well. They're all trying to figure out where Saddlestring is and how they can get here with a satellite truck."

"Do they know about the storm?" a deputy asked.

Strickland nodded her head. "I told them about it, but most of them were already watching the weather. I guess this one's supposed to be huge, much worse than the Christmas storm."

Joe heard men mumble about the severe winter storm warning, and predictions of three to five feet of snow in the mountains.

"Which poses an opportunity, gentlemen," Munker interjected. "The last thing we want is for this to turn into a standoff that's the subject of every fucking twenty-four-hour news show in America. We cannot let these Sovereigns use the media to create sympathy, which they will do given the opportunity. They cannot be provided a forum for their twisted, antigovernment ravings. Believe me, I know. I was at Waco. I was at Ruby Ridge. I was in Garfield County, Montana, when the Freemen held out. If the press is here, we lose all tactical advantage. And there will be no possible way in hell for an efficient solution."

Munker's face was red and he was practically snarling.

"I've been there, fellows. I've been there when dildo Freemen wearing hoods patrolled their ranch for the cameras, making us look like a bunch of wussy assholes. I was there when info-babes showed up while the fire was still burning at Waco to ask us if the force we used was unreasonable.

"This storm is supposed to last at least three days. It's likely the airstrip will be closed and the roads will be closed. If film crews can't get here, it means there isn't any news. That's how it works. So we have a short window of time to act. In the past, too many of these situations have degenerated into fucking situation comedies. We can't let that happen here, gentlemen. And lady," he said, deferring to Melinda Strickland.

"Ladies!" Elle Broxton-Howard shouted, raising her hand next to Joe. There was a titter of laughter. Most of the men who turned to look at Broxton-Howard were still looking at her when Melinda Strickland spoke again.

"When I came here, I said we were going to stand up to these antigovernment outlaws," Strickland said, looking to Broxton-Howard to make sure the reporter had her pad out. "Some mocked me. Some doubted the seriousness of the situation. Now we know just how serious this situation is!"

Robey Hersig's assistant, an ancient clerk named Bud Lipsey, wearing a gray Stetson and horn-rimmed glasses, blew into the room. He raised a manila folder.

"The search warrant has been signed by Judge Pennock," Lipsey announced.

Munker smiled. Joe saw it as a leer.

"Let's regroup at noon," he said. "The sheriff, Ms. Strickland, and I will set our strategy and make assignments."

*   *   *

JOE LEANED AGAINST THE WALL and rubbed his face with his hands. He couldn't believe what was happening. Law-enforcement personnel filed out of the building charged with a sense of purpose. There was back-slapping and shoulder-punching. A small army had been assembled, to be led by Munker, Strickland, and Barnum against the Sovereign compound. It all felt horribly wrong. The room was too hot. Somebody needed to turn the ther-mostat down or open a window.

When he opened his eyes, Elle Broxton-Howard was standing in front of him.

"Did you get my fax?" she asked.

Not now, he thought.

"We don't have any brown rice."

She smiled. "I can bring some. Or better yet, we don't do the interview at your house. I just need some quotes on how you trapped that bad guy. And I want to know more about what Mr. Munker was saying about the steering wheel. Is that true?"

Joe fought back an urge to shove her. "It's true."

She was joined by Melinda Strickland. Strickland was obviously concerned, which, to Joe, looked as patently false as all of her public emotions. It looked like she'd said to herself, *"Now put on your frowny face."*

"Joe, we really have to talk."

Joe looked up. Elle Broxton-Howard stepped to the side. Munker and Barnum were still at the podium, but they were both looking toward Joe and Melinda Strick-land, awaiting the outcome of what no doubt had been previously discussed among the three of them.

"Joe, we all really appreciate what you did when you arrested Rope Latham, but there are some issues."

In his peripheral vision, he saw Broxton-Howard scribbling the sentence in her pad. So this was for *her* benefit, Joe realized.

"What issues?" he asked. He hated words like "issues."

"It's interesting that you didn't get one of the liens or subpoenas like all of the rest of us did," she said. "Or did you?"

He shook his head no.

"Joe, don't you feel that maybe you've got too many personal issues in this situation? Like with that little girl and all? Like maybe, you know, maybe you're a little too close to the Sovereigns up there, and that it would be best not to participate in the search and all?"

He stared at her. Broxton-Howard wrote.

"This whole sad affair started when, unfortunately, Lamar Gardiner escaped from you. The arrest of Rope Latham was good and all, but maybe you should sort of take a break and get some rest and leave it up to the professionals."

A hot surge began to crawl up Joe's neck as he looked at Melinda Strickland, and beyond her at Munker. The flush spread through his chest, ran down his arms, and settled behind his eyes. He stared at them both with blinders on, his rage coursing through him.

"I can see what's happening here," he said. His voice sounded strained, even to him. "It's a case of target fixation, just like when Lamar Gardiner saw more elk than he had ever seen in one place before. Like when he was reloading with cigarettes so he could shoot and kill some more."

"Joe . . ."

"You see a chance to crush people like you've always wanted to do. You've found a situation where you think you're justified in doing it. You people hate so much you forget to *think*. There are big problems here. The first is that you've brought in a psychopath to run things." He nodded toward Munker. "The second is that I have a child up there in that compound. As you know."

From the front of the room, Dick Munker scoffed. He had been listening all along. "From what I understand she's not even yours."

Rage all but consumed him. He despised the fact that Munker and Strickland had discussed Joe and Marybeth's situation with April as freely as they had. Although the matter was not private, given the circumstances, he thought it should be treated that way. When he closed his eyes, spangles of red cascaded like fireworks down the insides of his eyelids. He felt someone grip his arm—Hersig—and he ripped his arm away.

It's not about children as property, he shouted to himself, *or who belongs to whom. It's not about that. It's about bringing up kids who become good human beings, so they won't turn out like the people standing in front of me.*

"Joe?" Hersig asked. Joe hadn't realized Robey was so close to him.

Joe opened his eyes. Melinda Strickland had stepped back, as had Elle Broxton-Howard. They had inadvertently cleared a path across the room to Dick Munker, who lit a cigarette behind the podium.

"Munker." His voice was hoarse.

Munker raised an eyebrow in response.

"If you do anything that hurts April even further, I'm going to paint the trees with your blood."

"My God!" Melinda Strickland said, looking to Broxton-Howard with alarm so her reaction would be noted.

"That goes for you, too," Joe said, shooting his eyes to Melinda Strickland. "You wanted a war and now you're going to get your wish."

"Joe, goddammit, go home," Hersig hissed into his ear. "Go home before Munker swears out a warrant on you for that threat that *we all heard.*"

The silence in the room was conspicuous.

Joe let himself be led toward the door by Robey Hersig, who stepped outside with him.

"You were way out of line in there," Hersig said, shaking his head. "What are you doing, Joe?"

Joe set his jaw to argue, but the red shroud of rage began to pull back from his eyes. "Maybe I don't know what I'm doing, Robey."

"Go home. Keep out of this."

"April is up there."

"So is Spud Cargill."

"I don't know that. I honestly don't believe that. It doesn't make sense."

"Joe . . ."

"We're taking McLanahan's word that he *might* have seen a guy who *might* have been Cargill driving past him yesterday afternoon. Based on that, all hell is breaking loose, to use your phrase."

"I know, I know," Hersig said wearily.

"Are we just going to let it happen?" Joe asked.

Hersig started to speak, then stopped. "Maybe it won't be so bad, Joe. That isn't exactly the cream of all mankind up there."

Joe's eyes flared. "Get the hell away from me, Robey."

Joe turned and stomped across the snow, knowing that if he didn't leave now, things were going to get much worse very quickly.

JOE CLEARED SADDLESTRING toward the mountains en route to . . . *where*? He didn't know. He felt as if he were under water. His thoughts and movements seemed sluggish. They were someone else's thoughts.

He pulled over. Huge white flakes lit on his windshield, turning instantly into beaded stars against the glass. It was snowing hard. He opened his window and stuck his head out. The snow descended on his face. It felt cool against his skin.

He stared wide-eyed into the sky. Snowflakes swirled as far as he could see. A few stung his eyes. He tried not to blink.

26

THE SNOW WAS NOW FALLING AT AN OVERWHELMING volume. As Joe drove toward Saddlestring with his defroster and windshield wipers on high, he fought a rising sense of desperation. The fresh snow crunched beneath his tires, and the tracks in the snow he had made on the way out of town were already filled in and covered over. Deer, passing shadows in the snowfall, silently climbed from the plains and draws into the timber of the foothills. Geese on the river found overhangs and brush. The looming, wide shoulders of the Bighorn Mountains that provided the constant, dependable horizon had vanished behind a curtain of deathly white. If it weren't for the dark metal delineator posts that bordered the two-lane highway, he would not have been able to see where the road was located.

He tried to think, tried to put things into perspective, tried to fight the bile that was rising in his throat. He had cooled down enough to feel ashamed of what he'd said at the Forest Service office. He had lost it, which was unusual for him. The weakness he had showed to Strickland

and Munker, and things he had said could come back to
haunt him. Strickland, Munker, or even Robey could file
a complaint with his supervisors. They could have him
arrested. Jeannie Keeley could use the outburst against
him when Joe tried to make the case that April would be
better off with him and Marybeth.

Joe cursed, and thumped the dashboard with the heel
of his hand.

THINK. Calm down and think.

Strickland and Munker were mounting an assault on
the Sovereign Citizen compound because Spud Cargill
was allegedly there. The judge had signed a search warrant based on probable cause. Joe couldn't imagine a scenario where Wade Brockius and the other Sovereigns
simply stood aside while the agents ransacked their "sovereign nation." The Sovereigns would defend their compound and from there, it would likely get out of control.

Spud Cargill was the key. If Joe could find him, arrest
him, or somehow prove that he wasn't in the compound—
the assault could be delayed until Munker found another excuse. By then, possibly, enough time could pass
to once again defuse the situation. Maybe by then the
storm would let up. Exposing the situation to the light
of day, with the possible help and/or interference of the
media, could delay or spoil Munker's immediate plans.
Maybe the Sovereigns would pack up and move on, taking their problems and their decades of miserable, irra-
tional, and violent emotional baggage with them. Then
they would be someone else's problem. The idea ap-
pealed to Joe, although he suffered a pang of guilt as
well.

But Spud Cargill was the key. The only way to keep
April out of danger, to delay things long enough for the
courts to work, was to find Spud Cargill.

To do this, Joe would need help.

He drove through one of the three red lights in Saddlestring without seeing it.

THE PARKING LOT AT THE Twelve Sleep County Municipal Library was empty except for four cars already topped with eight inches of snow. Marybeth's van was one of them.

Joe pulled beside it and jumped out. He left his pickup running.

The library was locked, and a hand-lettered sign had been taped to the double doors saying that they had closed for the day due to the weather. Joe pressed his face to the glass and knocked loudly on the door. The lights inside had already been dimmed. A woman inside, one of Marybeth's co-workers, saw him and squinted. She started to shoo him away when Marybeth joined her, smiled, and approached the door with a set of keys.

"The librarian is sending everyone home," Marybeth said, letting him in. "They've released the kids from school, and I guess the roads and airport are already closed."

Joe entered after shaking snow from his coat and hat. He nodded hello to the other employees, who were gathering their coats and gloves to go home.

"Marybeth, we need to talk."

Her face showed instant concern. There was a sadness in her eyes that quickly emerged. It was a sadness that had not been very far from the surface since April had been taken.

Aware that the other library employees were hovering, Marybeth led Joe to a small, dark conference room. She told the others to go ahead and leave, and that she would lock up.

When she closed the door, he told her what had happened at the meeting.

"You said *that*? Joe!"

"I know," he said. "But I could smell blood in that room, Marybeth. It got to me."

Marybeth sighed and leaned back against a table, studying him, waiting for what would come next. He was taken by her profound sadness. It hurt him that she felt this way. Which meant he had to do something about it. It was his duty to fix it.

"I'm here for your permission," he said.

"For what?"

"To do what I think best."

"What? You don't need my permission for that."

Joe shook his head. "I've been giving this a lot of thought. For the past month, it's been eating at me."

She didn't understand.

"Marybeth, I've been a bad husband and father. I haven't protected April, or you, or our family. I've let lawyers do it. I've asked Robey about it, hoping he would do something. I've gone the easy, legal route."

"But Joe . . ."

"Nobody cares for April like we do. The judge doesn't care, the lawyers don't care. To them, it's just more paperwork, another case. Robey tries to care, but he's busy. Now there are things happening where lawyers aren't going to help us."

Joe stepped forward and gently grasped Marybeth by her shoulders. "I'm not sure I can do any good, honey. But I can try."

Marybeth was silent for a moment. Then she spoke gently. "You haven't been a bad father or husband, Joe."

He was pleased that she said it, but not sure he agreed with her. "The most important thing is that April is safe," he said. "It doesn't matter if she's with us or that awful woman. Those things can be sorted out later. For now, we need to see that she's safe."

Marybeth's eyes softened. "I agree," she whispered.

"We can't rely on the sheriff or the lawyers for this. We can't rely on *anybody*."

"What are you going to do?"

"I'm not sure yet," he confessed. "But I know that the reason Melinda Strickland and her stormtroopers are going to confront the Sovereigns is because they think Spud Cargill is up there. If I can get to him first, or prove he isn't really up there, there's no reason for them to do it."

"I trust you," she said. "I trust you more than anyone I've ever known. Do what you have to do."

"Are you sure? I'm not sure that I trust myself."

"Go, Joe."

He kissed her, and they left the library together. While she started her car, he brushed the snow off her windshield and made sure she had traction to pull away. He told her to keep her cell phone on and call him if she had any trouble getting home.

As she started to leave the parking lot, he ran through the snow to stop her. She rolled the window down. He reached in and squeezed her hand.

"Marybeth . . ." He had trouble finding the words.

"Say it, Joe."

"Marybeth, I can't promise I can save her."

MARYBETH LEFT THE PARKING LOT and turned onto the unplowed street, and Joe watched until the snowfall absorbed her taillights.

He could never remember Saddlestring being as quiet as it was now. The only thing he could hear was the low burbling of the exhaust pipe of his pickup.

Residents had retreated to their houses and woodstoves. Stores, schools, and offices had closed. The snow absorbed all sound, and stilled all motion. There was no traffic.

Joe fought back a horrendous feeling of inevitable doom.

Then he climbed into his pickup and roared out of the parking lot.

27

THINK.

Joe had no clear idea where he should go or how he should proceed. He drove through Saddlestring on streets that were becoming more impassable by the minute. It was the kind of once-every-fifty-years storm where sending the plows out was pointless until it was over.

He drove by Bighorn Roofing to confirm that it was dark and locked. The same with Spud Cargill's home. He knew he was treading old ground.

He thought of interviewing Mrs. Gardiner again, just to see if she could provide anything new, but dismissed the idea as useless. He wasn't sure she was still in town and not en route to Nebraska.

Rope Latham might know something, he thought. Latham might reveal where his friend was likely to run. No doubt Barnum and Munker had asked Rope about his partner, but if he had said anything to them, it hadn't resulted in anything. Now Latham was in jail, in the county building, guarded by sheriff's deputies. Barnum's crew might not let Joe in to see him, or might delay a meeting throughout the day. Joe didn't think he had the time to waste right now. Also, Rope Latham wouldn't exactly have special feelings for the man who had arrested him, and if he was going to talk, it probably wasn't going to be to him.

Using his cell phone, Joe made sure Marybeth had made it home. She was there, but said the county had closed the road in back of her. And her van was stuck in the driveway.

On a chance, he tried another number.

"County attorney's office."

"Robey? You're there."

"Ah, Joe . . ." he said it in a way that suggested he wished it was just about anybody else who was calling him.

"Robey, you need to help me."

Silence.

"Robey?"

"I shouldn't even be talking to you, Joe, after what you said this morning. How you treated me. I'll just assume that you're a little off your rocker right now. Can I assume that?"

Joe nodded, even though Hersig couldn't see it. "I guess you can assume that. I guess I get that way when I see a bloodbath coming."

"Oh, for Christ's sake, Joe . . ."

"Robey."

"What?"

"Are Strickland and Munker still gathering the troops? Considering the weather, I mean?"

"You are to stay away from that meeting, Joe. You're likely to be arrested if you even show up."

"So that's a yes."

"YES!"

Joe slowed to a stop in the middle of the street. There

was no traffic to impede. "How are they going to get up the mountain? I just talked with Marybeth, and she said Bighorn Road is already closed."

"I don't know all the details, Joe. This isn't exactly my department. But I heard Barnum put in a request for those Sno-Cats again. And the Sheriff's Department has snowmobiles of their own. My understanding is that they'll roll as soon as they can get enough vehicles."

THINK.

The first place Joe had ever noticed Rope Latham and Spud Cargill together was during the Christmas Eve service at the First Alpine Church of Saddlestring. He'd been concerned with the presence of the Sovereigns at the time, and hadn't given it much consideration until now.

Two single men, business partners, had gone to church together. That was a bit unusual in itself. And although he didn't know either man well, he couldn't say that the roofers showed any outward signs of deep religiosity. One never knew for sure about such things, he thought, but neither seemed to approach business or life in a very God-fearing way. Unprovoked murder and assault for unpaid bills weren't exactly Christian acts.

But the First Alpine Church was more than just another denomination. It was "unconventional." Joe had heard that the weekly sermons by the Reverend B. J. Cobb were equal parts Gospel and God Damn the Government. It was the latter part, he surmised, that had drawn Spud Cargill.

Joe flipped a U-turn in the middle of the empty street and felt the back end of the truck fishtail in the snow. When it gripped, he gunned the truck eastward toward the edge of town.

*   *   *

ONE OF THE ADVANTAGES OF the storm, Joe thought, was that it drove everyone home and indoors. In normal circumstances, a search for the Reverend B. J. Cobb would have consisted of visiting various work sites where his contract welding unit might be set up. But today, Cobb would likely be home like everybody else. Home was a double-wide trailer behind the church.

Joe parked in front of the church and waded through the snow toward the double-wide. There were no fresh tracks of any kind around either structure. A snowmobile had been driven out from the garage and parked near the road, a wise precaution if an emergency came up.

He banged on the metal door and waited.

B. J. Cobb opened it wearing a ratty terrycloth bathrobe over a sweatshirt and stained white painter's pants. He was unshaven. The odor of simmering chili wafted out of the door.

"Hello, sir," Cobb said, not unfriendly.

Joe nodded and said he didn't mean to bother him at home. "Can I ask you some questions?"

Cobb smiled and looked up over Joe's head at the falling snow. "It seems like today you should be home with your family, waiting this out, instead of standing in it."

"If you let me in, I wouldn't be standing in it," Joe said.

Cobb looked down. He didn't invite Joe inside, which annoyed Joe slightly.

"What can I help you with?"

"Spud Cargill. He was a member of your church. I saw him there Christmas Eve."

Cobb nodded, and pulled his bathrobe together across his chest.

"B. J., would you please close that door?" Mrs. Eunice Cobb implored from somewhere inside the trailer. "You're letting all the heat out!"

"The game warden is here," Cobb called over his shoulder. "He's got questions about Spud."

That silenced Mrs. Cobb, and she did not reply. Cobb turned back.

"Yes, Spud was a member of the congregation. He faithfully attended church about two times a year, three in good years. He wasn't exactly a deacon in our church. You know, Mr. Pickett, I already answered these questions for the sheriff."

Joe nodded. "Did the sheriff ask you if you knew where Spud might hide out?"

"Of course he did."

"And your answer was . . ."

"My answer was that it was none of his damned business."

Joe grunted and looked away. *What a storm,* he thought.

"You know that Spud murdered a man."

Cobb chuckled. "You mean Elmer Fedd?"

"Lamar Gardiner," Joe corrected, his voice flat.

"So I've heard," Cobb said, while finding the ties to his robe and making a loose knot. "Now, Mr. Pickett, I don't mean to be obtuse. I admire your tenacity, and I've heard you are an honest man. That's rare. But I have strong feelings about state interference in people's lives. It's not my *obligation* to help out the state. It's the state's obligation to provide services for me, the taxpayer and citizen. I object to the kind of power the federal agencies wield here."

"Still doesn't mean Lamar Gardiner should have been murdered," Joe said.

Cobb considered that. "You're probably right."

"And you know what?" Joe asked, shaking the snow

off his coat. He raised his head and fixed his eyes on
Cobb's. "I'm not really here to debate this question with
you, Mr. Cobb. I don't really care all that much about
Spud Cargill, either, if you want to know the truth. I'm
here because I've got a little girl up there in that compound who might get hurt if the FBI and the Forest Service people have their way and raid it because *they* think
he's there. So if I can find out where Spud is—or isn't—I
might be able to help my little girl."

Cobb's expression changed. There was now a hint of
confusion, as if he were weighing a dilemma. He searched
Joe's face, then returned to his eyes.

"I didn't know that," Cobb said softly.

"Don't get me wrong," Joe said. "We don't think the
same way, you and me. But in this case, I want to stop
the Feds as much as you do. Just for a different reason."

Cobb seemed to be considering something.

"Honey . . ." Mrs. Cobb said softly from inside. "I'm
sorry, but I'm *freezing.*"

Cobb started to speak, then stopped. Then he set his
mouth hard and rubbed his buzz-cut hair with the palm
of his hand.

"Is he up there, Mr. Cobb?" Joe asked.

Cobb stepped back and felt for the handle of the door.
Is he going to shut it in my face? Joe wondered.

"You are a man of God," Joe said. "Convince Spud to
turn himself in."

"I am and he won't."

Joe tried to hide his elation. This meant that Cobb
was—or had been—in contact with Spud Cargill. It also
meant that Cobb could be arrested for assisting a fugitive. Both men knew that.

"It's called sanctuary, Mr. Pickett," Cobb said. "Spud
believes in it. So do I. And I can't help you any further."

"So he's here," Joe said softly.

Cobb shook his head. "He was here. But he's not any-more."

Before Cobb closed the door and Joe heard a lock snap shut, Cobb raised his eyes and looked over Joe's shoulder in the direction of the mountains.

THE ROAD TO NATE ROMANOWSKI'S cabin was almost impenetrable, even though Joe had put chains on his tires before trying it. Four times, he got stuck. What should have taken an hour had taken three. It was mid-afternoon, although he couldn't tell that by the sun or the sky. It was just as dark, and the snow was coming down just as hard, as it had been all day.

Joe had tried to call ahead but got a message that Nate's phone was out of service. He remembered be-latedly that the telephone had been damaged during the search of the cabin, that pieces of it had been scattered across the kitchen counter. He cursed while he dug un-der the front axle with a shovel to clear the packed snow that had once again stopped him. He hated to waste the time it took to dig himself out. Every hour that went by was an hour closer to the assembling of Munker and Strickland's assault team in town.

Joe's plan, formed as he left Cobb's trailer, was to ask Nate if he would go up to the compound with him. Joe had learned through experience that backup in volatile situations was essential. Not having backup at Savage Run had nearly killed him, and it had resulted in the deaths of others. He had vowed never to approach a pre-dicament like that again without help. And Nate and his big gun might provide help.

Finally, Joe was able to rock the pickup and break through the snowbank and over the rise to the river.

Nate's cabin was dark and socked in, and his Jeep was

gone. The complete absence of tracks suggested that Nate had been gone for at least a day.

Joe cursed again and thumped the truck seat with his hand. Pulling the evidence notebook from his pocket, he wrote out a note to Nate and attached it to the front door with a rusty penknife he found in his glove box. He also pinned a business card with his cell and home telephone numbers on it.

Nate:
　You offered help. I need it now.
Joe Pickett

"Thanks for everything, Nate," he growled, turning the pickup around. He drove back out in his own tracks.

28

FOR SHERIDAN PICKETT, THERE WAS USUALLY NOTHING more invigorating, or liberating, than having school let out because of snow. The announcement over the intercom had been received with unabashed cheers and whistles, and was followed by a mad scramble of books and uneaten lunches being thrown into backpacks.

Sheridan couldn't share in the enthusiasm, though. A snow day meant nothing with her sister April gone.

Outside, the small fleet of buses had been lined up on the street, their engines idling, great clouds of exhaust rising up to meet the heavy snow.

Now she was home, safe and warm, curled up on the couch in her sweats reading an introductory book about falconry that had appeared in their mailbox the day before in an envelope addressed to her. Paper-clipped to the book jacket was a note written on the back of a beer coaster with foreign printing on it.

> *Sheridan:*
> *People don't choose the art of falconry like they choose a sport or a hobby. Falconry chooses them. After*

*meeting you, I think you might be chosen. Please read
this book carefully, and if you're still interested I can
teach you.*
Nate Romanowski

She raised the coaster to her nose for the fourth time
that afternoon and sniffed it. It still smelled faintly of
beer. She tried to imagine where he'd gotten it. The
printing on the coaster was in English and Arabic.

She opened the battered old book and looked at the
photo plates of falcons, hawks, and eagles. The birds cap-
tivated her.

When the telephone rang, Missy appeared from the
hallway and took it off the hook as Sheridan was reaching
for it. Sheridan watched her grandmother with annoyance.

Missy handed the telephone toward Sheridan. "It's
some little girl for you."

As Sheridan took the receiver, Missy bent down near
her. "I'm expecting a call from Bud Longbrake, so don't
be long."

Sheridan made a face and turned away from Missy.

"Sherry?"

Sheridan felt a jolt shoot through her body. She immediately recognized the tiny, distant voice, where Missy
had not.

"April?"

"Hi."

"I don't know what to say!" Sheridan looked around
the room. She remembered her mother had said something about going outside to take care of their horses.
Lucy was in their room, putting on makeup in front of a
mirror just for fun.

"How are you guys doing?" April asked. "I miss you
guys."

"We all miss you, too. Where are you?"

"Up here. Up here in the snow. It's really cold."

"Then come home!" Sheridan laughed nervously.

April sighed. "I wish I could." There was a beat of silence, and Sheridan could hear static growing. It was a poor connection.

"I'm not supposed to use the phone. My mom will really get mad if she finds out I'm talking to you."

"Where is she?"

"Oh, everybody is at a meeting. Mom, Clem . . ."

"Who's Clem?"

"A guy who lives with us. I don't like him much, but he's the only person who knows how to keep the heater running."

Sheridan noticed that April's Southern accent was coming back. Sheridan had forgotten that April had had it when she first moved in with them.

"I miss you guys a lot." She sounded pathetic.

"April, are you coming home?"

April sighed. "I really do want to. I cry a lot. I like my mom and all, but . . ."

"What's it like there?" Sheridan asked. She was in the kitchen now, parting the curtains. The snow was coming down so hard that the corral and shelter were smudges in the snow. She couldn't see her mother.

"It's cold up here. Really cold. I just stay inside all day. Last night, there were awful sounds outside that kept everybody awake. Clem said it was rabbits being skinned alive."

"You're kidding!"

"No. How's Lucy?"

Sheridan tried to picture April as she talked. She pictured her in a corner, wearing rags. For some reason, Sheridan couldn't see April's face, just her tangled blonde hair. The image of April without a face made Sheridan shiver.

"Lucy's fine. Goofy as always. She's been dressing up with Grandmother Missy and going to town. Right now she's in our room putting on makeup."

April laughed a little. "She's our little girlie-girl, isn't she?"

Sheridan felt tears welling in her eyes. April seemed so close, but she wasn't.

"Do you want me to go get her? Do you want to talk to her?"

Over the phone, Sheridan heard the sounds of adults talking in the background. Their voices were muffled.

"Uh-oh, somebody's coming," April said frantically, her voice climbing in register. " 'Bye, Sherry. Tell Lucy I miss her. TellMomandDadIlovethem . . ."

The phone disconnected, and Sheridan stood there, tears rolling down her cheeks.

"Good-bye, April," she said to the dead telephone.

SHERIDAN HEARD THE HIGH WHINING sound of a snow-mobile outside. She ran across the living room and saw out the window that her dad was home. His pickup was in the driveway, and he was driving his snow machine from the garage up a ramp into the bed of the truck.

Without putting on her coat or boots, she stepped outside on the front porch in the deep snow. Even though she was wearing only socks, she couldn't feel the cold.

Her dad saw her and killed the engine of the machine. He stood up in the back of his truck, looking at her like she was crazy.

"You need to get inside and close the door, Sheridan," he said. "What's going on?"

"Dad, I just talked with April."

"You *what*?"

"You've got to save her, Dad. You've *got* to."

29

JOE PICKETT MOVED SILENTLY THROUGH THE TREES IN the dark. Although the moon was obscured by the storm clouds, there was enough ambient light that the virgin snow appeared a dark blue. The trunks of trees rose from it and the branches melded into the night sky. The snow had decreased in its fury, although it had not stopped. It sifted dust-like through the branches, so powdery that it sometimes hung suspended in the air. The temperature had dropped into the low teens, cold enough to evince an occasional pop or moan from freezing timber.

He was on Battle Mountain, approaching the Sovereign Citizen compound on foot from the north. He was not yet close enough to see lights or hear voices. He was there to arrest Spud or save April, or both. He was not thinking clearly.

Joe had been prevented from reaching the compound via Bighorn Road by two things. The first was the snow, which had literally rendered the road impassable. The second was the sheriff's Blazer, belonging to Deputy Mc-Lanahan, parked at the beginning of the summit. They had relocated the roadblocks farther down the mountain, but they were roadblocks nevertheless. Joe wasn't sure he could talk his way through it, or that he even wanted to try. It was obvious that the assault would be at least a day away, given the conditions. Even Munker wouldn't be hot-blooded enough to confront the camp in the dark, Joe reasoned. The Sno-Cats they would use in the morning had been assembled, and were parked shoulder to shoulder near the Blazer. Joe had seen them through his binoculars, and had seen both Munker and Portenson checking out the Sno-Cats from the backs of borrowed Forest Service snowmobiles. Joe had driven away, hoping he hadn't been seen, and had taken the other road.

As it darkened, Joe had driven as far as he could up Timberline Road until the snow got so deep that he almost got stuck again. Rather than try to go any farther with the night coming on, he pulled out the ramps and backed his snowmobile out of the pickup. Then he mounted the snowmobile and roared into the black timber. He cut through the forest rather than go around it, through a huge, dark, wooded wilderness that had been declared officially closed by Lamar Gardiner's Forest Service. The sledding had been a challenge. The snow was untracked, and so fresh and deep that at times the machine bogged down in it, the rear tracks digging down into the snow rather than hurling him over the top of it. The snout of the machine would raise and point to the sky as the snowmobile foundered in the powder. When this happened, Joe's adrenaline rushed through him and he threw his weight forward or back with controlled violence, levering himself free and allowing the track to grip and hurl him forward. He knew that if he got stuck in snow this deep, in temperatures this low, he might never get out alive. No one knew where he was, and the Sovereigns certainly weren't expecting him.

If I get stuck, Joe said to himself in a mantra, *I die.*

And he could not slow down, because when he did, sometimes involuntarily as a result of trying to pick his route through dark timber with the single headlight, he could feel the machine start to sink and settle into the four-foot-thick powder. The only way to keep moving and not get stuck was to keep the machine hurtling forward over the top. So he had run the engine much faster than he was comfortable with, keeping the headlight pointing south, sometimes clipping trees so closely that he was showered with bark and snow from their branches.

Miraculously, he had made it through the timber and out the other side. The machine's engine was loud, however, and he didn't want the Sovereigns to hear him coming, so he had shut it down near the top of the mountain beneath a granite outcropping that had shielded the ground from much of the snowfall. Before leaving it, he had filled the tank with gasoline from a can he'd strapped on the back of the machine earlier. Buckling on oval snowshoes, he had left the snowmobile and its loud engine and worked his way south in silence.

A THIN SHEEN OF SWEAT served as the first layer between his skin and his polypropylene underwear. Walking on snowshoes in deep powder snow was hard work. He tried to control his temperature by zipping and unzipping his parka as he walked. The cold wasn't a problem as long as he was moving but once he stopped, it might be.

He felt more than saw a dark presence in front of him in the trees, and he froze. He thought immediately about his weapon, which was secured and zipped up under his parka. It would be hard to get at. His eyes strained in the quarter-light and he saw movement and heard a footfall. His scalp crawled under his hat. Then the huge cow moose turned broadside across his field of vision, daintily high-stepping through the snow with her long legs that were perfect for these conditions.

He exhaled, and unclenched. He hadn't even realized he was holding his breath.

HIS INTENTION WAS TO GET close enough to the compound to discern whether or not Spud Cargill was there. He even considered knocking on Wade Brockius's trailer door and asking outright. He struggled with what he should and shouldn't tell the Sovereigns about the impending raid, or if he should tell them anything at all. Joe knew that if he tipped the Sovereigns off about the raid and Cargill escaped, Munker would undoubtedly see to it that Joe went to prison. *Maybe I would deserve to,* Joe thought.

Damn that Nate Romanowski, he cursed. *THIS is the kind of thing I could have used some help with!*

He thought about the telephone call Sheridan had received from April. It had broken his heart to see Sheridan's face. For his daughter to tell him "You've got to save her, Dad," tore him up inside. Sheridan, like Marybeth, trusted him completely. But Marybeth was more realistic about her expectations. Sheridan was his daughter, and they had a special bond. She was confident that he could save April. After all, he was her *dad.* He winced, and sighed. He had always tried to live up to her expectations but this time, he wasn't sure he could.

Ahead of him there was a low muffled voice, and Joe sunk to his haunches in the deep snow. He was suddenly alert. He stayed still until his heart slowed and his breath evened out from the exertion. As gently as he could, he eased the zipper of his parka down and reached into his jacket for his service-issue .40 Beretta, unsnapped it from his holster, and withdrew it. Using his clothing to mute the sounds, he jacked a cartridge into the chamber and eased the hammer back down. He slipped the Beretta into his front parka pocket, where it would be easier to get at than in the holster under his coat, and stood back up. He stuffed his mittens into his other pocket, leaving only his thin liner gloves on his hands. If the Sovereigns knew what a poor pistol shot he was, he thought wryly, they would know they had nothing at all to worry about.

His breath billowed as he approached the compound. He could now make out squares of yellow light from windows through the trees. The light wasn't bright, though, like electric lights would be. *They must be using lanterns and propane,* he thought. Then he remembered that Munker had cut off their electricity.

As he got closer to the compound, he could hear the hiss of propane from two dozen metal tanks. He found a thick spruce with a jutting V-shaped branch that he could hide behind near the compound. Normally, the branch would have been too high for Joe to see over. But with the three feet of snow as a step stool, he rested his chest against the trunk and peered through the notch.

Joe couldn't see anyone outside their trailers and RVs. He noted the series of tramped-down paths that connected the units through the snow, and led to other facilities throughout the camp. He estimated that the paths were at least three feet in depth, although they could be deeper. A courtyard of sorts in the center of the compound where propane tanks were located had been crudely plowed. Only after studying the units within the camp for a while did Joe realize that there was at least one snowmobile, and sometimes two, parked near the entrance of each dwelling. Many of the snowmobiles were protected (or hidden) with blankets or tarps, which in turn were covered with at least a foot of fresh snowfall.

So the Sovereigns could get away if they had to, he thought, *even in these conditions. Interesting.*

The metallic sound of a trailer door being opened carried across the camp. He heard it shut, then heard the crunch of snow beneath boots. The figure of a man moved across the squares of light, and he could see the profile of someone with a beard and broken nose. It wasn't Spud Cargill. The man walked through the center of camp toward a set of outdoor Forest Service toilets. After a few minutes, the man came back outside and returned to his trailer.

Okay, Joe thought. *That's where everybody needs to go at some point tonight.*

TWO HOURS WENT BY AND the cold settled in. Despite his heavy Sorel pac boots and two pairs of socks, his feet were starting to get cold. He worked his toes to keep the circulation going.

Twelve people, most of them men, had exited trailers or campers and trudged to the toilets. In the stillness, he heard them cough, hack, and make disgusting sounds in the toilets. None of them was Spud Cargill. None of them was Wade Brockius. None of them was April.

THEN SHE WAS THERE. JOE had almost fallen asleep despite the cold and his awkward stance. But when he saw the small woman, Jeannie Keeley, emerge from a trailer with a small blonde girl, he knew it was April.

He watched and listened. Their footfalls weren't as percussive in the frozen snow as the men's had been. When they passed the nearest window, he ignored Jeannie and saw April's frail profile against the light. The glimpse didn't reveal much. He couldn't have seen bruises, if they were there, or pain on her face. She just seemed vacant, glassy-eyed. Her snowboots shuffled. Jeannie led her by the hand to the outdoor toilet.

April went inside and shut the door. Jeannie stood outside and waited, smoking a cigarette.

When April was through, Jeannie took her hand and they walked back together. April raised her face, which caught some light from a window, and said something to Jeannie. Jeannie laughed, and bent her head down to April and said something back, which caused April to laugh. The girl had a husky laugh, a belly laugh that Joe loved to hear. But the sound of it now filled him with violently mixed emotions.

They entered the trailer and shut the door, and April was gone.

Joe blinked.

If he wouldn't have known who they were, or what the circumstances were, he would have described the scene as heartwarming. The mother, Jeannie, obviously cared enough about the welfare of her daughter to walk her to and from the outhouse. They held hands, and April reached up for Jeannie's hand when she exited. The joke, whatever it was, was appreciated by her mother. And her mother bent down to share something that made both of them giggle.

Joe wasn't sure this is what he had wanted to see. He had envisioned a scenario where April, in tears, was dragged through the camp. If he'd seen that, he could also see himself running into the camp, throwing Jeannie aside, and rescuing April. He would carry her through the snow to the snowmobile and roar down the mountain. But that hadn't happened. Not at all.

He couldn't believe that April was in a better place.

That was inconceivable. But unless he literally stormed into the trailer and took her—kidnapped her—there was little he could do.

He was freezing, and conflicted. There was nothing he could do here, and Joe shook snow from his parka and prepared to go back to his snowmobile.

WHEN "DANKE SCHOEN" STARTED UP, Joe turned in surprise and dropped a glove in the snow. He had not been four feet from the tree he had been hiding in when the song blasted through the night and scared him. He stood and listened, stunned. Where was it coming from? Then he remembered the speakers he had seen when he last visited the compound.

From inside trailers, he heard shouted curses. Someone threw something heavy into a wall. If the intention of the song was to drive the Sovereigns crazy, Joe thought, it appeared to be working.

A door flew open and a man Joe didn't recognize stood framed in the light of his propane lamp. He swung an automatic rifle up across his body and leaned into it. A furious burst of fire lit up the night. Although the man was shooting at the speakers—and hitting them, judging by the sharp pings of metal—and not toward Joe, Joe sunk to his haunches and dug for his Beretta.

Another burst shredded the speakers with holes, but did little to stop the sound.

The song ended and, after a brief pause, started up again. Only this time it was louder.

Joe heard a sudden rustle close behind him, but he was too slow, and too cold, to react. He felt a heavy blow above his ear that sent him sprawling clumsily forward, snow filling his nose and mouth.

*   *   *

HE NEVER ACTUALLY LOST CONSCIOUSNESS, but the orange flashes that burst across his eyes and the thundering pulses of pain in his head prevented him from fighting back as he was dragged from his place in the trees into the compound.

Two men wearing oversized white fatigues and carrying scoped SKS rifles wrapped in white tape pulled him by his arms. Snow and ice jammed into his collar and into the top of his pants. One of them had taken his pistol.

Sliding easier now over the packed snow of the compound, Joe tried to twist away. They immediately let go of him, and kicked him in the ribs with their heavy winter boots.

The first kick was true, knocking the air out of him and leaving him writhing in the snow. He was suprisingly lucid, he realized. He knew what was going on around him as if he were watching it from somewhere else—he just couldn't do much about it. It wouldn't be that much of a surprise to him if someone pressed the cold muzzle of a shotgun to his neck and fired. Oddly, he didn't fear it. That just seemed like part of the deal.

"Stop, I think I know him." It was Wade Brockius. His voice was unmistakable.

Joe heard the crunching of snow from across the compound.

One of the men kicked him again, although not as effectively this time. Joe partially blocked it, and absorbed most of the blow in his forearms. "Asshole," the man spat.

Joe rolled and blinked as Brockius shined a flashlight in his eyes.

"Yeah, I know him. He's that game warden."

"We caught him at the edge of camp, bobbing and weaving when Clem shot at that speaker."

Joe suddenly realized that the music was still playing, and even louder. Still "Danke Schoen." But here was a hideous screaming along with it.

Joe started to sit up, but the pain in his head roared back and he sank down onto an elbow, waiting for his sudden nausea to recede. He kept his free arm up, wary of more kicks. Brockius knelt and wrapped a large arm around Joe and helped him to sit upright, to Joe's relief. Joe's mouth was full of hot blood and melting snow. He spit a dark stream out between his knees.

"Don't go anywhere quite yet, boys," Brockius said to the two men.

"Do you have to listen to that every night?" Joe asked, testing his voice. It sounded shaky.

"Since last night," Brockius said. "I think we're going to be serenaded by Wayne Newton every night now."

"Clem shot the hell out of those speakers," one of the men in white said. "But it didn't do any good."

"We'll cut the fucking wires," the other said.

Brockius nodded absently, but his eyes stayed on Joe.

"Mind if I come in?" Joe asked. "It's pretty cold out here."

Brockius considered it, then shook his head.

"You're the second person today who wouldn't invite me in," Joe said absently. "I don't know what to think about that."

Brockius showed a slight smile. "There are some things in my trailer I really don't want anyone to see."

Joe thought: *weapons*. The ATF had conducted raids for less. Either that, or Brockius's fax machine was loaded to broadcast more subpoenas and liens. Or both.

"What in the hell are you doing here?" Brockius asked.

Joe thought carefully before he spoke. The two men in white continued to crowd him. They blocked out the light where he sat.

"I wanted to see for myself if April was here and in good health."

"She is. I already told you that."

Joe looked up. "And I wanted to see if Spud Cargill was up here."

Brockius cursed, and shook his head. "Why does everybody think that man is up here, goddammit!"

"Because there was a report that he was," Joe said. "And because if he is up here, there will be . . . trouble."

"Trouble we can handle," one of the men in white said.

The other one chuckled at that.

"Look," Brockius said, his voice commanding as he leaned close to Joe. Joe could smell onions on his breath. "I'm going to tell you the truth, because I don't ever want you up here again. You could have gotten yourself killed real easily."

"That's right," the more obnoxious of the two men in white agreed. Again, the other chuckled.

"Spud. Cargill. Is. Not. Here."

Joe studied Brockius's face, looking into his soulful eyes.

"That man tried to join us last night. He *did* come here. I spoke with him, and I turned him away."

"Why didn't you tell the Feds that?"

Brockius rolled his eyes and roared, "I DID TELL THEM HE WASN'T HERE."

"They just didn't believe you," Joe said softly.

"How unlike them," Brockius spat.

"Where did Spud go when you told him to leave?"

Brockius shrugged. "To wherever he came from, I guess."

Joe felt a wave of exhaustion wash over him. He was no closer to finding Spud now than he had been when he started. The pain in his head had reduced to a steady thump in his right temple. Joe reached up with a bare hand and cleaned packed snow out of his ear.

"Did you hear me?" Brockius asked.

"Yes. And I believe you," Joe said.

"Jackbooted thugs," Obnoxious White growled. "People that hide behind their regulations and their badges while they're skinning a rabbit on a tape."

Yes, Joe realized. That was the horrible squealing sound he heard with "Danke Schoen."

There was a long minute where no one spoke. The screaming of the rabbit was like icy metal rubbing along Joe's spine. Finally, it stopped.

"It's going to start up again," Obnoxious White said. "Is it all right with you if I go cut that fucking wire?"

Brockius looked up. "Watch out for booby traps in the trees. I wouldn't put it past them to trip-wire the trees."

Obnoxious White snapped on a flashlight that was taped to the barrel of his SKS rifle and walked away toward the fence and the road.

"Do you mind if I say hello to April?" Joe asked. "I saw her earlier."

"You mean you spied on her."

Joe nodded. "Yes, I did."

"Did she seem happy to you?"

Joe hesitated. "She didn't seem unhappy."

"Then your question is answered. You can go now."

Brockius helped Joe to his feet. His legs felt weak. He had lost one of his snowshoes. While his head still pounded, the pain in his ribs hurt worse. He could feel a stabbing sensation with each deep breath.

"Your man broke my rib, I think."

"You're lucky it wasn't your head."

"He did a pretty good number on my head, too," Joe said, feeling slightly giddy for some reason.

Brockius walked Joe toward the edge of the compound where he had been dragged from. The other man in white stayed for a moment, then handed Joe's pistol to Brockius before going to help Obnoxious White cut the wires. Obviously, the wires hadn't been found yet, because the song started up again.

"Can you get back by yourself?" Brockius asked. "Are you okay to do that?"

"I think so," Joe said, wincing from the rib pain.

"The roads are blocked and guarded. There's no way we could take you down, even if we wanted to. This snow has trapped us here."

"Will you leave when it stops snowing?"

Brockius stopped. Joe looked at him. The man had a kindly face. Joe couldn't help liking him, despite himself.

"I think we might," Brockius said softly. "We had a meeting about that this afternoon. But I can't speak for everyone yet."

"It would be a good idea," Joe said, not wanting to tip off Brockius about Munker. This was as far as he would go.

But if the Sovereigns leave, Joe thought, *April will be with them.*

"My wife and I will still try to get April back," Joe said.

"I don't doubt that for a minute." Brockius smiled.

"My wife is a very determined woman," Joe added.

Brockius nodded, but said nothing, as he shined his flashlight on the snow where Joe had been dragged. He held the beam when it found Joe's missing snowshoe.

While he buckled it on, Joe said that one of the men in white had taken his weapon. "I need that back."

Brockius again shook his head.

"I can't hit anything with it anyway," Joe said, mumbling, and Brockius laughed.

"That was pretty ballsy of you to enter our camp the way you did. I'm impressed as hell. I never would have thought someone would come through the forest like that."

Joe shrugged.

Suddenly, the music stopped. Cheers went up from trailers and campers throughout the compound.

"Thank God for that," Brockius whistled.

Joe stood. Both snowshoes were secure. It seemed immensely quiet now. Snow still sifted through the trees, so fine that it cast halos around the lights.

"I really did think Spud Cargill was here," Joe said. "The Reverend Cobb in town said that he had provided Spud sanctuary. I think he was looking for sanctuary here, too."

Brockius looked puzzled for a moment. "This is not sanctuary."

"But he said . . ."

"A church is a sanctuary. This is not a church. This is a way station on the road to hell."

Instantly, Joe forgot the pain in his head and in his throbbing ribs, and the cold.

"I know where he is now," Joe said, his voice rising. "It's time to end this thing."

A slow, sad smile broke across Wade Brockius's face.

"Then you may need this," Brockius said, handing Joe his weapon back butt first.

Joe nodded his thanks, holstered the pistol, and turned back toward the dark timber he had come from.

30

IT WAS FOUR-THIRTY IN THE MORNING WHEN JOE HAD A
moment of panic and realized he might be lost. He was
in his pickup, working his way down the mountain, fix-
ated on the barely perceptible tracks in the road. He
thought he knew where he was and expected to see the
scattered lights of Saddlestring on the valley floor
through his windshield, but he saw nothing. Had he
somehow taken the wrong road? His sense of direction
was confounded by the snowstorm and the darkness and
the messianic swirl of huge snowflakes in his headlights.
Only when he glanced down at the dash-mounted GPS
unit did he confirm that he was going in the right direction, and he sighed, his short-lived panic subsiding. The
glow of the town lights had been sucked up by the snowfall, leaving only a faint smudge of off-color in a black-
and-white night.

Joe was exhausted, frustrated, and injured. If it weren't
for concentrating and driving precisely in the tracks he'd
made previously when he went up the mountain, he
wouldn't have had a chance of getting back down. He

drove much faster than he was comfortable with, given the conditions and his impaired field of vision, but whenever he slowed he felt the tires digging too deeply into the snowpack. Even while driving fast and staying in his already-cut trail, he had gotten stuck twice. Both times he was high-centered. The first time he dug out, clearing hard-packed snow from beneath the front and back differentials, his head hummed with thoughts of having seen April, the pounding he had taken, and Spud Cargill. The second time, he was so exhausted he could barely lift the shovel out of the bed of the truck, and he seriously considered climbing back in with the engine running and the heater blowing and going to sleep for the rest of the night. But when he considered the rate of snowfall, he calculated that the exhaust pipe would be covered up within a few hours. Carbon monoxide fumes would overwhelm him while he slept, and that would be that. There was something slightly inviting in the thought, but he fought it. He slapped himself awake, wincing when he did it because of his broken rib (he was sure of it now), and he dug himself out once again.

Hours were going by. The assault team would be assembling. But conditions and circumstances kept slowing Joe down. It reminded him of dreams he'd had as a pre-teen on nights when his parents were drunk and fighting and he slept between bursts of angry accusations and crashing glass. In his dreams, he would be running, or swimming, or riding his bike as fast as he could—but he could make no progress. The harder he ran, swam, or pedaled, the closer he seemed to be to the house he was leaving. He would wake up in tears, seized by the sense of futility and frustration. He recalled that frustration now, only this time it was much worse than anything he had ever dreamed.

Joe played the scene with April and Jeannie over and

over again in his mind. If only Jeannie had misbehaved, or if April had tried to resist or run, things could have been different. Now, his only hope was to extend the time it would take to find a resolution, and the only way to do that was to find Spud Cargill and force a cancellation of the raid.

He finally cleared the timber and the deepest snow and broke out into the foothills. The wall of trees receded in his rearview mirror. The sagebrush that carpeted the hills was completely covered with snow, and the lack of trees and brush created a spatial lack of perspective. Joe felt the tires dig down through the snow and grip actual frozen ground for the first time in hours, and he gained a sense of control. Still, though, it was wide-open country, and solid white for as far as he could see. Any wind at all would sweep the deep powder into high ridges and crests and make the going impossible.

In his fatigue, the dark form of the snow-covered Jeep that was stuck in the snow almost didn't register with him. It was only when he pulled alongside it and rolled down his window did he recognize the Jeep, and notice that it was running.

The plastic windows were steamed from the inside, and snow had accumulated on the top where there weren't holes or rips. Steam, looking like smoke from a chimney, rose from the top and dissipated into the cold night air. Joe rolled down the passenger window and leaned across his seat.

"Nate?" he called from his window, but there was no response. After a moment, Joe laid on his horn.

A gloved hand cleared steam from the inside of a plastic window in the Jeep, and was followed by two wide eyes that sleepily settled on Joe.

"Joe!" said a voice from inside the vehicle. "I didn't hear you. I was sleeping."

The door opened and Nate Romanowski grinned. An inch of snow, looking like frosting, crowned his watch cap. He held Joe's note in his big hand, and waved it at him.

"Got your note. I stopped at your house and your wife told me this is where you were. I was able to get this far before I got stuck. So," he said, "do you need help after all?"

"I do."

But Joe wasn't sure what help he needed, exactly, or what Nate's role should be. Whatever he was going to use Nate for, though, it would be better to have him in the truck with him.

"Why don't you get in my truck, then?" Joe called. "I've got all four tires chained up and I'm pointed downhill. I think I can make it to town. We can come back up and dig out your Jeep later."

Nate nodded once, then retrieved a daypack from his Jeep and waded through the thigh-high snow to climb into the cab.

"What in the hell happened to you?" Nate asked, looking Joe over.

"I got pounded on by a couple of the Sovereigns," he said. "I deserved it."

Joe slipped the pickup into gear and rolled forward to a dead stop in the deep snow.

"Uh-oh," Nate growled.

Not responding, Joe shoved the pickup into reverse and gunned the engine, backtracking a few feet. Then he rammed it back into drive and hit the snow again with jarring force. The truck broke through, and Joe kept going.

"I'm not stopping again," Joe said. "For anything."

*   *   *

"JOE, I LEARNED A LOT about Melinda Strickland and Dick Munker in Idaho. None of it is good."

"That's where you went? Idaho?"

"I didn't know you needed me here," Nate said defensively. "You said as much. And yes, Idaho. Seventy percent of the state is federally owned and managed. If there's any place where the locals know about specific federal land managers, it's Idaho. I've got some friends there, and I was curious about Strickland and Munker." He paused for a moment.

"Go on," Joe said. He wanted to hear the story, but he also needed Nate to keep talking to help him stay awake and alert.

"I don't want to scare you, Joe, but the fact is you're going to need all the friends you've got against these two."

Joe grunted. That wasn't very encouraging.

"You want some hot coffee?" Nate asked, digging into his pack.

Joe nodded.

"Melinda Strickland is even worse than I thought," Nate said while he poured the steaming coffee into Joe's travel mug. "The people I talked to down there think she's evil and insane. What they don't know is if she started out evil and went insane, or started out insane so she doesn't realize what she's doing."

Joe gulped the coffee, not caring that it was scalding his tongue. His body ached and his back was stiffening. He wasn't sure how long he'd be able to tolerate the exertion it took him to keep the truck from bucking out of the tracks and off into a snowbank. He knew he should have asked Nate to drive, but it was too late for that; he wasn't going to stop and run the risk of getting stuck.

"Just give me facts, Nate, not analysis," Joe barked. "We don't need psychobabble. We don't have a lot of time, and I'm not sure I've decided how to play this yet."

Nate refilled Joe's cup and fitted it into the holder. As the cab finally began to warm up, he unzipped his parka.

"Melinda Strickland is the daughter of a senator from Oregon. She's a trust-fund kid," Nate said. "Her dad greased the skids for her to enter the federal government after she'd bounced around the Pacific Northwest and through various agencies in Washington, D.C. Apparently, she spent a few years in various institutions as well. Drug and alcohol problems. But the rumor is she's a card-carrying paranoid."

Joe shot a glance at Nate that he hoped reminded him to stick to facts.

"Even though she probably makes a good impression on some people at first, she's a classic loose cannon, not capable of working with people. In a nutshell, she's consistently treated her colleagues and co-workers like pieces of shit, saying things about them, playing one off of the other, and just general nastiness. She was involved in a bunch of lawsuits when she worked for the Department of Agriculture because of things she said and did to people. Her idea of management is to make subordinates cry. Oh, and she's a pathological liar."

Joe glanced over at Nate and could see that under his parka he was wearing his shoulder holster.

"Once she got into the Forest Service, she started bouncing all around the country. She left a mess everywhere she went. She's the type that creates chaos out of order. No one knows what deep-seated problems make her the way she is, but the way the Forest Service handled it is how they generally handle things in the big government agencies."

"Transferring her so she's somebody else's problem?" Joe asked. He knew how the game was played.

"Exactly," Nate said. He spoke in a low, rhythmic cadence and rarely raised his voice. "She was in Oregon,

Montana, New Mexico, Nevada, South Dakota, Idaho twice, and then somewhere in Colorado. You know how it works—we all do. Longtime federal employees—especially if they're middle-aged women and they like to threaten lawsuits and they're daughters of senators—just don't get fired very easily. Her big bosses are political appointees who know that if they can bury the problem for a while, the next administration will have to deal with it. Meanwhile, local communities are subjected to her and her *ways*."

"Specifically?" Joe asked.

"Well, in Nevada she became convinced that a couple of the local ranchers with grazing leases were out to kill her dog. So she had them followed twenty-four hours a day by Forest Service rangers. This was in a town of three hundred people, where there were, like, two places to eat. And everywhere these ranchers went, two uniformed Feds went with them. Finally, one of the ranchers got drunk and forced a shoot-out. Both ranchers went down, and one Fed."

Joe shook his head sadly, and instantly regretted it as a throbbing pain burned into the back of his skull.

"Finally," Nate said, "The Forest Service ran out of places to hide her, and they were going to bring her up on harassment charges—finally hold her accountable for something—because she called a Latino contractor a "fat spic" in front of witnesses. Then her daddy stepped in and they figured out this new job for her. They made it up just for her—a position with a nice title but no staff or budget. It was a perfect place to stick her where she couldn't do any damage. My contacts said that even *that* was a mistake, because when the administration changed, she convinced somebody to shuffle the budget and get her some funding. All of a sudden she's got a travel budget, and in her mind a star was finally born. By the time the agency figured out what she'd done in a vacuum, that Elle what's-her-name had latched onto her to do a profile and their hands were tied. They couldn't get rid of the woman while she was being lionized by a journalist, so they just sort of let it go."

"And now we've got her," Joe said. His eyes burned with lack of sleep, and he felt a heightened sense of tension rising in his chest as they neared Saddlestring.

"They take a woman who *hates* people and put her in charge of a task force to go after rednecks who hate the government," Nate said. "This is what I love about the Feds."

Joe asked Nate to give him a minute and quickly called Marybeth on his cell phone. When she picked up, she sounded as if she had been up all night.

"I'm off the mountain and I've got Nate with me," he said. "Yes, I'm fine," he lied.

"DICK MUNKER," JOE SAID. "WHAT'S his story?"

Nate whistled. "It would be a good thing," he said, "If Dick Munker went away."

"Meaning?"

"The guy is a bitter, sadistic asshole," Nate said. "They knew this guy real well in Idaho, because he's one of the FBI sharpshooters the state was trying to put in jail for Ruby Ridge. He was one of the triggermen. The first guy to shoot, it was alleged. Unfortunately, the case got dismissed because of jurisdictional problems. Munker did get demoted, and like Melinda Strickland he's been bounced around the country in the hope that he'd retire so they wouldn't have to take administrative action. The FBI hates to call attention to itself and its problem agents—especially these days—so they do everything they can to keep things quiet when they have a psycho on the payroll."

Nate shook his head. "Melinda Strickland and Dick Munker are made for each other."

Joe didn't respond. The fear that had clenched his stomach for the past few hours was gripping harder. He held tight to the steering wheel and pushed on through the spinning snow, praying that he wasn't already too late. He needed to come up with a plan and he didn't have much time.

WHEN THEY ENTERED SADDLESTRING IT was still dark, although there was now a gray morning glow in the eastern sky. The town was encased in snow and ice. The chains on the tires of Joe's truck were singing because there was so much packed snow in the wheel wells. Joe was amazed they had made it without getting stuck.

Joe briefed Nate on the situation as he saw it, and went over the plan he had come up with. He told Nate that he needed him there for support and backup only. Nate nodded and smiled slyly, leaving Joe with a queasy feeling.

He didn't go far into town. He turned off the road and into the parking lot of the First Alpine Church.

The church was sanctuary once again, Joe now knew, for Spud Cargill.

31

AS JOE PULLED INTO THE SMALL PARKING AREA FOR THE church and the Reverend B. J. Cobb's trailer, he pointed out to Nate that there was no wood smoke coming from the tin stovepipe atop the church.

"It's too cold," Joe said, thinking aloud, "for someone to be inside the church without a morning fire. So if Spud is here, he'll be in the double-wide."

Nate grunted his agreement.

As they pulled to a stop in front of the trailer, something bothered Joe, but he couldn't put his finger on it. Then he remembered.

"Yesterday when I was here," Joe said, "there was a snowmobile parked out by the road. It's not there now."

"You think Spud took it?" Nate asked, zipping up his parka and preparing to open the truck door.

"We'll find out, I guess," Joe said, jumping out of the truck into the snow. He left his .40 Beretta in his holster and pulled the only weapon that he was comfortable with, his twelve-gauge Remington Wingmaster shotgun, out from behind the bench seat. Turning toward the trailer, he spun it upside down in his gloves to make sure it was loaded. The bright brass of a double-ought shell winked at him.

While Joe approached the front door of Cobb's trailer, Nate Romanowski pushed though the deep snow around the back where there was another door. Joe gave Nate a minute to get around before mounting the steps.

He knocked with enough force to send a line of icicles crashing from the eaves. Toward the back of the trailer, yellow light filled a curtained window. Joe assumed it was the bedroom. He stepped aside on the porch in case Cobb or Spud decided to fire through the door.

Joe heard heavy footfalls inside and watched the door handle turn. There was a kissing sound as it opened and broke through a thin seal of snow and ice. Joe raised the barrel of the shotgun, the butt firmly against his cheek, and aimed it at eye-level where he expected Cobb to stick his head out.

The door opened and the Reverend Cobb's cinder-block head jutted out into the half-light of dawn, his eyes squinting against the falling snow. The muzzle of Joe's shotgun was six inches away from Cobb's ear.

"Throw down your weapon if you have one," Joe said quietly, as Cobb's eyes swiveled toward the black mouth of the shotgun.

A nine-millimeter handgun dropped with a thud on the porch, vanishing into the snow but leaving a distinct profile outline.

"That's not necessary, Joe," Cobb said, keeping his voice even.

"Step outside where I can see you," Joe ordered. He did not trust Cobb not to have another weapon on him, or not to jump back and slam the door shut.

"You can't enter a man's house without probable cause, Joe," Cobb cautioned.

"I'm not," Joe said. "I'm asking you to come outside. And if you don't do it, we've got a problem."

Cobb gave a slight smile and briefly closed his eyes. His face was pink and warm from sleep, and snowflakes melted on his cheeks.

"Okay," Cobb said, opening his eyes. "My hands are up and I'm coming out. Don't do anything stupid."

"No promises," Joe said, immensely relieved that Cobb was cooperating.

Cobb stepped out on the porch in his slippers. He wore the same bathrobe Joe had seen him in the day before. His hands were raised and his expression was calm, but tired. There was a hint of defeat in the way he slumped his shoulders.

"I was wondering what happened to you yesterday after we talked," Cobb said.

"I went up to the compund," Joe responded, a little defensively. "I was too late to find Spud. The Sovereigns had already refused him a place to hide out, and they sent him away."

Cobb nodded. "I figured they probably wouldn't let him in. I was conflicted about telling you too much, though. I don't approve of what he did. I don't even like Spud much. But I have a real problem with the way the Feds are conducting themselves. We don't need another Gestapo."

Joe repressed the urge to hit Cobb across the face with the butt of his shotgun.

"Goddamn you, Cobb, just put that antigovernment crap away for a few minutes," Joe hissed. "I know about all that, and I don't care about any of it. All that matters to me right now is my little girl. You've just wasted twelve hours of my time when you had a pretty good idea he was coming back here." Joe angrily racked his shotgun, and pressed the muzzle against Cobb's ear.

Cobb flinched away from the icy metal on his bare skin, and Joe saw his eyes bulge with fear. Joe didn't mind that at all.

"I've always liked you, B. J.," Joe said, pressing the muzzle even harder. "I'm not sure why. But if you don't start telling me the truth, and I mean *every bit of it*, things are going to get real Western real fast."

Cobb closed his eyes briefly and Joe heard a wracking breath. He pushed the shotgun forward, so that now the side of Cobb's head was pinned against the opposite doorjamb and his closest ear was cupped around the muzzle and misshapen.

"Okay, Joe," Cobb said softly.

Joe felt a rush of relief mixed with a whiff of shame for what he had just done to Cobb. He eased up on the pressure he had been using.

"Is he inside?" Joe asked.

Cobb shook his head, and rubbed his ear. "He was in the church for the past few days. But I haven't seen him since he left."

"Then he . . ." Joe started to ask when Nate shouted from the back of the trailer.

"Joe! There he is."

Turning, Joe looked through the heavy snowfall toward the church. A door was open, and a single shadowy form—Spud Cargill—was trying to run across an open field away from them. He had obviously been in the church when Joe and Nate arrived, huddling in the cold without a fire, and had just run out the back door behind the pulpit.

"Yes, there he is," Cobb said with resignation. "He must have known I wouldn't let him into my home."

Joe looked back to Cobb. The Reverend was shaking his head sadly, still rubbing his ear, but slumping as if he had given up. There didn't seem to be any fight in him.

Joe made a quick decision that Cobb would stay put and wouldn't be a threat, since he had, in effect, already given Spud's location away.

Joe lowered the shotgun and jumped off the porch, turning his back to Cobb.

"Go inside and stay put," Joe shouted over his shoulder. "You've got no part in this anymore."

"Don't hurt him," Cobb implored. "He's an idiot, but there's no reason to hurt him."

Joe said nothing. Nate met him in the yard between the trailer and the church, breathing hard from bulling his way through the deep snow. Joe crossed in front of Nate on his way to his pickup.

As Joe threw down the ramps and fired up his snowmobile, he squinted through the storm. Spud Cargill was getting far enough away that with the hard-falling snow he was little more than a shadow in the field.

"Spud Cargill, STOP!" Joe shouted. "Don't make us come after you!"

Joe shouted several more times as he backed the machine out of the truck. Cargill didn't respond. He was struggling through the snow, high-stepping and stumbling. Several times, he pitched forward and vanished out of sight for an instant.

Joe idled the snowmobile alongside Nate.

"I can hit him from here," Nate said, sliding his .454 out of his shoulder holster.

"No!" Joe said. "I'm going to go get him."

"I could blow a leg off and shut him down."

"Nate!"

Nate smiled slightly and shrugged. "I'll cover you in case he's crabby."

"That's a deal."

As Joe roared by, he saw Nate out of the corner of his

eye with his big pistol extended over a log, the sights, no doubt, on the back of Spud Cargill's head.

Joe quickly closed the gap between himself and Cargill. Joe drove one-handed, his right hand on the throttle and his left holding the shotgun. The snow was thigh-deep, and Spud Cargill was flushed and sweating. His eyes were wild. He didn't have gloves or a hat. Joe couldn't see if Spud had a weapon or not. Joe veered around him, cutting him off, then pointed the shotgun at Cargill's chest.

"That's enough," Joe said.

Cargill stopped, wheezing, his breath billowing from his nostrils like dual exhausts. Slowly, Cargill bent forward and grasped his knees in an effort to catch his breath.

"Turn around and head back."

Cargill's hand came up with a tiny double-barreled Derringer in it. Joe flopped back flat on his seat as the little pistol cracked and the bullet missed. Still on his back but grasping the hand grip, Joe buried the throttle with his thumb and the snowmobile howled and pounced forward. The collision with Spud Cargill smashed the plastic windshield and cracked the fiberglass hood. Joe felt Cargill's body thump beneath the tracks as the snowmobile passed over him.

Once Joe was clear, he sat back up and circled back.

A hand pushed its way out of the tracked snow, and then a knee. Joe drove up alongside and grabbed the hand. With tremendous effort, he pulled Spud Cargill from the snow. Cargill came up with his mouth, eyes, and ears packed with snow but his hands empty of little guns. The tracks of the snowmobile had shredded the front of his coat.

It wasn't until then that Joe realized how absolutely terrified he had been, and how instinctual and unplanned his reaction was.

While Spud coughed and sputtered, Joe reached up and grabbed Cargill's coat collar from the back. *"Miranda rights!"* Joe spat, not having the time, energy, or inclination to say more at the moment. Spud started to speak, but with a firm grasp of the coat, Joe gunned the snowmobile and rode it back to the church, dragging a flailing and screaming Spud Cargill alongside. As Joe rode back, he saw that Spud's pickup was on the side of the church, obscured from the road and covered by a tarp that was now heavy with snow.

Nate stepped away from the church as Joe rode up and let go of the coat. Cargill rolled twice in the snow, coming to rest facedown at Nate's feet.

"Damn nice work," Nate said, smiling.

"I thought you were going to cover me," Joe snapped, his adrenaline still on high.

"If I'd shot, I would have hit both of you," Nate said sourly. "You were right in my line of fire."

Joe started to argue, then realized Nate was right.

"Anyway . . . ," Joe said.

"You got him," Nate said, finishing Joe's sentence. Nate stepped forward, rolled Spud Cargill over with his boot then bent down and expertly searched Cargill from his coat to his shoes. He found a folded Buck knife in a trouser pocket and a thin thowing knife in a sheath in Spud's boot. Nate put them both in his parka pocket.

"No more weapons."

"He's an idiot," Joe said. Then, to Spud: "You have caused me and my family more pain and heartache than you can ever imagine. I'm just real happy to see you, Spud."

"The hell you *talking* about?" Spud mumbled, genuinely confused. "Never went after you . . . or *any* of the state agencies."

Joe didn't have time to explain, and didn't think Spud was owed an explanation.

THEY WERE STILL IN THE church parking lot. The three of them were wedged into the cab of Joe's pickup with Spud in the middle between Joe and Nate.

Spud Cargill was wet and ragged, and he complained to Joe that the handcuffs were too tight. Nate responded by elbowing Spud sharply in the mouth and snapping his head back.

"Shut up," Nate hissed. Cargill shut up. Joe glared at Nate, but said nothing.

The motor was running and the heat was on, and Joe breathed easier as he unhooked his radio mike from the cradle and called for dispatch.

There was now enough morning light to see . . . just about nothing. The snow was falling hard again, and the air was filled with nickel-sized flakes.

"Dispatch." It was Wendy, a longtime county employee and conspiracy buff.

"This is Game Warden Joe Pickett," he said. "Can you patch me through to Sheriff Barnum?"

"No can do."

Joe waited for more. There wasn't any.

"Excuse me?"

"No can do."

"Then patch me through to anybody. It doesn't have to be Barnum."

"No can do."

"Wendy, damn you . . ."

Another voice came on. Joe recognized it as Tony Portenson, Munker's partner.

"Call me back on a landline," Portenson said.

*   *   *

FURIOUS, JOE LEFT CARGILL WITH Nate in the pickup.

"Don't leave me with *him*!" Cargill pleaded as Joe slammed the door.

He knocked again on the trailer door and asked the Reverend Cobb if he could use his telephone.

"I see you found Spud," Cobb said, looking over Joe's shoulder toward the pickup.

"Yup."

Cobb stepped aside so Joe could enter. He was still obviously wary, and gave Joe a wider berth than necessary.

"You scared me a little out there, Joe," Cobb said, reaching again for his ear. Joe noted that the round imprint of the barrel could be seen on Cobb's earlobe.

"I'm sorry about that," Joe said earnestly.

Cobb shook his head, then nodded toward the window. "He tried to get the Sovereigns to shelter him, but they wouldn't. I don't blame them, but then I would have been rid of him."

"That's what they told me," Joe said. But something didn't fit. He thought of the porch steps he had come up when he approached the trailer that morning. They were completely untracked. How could Spud have told Cobb about what had happened? Joe had the impression that Spud had entered the church in secret. "Did Spud tell you that?"

Cobb shook his head.

"So you're in contact with the Sovereigns. How? By telephone?"

Cobb sipped from a mug of coffee. He nodded toward a PC in a darkened corner of the trailer. The computer was on, a screen-saver undulating on its monitor. "E-mail," Cobb said.

"With who? Wade Brockius?"

Cobb looked away. "Wade and I have corresponded for years. He's a brilliant man and a good friend."

"Are you the one who suggested they come to Twelve Sleep County?"

"Yes," Cobb said. "I thought they would be safe here. Now I wish to God they had never come."

Joe sighed. "You're not the only one."

Cobb handed Joe the telephone receiver and shuffled away in the direction of the computer to give Joe some privacy. Joe walked into the darkened kitchen, as far as the cord would allow him to go. He dialed the sheriff's office.

"Portenson."

"Joe Pickett. Can you tell me what's going on?"

Portenson's voice sounded tired. "All law-enforcement personnel in Twelve Sleep County are under orders to maintain radio silence."

Joe had never heard of this happening before. "Why?"

Portenson hesitated. "The assault team left this morning in the Sno-Cats. Agent Munker was afraid the Sovereigns had scanners up there and that they would overhear the chatter and know they were coming."

Joe felt his skin crawl. "They've already left?"

"They assembled at four this morning and rolled at five."

Joe did a quick calculation. The Sno-Cats, he determined, would be at the Sovereign compound within the hour.

"Portenson, can you reach them?"

"I told you, their radios are off."

Joe held the telephone away from his ear for a moment and looked at it. Then he jerked it back. "I'VE GOT SPUD CARGILL!" Joe shouted. "I arrested him at a church fifteen minutes ago. He's NOT at that compound."

"Oh, shit."

"Oh, shit is right," Joe said. "How can we reach them to call off the raid? *Think!*"

"Oh shit, oh shit, *oh shit*," Portenson repeated, his sense of alarm coming through the receiver.

"Hold it," Joe said suddenly. "Why aren't you with them?"

"I couldn't go."

"What do you mean."

"I mean I fucking couldn't make myself go!" Portenson cried. "I quit! I think this whole operation is a cluster-fuck in the making, just like Ruby Ridge and Waco. I insisted that we wait for approval from the director before moving on the compound, but the director's overseas and won't be back till Monday. Munker and Melinda Strickland refused to wait even three days because they're afraid the press will be here by then!"

Joe listened silently. Rage and desperation began to fill him again.

"Melinda Strickland, that nut, wouldn't even compromise with me and go on Saturday, you know why?"

Joe said nothing.

"Because she said she doesn't want to work on the weekend! Can you fucking believe it? She only kills people when she's on the clock! You should have seen her this morning, it was unbelievable. She was sitting in the backseat of the Sno-Cat all bundled in blankets like she was going on a fucking sleigh ride. And she had that damned dog with her. She's crazy, and so is Munker. I hate this operation. I hate this town. *I HATE THIS GODDAMNED SNOW!*"

Joe hung up on Portenson in mid-rant.

While he had raced down Timberline Road just a few hours before, the small convoy of Sno-Cats and snowmobiles had been rumbling up the mountain on Bighorn

Road toward the compound. He had not only missed Cargill coming down, he had missed the assault team going up. He slammed the counter with the heel of his hand and made the coffeemaker dance.

Joe opened the front door and stood on the porch. Nate saw him through the windshield and lowered his window.

"They've already left for the compound," Joe said flatly.

If Nate registered any alarm, Joe couldn't see it in his face.

"Nate, will you please check to see if Spud has his wallet? I'm going to need his identification to prove to Munker and Strickland that we've actually got him in custody."

Nate nodded. "Are we going to try to head them off?"

"*I'm* going to try," Joe said. "You have even less credibility with those folks than I do. I need you to take Cargill to the county building and make sure he gets booked into jail. Just ask for Tony Portenson. I just talked with him; he's at the building."

Suddenly, there was a flurry inside the cab of the truck as Spud Cargill tried to cold-cock Nate while he was talking to Joe. Joe saw Nate's head jerk from a blow. But instead of panicking, Nate signaled to Joe that everything was okay and closed the window. Nate turned his attention to Spud Cargill.

Joe was amazed.

"WARDEN?" IT WAS B. J. Cobb from inside the trailer.

Joe turned, assuming Cobb was going to ask him to close the door.

"You need to come see this." Cobb's voice was deadly cold.

Joe stepped back in and walked with Cobb across the cluttered living room. Cobb sat down in front of his computer.

On the monitor, an e-mail program was fired up. In the "Inbox" was a message from W. Brockius to B. J. Cobb.

The subject line of the e-mail was:

THEY'RE HERE.

The body of the message was short:

THEY'VE ESTABLISHED A PERIMETER. HELP US, MY LOVE.

Joe was just about to ask Cobb why the e-mail said "MY LOVE" when he heard a scream outside that set his teeth on edge.

JOE LEFT THE TRAILER AND shut the door, looking for the source of the scream. Nate Romanowski was now outside the pickup, rubbing his bare hands with snow.

"What was that?" Joe asked.

Nate gestured toward Joe's truck. Inside the cab, Spud Cargill was holding his hands to the sides of his head, his eyes white and wild, his mouth wide open. He looked like the painting by Edvard Munch. He screamed again.

"I got his wallet, but I didn't think that would be enough," Nate said. "Munker would just think you found his wallet in his house or workplace."

Oh no . . . , Joe thought. "Nate . . ."

Romanowski held his palm out. "So I got you his ear."

32

JOE SEETHED AS HE ATTACHED HIS SHOTGUN TO THE back of the snowmobile with bungee cords in the parking lot of the church. He could not believe that the assault team had launched in the bad weather, and he was furious that he had wasted so many hours chasing Spud up the mountain, down the mountain, and back to where he'd started in the first place.

Nate Romanowski declared that he should go to the compound as well. "You might need me," he said.

Still reeling from pocketing Spud's severed ear, Joe snarled at Nate.

"You cut off his ear!"

"Hey, once you think about it you'll agree with me that it was a good idea. Hell, you took the ear, didn't you?" Nate said. "The little bastard deserved it. Think about everything he set in motion in this valley."

Joe breathed deeply and collected himself. Nate was right, but the whole episode—his own behavior and Nate's—still disturbed him. Joe pulled on his thick snowmobile suit and started zipping the sleeves and pant legs tight.

"Nate, I need you to take Spud to jail so we know where to find him. I can't spare the time it would take to book him in."

Nate began to protest, but Joe cut him off.

"Just sit Portenson down and tell him the whole story. Maybe he can figure out a way to intervene. Maybe he can contact his director, or talk some sense into Melinda Strickland or Munker."

"I'm not sure you know what you're dealing with here, Joe," Nate said.

Joe had no response, but pulled his black helmet on.

"Don't worry, Joe, I'll take him to jail. And I'll give Marybeth a call."

"Good," Joe said, turning the key in the ignition. "Thank you. You've been more than enough help already."

Nate saluted, and grinned crookedly. Joe wondered whether or not Spud Cargill would make it to jail in one piece. Actually, he conceded to himself, he didn't really care that much either way.

ON THE SNOWMOBILE, JOE PICKETT rocketed through Saddlestring and out the other side on unplowed streets with no traffic. Despite the protection of his helmet and Plexiglas shield, his face stung from the cold wind and the pinpricks of snow. The windscreen had been smashed by Spud Cargill. The crack in the snowmobile's hood concerned him, but there didn't seem to be any indication of engine damage. The tank was full, and Joe thought that would be enough gasoline to get him to the compound. In his parka pocket was Spud Cargill's wallet and driver's license, as well as his ear.

The Sno-Cats had groomed a packed and smooth trail up the mountain road, and Joe increased his speed. Dark trees flashed by on both sides. He shot a look at his speedometer: seventy miles per hour. Even in the summer, the speed limit for Bighorn Road in the forest was forty-five.

Help me save her, he prayed.

LORD, HE WAS TIRED.

The high, angry whine of the engine served as a soundtrack to his aching muscles, broken rib, and pounding head. He had not slept for twenty hours, and he rode right through spinning, improbable, multicolored hallucinations that wavered ahead of him in the dawn. More than once, he leaned into what he thought was a turn in the road only to realize, at the last possible second, that the road went the other way.

Despite the icy wind in his face that made his eyes water and blurred his vision, Joe's mind raced.

He thought about the words on Cobb's computer screen: THEY'VE ESTABLISHED A PERIMETER. HELP US, MY LOVE. "My love"? Cobb had said he admired Brockius, but . . .

Joe shook it out of his mind. At this point he wasn't sure that it mattered. Maybe later, once April was safe. There was no time now.

If he could somehow buy an hour back, he thought, he would pay anything.

Spud's driver's license should do it, he thought. The ear definitely would, as unorthodox as it was. Even if Munker and Strickland didn't back off, surely Sheriff Barnum would move to retreat or delay the assault, wouldn't he? Not because he cared a whit about the Sovereigns, but because Barnum was politically sensitive and the next sheriff's election was a year away. Barnum didn't have as much invested in this thing as Strickland and Munker did. Barnum could come out looking good by putting his foot down, stopping the assault by pulling his deputies out of it. That was how Barnum operated, after all. He wanted to look good. *Robey!* Maybe Robey was up there, Joe hoped. Robey could shut things down in a hurry and threaten action against Melinda Strickland and Munker if they didn't back off. Although Strickland didn't care much about the law, she might listen if Robey convinced Barnum to pull his men out.

He hadn't really thought through what Romanowski had told him about Melinda Strickland and Dick Munker, but he knew they spelled trouble. The thought of Melinda Strickland sitting, as Tony Portenson had described her, bundled in blankets and cuddling her dog as she ordered her minions to ascend the mountain, made him coldly angry.

Because he wasn't paying attention, he almost missed a turn; he would have been launched over a bank into a deep slough. But he corrected himself at the last moment and leaned into the track of the road.

Think of something else, he pleaded to himself. *Something better.*

So he tried to imagine how he would feel coming back down this road in a little while with April bundled up in his lap. Under his helmet, he smiled. And he vowed to make that scenario real.

A MAN ON A SNOWMOBILE blocked the road that led to the compound, and Joe figured he'd probably heard him coming from miles away. The man wore a heavy black snowmobile suit and had an assault rifle clamped under his arm, and he waved his hand for Joe to stop. Joe slowed—his broken rib and the muscles in his back were screaming from riding so hard and so fast—and he unbent from his forward lean while the snowmobile wound down. Joe stopped a few feet in front of the man. Early-morning light filtered through the canopy of pine trees but was absorbed by the heavy snowfall, giving the morning a creamy gray cast.

"Turn it off," the man ordered, nodding at Joe's snowmobile, which sizzled and popped as it idled.

Joe ignored him and raised the shield on his helmet with a squeak that broke a film of ice from the hinges. Joe's breath billowed in the cold from the exertion of the ride.

"Oh, it's you," the man said. "I recognize you from the meeting at the Forest Service."

"Are they up there?" Joe asked anxiously.

The man nodded. Joe recognized him as Saddlestring police, but didn't know his name.

"Anything happening yet?"

"I haven't heard anything. No shots fired," the officer said. "Our radios are off, so I don't know if they're negotiating or what."

Joe exhaled deeply. *Thank God,* he thought, *I'm not too late.* "I've got an emergency message for Sheriff Barnum."

"I can't let you in," the officer said.

"I said it was an emergency, deputy." Joe's voice took on a mean edge that he didn't recognize. "No one has been able to reach him because all the radios are turned off."

The officer hesitated. "I can't exactly call ahead and ask about this."

"No, you can't," Joe said. "Which is why I'm going."

"Well . . ."

Joe flipped down his shield and roared around the officer and up the road. In his cracked rearview mirror, Joe saw the policeman throw up his hands and kick at the snow in frustration.

*   *   *

THE SNO-CATS WERE NOSE-TO-TAIL ON the road in front of the Sovereign compound, forming a glass-and-steel skirmish line, and snowmobiles were scattered at all angles behind them. Joe slowed and rose in his seat as he approached, trying to assess the situation as he squinted through watery eyes and snowfall so heavy that it obscured the scene like smoke.

As he approached the gathering of vehicles, he saw that the assault team all wore identical black snowmobile suits and black helmets, just like his own. Inside those suits were Highway Patrol troopers, Forest Service rangers, sheriff's deputies, Saddlestring P.D., maybe even more FBI—but he couldn't tell who was who. He wanted to start with local guys who might know and trust him, but he had no idea where to begin. Obscured by their suits and helmets, Joe thought, these men could be capable of anything.

Most of the men were huddled behind the steel wall of the Sno-Cats with their weapons pointed across the hoods of the vehicles toward the compound. Someone in a black snowmobile suit waved at him—he couldn't tell who—and another stepped away from the line and blocked his path.

"Who in the hell are *you?*" the man asked, and reached over and flipped Joe's shield up. Angrily, Joe leaned forward on the handlebars and reciprocated, and the man stepped back as if slapped. It was Deputy McLanahan. Joe could see his dumb, rodent eyes and the bruises on his face.

"Where is Barnum?"

"Why in the hell are you here?" McLanahan asked.

"I asked you a question, McLanahan."

McLanahan squared his shoulders as if he were about to charge.

Joe instinctively reached back for his shotgun, which was still attached to the seat with bungee cords. McLanahan hesitated.

"Knock it off, deputy," Joe said. "I need to talk to the sheriff NOW! Spud Cargill isn't up here. I can prove it."

Confusion overtook McLanahan's tough-guy face.

"What?"

"He was at the church all along. The First Alpine Church. He tried to come up here but they wouldn't let him in. I arrested him and he's in your jail. Now, step aside."

"Bullshit."

"I can prove it," Joe shouted, turning the handlebars so the front skis pointed right at McLanahan. Joe engaged the gears and raced the engine. McLanahan knew enough about snowmobiles to know that Joe was poised to run right over the top of him if he didn't answer. "Now, where's Barnum?"

McLanahan stepped aside and pointed. Joe should have noticed it earlier—a single Sno-Cat parked behind the skirmish line. *That would be the one holding the leaders, the one out of fire,* he thought. He revved his engine and covered the fifty yards in a flash.

Joe shut down his engine, leaped off, and ran around the Sno-Cat. Its exhaust burbled in the cold. Joe threw open the door and stuck his head inside, and it took a moment for his eyes to adjust.

Sheriff Barnum sat in the front seat, behind the wheel. Elle Broxton-Howard sat next to him in her faux fur-lined parka. Melinda Strickland took up the entire backseat, just as Portenson had described, her cocker spaniel snuggled into the blankets with her. She held a small two-way radio in her gloved hand. All of them were shocked to see him.

"You scared me!" Strickland said. "I wasn't expecting you, ya know?"

"Jesus, Pickett. What are you doing up here?" Barnum growled. "You've got no jurisdiction in an operation like this."

"Is Robey here anywhere?" Joe asked.

"Nope," Barnum said.

"Listen," Joe said, trying to calm himself, wishing he could have started this with Robey present. He was out of breath, and shaky from the ride up the mountain. "Spud Cargill is in the county jail. I arrested him about an hour and a half ago."

The three of them looked at each other in disbelief.

"We couldn't call you to let you know because you were running silent, for some stupid reason," Joe said, looking from Barnum to Strickland to gauge their reaction to the news.

Then Joe realized: Where was Dick Munker? *Probably on the other end of Strickland's radio,* he thought.

"You're not pulling our chain, are you?" Barnum asked.

Joe fought an urge to smash Barnum in the mouth. He shook it off and briefly looked away, before turning his focus back to Barnum. *Someday,* Joe said to himself, drilling Barnum with his eyes, *you and I are going to go at it.*

"No, he's in jail," Joe said. "Look. I can prove it." While he dug into his pocket, he told them about finding Cargill at the church and running him down.

Pulling the worn black wallet out of his pocket, he flipped it open to Cargill's Wyoming driver's license. "I took this off him."

Melinda Strickland reached for it and looked at the

license with distaste. "I don't know what to think," she said. A hint of confusion that Joe welcomed clouded her features.

"Are you sure you didn't find that in his truck or at his house?" Barnum asked, raising his eyebrows as if he had just come upon a clever discovery.

Again, Joe had to hold himself back. Nate had been right.

With his glove, Joe reached into his parka. Cargill's ear felt like a thin, greasy slice of apple. He flipped it onto Barnum's lap like a poker chip.

"Here's his ear."

"Oh, my God!" Melinda Strickland cried.

"That is absolutely disgusting," Broxton-Howard said, hiding her face in her hands.

Barnum smiled sardonically, and shook his head in something like admiration.

"NOW, WHERE'S MUNKER?" JOE DEMANDED.

Melinda Strickland looked to Sheriff Barnum for help.

"He's in a position to fire on the compound," Barnum said.

"Where?"

Barnum nodded vaguely toward the fence.

"Call him in," Joe said.

Again, Melinda Strickland looked to Barnum. Joe again saw her confused face. Barnum nodded, and she raised the two-way to her mouth. *Why is she looking to Barnum,* Joe wondered, *if she's running this operation?*

"Dick, can you hear me?" she asked. Joe noted that she used no official radio protocol.

Everyone in the Sno-Cat now watched her.

"Dick? Come in, Dick."

"He said he'd keep his radio on," Barnum muttered.

After a beat, there was a chirp from Strickland's radio. "That means he can hear us but he doesn't want to talk," she explained to Joe. "He's in a position where they can't see him and he doesn't want to give himself away."

Joe nearly reached into the backseat and throttled her.

"Give me the radio," he said, reaching for it. Reluctantly, she handed it over.

Joe grabbed it and keyed the mike. "Munker, wherever you are, this is Joe Pickett. Your little show is over. Spud Cargill is in custody in Saddlestring with Agent Portenson. I repeat, Spud Cargill is NOT HERE." Joe spoke as clearly as he could, trying to keep the rage out.

Silence.

Joe withdrew his head from the Sno-Cat and looked over the hood of the next vehicle into the falling snow and distant shadows of the trailers in the compound. He stood behind the open door and felt warmth from the cab radiate out. The silence was remarkable. Even with the Sno-Cat's engine idling, the heavy snow hushed everything. Joe noticed that two members of the assault team—he couldn't tell who they were, of course—must have heard him talking to Munker, because they now looked back at him, and at each other. *They're wondering what's going on,* he thought, *waiting to see if the raid's being called off.*

Joe searched the shadowed trees and the meadow for a sign of Dick Munker. Between the Sno-Cats and the fence was a ditch.

Joe guessed that Munker would hide in that ditch so he could rest his sniper's rifle on the opposite bank and see into the compound. There was enough snow-covered brush to hide behind, Joe noticed, and Munker would likely be in all-white winter gear.

The two-way crackled to life. "This is Munker. They've got a hostage."

Joe stared at the radio in disbelief. What was *this*?

Then he raised it to his mouth, still scanning the silent meadow for Munker. "What are you talking about, Munker?"

"Give me back the radio," Strickland whined from inside, putting her dog aside so she could reach for it.

Joe turned his back to her.

"What hostage?" Joe asked.

Munker's voice was a whisper. Joe assumed Munker had it pressed against his lips to muffle his voice even further. "She's the wife of that crazy minister in Saddlestring. Mrs. Cobb. I can see her in the trailer."

Instantly, Joe understood, and his blood ran cold. He understood why Eunice Cobb hadn't been with B. J. in the morning. He understood "My Love." He understood where the Cobbs' missing snowmobile had gone. She had come to the compound the night before to warn them in person after Joe's visit, rather than e-mail. Maybe she had come up to assure the Sovereigns that they shouldn't harbor Spud. For whatever reason—the increasing storm, or the fact that a convoy of law-enforcement personnel were coming up the road—she'd been forced to stay the night. *She was probably in Brockius's trailer when I came to the camp,* he thought. *She was the reason Brockius didn't invite me in.*

"How do you know she's a hostage?" Joe asked. "How do you know she isn't just visiting?"

"You're one stupid motherfucker," Munker replied in his deep cigarette-coated voice.

"Give me that!" Melinda Strickland said, reaching around Joe and snatching the radio from his hand. She settled back into the rear of the Sno-Cat.

A hot, white veil of rage covered Joe's eyes, and it was all he could do to keep from launching himself into the cab. He sucked in a deep gulp of cold air and falling snow, forcing himself to stay in control of his actions. When he looked up, Barnum was eyeing him, as if waiting to see what Joe would do next. Panic flooded Joe as he looked into the cab and saw that Melinda Strickland was clutching the radio tightly to her chest. There was no way he was going to get it back without breaking her fingers.

Joe turned to Barnum.

"She's no hostage, for God's sake. Mrs. Cobb and her husband have been in contact with these Sovereigns since the beginning. They're all part of the black-helicopter crowd. It makes sense when you think about it."

Barnum raised his eyebrows and shrugged in a "Who knows?" gesture.

"Barnum, you need to call your deputies off," Joe said, glaring at Barnum's passive face. "Pull them off and they can't continue the raid."

"Hell, Joe, I don't even know which ones are mine and which ones ain't," Barnum said, staring back. "They all look alike to me out here."

Joe was too surprised to move for a moment.

"Besides," Barnum said, reaching for the handle of the door, "It'll be interesting to see how this thing plays out."

Barnum slammed the door shut before Joe could stop him and he heard the lock click. He couldn't fathom what was happening. He stood outside the cab of the Sno-Cat, furious, and depressingly alone.

THINK.

Joe was beside himself. No matter what he did, it wasn't enough. He had never been in a situation that seemed so . . . inevitable.

*   *   *

A SUDDEN SCRATCH OF STATIC ruptured the silence that had reclaimed the scene after Joe's outburst. Joe could hear the radio clearly through an open window in the Sno-Cat that had been cracked an inch to prevent the glass from steaming up inside.

"I can see Wade Brockius through the window of a trailer," Munker reported over the radio. "He's pacing."

"Can you see the hostage?" Strickland asked.

"Not for the last few minutes."

"If you took him out, could we rush the trailer and save her?"

"No. There are too many damned Sovereigns hidden in the trees."

Joe couldn't believe what he was hearing. He had been slumped against the outside of the command Sno-Cat, but he now stood up. He rubbed his face hard. He didn't know the procedure for a hostage situation—they didn't teach that to game wardens—but he knew this wasn't it. This was madness.

He reached into his suit and found his compact binoculars. Moving away from the Sno-Cat, he scanned the compound. The nose of Brockius's trailer faced the road. Through the thin curtains, he could see Brockius just as Munker had described.

Then he saw someone else.

Jeannie Keeley was now at the window, pulling the curtain aside to look out. Her face looked tense, and angry. Beneath her chin was another, smaller, paler face. April.

"Fire a warning shot," Melinda Strickland told Munker.

"A *warning shot*?" Joe screamed. "What are you . . ."

Before Joe could react, he saw a movement in the ditch behind a knot of brush. The slim black barrel of a rifle slid out of blinding whiteness and swung slowly toward the trailer window. Joe screamed "NO!" as he involuntarily launched himself from the cover of the vehicles in the direction of the shooter. As he ran, he watched in absolute horror as the barrel stopped on a target and fired. The shot boomed across the mountain, jarring the dreamlike snowy morning violently awake.

Immediately after the shot, Joe realized what he had just done, how he had exposed himself completely in the open road with the assault team behind him and the hidden Sovereigns somewhere in front. Maybe the Sovereigns were as shocked as he was, he thought, since no one had fired back.

But within the hush of the snowfall and the faint returning echo of the shot, there was a high-pitched hiss. It took a moment for Joe to focus on the sound, and when he did, he realized that its origin was a newly severed pipe that had run between a large propane tank on the side of the trailer and the trailer itself. The thin copper tubing rose from the snow and bent toward the trailer like a rattlesnake ready to strike. He could clearly see an open space between the broken tip of the tubing and the fitting on the side of the trailer where the pipe should have been attached. High-pressure gas was shooting into the side vents of the trailer.

No! Joe thought. Munker *couldn't* have . . .

He looked up to see a flurry of movement behind the curtains inside the trailer a split-second before there was a sudden, sickening *WHUMP* that seemed to suck all the air off the mountain. The explosion came from inside the trailer, blowing out the window glass and instantly crushing two tires so the trailer rocked and heaved to one side like a wounded animal. The hissing gas from the severed pipe was now on fire, and it became a furious gout of flame aimed at the thin metal skin of the trailer.

Suddenly, a burning figure ran from the trailer, its gyrations framed by fire, and crumpled into the snow.

Joe stood transfixed, staring at the window where he had last seen April. It was now a blazing hole.

He did not move as the shouting started from both the compound in front of him and the assault team behind him, as Sovereigns who had been hiding behind trees and under the snow screamed curses, as several of them fired back, the rounds smashing through the windows or pinging against the thin metal skins of the Sno-Cats. He heard the sharp *snap* of bullets through the air around him.

The propane tanks near the burning trailer now flared and exploded, launching rolling orange fireballs veined with black smoke into the air. The trailer burned furiously, the wall consumed so fast that the black metal skeleton of the frame was already showing.

Joe's hands hung limply at his sides. Despite the distance, he could feel the warmth of the fire on his face. Tears streamed down his cheeks, mixed with melting snowflakes.

"Got 'em," he heard Munker say from somewhere in front of him in the snow.

Rage, vicious and hot, swept through Joe, and he started running straight ahead toward the compound, scanning the trees and ground in front of him for Munker. Joe plunged into the ditch, flailing through the snow, finally catching sight of Munker standing among thick trees on the other side of the ditch, with his back to the Sno-Cats. Munker was watching the Sovereign compound with his rifle by his side, smoking a cigarette.

Joe charged out of the ditch toward Munker when he suddenly felt something sharp against his legs, jerking him backwards into the snow. He looked down and realized he had run straight into the barbed wire the Sovereigns had strung around the perimeter of the compound. Joe knew he was cut—he could see the rips in his pants, could feel hot blood running down his leg—but oddly the pain didn't register. Scrambling to his feet, he grabbed the wire and threw it over his head as he mounted the ditch. A guttural sound that was completely unfamiliar to him came out of his throat.

Munker heard the roar and turned, his eyes widening at the sight of Joe crashing through the deep snow toward him. As Joe narrowed the distance, wondering if he'd have time to unzip his suit and pull his Beretta from its holster, Munker calmly tossed the cigarette aside and worked the bolt on his rifle while he raised it.

An ear-shattering concussion came from somewhere behind Joe, and something big hit the stand of trees around Munker. The impact rocked the big tree behind Munker, sending a small mountain of snow cascading through its branches that covered Munker and whited him out.

Joe turned, trying to grasp what had just happened. He could see someone standing atop a wooded rise behind the Sno-Cats, in an open area between two stands of dark spruce. The man wore a black snowmobile suit and helmet like everyone else, and he stood behind a snowmobile for cover. Despite the shroud of thickly falling snow, Joe caught a glimpse of the man sweeping a huge silver handgun across the chaos of the assault team diving for cover between Sno-Cats and behind snowmobiles on the skirmish line. The team was now shouting, trying to figure out who was attacking them and where the assault was coming from.

Holding the revolver with both hands, Nate Romanowski began firing methodically from the top of the hill. He was putting a bullet or two into the engine block of each of the Sno-Cats. The smashing impact rocked the vehicles, sending deputies who were hiding behind them diving into the snow. Joe watched as Romanowski speed-loaded, moved to the side, and started firing again.

Joe looked over his shoulder and saw that the Sovereigns were using the diversion to scramble as well, running for their vehicles in the compound.

"I see him!" one of the deputies shouted, sending a burst of automatic fire up through the trees. Joe heard bullets smacking frozen tree trunks and saw eruptions of heavy snow bloom from the branches and fall to the ground. Romanowski responded by shooting the hood of a snowmobile closest to the deputy, causing the machine to bounce a few inches into the air.

Joe didn't hear anything behind him until something clubbed his neck and sent him sprawling, and turned the world into exquisite aquamarine.

HE COULD HEAR GUNSHOTS, SHOUTS, and motors being started somewhere in another world. He wasn't part of it anymore. There was a dull hum in both ears, and a stinging feeling in his face. When he opened his mouth to breathe, there was no air. He opened his eyes to beautiful, comforting light blue. Then his anger, and the pain, brought him back and he realized he was where Munker had left him—facedown, smothering in deep snow.

Joe thrashed in the snow, moaning, not sure for a moment where *up* was. As his senses surged back, he felt not only the dull roar at the base of his skull but also the searing bite of his broken rib, the barbed-wire slashes on his legs—and an overwhelming, almost physical hurt he felt over April.

WHEN JOE WAS ABLE TO sit up, Nate Romanowski was gone, but Joe could hear the whine of a snowmobile from where he had stood. And on the road, Dick Munker mounted an undamaged Sheriff's Department snowmobile and sped off toward the hill. Nate hadn't hit Munker with that first shot after all.

JOE STAGGERED THROUGH THE DEEP snow until he reached the packed powder of the roadbed and climbed back up. The stench of the burning trailer filled his nose and mouth.

As he reached his snowmobile, Melinda Strickland and Elle Broxton-Howard ran toward him. Strickland's little dog leaped like a jackrabbit to keep up with her in the snow. Joe noted that Barnum was huddled over a disabled snowmobile and didn't look his way.

"Joe, I . . . ," Strickland started to say, but Joe ignored her. He noticed that both Strickland and Broxton-Howard's clothing winked from bits of glass in the folds and creases. He guessed they had huddled on the floorboards of the Sno-Cat when the windows were shot out.

He pulled his shotgun from beneath the elastic cords on the back of his snowmobile and racked the pump. Strickland stopped, puzzled.

Fire a warning shot, she had told Munker. His eyes bored holes into her, but she looked back blankly.

"Get out of the way," Joe said, starting the engine. Both women quickly and clumsily stepped aside for him as he roared into the trees on Munker's tracks.

As he topped the rise where he had last seen Romanowski, he looked over his shoulder at the skirmish line and compound far below. Black-clad members of the assault team stood around their disabled vehicles, some gesturing, most still. In the compound, the big roll of black smoke obscured the remains of Wade Brockius's trailer. The rest of the compound was now empty of Sovereigns.

33

FOLLOWING THE TWO SNOWMOBILES THROUGH THE trees was easy, and Joe did it through half-lidded eyes that were burning in their sockets and with a twelve-gauge shotgun across his lap. Munker had stayed exactly in Nate's tracks, packing the trail even harder, and Joe knew he would gain speed on both of them.

He had no helmet, and the wind and snow tore at his exposed face and ears and pasted his hair back. He paid no attention to it, concentrating instead on the track in front of him and anticipating the first sight of Munker ahead. He had no doubts about what to do when he caught up to him. Focus was not a problem now.

He followed the tracks across an open meadow and back into the dark timber on the other side. Because he couldn't hear anything but his own motor, he couldn't tell if Munker had Nate in his sights or if he, like Joe, was simply following the trail.

The trees got thicker, flashing by on each side, and Joe had to slow down to stay in the track and not to hurtle into the timber. Nate had obviously tried to shake

Munker by diving into the deep woods, making hairpin turns around pine trees, and ducking under low-hanging branches. The trail zigzagged through the trees, sometimes banking sharply near trunks or outcroppings.

The single thought in Joe's mind was to find Dick Munker and kill him. He knew it would mean prison. He didn't care. Today Agent Dick Munker of the FBI needed to die by Joe's hand.

The terrain suddenly cleared, and the track went up the middle of a treeless hill. Joe hit his accelerator and the snowmobile whined, blindly surging up the rise.

He was going so fast, that he almost didn't see the tracks he was following split in two as he plunged down the hill's other side. One track had turned sharply to the right and the other plunged straight down the steep ridge into a dark and tangled mass of violently uprooted trees. Out of control, Joe rocketed down the slope, trying to avoid the trees while decelerating with one hand and crushing the handbrake with the other. He caught a glimpse of a smashed snowmobile below him, pieces of it scattered in the tangle of downed trees, and the black shape of a body in the snow. The body was sprawled out flat on its back, as if making a snow angel. When Joe's machine finally stopped, his left front ski was six inches from Dick Munker's head. Hanging in the air directly in front of him, where his windshield should have been, was the broken-off end of an upturned lodgepole pine that would have skewered Joe if he hadn't been able to stop.

Joe killed the engine and climbed off his snowmobile. He instantly sunk into the snow to his waist. Using a heavy-legged swimming motion, he approached Dick Munker.

It was clear from the two sets of tracks what had happened. Munker had followed Romanowski's trail over the ridge and plunged down into the maw of a violent forest blowdown. Trunks and branches had been wrenched and snapped, and were nakedly exposed. A stout branch had impaled the hood of Munker's snowmobile and thrown Munker into the blowdown. Romanowski had no doubt led him to this spot deliberately.

Munker's eyes were on Joe as he waded to him. Joe detected no movement from Munker other than in those eyes. Only when he was practically on top of Munker did Joe catch the ripe scent of hot blood and notice the steam wafting from the crotch of Munker's white camouflage suit. Joe stared. It was Munker's upper thigh, near his groin. A sharp branch had pierced Munker's suit.

"Didn't make the turn, huh?" Joe said dully, lowering the muzzle of his shotgun to Munker's forehead. Both heard the dull snap of the safety being thumbed off.

Munker started to say something, but decided against it. His sharp eyes moved from the muzzle to Joe's face. Joe noticed that a little clump of snow was packed into Munker's nostril.

"You murdered my daughter," Joe said. "No one in that compound needed to die."

"She wasn't even yours, was she?" Munker asked weakly. His eyes showed contempt.

Joe grimaced. This man *wanted* to die.

"Joe, don't do it."

It was Nate. He must have shut off his machine in the trees and struggled back through the snow on foot to check on Munker. Joe hadn't heard him coming.

"Why shouldn't I, Nate?" Joe said, feeling strangely giddy. He looked down to see if Munker was moving yet, trying to slap the shotgun away. But all that moved were Munker's sharp eyes.

Nate stopped to catch his breath. He leaned against one of the downed trees, puffing steam that billowed like a halo around his head.

"Because you're not scum like Munker. You don't murder people in cold blood."

"I do now," Joe said. God, his head hurt.

"You're a good guy, Joe. You don't do things like this."

Joe looked up. "I'm tired, Nate. I just lost a daughter."

Nate nodded. "If you shoot this guy, who will take care of Marybeth? What about Sheridan? And Lucy? Her name's Lucy, right?"

"Right." Joe thought Nate was being horribly unfair.

"Who will take care of them? They need their dad."

"Goddamn you, Nate."

Romanowski grinned slightly.

"Besides, I think Munker here severed an artery, and he's probably a few quarts low already. My guess is that he'll go naturally and quietly in your heroic attempt to rescue him."

Joe looked down, and knew that Nate was right. Munker's eyes blazed, but his face was ashen. His lips were already blue. The snow packed into his nose had not melted.

Joe cursed bitterly, raising the shotgun.

"Can you help me lift him up, please?" Joe asked Nate.

AS JOE ROARED AWAY FROM the blowdown with Dick Munker slumped in the seat in front of him, he had second thoughts about Nate's idea. As far as Joe could tell, Munker's life was worth nothing. Joe couldn't think of any value that Munker had brought into the world. Nevertheless, he gunned the engine, hoping against hope that he could deliver the FBI agent to the skirmish line alive. It was more than acceptable if Munker died while

Joe transported him, he thought. But he had to give it his all. He couldn't deliberately slow down and dawdle while Munker suffered. That went against his grain, as much as Joe hated the man. Joe knew it didn't make sense, but he would have rather blasted Munker with his shotgun than be responsible for his death because he'd driven back in a half-assed way.

But Dick Munker died before Joe even got him as far as the meadow they had crossed. Joe knew it the instant it happened, because Munker stiffened and then went limp and heavy and nearly fell off of Joe's snowmobile. Joe stopped, and used his bungee cords to secure the body before continuing on to the compound.

JOE PICKETT LEANED AGAINST HIS snowmobile and watched the deputies load Munker's body into the back of the only Sno-Cat that was still operational. Across the fence, the compound was deserted. Joe watched a few of the assault team check out trailers and RVs that were now empty. Nate's intervention, and the chaos that resulted, had allowed the Sovereigns to proceed with a clearly well-rehearsed escape plan. They had vanished, leaving their belongings and vehicles. Nate's disabling of almost all of the sheriff's Sno-Cats and snowmobiles had prevented any attempt at chasing them down. All that was left were their deserted homes, dozens of exiting snowmobile tracks, and the smoking remains of Wade Brockius's trailer.

"You tried to save him," Elle Broxton-Howard said, putting her arm around Joe.

"Yup," he said. He hadn't been thinking about Dick Munker.

"Too bad about that little girl."

Joe shook her arm off and walked far away from her,

far away from everybody. He couldn't even speak. He stared at the smoldering carcass of the trailer. It had scorched the snow and exposed the earth beneath it— dark earth and green grass that didn't belong here. Melted snow mixed with soot had cut miniature troughs, like spindly black fingers, down the hillside. When he stared at the black framework, all he could see was the face of April Keeley as he last saw her. She was looking out of the window, her head tucked under the chin of her mother. April's face had been emotionless, and haunted. April had always been haunted. She had never, it seemed, had much of a chance, no matter how hard he and Marybeth had tried. He had failed her, and as a result, she was gone. It tore his heart out.

Joe stood there as the snow swirled around him, then felt a wracking sob burst in his chest taking his remaining strength away. His knees buckled and his hands dropped to his sides and he sank down into the snow, hung his head, and cried.

PART FOUR

Snow Ghosts

34

TWO MONTHS HAD PASSED, AND EXCEPT FOR AN OCCA-
sional morning dusting, it hadn't snowed. Even in
March, normally the snowiest month of the year in Wyoming, it didn't snow. A combination of high-altitude
sunshine and warm Chinook winds that swept down and
roared across the face of the Rockies had melted the
snow on the valley floor, although there were still six to
ten feet of snow in the mountains.

At the Sovereign Citizen compound, the disabled
Sno-Cats still sat as silent hulks. The empty trailers,
campers, and vehicles of the Sovereigns hadn't been removed either, and probably wouldn't be until late spring,
when the mountain roads were open and tractors and
flat-bed trucks could get up there.

Except for investigators and a very few journalists,
there had been almost no visitors to the compound since
it had erupted. For all practical purposes, it looked the
same as it had on that day in January.

*   *   *

AN INTERNAL FOREST SERVICE INVESTIGATION had been launched immediately to determine whether or not policies had been breached and regulations followed. The FBI announced a similar investigation into the actions of Special Agent Dick Munker.

Robey Hersig had tentatively put out feelers to the attorney general in Cheyenne about an investigation on a statewide level. He was rebuffed on the basis that it was a federal matter.

Wade Brockius was among those found in the burned trailer. His body lay on top of Jeannie Keeley's as if he had been trying to shield her, and April's body was found beside her mother. Eunice Cobb's body was also found and identified. She had been the victim who had run burning from the trailer. The Reverend B. J. Cobb announced that he intended to file a wrongful-death suit against the U.S. Forest Service and the FBI, and that he would start a legal expense fund based at his church. Cobb had been told to expect that the suit would take as long as five years to culminate in a trial, if it ever went that far.

Cobb had noisily objected to the "internal" nature of the investigations carried out by the federal agencies. He called for an independent investigation instead and proposed that the U.S. Justice Department should form a task force. His proposal gained no traction.

In the meantime, Melinda Strickland had remained in Saddlestring. She had been named interim district supervisor, and had taken over Lamar Gardiner's office and desk. Two female employees had already filed a grievance, claiming that Strickland had hurled books at them in a rage.

JOE AND MARYBETH PICKETT PAID for the funerals of April and Jeannie Keeley with money they didn't have.

Although they still had legal bills from the lawyer they had hired to get April back, they went further into debt to pay for the plots and coffins in the Twelve Sleep County cemetery. The plots were located next to the grave of Ote Keeley, the murdered outfitter who had been buried in his pickup four years before. The fact that they paid for the funerals raised some eyebrows in Saddlestring, and it became a topic of conversation at the Burg-O-Pardner restaurant.

THE "SHOOT-OUT AT BATTLE MOUNTAIN," as it had been dubbed, faded quickly as a mainstream national news story, and didn't linger much longer than that within the state and region, except within pockets of the suspicious and dispossessed. Robey Hersig explained to Joe that the reasons for this had been the inaccessibility of the compound, the lack of media buildup, more pressing war news, and the absence of television coverage. Without visuals, Hersig said, there was no news. He gave the late Dick Munker credit for that.

Therefore, what happened at Battle Mountain didn't rank in the national conscience with Waco, Ruby Ridge, or the Montana Freemen standoff. Although the incident raged through Internet forums and simmered beneath the surface throughout the Mountain West, the lack of good information relegated the story to the back pages of newspapers. Robey told Joe that a few of the Sovereigns who had fled that day had contacted journalists in different parts of the country to offer their stories, but were generally deemed less than credible.

Melinda Strickland was hailed as a hero in a long-form feature in *Rumour* magazine written by Elle Broxton-Howard. Another feature in *Us* magazine—"Lady Ranger Bucks the System and Saves a Forest"—showed a photo of a shoeless Melinda Strickland on the couch in her home, with streaky blonde hair, hugging her dog. A cable-television news crew came to Saddlestring and did a feel-good feature on Broxton-Howard and Melinda Strickland for a newsmagazine show.

As a result, Broxton-Howard's U.S.-based publicist parlayed the segment, which showcased his client's good looks, her on-screen presence, and an accent that seemed to have grown more refined and pronounced since she left Saddlestring, into a series of talk-show and twenty-four-hour cable-news bookings. Elle Broxton-Howard could now be seen on television several nights a week as a paid analyst specializing in gender and environmental issues.

Since January, Broxton-Howard had left three messages for Joe on his office answering machine. She still wanted to do his story, she said. She "smelled" a six-figure movie option. They could work out the details later, when they met, she said. Joe had yet to return her calls.

One night, while Marybeth was idly channel-surfing, Broxton-Howard's face appeared on their television screen. Marybeth scowled at Joe and quickly changed the channel.

BUD LONGBRAKE'S WIFE, THE WOMAN who had been Nate Romanowski's secret lover and who had gone on a world cruise, sent divorce papers from somewhere in Nevada to her husband. He signed them. A week after that, Missy Vankueren moved to the Longbrake ranch.

NATE ROMANOWSKI HAD VANISHED. JOE was surprised to find out that Nate had not been identified by the assault team as the man who had fired on them. His bulky snowmobile suit and helmet had disguised him. They mistakenly assumed that the shooter had been a Sovereign who had somehow flanked them. Ballistics reports couldn't positively identify the huge slugs that had disabled the Sno-Cats because the bullets were damaged beyond recognition. Joe realized that only two people could have positively identified Nate Romanowski as the shooter—Dick Munker and himself.

JOE TOLD STATE AND FEDERAL investigators everything he knew about the incident that day and the buildup to it, with the exceptions of Nate Romanowski's identity and the conversation Joe had had with Romanowski as Dick Munker lay dying. He knew that his account was at odds with those of other witnesses, namely Melinda Strickland, Sheriff Barnum, Elle Broxton-Howard, and a half-dozen deputies. Joe was the only witness to claim that Munker's "warning shot" damaged the propane pipe, or that Munker had manufactured the hostage situation on the fly when told that Spud Cargill was in custody. According to the others, the warning shot had been exactly that, as far as they knew. No one else claimed to have seen a severed copper gas line or heard escaping propane gas. Joe didn't think the members of the assault team were lying—after all, they had been bundled up and wearing helmets that blocked sound, and none of them had been as close as Joe was on the road to the trailer and the severed pipe. The heat of the fire had damaged the pipe that Joe claimed was severed, literally melting it into the snow so Joe had no way to prove his allegations. Despite this, he hoped that his account would not be dismissed.

Several of the investigators asked Joe pointedly, and with obvious skepticism, if he wasn't too far away to see with certainty what had happened when Munker fired. They also speculated aloud that perhaps his personal interest in the entire event—and his obvious animosity toward Dick Munker and Melinda Strickland—had colored his interpretation. The working theory reached by DCI and the FBI was that the trailer burned from the accidental or intentional ignition of materials within the trailer itself.

One of the FBI investigators, a small man named Wendt, told Joe in confidence that he believed him. He also told Joe that his account would be difficult, if not impossible, to prove. Wendt said he was afraid that the internal investigation would be written from the point of view that Munker was a hero who had died in the line of duty. However it went, he said, Joe would also be commended for his attempt to save Munker's life.

Joe didn't hold out much hope, but part of him wanted to believe that further investigation would somehow corroborate his version and justice would be done. He hoped that a deputy or other member of the assault team would confirm his account, or at least parts of it. Someone, he thought, *must* have heard the hissing of gas. Maybe time, and guilt, would make someone step forward. But he knew how unlikely that was, and he knew from experience how law-enforcement personnel stuck together and told the same story.

FOR JOE AND MARYBETH PICKETT, the two months following the death of April went by in a kind of bitter, dreamy fog. Joe relived the two days leading up to the deaths over and over, picking apart his feverish moves and decisions. He deeply regretted not pressing Cobb further when he'd first gone to his house, and not questioning Cobb's reference to "sanctuary" that day. Cobb had misled him, but Joe had allowed himself to be misled. Because he hadn't understood what Cobb was hinting at, he had gone on an errant trail and wasted almost sixteen hours when he could have intercepted Spud coming down the mountain. It gnawed at him.

Many nights, he didn't sleep more than a few hours at a stretch. Several times, when he couldn't sleep, he would wander downstairs to his office and rewrite his letter of resignation. He had once sealed it and stamped it—only to retrieve it from his OUT basket the next morning. He had also written—but not submitted—a request to be reassigned to another district. The thought of sharing Twelve Sleep Valley with Melinda Strickland was loathsome.

Marybeth was mercurial, her moods swinging from pure anger to a resigned depression that was new, and disturbing, to Joe. On the nights when Marybeth locked herself in the bedroom, Joe cooked dinner for his girls and told them that their mother wasn't feeling well. Sheridan had stared him down on that one, and had known without asking that he was using illness as an excuse.

Once, late at night, as Joe printed out the latest version of his resignation letter, he heard sounds from down the hallway. Marybeth had led Sheridan and Lucy into Joe and Marybeth's bedroom to sleep, and was shuffling things in the children's bedroom with a vengeance. When Joe found her, she was in the process of removing every last sign of April. She had bagged all of April's clothes, school papers, and toys, and was now stripping the bed. He watched with sadness as she scrubbed down the walls near April's bed, as if to remove any physical evidence of April having been there.

"I haven't cleaned her sheets since she left," Marybeth told him, her eyes strangely alert. "I don't know why I haven't done that. But I need to wash them and put them away now."

Joe had watched her, not knowing what to do. When Marybeth finally paused long enough to cry, he held her.

"I've never hated a woman as much as I hate her," Marybeth said. Joe knew she meant Melinda Strickland.

Joe had never seen her so angry, or so bitter.

"She'll go to jail. The investigation will prove that," Joe assured Marybeth, stroking her hair and hoping that somehow he was right. "It won't bring April back, but at least Melinda Strickland will pay."

Marybeth leaned her head back and met his eyes. "She never even sent a note. Think about that, Joe. Think how cold her heart is."

Joe just nodded, knowing there was nothing to say.

ON THE WAY HOME FROM the last basketball practice of the season, Sheridan sat quietly in the cab of the pickup, absently patting Maxine's head. Joe, driving, cast wary glances at the sky that filled the top half of his windshield. Thunderheads were moving in. It looked like snow.

"Dad?"

"Yes."

"Is Mom going to be okay?"

Joe paused. "She's going to be all right. It takes a while."

"I miss April, too."

"So do I, honey."

"I know we're not going to get April back," Sheridan said. "But I do want my mom back."

Joe reached over and put his hand on Sheridan's shoulder. Her hair was still damp from practice.

"Dad, can I ask you something?"

Joe nodded.

"Are you and Mom mad at me for not watching April closer that day in school? For letting Jeannie Keeley take her away?"

Joe was hurt by the question, and pulled quickly to the side of the road so he could turn in his seat and face her.

"No, honey, of course we're not angry with you," he assured her. "It wasn't your fault."

"But I was responsible for her," Sheridan said, fighting tears that seemed to come, Joe thought, much more easily than they used to.

"That's never even crossed our minds, Sheridan," Joe said. "Never."

As they pulled out into the road, Joe restrained a heavy sigh. He felt badly that he hadn't seen this coming, hadn't thought to talk to Sheridan about this earlier. *Of course she would feel this way,* he thought. Despite her maturity, despite what she's been through, *she's still a child,* he thought. And she naturally wondered if the difficulties her parents were having were somehow her doing.

It had been rough on Sheridan and Lucy, Joe knew. They missed April, and they missed the way their mother used to be. Marybeth had seesawed between snapping at them and smothering them with physical affection. Lucy had complained to him that she didn't know what to say to her mother because she never knew what reaction she would get.

Joe knew he was far from faultless as well. He felt distant, and uninterested in so many of the things that used to give him joy. His thoughts were still up there on the mountain, in the compound, in the snow. He sometimes forgot that the living members of his family were in front of him and needed his attention.

"Your mom will be all right," Joe said. "She's tough."

Sheridan nodded.

"We've never really talked about what happened up there on the mountain, Dad," she said. "It seems like the good guys turned out to be the bad guys, and the bad guys weren't all that bad."

Joe smiled. "That's a pretty good way to put it."

"I can't really sort it out," Sheridan confessed.

"Sheridan, it's all about accountability," he said after a pause. It was something he had thought a lot about recently.

"What's that mean?"

"It means that people should be accountable for their actions. They *have* to be accountable. There need to be consequences for thoughtless or cruel behavior," Joe said, wondering if he'd said too much. He didn't want her to think he was plotting revenge.

Sheridan sat silently for a few moments.

"Who is accountable for me losing a sister for no good reason?"

Joe frowned. "I am, to a certain degree . . ."

"No, you're not!"

"Yes, honey, I am," Joe said, looking straight ahead out the window. "I didn't protect her as well as I should have. I didn't get her back."

"Dad!" Tears rolled down Sheridan's face.

"Others are even more accountable," he said.

THAT EVENING, AFTER DINNER, THE telephone rang. It was Robey Hersig.

"Joe," Hersig said.

Joe could tell that something was wrong. There was no greeting, no small talk, no mention of the coming storm.

"Yup."

"We got an early look at the findings of the joint FBI and Forest Service investigation. Munker and Melinda Strickland were not only exonerated, they were commended for their actions. There will be a formal announcement tomorrow."

Joe squeezed the receiver as if to crush it.

"How could this happen, Robey?"

"Joe, you've got to stay calm."

"I'm calm."

He looked up to see Marybeth staring at him from where she had turned near the sink. It was obvious she could tell what was happening by reading his face. Joe watched as her expression went cold and her fists clenched.

"Don't do anything foolish," Hersig said. "We knew this was a possibility. You and I discussed it. With an internal investigation and all . . . well, they weren't too likely to find that their own people screwed up. Remember, these are the Feds—the FBI. We knew that going in."

Joe said nothing.

"Joe, promise me you'll stay calm."

MARYBETH HAD RUN UPSTAIRS TO the bedroom and closed the door after Joe told her what Hersig had reported. He needed to give her some time, he thought, before he went up there. He needed some time to figure out what to say that wasn't angry and bitter. Grabbing his coat from the rack in the mudroom, he went outside into the dark to try to clear his head.

It was cold, and there was humidity in the air. The stars were blocked out by clouds. After two months, there would be snow coming again. For some reason, he welcomed it. He zipped his coat as he strode up the walk toward the picket fence.

Joe heard a muffled rustling of bird's wings in the dark and stopped with one hand on the gate. He turned. Next to Joe's pickup in the driveway, Nate Romanowski sat on the hood of an ancient Buick Riviera with Idaho license plates. His peregrine was perched on his fist.

"Have you ever considered just knocking on the door?" Joe asked.

"Thanks for keeping me out of it," Nate said, ignoring Joe's question.

"You were helping me," Joe said, closing the gate behind him and approaching Nate and the Buick. "It was the least I could do."

"I heard about the results of the investigation," Nate said, shaking his head. "Their first rule of survival is that they protect their own."

"How in the hell did you know about it? I just heard."

"My contacts in Idaho," Nate said. "The decision was a foregone conclusion six weeks ago. All the Feds knew about it. Office gossip. It just took them a while to write it up with the proper spin."

Joe sat next to Nate on the hood of the Riviera. He sighed deeply, and fought an urge to hurl himself into something hard. He realized how much he had hoped for a miracle after the investigation, and how naïve that hope had been.

"It would be a good thing," Nate said, "if Melinda Strickland went away."

Joe turned and looked hard at Nate. This time, he didn't argue. Joe thought about his family inside the house, and how rough the past two months had been for them all. This wouldn't set things right, or take them back to where they were. But he thought about what he'd told Sheridan about accountability.

"I can take care of it," Nate said.

"No," Joe said hesitantly.

"You don't know what you want, do you?"

"I want her out of this state," Joe said. "I want her out of the Forest Service. I want her to pay something. And I don't mean money. I mean her job at the very least."

"She's evil." Nate frowned. "Leaving her on the street will result in somebody else getting hurt wherever she lands."

Joe thought about it. "That's as far as I'm willing to go, Nate."

"You're sure?" Nate asked.

Joe nodded. He was well aware of the fact that he was crossing a line. But, he thought, it was a line that needed to be crossed in these circumstances. If he was wrong, there would be a world of trouble for him. If he was right, there could still be trouble. The easy and safe thing would be to simply let things run their course. But that was something he couldn't do.

"Maybe a little more," Joe said, feeling both elated and guilty at the same time.

"There's my boy." Nate smiled and nodded and clapped Joe on the back of his coat. "Then we need to persuade her to retire and leave," Nate said. "So we need leverage. How well do you know her?"

"Not well enough," Joe said. "I'm not sure anyone really knows her."

"But you know her well enough to have a good idea about what she likes, what's important to her, right?"

Joe thought about it. He thought of two things. They went inside to Joe's office and Joe asked Nate to wait a moment. He went upstairs to check on Marybeth. She had been crying. Joe tried to comfort her, but she didn't want comforting. Seeing her like that steeled Joe's determination to *do something*. He left Marybeth, went downstairs to the kitchen. He grabbed a bottle of bourbon, dropped ice into two waterglasses, and carried it all into his office. He shut the door.

For the next two hours, they discussed it. Eventually, they agreed on a plan.

It began to snow.

35

AT 4:52 THE NEXT AFTERNOON, JOE PICKETT ENTERED the U.S. Forest Service office in Saddlestring and sat down on a vinyl couch that looked as if it had been purchased during the Ford Administration. While he brushed snowflakes off the manila folder he had brought with him, he smiled at the receptionist.

"I'm here to see Melinda Strickland."

The receptionist glanced at the clock on the wall. The office would close in eight minutes. She had already put her purse on her desk and gathered up her coat. Joe knew from experience that no one in the office worked a minute past five. It was the same situation at most state and federal offices.

"Is she expecting you?"

"She should be," Joe said, "but I doubt it."

"Your name?"

"Joe Pickett. And please tell her it's important."

The receptionist was a new employee, someone recently hired by Melinda Strickland to replace the last receptionist, who was one of the two women who had filed the grievance. Joe recognized her from a previous job she had held in a local credit union. She was unsmiling, and squat, brusque. He watched her as she rapped on Melinda Strickland's closed door. Then she went inside and shut the door behind her.

Joe heard the murmur of voices, one of them raising in pitch. In a moment, the door reopened and the receptionist returned to her desk for her purse and coat.

"She asked that you make an appointment for later in the week."

"I see," Joe said. "Did you tell her it was important?"

The receptionist glared at Joe.

"Yes."

"Did you tell her it was about her *dog*?"

She was suddenly flustered. As Joe had suspected, the receptionist had been there long enough to realize the special relationship Strickland had with her cocker spaniel.

"No. What about her dog?"

Joe shook his head. "I need to talk with Ms. Strickland privately, please."

The receptionist huffed and turned on her heel and went back into Strickland's office. Behind him, Joe heard a brief rush of employees turning off lights and closing office doors. It was five, and they streamed out of the building so quickly that the outside door never shut between them.

Melinda Strickland opened her door, clearly agitated. She stood to one side to let the receptionist back through so she could go home. Strickland's hair was the coppery color it had been when Joe first met her three months before.

"What is this about Bette?"

Joe had forgotten the name of her cocker spaniel. He stood up.

"Do you have a minute?" he asked.

Strickland's eyes flashed. She hated surprises, but she loved her dog. Joe knew that.

"Ms. Strickland . . . ?" the receptionist asked, poised behind her desk.

"Yes, go on home," Strickland snapped at her employee. "I'll lock things up in a minute."

Joe pushed by Melinda Strickland in her doorway and walked into her office. The room was in a shambles. Papers, notebooks, and mail were piled on the chairs, on the desk, and in the corners. She had made quite a mess in a short period of time. He cleared a hardback chair of papers and sat down across from her desk to wait for her.

Peeved that he had entered her office uninvited, she strode around her desk and sat down facing him. *"What?"* she demanded.

He coolly looked around the room. The only things of a personal nature on the side wall were a framed cover of *Rumour* magazine and a photo of Bette.

"Joe, I . . ."

"Your actions killed my daughter," Joe said simply, letting the words drop like stones.

She recoiled as if stung.

"You and I both know what happened up there on the mountain," he said, holding her eyes until she looked away. "Your agency exonerated you. But we're talking about the real world now. I was there. You caused her death, and the death of three other people."

"I don't know what you're talking about," she spat. "You are a sick man." She looked everywhere in the room except at Joe.

"You didn't even send my wife a note."

"Leave my office this instant, Warden Pickett."

Joe leaned forward and cleared a spot on her desk for the manila folder he had brought with him. He placed it there but didn't open it.

"There's no way you can bring April back," Joe said. "But there are a couple of things you can do to at least partially absolve your guilt."

Her hands thumped on the desktop. "I'm guilty of nothing!"

"Of course, it's not even close to enough . . . ," Joe continued, opening the folder as if Strickland hadn't spoken, ". . . but it's something. It will make my wife feel better. And it will make me feel better. It might even make *you* feel better."

"Get out of my office!" Strickland screeched, her face contorted with rage. It was clear to Joe she wasn't used to people ignoring her orders.

Joe went on, directing his attention again to the paper he was reading. "The first document here is a press release creating the April Keeley Foundation for Children," he said. He glanced up and saw that she was listening, although her face was white and tense. "The initial twenty-five thousand dollars for the Foundation is to be donated by you from the trust fund your father set up for you. If you can give more than that, it would be even better."

He searched the document so he could quote directly from it. "The purpose of the Foundation is to 'advocate for better protection and legislation for children in foster care.' You'll be a hero again. Maybe there will be a story in a magazine about you not only saving a forest but also protecting foster children."

"What is this?" she said. "Where did you get that?"

"I wrote it up last night," he said, shrugging. "Press releases are not my specialty, but I think it's okay."

"What am I supposed to do with it?"

"Release it under your signature. Then call one of your press conferences and announce it." An edge of sarcasm had crept into his voice, and a slight smile tugged at his mouth.

Strickland was clearly aghast. Joe hadn't seen her face so contorted before.

"And something else," he said, removing the other document from the folder. "Your resignation letter. You can sign it and announce it during your press conference. It will look like you're quitting in order to do good work for children. Everybody likes *that*. The real reason will be our little secret."

The resignation letter had been easy to write for Joe. He had simply used the one *he* had been working on, and changed the names.

"Sign these, and we can both go home," Joe said, placing the documents in front of her.

"This is sick."

"No, it's not sick."

"I should call the sheriff."

"No, you should sign these documents. There's a copy for you and one for me."

Joe leaned forward in his chair, and any semblance of a smile left his face. "Look, call the sheriff if you want. Tell him I'm threatening you with two pieces of paper. Tell him why this is so upsetting to you, that I would want you to create a foundation for children. That should play pretty well with the media as well, don't you think?"

Strickland erupted violently, lashing out with the back of her hand and sending a stack of paperwork that was piled on the edge of the desk fluttering toward the wall like a flock of wounded birds.

"GET OUT OF MY OFFICE!" she shrieked. "JUST *GET OUT!*"

Joe snatched the release and the letter before she

could destroy them. Watching her carefully, he leaned back in his chair and shouted over his shoulder.

"Nate!"

He watched her eyes as they swung from him over his shoulder toward the door. He heard a shuffle behind him, and watched as her eyes widened and the blood drained from her face.

Joe glanced back. Nate Romanowski stood inside the office now. He cradled Bette in one arm and held the gaping muzzle of his .454 Casull to the head of the cocker spaniel.

"Sign your name," Nate said, "or the little dog gets it."

Despite the situation, Joe almost smiled.

"You're *monsters*!" Strickland whispered. "My poor Bette."

Joe turned back to her. Silently, he slid the documents back onto her desk. He took a pen from his shirt pocket and took its cap off. Handing her the pen, he said, "Let's get this done."

Relief surged through him as she absently reached out for the pen.

He turned the documents around and pointed to the blank signature lines. Strickland leaned forward and her hand hovered over the papers for a moment, but then he saw something dark and malevolent wash over her face angrily twist her features. Suddenly, she threw the pen aside.

"Go ahead and kill the dog," she snarled. "I'm not signing anything. What's in this for me? Huh? What do *I* get out of this? *Nothing!* Fucking *nothing*."

Joe hoped she was bluffing. But when he looked into her eyes, into the cold fury of madness, he knew she wasn't. He had horribly miscalculated.

Behind him, he heard the metallic click of the hammer being pulled back on the revolver.

But Nate cocking the revolver made no difference. When he looked at Melinda Strickland, he saw a grotesque shell filled with venom and bile. He did not see a glimmer of human feelings. Even the death of her dog, the only thing she appeared to have feelings for, could not break through the armor of her narcissism. He was outmatched, and felt utterly defeated. He knew he wasn't capable of pushing this any further. To do so would be to join her in her malediction.

"Nate, let the dog go," Joe said, sighing.

"What?" Nate's voice was hard with anger. "What are you saying?"

"Let the dog go."

"Joe, you've got to go through with . . ."

He rose and turned. "It's not going to work."

Nate narrowed his eyes as he studied the leering face of Melinda Strickland, then came to the same conclusion Joe had. The dog licked his hand.

Nate released the hammer and shoved his revolver back into his shoulder holster with indignation. He bent and freed the dog.

"Get out of my office," Strickland said coldly, triumphantly. "Both of you."

Then she called her dog.

Joe walked past Nate into the reception area. He was crushed, humiliated. Nate joined him a beat later. They stared at each other in the reception area, both confounded by what had just happened.

"Bette, damn you, come *here*!" Strickland shouted from inside her office.

Instead, the cocker spaniel tore through the door and leaped toward Nate. The dog wanted him to hold her again.

36

JOE PICKETT STOOD AT THE BAR IN THE STOCKMAN'S and ordered his third Jim Beam on the rocks. While darkness came and the snow fell outside and drinkers entered complaining about the weather, he stared at his face in the cracked mirror.

He felt impotent and defeated, and the slow warmth of the bourbon spreading through him didn't assuage his humiliation. When the glass came he threw back his head and drained it, then signaled to the bartender. The man looked skeptically at Joe for a moment, but poured another drink.

It was probably dinnertime at home, but it didn't register with him. Pool balls clicked in the back of the bar, but he barely heard them. He realized that somehow he had lost Nate as he walked the three blocks from the Forest Service office to the Stockman's, and he hadn't looked around for him until he was seated on the red leather stool. He didn't want to think anymore. He wanted another drink.

He had never felt like such a failure. He was a poor

father and a poor husband. He hadn't protected April and she was dead as a result. She had died because of lack of protection, like winterkill. Now, in confronting Melinda Strickland, he had failed April once again.

Would it have been different if it had been Sheridan or Lucy instead of April? Joe wondered. Would he have reacted differently, been more aggressive early on and not depended on the legal system to work, if it had been one of his own flesh-and-blood daughters up there? Would he have "turned cowboy," as Nate once put it, if it hadn't been April? The question tortured him.

He stared at his face in the mirror. He wasn't sure he liked what he saw.

"WAITING FOR YOUR WIFE TO join you?"

The question startled Joe out of his malaise, and he spilled his drink on the bar. It was Herman Klein, the rancher. Joe hadn't seen him walk into the Stockman's, but he'd been so deep in thought that he hadn't been noticing much. He was now on his fifth drink, and the bar lights were starting to shimmy.

"Nope. Have a seat." Joe recognized the birth of a slur when he said "seat."

Klein sat and removed his hat to shake the snow off.

"I'm glad to see this storm," Klein said, ordering a shot and a beer and another drink for Joe. Joe ignored the skeptical glare of the bartender, who wiped up the spill with a rag. "We need the moisture. That's a strange thing to say after this January, but it's true."

Joe nodded. He felt a burbling in his stomach. He wondered if he would need to throw up.

They drank for a moment.

"Why did you ask about Marybeth?" Joe said.

Klein raised his eyebrows. "Because I never see you in

here, and I saw her getting out of her van down the block. I just figured you were meeting her."

It took a moment for this information to filter through Joe's lethargic brain. Then he was puzzled. What would Marybeth be doing in town? The kids would have been home from school for the last few hours, and she should have been at home with them. Was she looking for Joe? He hadn't called her, after all. In fact, he had told her nothing of the plan he and Nate had come up with. It was rare for him not to consult with her, but this had seemed like something she didn't need right now. Or more rightly, something *he* didn't need. In the back of his mind, knowing her feelings, he had been a little afraid of how far she would have wanted to go with Strickland. It wasn't something he wanted to see in his wife, if he could help it, or something he wanted to give her the opportunity to act upon.

"How long ago was that?" Joe asked Klein.

He shrugged. "Half-hour, I guess."

Joe had left his truck at the Forest Service office. Maybe, he thought, she saw it there on her way home from her job at the library and stopped. *Uh-oh.*

Hastily but clumsily, he slid off his stool and threw his last twenty on the bar.

"Gotta go," he mumbled, sliding his coat up over his shoulders.

"You need a ride somewhere?" Klein asked, assessing Joe's condition.

"I'm fine."

Joe pretended not to hear Klein's protestations as he weaved his way toward the door.

He spilled out into the darkness, his boots sliding on the three inches of fresh powder on the pavement. He clamped down his hat and buttoned his coat as he walked as quickly as he could down the street.

If Marybeth saw his pickup in front of the Forest Service office, she would probably go inside. Would Melinda Strickland still be there? If that was the case, Joe could only guess what could happen. *I've never hated a woman as much as I hate her*, Marybeth had said. But Melinda Strickland would surely have left her office right after he and Nate left, wouldn't she? Wouldn't she?

He wished he were sober.

He rounded the corner and could see through the waves of snow that a Sheriff's Department Blazer, lights flashing, and a Saddlestring Police Department cruiser were parked in front of the Forest Service office. Blue and red wig-wag lights painted the street. The door of the Blazer hung open, as if the deputy had just jumped out. Joe's truck was still parked in front, as was Melinda Strickland's green Bronco. Marybeth's van was not there, and he breathed a sigh of relief.

HE DID NOT WANT TO see Melinda Strickland again. Had she called the sheriff on him? Had something happened between her and Marybeth after he'd left?

Joe approached the building and eased the door open far enough to stick his head inside. The bourbon had made him bold—or foolhardy, he thought. Probably both. Inside, it was just as he had left it, except that Deputy Reed stood in the reception area, his radio raised to his mouth. The Saddlestring policeman sat on the vinyl couch, still bundled in his winter coat, with a vacant, drained look on his face, like he had seen something awful.

"Sheriff Barnum?" Reed said into the radio, "How fast can you get over to the Forest Service building? We just got a call about the fact that the door was left open and the lights were on at seven at night, so I checked it out and . . . well, *we've got a situation*."

Joe looked quizzically at Reed, and Reed nodded toward the hallway where Melinda Strickland's office was. Her door, like the front, was ajar.

He stepped inside and walked across the reception area. The Saddlestring cop was upset. Something he had seen down the hall made him lurch to one side and throw up in a small garbage can. Joe was grateful that both Reed and the cop were too preoccupied to ask him why he was there.

Joe rounded the reception desk and looked into Melinda Strickland's office. What he saw seared the alcohol out of his system.

Strickland was still in her chair, but was slumped face-down over her desk in a dark red pool of blood. The wall with the framed cover of *Rumour* and photo of Bette was spattered with blood, brains, and stringy swatches of copper-colored hair. Strickland's stainless-steel nine-millimeter Ruger semiautomatic pistol was clutched in her hand on top of the desk. A single shell casing on the carpet reflected the overhead light. The room smelled of hot blood.

Joe gagged, then swallowed. The bourbon tasted so bitter this time that he nearly choked on it.

He *knew* it wasn't suicide. Just a couple of hours before, he had stared into that woman's soul and there was nothing there to see. Strickland had not succumbed to some sudden pang of guilt. No, Joe thought, someone had made it *look* like a suicide.

He started to push the door open farther but it stiffened. It wouldn't open enough for him to get through. He looked down and saw that he had shoved the bottom of the door over something that had jammed it.

In a fog, he bent down to clear the door. He pulled the obstruction free, and looked at it.

It seemed as if something had sucked all the air out of

his lungs and out of the room itself. He wasn't entirely sure the groan he heard was his own.

The item jamming the door was a single Canadian-made Watson riding glove. It was one-half of Joe's Christmas present to Marybeth.

37

JOE CHECKED BOTH WAYS AS HE LEFT THE FOREST SER-
vice office in the heavy snowfall. There was no traffic on
the street. He heard a siren fire up several blocks away.
That would be either Barnum or the police chief. The
glove was jammed in Joe's pocket.

He was soon out of town and rolling on Bighorn
Road toward his home before he allowed himself to
think. He was ashamed of what he was thinking. It was
unfathomable.

MARYBETH'S VAN WAS PARKED IN front of the garage and
the porch light was on, but the windows were dark.
When he entered, he noticed immediately that the house
was cool and that the thermostat had not been turned up
since they had left in the morning.

Sheridan and Lucy, who should have been watching
television or doing homework, were nowhere to be seen.

"Marybeth?"

"Up here." Her voice was faint. She was upstairs.

He bounded up the stairs and found his family in the bedroom. Lucy was sleeping on the top of the covers at the foot of the bed, and Sheridan and Marybeth were sitting on the side of the bed cuddling.

"Are you okay?" he asked.

"We were just talking about April," Sheridan said, her voice solemn. "We were feeling kind of sad tonight."

Joe looked at Marybeth, trying to read her. She looked drained and wan. She did not look up at him.

"Have you eaten?" he asked.

Sheridan shook her head.

"Please take Lucy downstairs and get yourselves something," Joe said. "We'll be down in a minute."

Marybeth untangled herself from Sheridan, but she wouldn't look at Joe.

When the girls were gone, Joe eased the door shut and sat next to Marybeth on the bed.

"You've been drinking," she said. "I can smell it."

Joe grunted.

"Marybeth, we have to talk about this," he said, pulling her glove from his coat pocket.

He watched her carefully when she looked at it.

"I didn't realize I lost it," she said, turning it over in her hand and squeezing it into a ball.

Joe felt something hot rising inside of him.

"You know where I found it, don't you?"

She nodded. Finally, she raised her eyes to his.

"I saw your truck," she said, her voice flat. "So I went inside the building. Melinda Strickland was sitting at her desk, and her blood was on the wall . . ."

The relief Joe felt was better than the bourbon ever was. Then he realized something that jarred him.

"You think *I* did it," Joe said.

The same emotion Joe had felt a moment before was mirrored in Marybeth's face.

"Joe, you didn't do it?"

He shook his head. "I found her like that after you did. And I saw this glove . . ."

"Oh," she cried, instantly aware of what he must have thought. "Oh, Joe, I knew you went there and I thought . . ."

They embraced in a furious swirl of redemption. Marybeth cried, and laughed, and cried again. After a few minutes, she pulled away.

"So did she kill herself?" she asked.

Joe shook his head. "Not a chance."

"Then who?"

He paused a beat.

"Nate."

She stood and walked to the window, looking out at the snow.

"He went back after we left, while I was in the bar. He must have watched me go into the Stockman's to make sure I'd have a good alibi before he went back to her office. I thought I had just lost him. I wasn't thinking very clearly at that point. Somehow, he got Melinda Strickland's gun away from her and shot her point-blank in the head."

"My God," Marybeth said, turning it over in her mind.

"He told me once that he didn't believe in the legal system, but he believed in justice," Joe said. "We tried it my way and it didn't work. His way worked."

"What are you going to do?"

Joe sighed, and rubbed his face. He felt Marybeth watching him anxiously, felt her searching his face for an indication of what he was thinking.

He looked up at her and spoke softly.

"I'm going to make Melinda Strickland a hero," he said.

She was clearly puzzled.

"There are some papers on her desk we left there. They'll find them when they investigate the crime scene. But it will take a few days to analyze everything. Tomorrow, I'll call Elle Broxton-Howard and give her that interview she wants. In fact, I'll give her the *mother* of all interviews—the exclusive inside story of Melinda Strickland's last day on earth. I'll tell her that ever since the shoot-out at Battle Mountain, Melinda Strickland has been tortured by the death of April Keeley, that it was eating away at her. Strickland told me all about it in the meeting we had in her office, when she described the foundation she was creating. Her secretary will corroborate the meeting.

"She just couldn't overcome the guilt," Joe said. "So she took her own life. Before she did, though, she wrote out her resignation and established the April Keeley Foundation as her legacy."

The story was taking shape as he spun it out, and he was becoming convinced it would work. He stopped for breath, and looked to Marybeth for confirmation.

Marybeth looked at him with eyes that shined. "Sometimes you amaze me," she said.

"It'll be a hell of a story," he said, shaking his head.

There was a long pause.

"What are you going to do about Nate?"

Joe thought, and hesitated for a moment. He had crossed a line. He couldn't go back and pretend he hadn't crossed it. He would have to ride it out.

"I'm going to ask him to teach Sheridan about falconry."

He rose and joined her at the window and they looked out at the storm. A burst of wind sent snow tumbling toward them, and Joe felt the lick of icy wind on his hand near the window frame. He would need to put some insulation in the crack later. He had forgotten about it.

He leaned forward and looked down into the front yard. The heavy, wet spring snow was being carried by the wind and was sticking to the sides of the fence and the power poles. There were three small Austrian pine trees in the front yard that Joe had put in the previous spring. The girls had helped him plant them and, at the time, each had claimed a tree. The tallest was Sheridan's, the next was April's, the smallest belonged to Lucy. Joe found himself staring at April's tree, watching the blowing snow pack hard into the branches, changing it into a snow ghost, and felt oddly comforted.

ACKNOWLEDGMENTS

I'm deeply indebted to those who gave their time and expertise to make this novel as accurate as possible. It should be noted, however, that any mistakes are mine alone.

Bob Baker of Freedom Arms in Freedom, Wyoming, demonstrated the quality workmanship and tremendous firepower of his fine revolvers. My ears are still ringing.

Gordon Crawford, one of my oldest friends, was the first to introduce me to the art of falconry. Gordon corrected my first-draft errors about falconry, and offered other valuable suggestions.

Mark and Mari Nelson once again assisted with details and procedures in regard to a real-life Wyoming game warden (and family), and provided me with professional guidance and encouragement.

Andy Whelchel, my agent, is always there behind the scenes, making things work.

Don Hajicek is the resident genius behind www.cjbox.net.

Attorney Thomas Lubnau, of Gillette, Wyoming, provided invaluable assistance in the legal issues involved with foster care and parental custody.

Ken Siman, my hardworking publicist, does an unbelievable job, and does not own a funeral home—at least not that I know of.

My deep appreciation, once again, goes to Martha Bushko, my brilliant editor. The professionals at G. P. Putnam's Sons and Berkley are the best of the best—Carole Baron, Dan Harvey, Leslie Gelbman, the entire team—and I am honored to have the privilege of working with them.

C. J. Box
Cheyenne, Wyoming

1

IT HAD BEEN A GOOD DAY OF FLY-FISHING UNTIL JOE Pickett and his daughters encountered a massive bull moose that appeared to be grinning at them.

Until then, Joe, Sheridan, and seven-year-old Lucy had spent the entire afternoon working their way up-stream on Crazy Woman Creek on a brilliant, early-September day. Maxine, their yellow Labrador, was with them. The tall streamside grass hummed with insects, hoppers mainly, and a high breeze swayed the crowns of the musky lodgepole pine forest.

They fished methodically, overtaking each other in wide loops away from the water, passing silently while the person they were passing cast at a pool or promising riffle. The water was lower than usual—it was a drought year—but the stream was clear and still very cold. Joe was in his late thirties, lean and of average height. His face and the backs of his hands were sunburned from being outside at altitude.

Hopscotching over dry river rocks, Joe had crossed the stream so he could keep a better eye on his girls as they worked the other side with their fly rods. Maxine shadowed Joe, as she always did, fighting her natural instinct to plunge into the water and retrieve fly casts.

Sheridan stood waist deep in brush upstream and was momentarily still, concentrating on tying a new hopper pattern to her tippet. Her glasses glinted in the afternoon sun, so Joe couldn't tell if she was watching him observe her. She wore her new fishing vest (a recent birthday present) over a T-shirt, baggy shorts, and water sandals for wading. A sweat-stained Wyoming Game and Fish Department cap—one of Joe's old ones—was pulled down tightly on her head. Her bare arms and legs were crosshatched with fresh scratches from thorns and branches she had crashed through to get closer to the water. She was a serious fly-fisher, and a serious girl over-all.

But while Sheridan was the fisher, Lucy seemed to be catching most of the fish, much to Sheridan's consternation. Lucy did not share her older sister's passion for fishing. She came because Joe insisted, and because he had promised her a good lunch. She wore a sundress and white sandals, her shiny blonde hair tied in a ponytail.

With each fish Lucy caught, Sheridan's glare toward her little sister intensified, and she moved farther upstream away from her. *It's not fair,* Joe knew she was thinking.

"Dad, come here and look at this," Sheridan called, breaking into his rumination. He pulled the slack tight on his rod and looped his line through his fingers before walking up the bank toward her. She was pointing down at something in the water beneath her feet.

It was a dead trout, white belly up, lodged between two exposed stones. The fish bobbed in a natural cul-de-sac dark with pine needles and sheaths of algae that had washed down with the current. He could tell from the wet, vinyl-like sheen on the fish's pale underside and the still-bright twin slashes of red beneath its gills that it hadn't been dead very long.

"That's a nice fish," Sheridan said to Joe. "A cutthroat. How big do you think it is?"

"Thirteen, fourteen inches," Joe replied. "It's a dandy." Instinctively, he reached down for Maxine's collar. He could feel her trembling under her skin through her coat, anxious to retrieve the dead fish.

"What do you think happened to it?" she asked. "Do you think somebody caught it and threw it back after it was dead?"

Joe shrugged, "Don't know." On a previous trip, Joe had instructed Sheridan how to properly release a fish back into the water after he caught it. He had shown her how to cradle it under its belly and lower it slowly into the water so that the natural current would revive it, and how to let the fish dart away under its own power once it was fit to do so.

She had asked him about the ethics of eating caught fish versus releasing them, and he told her that fish were for eating but that there was no reason to be greedy, and that keeping dead fish in a hot creel all day and throwing them away later because they were ruined was an ethical problem, if not a legal one. He knew this is what she was thinking about when she pointed out the dead fish.

IT WASN'T LONG BEFORE SHERIDAN pointed out another dead fish. It hadn't been dead as long as the other one, Joe noted, because it floated on its side, flaunting the rainbow colors that gave the fish its name. It had not yet turned belly-up. This fish was not as large as the first, but still impressive.

Sheridan was righteously indignant.

"Something is killing these fish, and it makes me mad," she said, her eyes flashing. Joe didn't like it either but was impressed by her outrage, although he didn't know whether her anger came from her outdoor ethics or if she was angry because someone was killing fish she felt *she* deserved to catch.

"Can you tell what's killing them?" she asked.

This time, he let Maxine retrieve the rainbow. The Lab unnecessarily launched herself into the water with a splash that soaked both of them, and came back with the trout in her mouth. Joe pried it loose from Maxine's jaws and turned it over in his palm. He could see nothing unusual about the fish.

"This isn't like finding a dead deer or elk, where I can check for bullets," he told Sheridan. "I can't see any wounds or disease on this fish. They may have been over-stressed after being caught by someone."

Sheridan huffed with disappointment, and strode upstream. Joe tossed the fish into a stand of willows behind him.

While he waited for Lucy to mosey her way closer, he reached behind him and felt the heavy sag of his .40 Beretta semiautomatic, his service weapon, hidden away in the large back pocket creel of his fishing vest. He also affirmed that his wallet-badge was there, as well as several strands of Flexcuffs. Although he wasn't working, he was still the game warden, and still charged with enforcing regulations.

That morning, as he packed, he had taken the unusual step of adding another item to his fishing-vest arsenal: bear spray. He strummed his fingers over the large aerosol can through the fabric of his vest. The bear spray was wicked stuff, ten times more powerful than the pepper spray used for disabling humans. A whiff of the spray, even at a distance, brought men to their knees. Joe thought about the series of reports and cryptic e-mails he'd received regarding a rogue 400-pound male grizzly that was causing havoc in northwestern Wyoming. For the past month, the bear had damaged cars, campsites, and cabins, but as yet there had been no human–bear encounters. The bear had originally been located near the east entrance of Yellowstone Park through a weakening signal from its radio collar, but he had not yet been sighted. When the "bear guys"—a team of Wyoming Game and Fish Department and U.S. Fish and Wildlife Service bear specialists—tried to cut it off, the bear eluded them and they lost the signal. Joe couldn't recall a runaway bear incident quite like this before. It was like the wilderness version of an escaped convict. He blamed the drought, as the biologists did, and the need for the grizzly to cover new ground in search of something, anything, to eat. It had not been lost on him that the damage reports indicated that the grizzly was moving to the east, through the Shoshone National Forest. If the bear kept up his march, he would enter the Bighorn Mountains, where grizzlies had not roamed for eighty years.

Joe disliked bringing his weapon and badge with him on his day off. He felt oddly ashamed that his daughters were seeing his day-to-day equipment as they caught fish and he cooked them over an open fire for lunch. It was different when he was out in the field, in his red chamois Game and Fish shirt and driving his green pickup, checking hunters and fishers. Now, he just wanted to be Dad.

WORKING THEIR WAY UPSTREAM, THEY stumbled upon another party. Sheridan saw them first and stopped, looking back for Joe. He could see flashes of color through the trees upstream, and he heard a cough.

Joe noticed a strange odor in the air when the wind

shifted. The odor was sickly sweet and metallic, and he winced when a particularly strong waft of it blew through.

Making sure Lucy was well behind them, Joe winked at Sheridan as he overtook her, and she fell in behind him as he closed in on the two fishers. He debated whether or not to show his badge before saying hello, and decided against it. Joe noticed the unpleasant odor again. It seemed to get worse as he walked upstream.

As he approached them, he felt Sheridan tug on his sleeve, and he turned and saw her point toward the water. A small brook trout, not more than six inches long, was floating on the top of the water on its side. It wasn't dead yet, and he could see its gills working as it pathetically tried to right itself and swim away.

"The fish killers," Sheridan whispered ominously at the man and woman in front of them, and he nodded to her in agreement.

The man looked to be in his late fifties, and was dressed as if he were a cover model for *Fly-Fisherman* magazine. He wore ultralight Gore-Tex waders and leather wading boots, a pale blue Coolmax shirt, and a fishing vest with dozens of bulging pockets filled with gear. A wooden net hung down his back from a ring on his collar. A leather-bound journal for documenting the species and size of the fish he caught was on a lanyard on his vest, as was a small digital camera for recording the catch. The man was large and ruddy, with a thick chest. He had a salt-and-pepper mustache and pale, watery eyes. He looked like a hungover CEO on vacation, Joe thought.

Behind and off to the side of the man was a much younger woman with blonde hair, long sunburned legs, and a fishing vest so new that the tag from the Bighorn Angler Fly Shop was still attached to the front zipper. She held her rod away from her body with the unease of someone holding a dead snake.

It was obvious, Joe thought, that the man was teaching the woman how to fish. Or, more accurately, the man was showing the woman what a fine fisherman *he* was. Joe assumed that the couple had stopped at the fly store on their way up the mountain and that the man had outfitted her with the new vest.

The man had been concentrating on dropping a fly into a deep pool but now glared at Joe and Sheridan, clearly annoyed that he had been disturbed.

"Jeff . . ." the woman cautioned in a low voice, attempting to get Jeff's attention.

"Good afternoon," Joe said and smiled. "How's fishing?"

Jeff stepped back from the stream in an exaggerated way. His movement wasn't aggressive but clearly designed to show Joe and Sheridan that he wasn't pleased with the interruption and that he planned to resume his cast as soon as possible.

"Thirty-fish day," Jeff said gruffly.

"Twenty-eight," the woman corrected, and Jeff instantly flashed a look at her.

"It's an *expression*," he said as if scolding a child. "Twenty-fish day, thirty-fish day, they're fucking *expressions*. It's what fishermen tell each other if one of them is rude enough to ask."

The woman shrank back and nodded.

Joe didn't like this guy. He knew the type: a flyfisherman who thought he knew everything and who could afford all of the equipment he read about in the magazines. Often, these men were fairly new to the sport. Too often, these men had never learned about outdoor etiquette, or common courtesy. To them it was all about thirty-fish days.

"Keeping any?" Joe asked, still smiling. He reached into the back pocket of his vest, bringing out his wallet-badge and holding it up so Jeff could understand why Joe was asking the question.

"There's a limit of six on this stream," Joe said. "Mind if I look at what you've kept?"

Jeff snorted and his face hardened.

"So you're the game warden?"

"Yes," Joe said. "And this is my daughter Sheridan."

"And his daughter Lucy," Lucy said, having caught up with them. "What's that smell, Dad?"

"And Lucy," Joe added, looking back at her. She was pinching her nose with her fingers. "So I would appreciate it if you watched your language around them."

Jeff started to say something but caught himself. Then he rolled his eyes heavenward.

"Tell you what," Joe said, looking at the woman— who appeared to be fearing a fight—and Jeff. "How about you show me your licenses and conservation stamps and I'll show you how to properly release a fish so that there aren't any more dead ones?"

The woman immediately began digging in her tight shorts, and Jeff seemed to make up his mind that he didn't really want a fight, either. Still glaring at Joe, he reached behind his back for his wallet.

Joe checked the licenses. Both were perfectly legal. She was from Colorado and had a temporary fishing license. Jeff O'Bannon was local, although Joe couldn't remember ever seeing him before. Joe noted that O'Bannon's address was on Red Cloud Road, which meant he lived in one of the new $500,000 ranchettes south of town in the Elkhorn Ranches subdivision. That didn't surprise Joe.

"Do you know what that awful smell is?" Joe asked conversationally as he handed the licenses back.

"It's a dead moose," Jeff O'Bannon said sullenly. "In that meadow up there." He gestured through the trees to the west, vaguely pointing with the peaked extra-long bill of his Orvis fishing cap. "That's one reason why we're fucking leaving."

"Jeff . . ." The woman cautioned.

O'Bannon growled at her, "There's no law against the word *fucking*."

Joe felt a rise of anger. "I think, Jeff, that I'll see you again some time out here," Joe said, leaning in close to Jeff. "Given your bad attitude, you'll probably be doing something wrong. I'll arrest you when you do."

O'Bannon started to step toward Joe but the woman held his arm. Joe slipped his hand in the back pocket of his fishing vest and thumbed off the safety bar on the bear spray.

"Aw, to hell with it," O'Bannon said, leaning back. "Let's get out of here, Cindy. He's already ruined my good mood."

Joe watched as Cindy breathed a long sigh of relief and shook her head in bewilderment for Joe's benefit, keeping out of Jeff's line of vision. Joe stepped aside as the man stormed past him, followed by Cindy.

"Bye, girls," Cindy called to Sheridan and Lucy, who watched the two walk downstream. Jeff led the way, snapping branches and cursing. Cindy tried to keep up.

"Dad, can we leave, too?" Lucy asked. "It stinks here."

"Go ahead and go downstream a little ways and get out of the smell if you want to," Joe said. "I need to check this moose out."

"We're going with you," Lucy honked back, still holding her nose. Joe turned to argue when he noticed that O'Bannon and Cindy hadn't moved very far downstream after all. O'Bannon stood in a clearing, glaring through pine branches at Joe while Cindy tugged at him.

"Okay," Joe said, knowing it was best to keep his girls near him.

*   *   *

THE MOOSE WASN'T HARD TO find, and the sight jarred
Joe. A full-grown bull moose lay on its side in the ankle-
high grass in the center of the meadow, which was walled
on three sides by dark trees that continued in force up
the mountain. The dead moose was horribly bloated to
nearly twice its normal size, its mottled purple skin
stretched nearly to breaking. Two black legs, knobby-
kneed and surprisingly long, were suspended over the
ground, like a chair that had been tipped over. Its face,
half-hidden in the grass, seemed to leer at him with bared
long teeth and a single, bulging, wide-open eye that
looked like it was primed and ready to fire right out of
the socket.

Joe turned on his heels and told his girls to stop so
they wouldn't see it. Too late.

Lucy shrieked, and covered her mouth with her hands.
Sheridan stared, her eyes wide, her mouth set grimly.

"It's alive!" Lucy cried.

"No it isn't," Sheridan countered. "But there's something wrong with it."

"Stay put," Joe said sternly. "I mean that."

Drawing a bandanna out of his Wranglers, he tied it
over his nose and mouth like a highwayman, and approached the bloated carcass. Sheridan was right, Joe
thought. There was something wrong with it. And there
was something else; he had a fuzzy, slightly dizzy feeling.
For a moment, he was light-headed, and thought that
perhaps he had moved too quickly or something. He
blinked, and when he looked around he saw faint, slow
motion sparkling in the air for a moment.

Shaking his head to try and clear it, Joe circled the
carcass, never getting closer than a few feet from it. The
animal had been mutilated. Its genitals and musk glands

had been cut out, and its rectum was cored. Half of its face had been removed, leaving a grinning skull and long, yellowed teeth. He could see where the skin and glands had been cut away, and noted that the incisions were smooth, almost surgical, in their precision. He could not imagine an animal, any animal, leaving wounds like that. Where the skin had been cut away the exposed flesh was dark purple and black, speckled with tiny commas of bright yellow. When he stopped and stared, he realized that the commas were writhing. Maggots. Besides the incisions, he could see no exterior wounds on the carcass.

Turning his head for a big gulp of air, he strode forward and squatted and grasped one of the bony, stiff forelegs. Grunting, he lifted, using the leg as a lever. He shinnied around the obscenely smiling face and massive, inverted palm-frond antlers and pulled, using his legs and back, trying to turn the stiff carcass. For a moment, the sheer weight of the animal stymied him, and he feared losing his footing and falling over it. Worse yet would be if the leg pulled loose from the putrefied shoulder, leaving a long, hairy club in his hands. But with a sickening kissing sound the body detached from the ground and began to roll toward him. He pulled hard on the leg and jumped back as the carcass flopped over in the grass. Gasses burbled inside the carcass, sounding like something subterranean. He searched the grass-matted hide for external injuries. Again, he found none.

He expected to see the flattened grass black with congealed blood, as was usually the case when he found animals that had been poached. The entry wound was often hard to see but the exit wound would bleed and drain into the turf, leaving a black-and-red pudding. But there was no blood underneath the moose at all, only more insects, madly scrambling, running from sunlight.

Joe stepped back and looked around. The grass was lush and thick in the meadow, and he noticed, for the first time, that there were no tracks of any kind in it. When he looked back on the slope he had walked up, his own footprints were glaringly obvious in the crushed, dry grass. It appeared that the moose had chosen the center of the meadow to suddenly drop dead. So what could possibly have removed the animal's genitals, glands, and face? And not left so much as a print?

He pulled the bandanna from his mouth and let it hang around his neck. His necropsy kit was in his pickup, which was a one-hour walk away. Dusk would be approaching soon, and he had promised Marybeth he would have the girls home in time for dinner and homework. Tomorrow, when he returned, he expected that with the kit and his metal detector he would find a bullet or two in the carcass. Usually, the lead caught up just beneath the hide on the opposite side of where the animal had been shot.

Joe walked back to where Sheridan and Lucy were standing. They had moved back down the hill from the meadow, close enough that they could watch him but far enough away that the smell of the carcass wouldn't make them sick to their stomachs. Jeff and Cindy were nowhere in sight.

As they worked their way down the slope to Crazy Woman Creek, his girls fired questions at him.

"Who killed the moose, Dad?" Lucy asked. "I like moose."

"Me too. And I don't know what killed it."

"Isn't that strange to find an animal just dead like that?" Lucy again.

"Very strange," Joe said. "Unless somebody shot it and left it."

"That's a crime, right? A big one?" Sheridan asked.

Joe nodded. "Wanton destruction of a game animal."

"I hope you find out who did it," Sheridan said, "and take away all of his stuff."

"Yup," Joe agreed, but his mind was racing. Besides the mutilation and the lack of tracks around the animal, something else bothered him that he couldn't put his finger on. But as the three of them walked downstream, he saw a raccoon ahead of them splash through a pool and vanish into a stand of trees. The raccoon had found one of the dead fish that Jeff had "released."

Suddenly, Joe stopped. That was it, he thought. The bull moose had been dead for at least several days, lying in the open, and *nothing* had fed on it. The mountains were filled with scavengers—eagles, coyotes, badgers, hawks, ravens, even mice—who were usually the first on the scene of a dead animal. Joe had discovered scores of game animals, which had been lost or left by hunters, by the squawking, feeding magpies that usually marked a kill. But the moose looked untouched, except for the incisions.

As a big fist of cumulous clouds punched across the sun and flattened the shadows and dropped the temperature by a quick ten degrees, Joe heard a snapping sound and turned slowly, looking back toward the meadow where they had found the moose. He could see nothing, but he felt a ripple through the hairs on the back of his neck.

"What is it, Dad?" Sheridan asked.

Joe shook his head, listening.

"I heard it," Lucy said. "It sounded like somebody stepped on a branch or a twig. Or maybe they were eating potato chips."

"Potato chips," Sheridan scoffed. "That's stupid."

"I'm not stupid."

"Girls." Joe admonished them, still trying to listen.

But he heard nothing beyond the liquid sound of the flowing breeze through the swaying crowns of the pine trees. He thought of how, in just a few moments, the mountain setting had changed from warm and welcoming to cold and oddly silent.

2

IT WAS A HALF HOUR BEFORE DUSK WHEN THEY ARRIVED at their small, two-story, state-owned home eight miles out of Saddlestring. Joe swung the pickup off Bighorn Road and parked it in front of the detached garage that needed painting. Sheridan and Lucy were out of the passenger door even before he set the brake, rushing across the grass in the front yard into the house to tell their mother what they had seen. Maxine bounded behind them but paused at the door to look back at Joe.

"Go ahead," Joe said, "I'm coming."

Assured, the Labrador bolted into the house.

After putting the rods, vests, and cooler into the garage, Joe walked around the house toward the corral. Toby, their eight-year-old paint gelding, nickered as soon as Joe was in sight, which meant he was hungry. Doc, their new sorrel yearling, nickered as well, following the older horse's lead. Joe shooed them aside as he entered the corral, then fed them two flake sections each of grass hay. He filled the trough and checked the gate on his

way out. While he did so, he wondered why Marybeth
hadn't fed them earlier, because she usually did.

As he opened the door at the back of the house, Sheridan stormed out of it in a dark mood.

"Did you tell your mom about the moose?" Joe asked
her.

"She's busy," Sheridan snapped, "maybe I should have
made an appointment."

"Sherry . . ." Joe admonished, but Sheridan was out
the back gate toward the corral.

He turned and entered the kitchen. Marybeth sat at
the kitchen table wearing a sweatshirt and jeans, surrounded by manila files, stacks of paper, facedown open
books, a calculator, and a laptop computer. Boxes of files
were stacked on either side of her chair, their lids on the
floor. She was concentrating on her laptop screen, and
barely acknowledged him as he entered the kitchen.

"Hey, babe," he greeted her and swept her blonde hair
away from the side of her face and kissed her on the cheek.

"Just a second," she said, tapping on her keyboard.

Joe felt a pang of annoyance. It was obvious that
nothing was cooking on the stove, and the oven light
was dark. The table was a shambles, and so was Marybeth. It wasn't as if he expected dinner on the table every
night. But she had asked him to be home early with the
girls, for dinner, and he had lived up to his part of the
bargain.

"Okay," she announced and snapped the screen down
on her laptop. "Got it."

"Got what?"

"The Logue Country Realty account is finally recon-
ciled," she said. "What a mess that one was."

"Well, good," he said flatly, opening the refrigerator
to see if a covered dish was ready to heat. Nope.

"I don't know how they stayed in business after they

bought it, Joe," she explained, filing bank statements and canceled checks into folders and envelopes. "The previous owners left them an unbelievable mess. Their cash flow was an absolute mystery for the last twelve quarters."

"Mmm."

There weren't even frozen pizzas in the freezer, he saw. Just some rock-hard packages of deer burger and elk roasts from the previous year, and a box of Popsicles that had been in the freezer as long as Joe could remember.

"I thought we'd go out tonight," Marybeth said. "Or maybe one of us could run into town to get something and bring it back."

He was surprised. "We can afford to?"

Marybeth's smile disappeared. "No, we really can't," she sighed. "Not until the end of the month, anyway."

"We could thaw out that burger in the microwave," Joe suggested.

"Do you mind grilling out?" she asked.

"That's fine," he said evenly.

"Honey . . ."

Joe held up his hand. "Don't worry about it. You got caught up in your work. It's okay."

For a second, he thought she would tear up. That happened more and more lately. But she didn't. Instead, she bit her lower lip and looked at him.

"Really," he said.

AS HE SCRAPED THE GRATE of the barbecue grill in the backyard, Joe battled with himself over his disappointment that there was no dinner planned and his growing worry about Marybeth and their marriage. There was no doubt that the violent death of April, their foster daughter, last winter had severely affected Marybeth. Joe had hoped that the dawn of spring would help Marybeth

heal but it hadn't. Spring had only brought the realization that their situation in general was no different than
it had been before.

Sometimes, he caught her staring. She would fix on
the window, or sometimes on something that seemed to
be between the window and her eyes. Her face would
look slightly wistful, and her eyes softened. A couple of
times he asked her what she was thinking about. When
he did, she shook her head as if shaking off a vision, and
said, "nothing."

He knew their finances troubled her, as they troubled
him. There was a statewide budget crunch, and salaries
had been frozen. In Joe's case, this meant he would make
$32,000 a year as far ahead as he could see. The long
hours he worked also meant that any kind of extra income was out of the question. The department provided
housing and equipment, but recently the house, which
had at one time seemed wonderful, felt like a trap.

After April died, Joe and Marybeth had discussed
their future. They needed normalcy, they agreed, they
needed routine. Faith and hope would return naturally,
because they were strong people and they loved each
other and, given time, they'd all heal. Joe had promised
to look at other job options, or request a change of districts within the state. A change of scenery might help,
they agreed. But he had not really researched the job
postings recently, because in his heart he loved his job
and never wanted to leave it. That reality shrouded him,
at times, with secret guilt.

Marybeth was no longer working at the library and
the stables, the two part-time jobs she had held. Even
combined, they were too low-paying, and involved too
much public contact, she told him. She was uncomfortable with library patrons who assessed her and asked her

questions about April, and the events that had led to her death.

But they needed additional income, and in the summer Marybeth had started her own business, setting up accounting, office management, and inventory control for small businesses in Saddlestring. Joe thought it was a perfect choice, with her education, toughness, and organizational skills. So far, her clients included Barrett's Pharmacy, Sandvick Taxidermy, the Saddlestring Burg-O-Pardner, and Logue Country Realty. She was working hard to get established, and the business was close to being a success.

Which made him feel even more guilty that he had been angry with her about dinner.

"TELL ME ABOUT THAT MOOSE," she asked after dinner, while they washed and rinsed dishes in the sink. Joe was surprised by the question, because Sheridan and Lucy had described the incident in such graphic detail while they were eating that Joe had asked them to stop.

"What about it?"

She smiled slyly. "For the past fifteen minutes, you've been thinking about it."

He flushed. "How do you know that?"

"You mean besides the fact that you've been staring off into space the entire time that we've been doing the dishes? Or that you're drying that glass for the fourth time?" she said, grinning. "You're standing right here but your mind is elsewhere."

"It isn't fair that you do that," he said, "because I can never tell what you're thinking about."

"As it should be," she said, giving him a mischievous hip-check as they stood side-by-side at the sink.

"The girls described it pretty accurately," he said. "Not much I can add to that."

"So why does it bother you?"

He rinsed a plate and slid it into the drying rack, pausing until he could articulate what he had been thinking about. "I've seen a lot of dead animals," he said, looking over his shoulder at her. "And, unfortunately, some dead human beings."

She nodded him on.

"But everything about that scene was, well, different—extremely so."

"Do you mean that you couldn't figure out what made the wounds?"

"That too," he said. "But you just don't find a dead moose in the middle of a meadow like that. There were no tracks; no indication that whoever shot it went to check it out afterward. Even the really bad poachers, the ones who leave the bodies on the ground, usually go check out the target."

"Maybe it was just sick and it died," she said reasonably.

Joe had turned and was leaning back against the sink with the towel still over his forearm.

He said, "Of course animals die of natural causes all the time. But you just never *find* them. You may find some bones if the skeleton hasn't been too scattered by predators, but you just don't happen upon animals that have died of old age. Or if you do, it's damned rare. Dying animals tend to seek out cover where nothing can find them. They don't just keel over in the middle of a meadow like that."

"But you don't know that it wasn't shot, or hit by lightning or something," she said.

"It wasn't lightning. There were no scorch marks. It may have been shot; I'll find that out tomorrow. But my gut tells me I won't find any lead."

"Maybe it was poisoned somehow?" Marybeth asked.

Joe was silent for a moment before answering, reviewing the scene in his head. He was pleased that Marybeth was so wrapped up in what had happened to the moose. She'd been so distracted by her new business that it had been a long time since she'd been interested in anything he'd been doing.

"Again, I think the bull would have sought cover to die. Unless the poison killed him so quick he just dropped, which doesn't sound very likely to me. And those wounds . . ."

"You described them as incisions earlier," Marybeth said.

"Yes, they were more like surgery than butchery. No animal I know of makes perfect cuts like that. And the parts that were cut away were removed from the scene, taken away. As if they were trophies of some kind."

Marybeth grimaced. "I'd hate to see *that* trophy collection."

Joe laughed uncomfortably, agreeing with her.

"It's almost as if the moose was dropped from the sky," Marybeth said.

"Aw, jeez," he moaned. "I was hoping you wouldn't say that."

She prodded him hard in the ribs with her finger. "But that's what you were thinking, weren't you, Joe?"

At first he thought about denying it. But she was so damnably keyed into his thoughts that he didn't dare.

"Yup," he said.

"I can't wait to hear what you find out," she said, turning and reaching through the wash water for the plug. "Should I ask my mother what she thinks about it?"

Joe bristled, as Marybeth knew he would, and she laughed to assure him she was kidding. Her mother, the former Missy Vankueren, was soon to marry a local rancher named Bud Longbrake. In addition to getting remarried (she had four ex-husbands), and discussing exactly how Joe had stifled Marybeth's potential, Missy's top passion was reading books and watching television shows and movies about the paranormal. She loved to speculate about situations and events around Twelve Sleep County—and the world—and ascribe supernatural explanations to them.

"Don't tell her, please," Joe begged, exaggerating his please, but not really. "You know how I hate that woo-woo crap."

"Speaking of woo-woo crap," Sheridan said as she entered the kitchen from where she'd been eavesdropping, "did I tell you I had that dream again?"

3

THE NEXT MORNING, MONDAY, JOE HIKED UP THE CRAZY Woman Creek drainage with his necropsy kit to discover that the grinning moose was no longer there. The absence of the dead moose in the meadow stopped him outright, and he stood still for a moment, surveying the crushed grass. He was thinking about Sheridan's dream, which made him uncomfortable. Joe refused to believe in aliens or creeping mist or anything else he couldn't see or touch. Had there been a time when he believed in monsters and things that went bump in the night? *Nope,* he thought. He had always been a skeptic. He remembered when neighborhood kids gathered around a Ouija board, and urged him to join them. Instead, he went fishing. When his friends stayed up late at night to watch creature movies, Joe fell asleep. Sheridan was different, though, and always had been. He hoped she'd outgrow the dreams.

SOMETHING HAD DRAGGED, OR CARRIED, the carcass away. The trail was obvious; a spoor of flattened grass led across the meadow in a stuttering S-curve toward the northern wall of pine trees. Puzzled, he followed it.

The mature bull moose weighed at least 600 pounds, he guessed. Whatever had moved it had tremendous strength. He wouldn't have been surprised to see a set of pickup or ATV tracks in the meadow, but they weren't there. He wondered if it could be the grizzly. As he walked silently across the meadow in the flattened grass track of the moose, he tried to peer ahead into the dark trees and see into them. He listened intently for sounds, and noted the absence of them. There were no chattering squirrels in the trees, or calling jays. Except for the low hum of insects in the grass near his feet and the high, airy flow of a cold fall breeze through the branches, it was deathly silent in the meadow. Again, he felt a chill run up his spine, which raised the hairs on his neck and forearms.

He couldn't explain the odd feeling he got again from the meadow. It felt as if something was physically pushing against him from all sides. Not hard, but steadily. The crisp fall mountain air tasted thicker than it should have, and when he breathed in, his lungs felt heavy and wet. He sensed a kind of shimmer in the air when he looked at the wall of trees and the granite mountains that pushed up behind them. He didn't like the feeling at all, and tried to shake it off.

Joe slipped the strap of the necropsy kit over his head so that his hands were free. He drew his semiautomatic weapon and worked the slide, seating a cartridge in the chamber. With his left hand, he unclipped the large can of bear spray from his belt and thumbed off the guard. He cautiously approached the wall of trees, his weapon in his right hand and the spray in his left. All of his senses were tuned to high, and he strained to see, hear, or smell anything that would give him a warning before it was too late.

That's when he saw the bear track in the center of the crushed grass. The huge paw was the size of a pie plate and had pushed down through the mat of grass into dark soil. He could see the heel imprint clearly; it was pressed into the dirt, as were the prints of all five toes. Nearly two inches from the end of the toe marks were sharp punctures in the ground, as if a curved garden rake had been swung overhead and embedded deeply into the earth. The creature that had made the tracks was the rogue grizzly bear, he was sure of it. None of the native black bears could leave a track that large. The odd thing, he thought, was that the track was pointed toward him, and not toward the wall of trees. Why wasn't the track heading away from the meadow?

Then he answered his own question. If the bear was dragging the moose out of the meadow, he would have clamped down on the moose's neck with his teeth and pulled it backward, like a puppy dragging a sock. The fact that the heel print was deeper than the claws indicated that the bear was struggling with the heavy carcass, backing up and digging deep into the earth for traction.

He glanced at the bear spray he carried and then at the .40 Beretta. *Too small,* he thought, *too puny.* Not only would he likely miss because he was such a poor shot with a handgun, but even if he hit his target it would probably do no more than make the bear angry.

He stood, thought, and shrugged, then plunged forward, toward the trees that lined the meadow. There was a hole in the brush where something—the bear?—had already blazed through. Branches had been bent and snapped back and broken. Entering the pool of shadow cast by the wall of pine trees, Joe squinted to see better. The forest was unnaturally dense and cluttered with wicked snarls of dry deadfall. The tree trunks were the thickness of the barrel of a baseball bat and extremely close together. Joe lowered his shoulder and pushed through.

The forest floor was dark, dry, and carpeted thickly with several inches of bronze pine needles. His boots sank with each step, and the earth was springy. The smell inside was a combination of dried pine, vegetative decay, and the sudden strong odor of the dead moose that for some reason Joe had not noticed until now.

As his eyes adjusted to the half-light filtering through the pine boughs, the carcass of the moose seemed to emerge on the forest floor right in front of him. The stench was suddenly overpowering, and Joe stepped back and thumped his shoulder blade against two tree trunks that prevented further flight. Holstering his gun, he held his breath while he dug a thick surgical face mask from the kit, pulled the rubber band over the back of his head, and fitted the mask over his nose and mouth. He smeared Vicks VapoRub across the front of the mask from a small plastic jar in the kit to further block the smell. Then he approached the carcass and got to work.

The carcass had obviously decomposed even more. Blooms of entrails had burst through several places in the abdomen of the moose, where the hide had been stretched so tightly that it split. Again, he marveled at the surgical precision of the incisions that had been made. He could see no wounds that he had missed the day before, except for the gouged rips in the neck from the teeth of the bear that had dragged it from the meadow. Joe photographed the wounds from several angles using his digital camera. The photos, he thought, didn't convey the dread and fear he felt. They looked clinical, and somehow cleaner than the real thing.

He put on thick rubber gloves and squatted next to the carcass with his kit open. Using dental charts, he noted the size of the pre-molars as well as their stain and wear and guessed that the bull was at least seven years old, in its prime. Pushing a stainless steel probe through the hide along the spine of the moose between the shoulders, then in the middle of the back, and finally between the haunches, he noted that the body fat of the animal was normal, even a little excessive. Joe thought it was unusual in a drought year that the moose seemed so robust and healthy. Whatever had happened to the moose, it was clear that it hadn't died from either starvation or old age.

He ran a telescopic metal detector over the animal from its tail to the rounded end of its bulbous snout. No metal. If the animal had been shot, the bullet had passed through the body. But there was no exit wound. Conventional high-powered hunting bullets were designed to mushroom inside the body and do horrendous damage inside. But they were engineered to stay inside the body somewhere, not to exit. There was the possibility, Joe thought, that the shooter was using specialized armor-piercing type rounds that could pass straight through. But he doubted that scenario. In fact, the more he studied the body, the less he could convince himself that somebody had shot it.

Using a razor, Joe sliced tissue samples from the places on the moose's hindquarters, neck, and head where its hide had been cut away. He dropped the strips of meat into thick paper envelopes to send to the lab in Laramie. Plastic would spoil the samples, and he didn't want his effort to go to waste. He duplicated the procedure with another set of envelopes he would send to another lab.

After he completed his work, he stood above the carcass and stared at it. If anything, the face stripped of its flesh seemed more gruesome in the dark silence of the forest floor. The smell of the decaying body was working its way through the mask, overpowering even the Vicks. Joe looked around, suddenly realizing that he had been so intent on collecting the samples and completing the necropsy that he hadn't thought about the grizzly. Was he out there now, somewhere in the shadows? Would he be coming back?

Why would the bear go to all the effort of dragging the huge corpse into the trees and not feed on it? Moose was highly choice meat, for hunters and for bears. If the bear wasn't hungry, why would he have worked so hard? If the bear intended to eat the moose later, why hadn't he buried the carcass or covered it with brush as bears usually did?

Joe zipped up his kit and retraced his steps. Nothing about this dead moose made sense. His only hope to solve the puzzle, he thought, was if the lab boys could come up with something from the photos and the samples. But even if the moose died of some strange disease, how would they account for the incisions and the missing skin, glands, and organs?

As he neared the meadow, the light fused yellow, and when he emerged from the forest he had the same feeling a swimmer does as he breaks the surface from below. In the meadow, Joe turned. He listened closely for the sounds of a bear approaching or, for that matter, any sound at all. There was none. But there was still that shimmer in the air, and the closed-in feeling of density.

Maybe, Joe thought, *somebody or something is watching me.* Maybe that was why he felt so unnatural and out of sorts in the meadow. He swept the forest with his eyes, trying to find something out of the ordinary. A set of eyes, perhaps, or the glint of the lenses from binoculars. He turned slowly in the center of the meadow, not far from where the moose had originally lain. He scanned the three walls of trees, and the creek bed, even the high, slick faces of the mountains. He saw nothing unusual. But he was thoroughly and ashamedly spooked.

Still clutching his weapon and the bear spray, Joe walked across the meadow and dropped down into Crazy Woman Creek. As he walked downstream, he felt the pressure lessen. Eventually, he couldn't feel it at all. The sun seemed warmer and brighter overhead. A raven cawed rudely somewhere on the opposite bank.

C.J. BOX

"One of today's solid-gold, A-list, must-read writers."

—Lee Child

For a complete list of titles and to sign up for our newsletter, please visit prh.com/CJBox